DESPERATE MEASURES

Kitty Neale was raised in South London and this working class area became the inspiration for her novels. In the 1980s she moved to Surrey with her husband and two children, but in 1998 there was a catalyst in her life when her son died, aged just 27. After joining other bereaved parents in a support group, Kitty was inspired to take up writing, and *Nobody's Girl* was recently a *Sunday Times* bestseller.

Kitty now lives in Spain with her husband and is working on her new novel for Avon, due to be published in summer 2009. To find out more about Kitty go to www.kittyneale.co.uk.

By the same author:

Nobody's Girl
Sins of the Father
Family Betrayal

KITTY NEALE

Desperate Measures

AVON

AVON

A Division of HarperCollins*Publishers*
77–85 Fulham Palace Road,
London W6 8JB

www.harpercollins.co.uk

A Paperback Original 2009

1

Copyright © Kitty Neal 2009

Kitty Neal asserts the moral right to
be identified as the author of this work

A catalogue record for this book is
available from the British Library

ISBN 978-0-00-787962-5

Typeset in Minion by Palimpsest Book Production Limited,
Grangemouth, Stirlingshire

Printed and bound in Great Britain by
Clays Ltd, St Ives plc

Mixed Sources
Product group from well-managed
forests and other controlled sources
www.fsc.org Cert no. SW-COC-001806
© 1996 Forest Stewardship Council

FSC is a non-profit international organisation established to promote the
responsible management of the world's forests. Products carrying the FSC
label are independently certified to assure consumers that they come
from forests that are managed to meet the social, economic and
ecological needs of present and future generations.

Find out more about HarperCollins and the environment at
www.harpercollins.co.uk/green

My thanks as always to my agent, Judith Murdoch, and the wonderful team at Avon/HarperCollins. Thanks also to my family and friends who always encourage me, and my wonderful readers for their kind words.

This book is for my adorable new great grandson, Michael Andrew Blofeld. May your life be a joyous one, my darling, full of love, laughter, and a smooth path to carry you forward on life's journey.

Prologue

The woman knew that what she wanted to do was justified, not just for her, but for the others that she had managed to bring into her small circle. It was a lovely day, the sun bright, yet impatiently she tugged her small dog's lead, too intent on finding her next recruit to appreciate her surroundings. Her life had been ruined and she'd been eaten up with bitterness – but now she had a mission.

She wasn't the only woman who'd suffered and it wasn't right, wasn't fair that these men had got away with it. Her goal now was to make them pay – to make *him* pay.

To that end she got up every morning, went to work, functioned – but it was as though she were living her life on automatic. Her plans and schemes had become the focus of her whole life and she couldn't rest until they'd been carried out. Since the day it had happened, since he'd destroyed her life, she'd wanted only one thing. Revenge.

Chapter One

Battersea, South London, 1969

Though it was early on Saturday morning there were already signs that it was going to be a lovely day, and the sunshine drew Betty out of her poky flat to the park on the opposite side of the road.

She walked for a while, but it was unusually warm for June and, feeling hot, Betty sat on a bench. The park began to fill and she frowned as two young women walked towards her, still unable to get used to the way youngsters dressed nowadays. They were both in A-line mini-dresses, one blonde, one dark, their hair cut short in the geometrical shapes made popular by the hairdresser Vidal Sassoon. Make-up was skilfully applied – heavy, but at least they weren't wearing the thick, black, false eyelashes that were at last going out of fashion.

Betty sighed. She was fifty-one now, but as a young woman a bit of powder and lipstick was all she'd been allowed to wear, and her clothes had been respectable, in the same style as her mother's. And not only that – what about underwear? These young girls didn't wear vests or corsets and, worse, sometimes they went without a brassiere. She shook her head. Anne, her twenty-nine-year-old daughter, accused her of being old-fashioned, saying that things were different now. Women were no longer shackled to men, Anne insisted. They had freedom, equality, the means to make their own way in the world.

The two young women walked past without sparing her so much as a glance, and Betty blinked away tears as a surge of loneliness swamped her. She watched a small, brown dog as it circled a tree, sniffing the trunk until, finally satisfied, it lifted its leg.

'Treacle, come here,' a woman's voice called.

Betty saw the dog's ears twitch, but intent on exploring fresh pastures the command was ignored. It trotted towards the bench she was sitting on, tail up, and obviously liking what it saw, reared up to place its paws on Betty's lap.

'Oh, I'm so sorry. Get down, Treacle.'

Whilst stroking the dog's head, Betty looked up at his owner. She'd seen the elegant, middle-aged woman before, had noticed her dark brown hair, styled into a French pleat that emphasised her high cheekbones. 'It's all right, I like dogs,' she assured her.

4

'Not everyone feels the same and he's a holy terror. I shouldn't have let him off the lead, but I'm trying to get him to obey me,' she chuckled. 'As you can see, it isn't working.'

'He looks so sweet.'

'Don't let that fool you,' the woman said as she sat down. Treacle immediately jumped onto her lap and she laughed as his tongue slobbered her face. 'Oh, what am I saying? He's a darling really but, as I said, he won't obey my commands.'

'What breed is he?'

'He's a Bitsa. You know, bits of this and bits of that.'

As Betty smiled, Treacle turned to look at her again, his head cocked, soft brown eyes intent on her face. He then left his owner, moving across to sit on Betty's lap, his tongue soft and wet on her cheek.

'He likes you,' the woman said. 'I'm Val by the way. Valerie Thorn.'

'I'm Betty. Betty Grayson.'

Treacle jumped down, heading for the nearest tree as Val said, 'It's nice to meet you at last. We live in the same block of flats and since you moved in I've been meaning to introduce myself, but, well, you know how it is.'

'Yes, all the tenants seem so busy and I hardly see them, but it's nice to meet you too. You're on the ground floor aren't you?'

'That's right, in a one-bedroom flat. I live alone. What about you?'

Betty's expression saddened. 'Yes, me too, though not by choice.'

Valerie Thorn's eyebrows rose, but then seeing that her dog was running off she rose swiftly to her feet. 'Blast, I'd best go after him. Treacle! Treacle,' she called, and after saying a hasty goodbye, she hurried off.

After this brief interlude, Betty was alone again. It wasn't unusual. Living in London was different from her life in Surrey, the pace of it much faster, all hustle and bustle, with everyone intent on their own business. Since moving into her flat in Ascot Court she found it the same as previous ones in London, the other tenants seeming not only busy, but distant and remote. All they'd exchanged were quick hellos, but at least she'd met one of them now and felt a surge of gratitude that Valerie Thorn had at least stopped to speak to her. She'd seen the woman a few times, judged her by appearance, her hard veneer, and had expected the woman to be brittle, perhaps standoffish. Instead she'd found her warm with a lovely sense of humour, and hoped that she'd bump into her again.

Betty stood up, deciding to go home in case one of her children rang, or even paid her a visit, which would be wonderful. As she walked towards the gate a young couple were coming towards her – hippies, the girl wearing a cotton, flowing maxi-dress, with strands of love beads around her neck. Her hair was long, fair and, with a flower tucked behind her ear, she looked carefree, happy. When Betty looked at her young man she saw that he was wearing a colourful kaftan, purple trousers and sandals, his hair almost as long as the girl's. Betty thought he looked disgraceful – if her son dressed like that she would die of shame.

The couple were intent on each other as they passed, their faces wreathed in smiles, and now Betty felt a surge of envy. They were in love. She had felt like that once – just once in her life; but oh, what a fool she had been – a blind, stupid fool.

Betty saw the red Mini pull up in front of the flats as soon as she left the park, and was delighted when her daughter climbed out. It never ceased to amaze her that Anne had her own car, or even that she could drive – something Betty would never have dreamed of achieving as a young woman and something she still couldn't master. Of course, when she was Anne's age few women drove; in fact, unless one was very well-off, a car was a rarity. She'd married Richard when she was eighteen years old and felt fortunate to have a bicycle, one that she rode to the local village, the basket on the front crammed with local produce as she cycled home. *Home.* Her stomach lurched. No, she couldn't think about it, not when Anne was standing there, a bright smile on her face.

'Hi, Mum. I can't stay long but I thought I'd pop round to see how you're doing.'

'I'd hardly call driving from Farnham popping round,' Betty said as they walked into the flats where, after climbing two flights of stairs, she opened her front door.

Anne followed her in, her face dropping as she took in the small living room. 'Oh, Mum, this is almost as bad as your last place.'

'It has a nice outlook and after the pittance I got as a settlement, it's all I can afford.'

'Please, Mum, don't start. We've had argument after argument about this, but you still refuse to see Dad's point of view.'

She clamped her lips together. Her daughter had always been a daddy's girl and, despite everything, she was quick to jump to Richard's defence. He had spoiled Anne, indulged her love of horse riding, but Betty knew that if she said any more Anne would leave. She hadn't seen her since moving into this flat, and the last thing she wanted was for her to leave after five minutes. Forcing a smile, she asked, 'What would you like to drink?'

'A bottle of Coke if you've got one.'

'Yes, of course I have,' Betty assured her as she went through to her tiny kitchenette. Coca-Cola was something Anne always asked for on her rare visits, so she kept a couple of bottles in the fridge for just such an occasion. Betty found the bottle opener, snapped off the top, and asked as she returned to the living room, 'Have you heard from your brother?'

'No, John's too busy with his latest conquest.'

'At least he isn't like his father.'

'Mum,' warned Anne.

Betty regretted the words as soon as they left her mouth, but it was hard to stay silent in the face of her daughter's loyalty to Richard. She felt that, like her, Anne should hate her father for what he'd done – that she should be on *her* side, but instead Anne had refused to cut him out of her life. When it happened, Anne had been twenty-five, living away from home, though still in Surrey, in a flat-share with another young woman. Her son, John, had been twenty-eight, a surveyor, but with her help he was buying a mews cottage. Unlike Anne he'd been sympathetic to Betty, severing all ties with his father. For that she was thankful, but with his busy career she rarely saw her son these days.

'How's Anthony?' Betty enquired, hoping that asking about Anne's boyfriend would mollify her daughter.

'He's still pushing to get married, but I'm happy to stay as we are. I mean, what's the point? It's only a ring and a piece of paper.'

Betty managed to hold her tongue this time. When Anne had met her boyfriend eighteen months ago they'd soon moved in together and she'd been shocked to the core, glad that she no longer lived in Farnham for her neighbours to witness her shame. It had also surprised her that, according to Anne, her father didn't object, but as he'd lived in sin until their divorce came through he was hardly a good example.

'What about children? You're twenty-nine now.'

'I'm up for promotion and a baby would ruin that. I'm happy to stay as we are.'

'You could still become pregnant. If that happens, surely you'll marry?'

'I'm on the pill so there's no chance of unwanted babies. Anyway, I'm not a hundred per cent sure that I want to spend the rest of my life with Tony. Living together is ideal. It's like a trial marriage and if things don't work out we can both walk away without regrets.'

Despite herself, Betty found that she envied her daughter. There had been no trial marriage for her – no chance to find out that her husband was a womaniser before he'd put a ring on her finger. Divorce had been frowned on too, so when she married Richard she'd expected it to be for life. Instead, at forty-seven years old, she'd been cruelly discarded, as though Richard had thrown out an old, worn-out coat.

'Mum, I've got to go.'

'But you've only just got here.'

'I work all week and only have weekends off, with little time to go riding. It was you who decided to move to London, so it's difficult for me. I'd like to see more of you, but it's a long drive and with so much to cram in each weekend, I'm pushed for time.'

Anne was part of the country scene and, with her, horses came first. 'I know and I'm sorry. It's just that I miss you.'

'And I miss you, Mum, but I really have got to go. Tony and I have booked a holiday to Spain and I need a couple of outfits. I couldn't find anything swish in Farnham so I'm off to Selfridges.'

'Spain! You're going abroad?'

'Yes, next Saturday, but only for a week. We got a good price on a flight with Laker Airways.'

'You're . . . you're flying?'

'Don't look so shocked. I know your idea of a holiday is a caravan in Margate, but things are changing nowadays, with more people going abroad. I doubt I'll see you again until we get back, but I'll send you a postcard.'

Anne then swallowed the last of her drink, picked up her bag, and left in a whirlwind before Betty got the chance to say a proper goodbye. With a small wave her daughter was gone, hurrying down the stairs while Betty managed to gather her wits in time to call, 'Have a good time.'

'Thanks, Mum.'

Betty closed the door. Never in her wildest dreams had she expected to holiday abroad, but as Anne had a career as a personnel officer with a large company in Farnham, and Tony was an engineer, no doubt they could afford it. Once again Betty felt a frisson of envy, which was soon followed by a familiar bitterness. Unlike her daughter, she'd never had a career, her life spent intent on being the perfect wife and mother. She had married Richard in 1936, and John had followed a year later. They hadn't been well-off and it was sometimes a struggle to make ends meet, but then war had been declared and Richard eventually called up. Anne was conceived when Richard had been on leave and when he returned to the fighting she'd been terrified of losing him.

When the war was over, she'd been overjoyed that Richard came home without a scratch, but he was different, more self-assured, and full of ideas to start up his own business. He'd been taught to drive, had been involved in vehicle maintenance, and had picked up the idea that cars were going to be the up-and-coming thing after the war, available not just to the wealthy, but the middle classes too. To start up the car dealership they had to make many sacrifices, yet she'd supported him one hundred per cent. Her neighbours were getting modern appliances, vacuum-cleaners, the latest electric boilers with mangles, but every penny that Richard made had to be ploughed back into the business. She'd continued to make do with hand-washing, had used brushes and brooms, with her little spare time spent knitting or sewing to make clothes for both herself and the children. She smiled grimly. Of course Richard had to make an impression, so he'd worn nice suits . . .

Her thoughts were interrupted as the telephone rang. She hurried to answer it, thrilled to hear her son's voice. 'John, how are you?'

Unaware that she had a huge grin on her face, Betty listened to her son, pleased to hear that he was doing well, though disappointed when he said that he was too busy to pay her a visit. 'But I haven't seen you for ages,' she protested.

John made his usual excuses, and then Betty told him, 'Anne called round today. She's booked a holiday to Spain.'

He didn't sound all that interested and soon said he had to go. Betty replaced the receiver, her smile now gone as she wandered over to the window. She looked across to the park, wishing that she still had a garden to fill her time. When married to Richard she'd spent hours gardening, growing fruit and vegetables to save money on food bills and, though it had been hard work, she'd grown to love it.

The sky was blue, with just a few white, puffy clouds, and now that Betty knew John wouldn't be paying her a visit, she was tempted to go out again. She could walk to the pond, feed the ducks – it would be better than sitting here alone. When she threw bread the ducks would leave the pond to crowd around her; they'd be aware of her existence, and at least for a short time she wouldn't feel as she always did in London – invisible.

Betty made herself a quick snack, and then stuffed a few slices of bread into a paper bag as her thoughts returned to her daughter. Unlike Anne, she couldn't remember the last time she'd had a holiday. If she'd been treated fairly, she too could have gone overseas, but thanks to Richard it was impossible. It wasn't fair, it just wasn't, but there was nothing she could do about it – Richard and his solicitor had seen to that.

Chapter Two

Valerie Thorn was standing at her window, her gaze following Betty Grayson as she left the flats. The woman had moved in upstairs about a month ago and since then Val had taken every opportunity to surreptitiously observe her. She had contrived to bump into the woman earlier in Battersea Park and at least now knew her name. Betty was a short, stocky woman, with a sad expression and brow-beaten manner. Her clothes were old-fashioned, her light brown hair tightly permed, and Val judged her to be in her middle fifties.

Was Betty a possible candidate? The woman certainly looked unhappy, lost, with few visitors, which boded well. When Betty said she lived alone, but not by choice, there'd been bitterness in her voice and it increased Val's interest. With her first plan already in mind, she knew it would take a third recruit for it to work, and if this woman was suitable, her group would be complete.

She would contrive to bump into Betty again, to open another conversation and perhaps make tentative overtures of friendship. If she could discover a shared interest it would break the ice, give them common ground, and then, when the time was right, she'd make her move.

Softly, softly catchee monkey, Val thought, turning away from the window. She'd been too wound up to eat breakfast, but now feeling peckish, her eyes avoided the empty mantelshelf as she went through to her tiny kitchenette to make a sandwich. It was her birthday, but she didn't have one single card on show. Her mother had died when Val was just twenty-six, followed only three years later by her father. He'd been hit by a lorry when carelessly crossing the road and she'd been left bereft.

As an only child there'd been no siblings to share her grief, just two distant aunts and a few cousins that she hardly saw. Heartbroken, she'd channelled all her energies into her career, and whilst gaining promotion she hoped that if her parents were looking down on her, they'd be proud of what she'd achieved. She'd been so busy with her career that she'd lost touch with her scant relatives, yet on days like this, when the postman didn't deliver even one card, she regretted it.

Val tried to push her unhappiness to one side but found it impossible. It was always the same on birthdays or Christmas, when, unbidden, memories of her happy childhood filled her mind. She'd been surrounded by laughter and love – but she wasn't a child now, she was a mature woman, and it was silly to let things like birthday cards upset her.

If her parents *were* watching over her, it upset Val that they would have seen her life destroyed – seen her foolishness and therefore her failure. Her unhappiness now festered into anger, the sandwich tasting like sawdust in her mouth. There were times when Val's rage almost consumed her and with a grunt she pushed her sandwich to one side. It was no good, she had to get out, to breathe fresh air and, as her possible candidate had gone to the park again, she would use the opportunity to bump into her. Val picked up the dog's lead, calling, 'Treacle, walkies.'

The dog's ears pricked up and he immediately ran to her side, and with his lead on Treacle eagerly pulled her towards the door. He was her one consolation in life and she didn't regret getting him from Battersea Dogs' Home. He might be a bit naughty, but he was loving and loyal – but then that thought brought *him* to mind again and her lips thinned.

Val left the flat, crossed the road to the park, her eyes peeled for Betty Grayson. It was still a glorious day and the park was full of people intent on making the most of the brilliant weather. She unclipped Treacle's lead and the dog scampered off ahead of her, but so far there was no sign of Betty. Val walked the paths, her eyes constantly on the look-out, but it was half an hour later before she saw the woman. Betty was sitting by the duck pond, partly concealed by the fronds of a willow tree.

Val drew in a deep gulp of air, forcing her shoulders to relax. Take it slowly – just be friendly, she told herself. She called Treacle and, knowing that the dog wouldn't be able to resist chasing the wildfowl that Betty was feeding, she clipped on his lead.

'Hello again,' Val said. 'Treacle wanted another walk, but I didn't expect to bump into you again.'

'It was too nice to stay indoors and lovely to have Battersea Park opposite our flats.'

'Yes, and with a dog but no garden, it's a godsend. Do you mind if I sit down?'

'Please do,' Betty said eagerly, her smile one of pleasure. With Treacle around the ducks had waddled quickly away, and after shoving a paper bag into her pocket, Betty bent to stroke the dog's head. 'I'd like a dog too, but as I work full time it wouldn't be fair to leave it in my flat all day.'

'Fortunately my employer is a lovely man and lets me take Treacle to work. He even got him a basket to sit beside my desk.'

'That's nice,' Betty said, then raised a hand to wipe it across her forehead. 'Goodness, it's hot.'

Treacle had moved to lie in the scant shade of the willow tree, panting, his tongue lolling, and

18

worriedly Val said, 'Yes, and I think it's a bit too much for Treacle. I'd best take him home. If you're ready to go, perhaps we could walk home together.'

Betty stood up, her expression eager. 'Yes, all right. I'd like that.'

With Treacle beside them, they began to stroll slowly, Betty speaking enthusiastically about the flowerbeds that lined the path. 'Look at those petunias. What a wonderful display. I used to have a large garden and miss it.'

'I'm afraid I know nothing about gardening, but they're certainly colourful.'

Betty indicated another flowerbed. 'They've used red geraniums in that one.'

They continued to chat about the plants, but when they arrived at the flats, Betty sort of hovered at the door, smiling tentatively. Val could sense the woman's loneliness, and hoped she'd accept her invitation as she said, 'It's my birthday today. If you aren't busy, would you like to join me for tea?'

'Oh, Happy Birthday and yes, I'd love to.'

'I expect you want to freshen up first. Give me half an hour to make some sandwiches and then pop down.'

Betty looked delighted as she climbed the stairs, calling, 'See you soon.'

Val went inside her own flat to make a plate of cucumber sandwiches, and then finding a packet of individual chocolate rolls she arranged them on a plate before gong to the bathroom to refresh her make-up.

Shortly afterwards the doorbell rang and Val tucked a stray lock of hair back into her French pleat as she answered it, a smile of welcome on her face. 'Come on in.'

Betty stepped inside, her eyes scanning the room. 'This is lovely – I just love your décor. Youngsters nowadays go for all the modern stuff with bright, garish wallpaper, whereas this is so soothing, so sophisticated.'

'I prefer soft colours and as I can't tackle wall-papering, I just gave it all a coat of paint. Would you like tea or coffee?'

'Tea please.'

'Sit yourself down. I won't be a tick,' Val said, going back to her small kitchenette.

When the tea was made she carried the tray through. 'I hope you like cucumber sandwiches.'

'Yes, lovely,' Betty said, whilst eyeing the plate of chocolate rolls with appreciation.

Val sat opposite, poured the tea into small, deli-cate china cups and then offered cubes of sugar from a bowl, complete with little silver tongs.

Betty took two lumps, then saying, 'Well, Happy Birthday again.'

'Thank you.'

'My daughter was waiting for me when I came

home from the park this morning. She couldn't stay long as she was off to buy new clothes for a holiday in Spain.'

'That's nice. Is she going with her husband?'

'Anne isn't married. She's going with her boyfriend.'

'Do you have other children?'

'Yes, a son, and he's single too.'

Val didn't want to sound too inquisitive, so said, 'I'm sure your daughter will love Spain. I once went to Barcelona and the architecture was stunning.'

'You're lucky. I've never been abroad.'

'Yes, well, nowadays I'm lucky if I can afford a day trip to Brighton.'

'Me too,' said Betty.

So, the woman was hard up, Val thought as she mentally stored this small piece of information. 'There are some lovely places in England and I've always been fond of Dorset. Do have a sandwich,' she encouraged, whilst fumbling for common ground. 'I suppose you heard that Judy Garland died on Monday?'

'Yes, I saw it in the newspaper. It said she died from an overdose of sleeping pills.'

'I was so sad to hear of her death. Since I saw her in *The Wizard of Oz* she's been one of my favourite actresses.'

'I loved her in *A Star is Born*,' Betty enthused.

'Do you go to the cinema much?'

'Not really, but I did go to see Maggie Smith in *The Prime of Miss Jean Brodie*.'

'Me too. I was so glad when it won the Oscar.'

Betty just nodded, munching on her sandwich and, when it was finished, Val held out the cakes.

'Thanks,' Betty said, taking one and biting into it with obvious relish.

Maybe food could be a common interest, Val thought. 'I'm not much of a cook. What about you?'

'I used to be, but as I only cook for myself now, it's usually something simple.'

'I love eating out, and often go to a little French restaurant in Chelsea.'

'I've never tried French food.'

'It's delicious, Betty, and if you aren't doing anything tomorrow, we could go there for lunch.'

Betty's eyes lit up for a moment, but then her face straightened as she said, 'I . . . I don't know. Is it expensive?'

'Not really, but don't worry, it's a family-run business and I know the owner. He usually gives me a discount.'

'In that case, I'd love to.'

'Wonderful,' Val said as she stood up to take a packet of cigarettes from the mantelshelf. Inviting Betty to tea had been a good move and she was pleased that there'd now be another opportunity to get to know her better. 'Would you like a cigarette?' she asked.

'No thanks, I don't smoke.'

'At six shillings a packet I know I should stop too, but I have managed to cut down.'

'Do you work locally?' Betty asked.

'I'm a receptionist for a solicitor in the King's Road.'

'It must be nice to work in an office and so interesting.'

'It can be sometimes, though most of my work is just routine. What do you do, Betty?'

'I'm just a sort of cleaner-cum-housekeeper in Kensington. I used to live in Surrey, but saw the job advertised in *The Lady*. I applied for it and got it, but it meant moving to London. My employer's away at the moment, but when in town he keeps me busy with his incessant demands.'

'He sounds a bit of an ogre,' Val sympathised.

'He's all right, but used to servants seeing to his every wish. His home is just amazing and it's such a shame that it remains empty for most of the year. He has a large staff, but when his wife died he retreated to his country home taking them with him. I was lucky to be taken on for his London house, but as I said, only as a sort of cleaner-cum-housekeeper.'

'If you're the only one there, don't you find it lonely?'

'Sometimes, but I keep myself busy. It's a very large house with plenty to do, and just polishing the silver can take all day. I'd love to work in an office like you, but I was a stay-at-home wife and mother so I'm not trained for anything else.'

'There's nothing wrong with being a housewife and mother,' Val said. She had caught the trace of bitterness in Betty's voice again, and though tempted to ask questions, it wouldn't do to rush things. 'Would you like another cup of tea?'

'I'd love one.'

'I'll just top up the pot,' Val said, taking it through to the kitchenette. So far she'd gleaned a little information, but if she didn't want to scare Betty off she would have to play this carefully. In her experience, Val had found that if you shared a confidence it was likely to be returned, but it was too early to try this ploy now. She would have to wait, but nevertheless crossed her fingers, hoping that Betty would turn out to be a suitable candidate.

Chapter Three

On Sunday, Betty climbed into Val's rather battered old car. 'It's smashing not to have to wait for a bus. This is lovely,' she said.

'I'd hardly call this old banger lovely,' Val said dryly, 'and it isn't a patch on the company car I used to have. Still, it'll get us there.'

Betty gazed at Val and, seeing how elegant she looked, felt old and frumpy beside her. Other than her home-made clothes, there had been one or two outfits she'd worn when entertaining, but they were nothing in comparison to the beautiful dresses worn by the wives of Richard's friends. Betty knew these women looked down on her, laughed at her behind her back, and so wherever possible she avoided them. The children became her life, the garden her refuge and her pleasure as she watched the things she had planted burst into life.

Yet now that she was alone, Betty craved friendship and companionship. It had been lovely to meet

Val – lovely to be invited out to lunch. Would they become friends? Oh, she hoped so and, who knows, maybe Val would be able to give her a few tips on style.

'Right, let's go,' Val said, smiling warmly as they drove off.

The sun was shining and they chatted happily as they drove over the Thames. In what felt like no time at all, they arrived at the restaurant where Val was treated like a long-lost friend.

'Valerie, how lovely to see you,' a dark-haired woman with a pretty French accent said. 'How is Mr Warriner?'

'He's fine, Yvette, and as busy as ever.'

'I'm not surprised. He's a wonderful solicitor. Now let me find you a nice table,' she said, leading them to one by the window.

Betty sat down, admiring the décor. The tables were covered with blue and white checked cloths, each with a small vase of fresh flowers in the centre. The chairs were raffia-backed, the seats in the same check material; though she had never seen a French bistro before, this was just how she would have imagined it.

Yvette handed them each a menu, saying, 'Raymond's special for today is daube de boeuf, but while you're making up your mind, what can I get you to drink?'

'Betty, would you like red or white wine?' Val asked.

'I'm afraid I don't drink. Would it be possible to have a glass of tonic water?'

'Of course,' Yvette said. 'What about you, Valerie?'

'I'll have a glass of your house red, please.'

Yvette bustled off and when Betty picked up the menu, she baulked. 'Oh dear, it's all in French.'

Val smiled, 'Don't worry, I can more or less tell you what's on offer. As you can see, it isn't overly expensive,' she added.

'How do you know the owners?'

'When Raymond and Yvette wanted to buy this place, the solicitor I work for handled the conveyance. There were a few sticky moments, with the seller wanting to up the price at the last moment. Raymond would have paid it, but Mr Warriner convinced him to hold out and so saved him a lot of money. Raymond and Yvette seem to think that I had some input, even though I've told them I'm only his receptionist.'

Betty nodded, her eyes returning to the menu. 'What's the special that Yvette mentioned? The daube of something?'

'Daube de boeuf. It's a sort of beef stew,' Val said as she too scanned the menu. 'I'm not sure whether to have that or the poulet Basque.'

'Sorry, the what?'

'It's a chicken stew with tomato and onions, but then again the quiche Lorraine is delicious too. If you want something light, it's ideal, a sort of open tart filled with egg, ham and cheese.'

'Yes, and as it's the least expensive, I think I'll have that.'

Yvette returned with the drinks and, after giving her their order, they sat back to wait. As Val smiled at her, Betty plucked up the courage to say, 'I wish I knew how to dress like you. That outfit you're wearing looks so elegant, but it must have cost the earth.'

'At one time I could afford to go to all the best shops, but those days are gone. This dress would have cost the earth if it was new, but it's actually second-hand.'

'Really? Goodness, I used to go to the occasional jumble sale in our village hall, but I never found anything like that.'

'It's from a shop that sells only top-quality second-hand clothes. Finding it has been a godsend.'

'Well I never. Mind you, even if I found it, I doubt there'd be anything to fit me.'

'They carry a range of sizes. If you like, I'll take you there.'

'Would you? Oh, thanks, Val.'

'If you're free, we could go next Saturday?'

'Can we make it in two weeks? I'm a bit short at the moment.'

'Yes, that's fine.'

Betty picked up her glass to take a sip of tonic

water, unable to help wondering about Val's past. She had at first appeared haughty, but in reality it was just the way she held herself, head high, a slight lift to her chin. Poised, Betty thought, like a model. Earlier Val had mentioned a company car, and now said that once she'd frequented the best shops. Something must have happened to change all that, but Betty didn't have the nerve to ask what. Maybe when they got to know each other a little better Val would confide in her. But for now she smiled with appreciation as Yvette returned to place a plate in front of her. 'It looks lovely.'

'Yes, it does, and thank you, Yvette,' said Val.

The two of them tucked in and Betty found the quiche Lorraine delicious. Between mouthfuls they talked about the merits of French cooking. She loved the salad dressing, and when Val told her how to make it she was determined to buy the ingredients.

In no time their plates were empty and when Yvette returned to clear them she asked, 'Can I get you anything else, and – as I know you love it, Val – perhaps a slice of tarte tatin?'

'Lovely, and Betty, you must have some too. It's a sort of apple tart, French style, and I'm sure you'll love it.'

Betty agreed to try it, and when it arrived they tucked in with relish. 'Wonderful,' she enthused, 'and thanks for bringing me here, Val.'

'You're welcome, and anyway it's nice not to eat alone for a change.'

Betty expected someone like Val to have a wide circle of friends or family, but it appeared that if she hadn't been invited to tea yesterday, Val would have spent her birthday alone. Unable to resist the question, she blurted out, 'Do you have any family?'

'I have a few distant relatives, but I haven't seen them in years.'

They continued to chat as they ate, Val going on to tell Betty that she had lost her parents many years ago. Betty found herself warming more and more to Val, so grateful for this budding friendship, and all too soon the meal was finished.

They split the bill, Yvette smiling warmly as she said goodbye. 'Come again soon, Valerie.'

'I will,' she said, kissing the pretty French woman on both cheeks before they left.

Betty had loved the meal but, though it hadn't been too expensive, she would still have to cut down on food for the rest of the week to cover the cost. It had been worth it, though, and lovely to be in Val's company, but her mood lowered now they were going home. The rest of the day stretched ahead of her, followed by a lonely evening, but she brightened when Val spoke.

'I'll have to take Treacle for a walk, but after that why don't you join me for a coffee?'

'Lovely, but it's my turn, so why don't you come up to my flat?'

'Yes, I'd like that,' Val said, smiling warmly.

They continued to chat but when they arrived home and climbed out of the car, Betty saw a young woman sitting on the wall outside the entrance to the flats. She looked scruffy, pale, and anxious as she jumped to her feet, rushing to Val's side. 'Oh . . . Val . . . Val,' she cried.

'Paula, what's wrong?'

'I . . . I saw him.'

'Come on, come in,' Val urged, and as they stepped inside, she said, 'Sorry, Betty. I . . . I'll see you later.'

Without waiting for a reply, Val ushered the girl into her flat, the door closing swiftly behind them, leaving Betty mystified. The girl hardly looked the type to be a friend of Val's. Who was she? And why was she so upset?

Chapter Four

Treacle yelped with excitement when Val and Paula walked in, his small tail wagging as he jumped up at Val's legs but, intent on Paula, she said impatiently, 'Get down, boy. I'll take you for a walk soon, but not now.'

'Oh . . . Val,' Paula cried again.

'Sit down,' Val urged, worried by the girl's obvious distress. 'Tell me what happened.'

'It was so hot in me bedsit and I felt stifled, so much so that I risked going out. I only went for a little walk, but . . . but I saw him.'

'Did he see you?'

'N-no, and before he got the chance I legged it. I . . . I ran, Val, almost all the way here.'

'Oh, darling, I'm sorry I wasn't in,' Val consoled.

'It ain't fair. He . . . he ruined my life and shouldn't be out there walking the streets.'

'I'll get you a drink,' Val offered as she rose to her feet, her thoughts taking her back to the first time she had met Paula Richardson. She'd been to Clapham Junction and was walking back to where her car was parked when she saw a young girl ahead of her, limping and in obvious pain. The girl then stopped, and as it looked like she couldn't walk any further, Val had gone to offer her assistance. That girl had been Paula. She had tripped badly, her ankle swollen, and despite her protests Val had insisted on driving her to casualty. Whilst waiting for X-ray results they had chatted; luckily it turned out that her ankle wasn't broken, just sprained. On the drive home, Paula had been quiet, but when they neared her street it was as though a long-held dam burst and she poured out the story of what had happened to her so many months earlier. As she'd listened, Val had been shocked, sickened by the girl's dreadful ordeal. Paula had looked so young, sounded so alone, a diminutive blue-eyed blonde who wasn't yet twenty. Paula's ordeal had awakened something in Val. She too had been hurt. Oh, not in such a dreadful way, but she was living with bitterness and hatred. Yet why should she? Why should Paula? Val had found that she wanted to do something, and, like an avenging angel, to hit back.

The chance meeting with Paula had sparked off Val's plans, but that had been eighteen months ago and they were still a long way from fruition. Paula had suffered so much, was still suffering, her need the greatest, and Val was determined that she should be the first to benefit from her plans. She wanted to give Paula her life back, to get on with it, her surge of impatience quickly stifled when Paula began to cry.

'Oh, darling, don't,' Val urged as she gave Paula a glass of sherry. 'You're safe now, and soon, I hope, you'll never have to be afraid again. The woman you saw is the one I told you about, and I'm hoping she'll be a suitable recruit. If she is, we can go ahead with our plans.'

'Oh, Val, I hope you're right. Before I met you, I . . . I didn't think I'd be able to go on.'

'Darling, don't say that. I know you were dreadfully depressed, close to ending it all, but there's no need now. We'll get him, you'll see.'

'And you think this woman will help?'

'With any luck, yes. Her name is Betty Grayson. She lives alone, and works as a housekeeper in Kensington. She also has two grown-up children.'

'Won't they be a problem?'

Val was pleased to see that Paula had calmed down. 'No, I don't think so. They live out of London and whilst I've been watching her, I've only seen the daughter once.'

'It sounds like you've done all right so far. Have you told Cheryl about her?'

'Not yet. She's on duty all day but I'll give her a ring this evening.'

Treacle began to clamour again, and knowing the signs that a walk couldn't wait, Val said, 'I'll have to take him out, but why don't you join me? After that, I'll run you home.'

'Yeah, all right, but I was hoping to stay a bit longer.'

'I'm sorry, darling, but Betty has invited me up to her place for coffee and, if we want to get things moving, I must take every opportunity to work on her.'

Paula's voice was lacklustre. 'Yeah, I suppose so, but will I see you next weekend?'

Val wanted to use the valuable time to get to know Betty, but with Paula looking at her so hopefully, she just couldn't refuse. 'How about next Saturday? I could pick you up at around eleven o'clock.'

'Great, and . . . and thanks, Val.'

The two of them left the flat to take Treacle for a walk, the dog almost dragging Val to the nearest tree. When they crossed into the park, Val let him off the lead for a run, whilst Paula's feet dragged, her eyes flicking nervously around her as they ambled along. Val hated to see her like this, the poor girl a nervous wreck, and felt a wave of determination to move things forward. She'd share a confidence with Betty and cross her fingers that it would be returned.

Impatient to get on with it, Val made it a short walk, then clipped on Treacle's lead to take him to her car. She opened the back door, the dog scrambling onto the seat. 'Good boy, and stay there,' she ordered.

Paula climbed in beside her. Obviously reluctant to be driven home, she said sadly, 'I hate me bedsit.'

'Why don't you look for a better one? It would give you something to do and take your mind off things.'

'I'd still feel like a prisoner, stuck in the house, too scared to go out.'

'Not for much longer,' Val said firmly, hoping she was right.

Soon they pulled up outside the tall, narrow house near Clapham Junction where Paula had a bedsit on the first floor. 'Bye, Val . . . and see you next week.'

Val said goodbye, but saw how Paula's shoulders were stooped with unhappiness as she climbed out of the car to walk to her door. A surge of rage made her heart pound. It was dreadful that Paula had to live like this, and Val's hands gripped the steering wheel as she drove off, her knuckles white. They had to move forward – had to – and now her thoughts focused on Betty and a way to draw the woman out.

When Val returned to the flats she went straight upstairs to knock on Betty's door.

'Val, come on in,' Betty invited, her face alight with pleasure. 'When I saw that young woman waiting for you, I wasn't sure you'd be up for coffee.'

'I'm a bit late, but Paula was upset and I had to

run her home. Do you mind if I bring Treacle in?'

'Of course not. It was awful to see the poor girl in such a state.'

'She's fine now,' Val said, unwilling as yet to talk about Paula, 'and just someone I took under my wing.'

In Betty's flat, Val saw ornaments in abundance, with a fussy crochet runner along the surface of the sideboard. There were embroidered linen chair-backs on the three-piece suite, fussy net curtains at the windows and, though it wasn't to Val's taste, it was homely, cosy – a perfect reflection of Betty's personality.

Treacle made a fuss of Betty as she bent down to stroke him, and then he made straight for the rug in front of the fireplace where he settled down immediately. 'Well, would you look at that?' Val said. 'He's made himself at home already.'

'He's lovely,' Betty said, smiling wistfully. 'Now, sit yourself down and I'll make us a drink. I'm afraid I've only got Camp coffee. Will that do?'

'Sorry, Betty, in that case I'd rather have tea.'

'Tea it is,' she said, bustling off to her kitchenette.

Val sat back, her eyes closing as she rehearsed what she was going to say. It wouldn't do to give too much away yet but, with any luck, if she spoke about her own situation, it would encourage Betty to do the same.

Betty returned with a tray, and along with the

tea there was a paper-doily-covered plate holding a selection of biscuits. Like the woman, the china was fussy, the teapot covered with a hand-knitted cosy.

When the tea was poured, Val sighed, saying, 'It's been a lovely weekend but back to work tomorrow. It's not a bad job, but my earnings are a fraction of what they used to be.'

'Haven't you always been a receptionist?'

'No, Betty. At one time I had a flourishing career. I started off as a sales rep for a company supplying laboratory equipment. I gained promotions and eventually became the sales manager.'

'Really? Goodness, that sounds exciting, but I know little about the commercial world.'

'It's amazing how far some women have come since the war ended. Now they have independence, with the opportunity to take up careers that were considered unsuitable for them before the conflict. Yet to gain promotion I'm sure that, like me, they had to fight every step of the way, to prove themselves as capable as men.'

'Yes, but my daughter is always telling me that things are different now, that women have more opportunities.'

'She's probably right. Mind you, sometimes I wish I hadn't concentrated so hard on a career. I missed out on marriage, on children, but I was ambitious. If I hadn't been such a fool, if I hadn't trusted a man . . .' Val smiled sadly, leaving the sentence unfinished.

'Why, what happened?'

'It's a long story and I don't want to bore you.'

'No, please, I'd love to hear about it.'

'All right, then. As I said, I was ambitious, and made sure I kept up with current trends in the marketplace, worked hard to find sources of information. It was an exciting time, with new developments in equipment that would require no manual operation. This would be an enormous breakthrough for the industry and started with a titration device patented in America.'

'Pardon? A what?'

'Sorry, Betty, it's all technical jargon – and no wonder you look bemused. I shouldn't have blinded you with science, so come on, let's talk about something else.'

'No, do carry on. It's just that I don't know anything about laboratory equipment. You . . . you mentioned a man?'

Betty seemed eager to hear more, but Val wondered how far to go. She took a deep breath, deciding to expand a little. 'Yes, there was a man, but he ruined my life. You see during my time as a sales rep, and occasionally as sales manager, I had to do a lot of travelling, sometimes staying overnight in hotels. As our equipment was for targeted markets, such as private laboratories, universities and hospitals, we sometimes came across reps from other companies. It was during an overnight stay that I met Mike Freeman. He was from another firm and it was just friendly rivalry at first, a bit of banter, but I have to admit I was attracted to him. We became involved, seeing each other at every opportunity. He was a sales manager too, with a team about the same size as mine, so it wasn't always easy. We continued to meet as often as possible for the next eighteen months, but then . . .' With a small shake of her head, Val's sentence trailed off.

Betty leaned forward, softly urging, 'Oh dear, what happened?' As always, Val found it hard to talk about Mike Freeman, and hoped she had said enough to encourage Betty to open up too. 'I . . . I'm sorry, Betty, it's so painful, and even now just talking about it upsets me. Please, can we change the subject?'

Betty looked disappointed, but her tone was sympathetic. 'You poor thing. Yes, talking about things can be painful and I know how you feel. Let's have another cup of tea and do help yourself to biscuits.'

It boded well that Betty understood how she felt, and though Val wanted to ask more, she held back, hoping that Betty would elaborate on her situation.

She took a biscuit, but after Betty had poured two more cups of tea she said nothing further on the subject, instead saying, 'I'm looking forward to going to that shop you told me about. You said they sell good-quality second-hand clothes. Where do they get them from?'

'I'm not really sure, but I would imagine from women who want only the latest fashions. They're dry-cleaned before going on sale, and though most are from last season, if you buy something classic, and maybe just dress it with beads or a scarf, it'll carry you through for years.'

'I'm not sure what you mean by classic, so would . . . would you help me to choose something?' Betty asked, going slightly pink.

'Yes, of course.'

'Oh, Val, thank you,' said Betty, gratefully.

After that the conversation remained on clothes, designers, and the sort of style that Val thought would suit Betty.

Val then rose to leave, disappointed that Betty hadn't confided in her any further, but she consoled herself with the thought that it was early days yet. 'Thanks for the tea. I know we're going shopping in a couple of weeks, but until then, if you aren't busy in the evenings, you can always pop down to see me.'

'I might just do that,' Betty said, looking pleased at the invitation. 'Or you can come up here to see me.'

'Yes, all right,' Val said. 'Come on, Treacle, time for your dinner.'

The dog trotted to her side and, after saying

goodbye to Betty, they returned downstairs. Val fed Treacle, and then curled on her sofa, feet tucked under her as she went over her plans – beginning with Paula. It would be risky, and she wasn't sure the others would be willing to go along with her ideas, but they would need Betty to pull it off. Had she been hurt? So badly that she'd agree to join them? God, Val hoped so.

Chapter Five

During the next couple of weeks, Val tried to concentrate on her work, but as usual found it boring. She
saw Betty at least four times in the evenings but,
worried that rushing things would frighten the
woman off, no further confidences had been
exchanged. Though they had little in common, they
were becoming relaxed in each other's company. Val
appreciated Betty's warm personality, her motherly
nature and, obviously lonely, Betty always seemed
so grateful to see her.

When Val started out, other than Paula, she hadn't
expected to grow attached to her recruits. She'd seen
them as a means to an end, a way to bring closure
– not just for Paula and herself, but for them too.
Instead she found herself becoming emotionally
involved, and that now included Betty too.

While trying to recruit Betty, she'd hadn't seen
much of Paula, but kept in telephone contact with
both her and Cheryl. So far there was little to tell

them, but after this trip to the second-hand shop, Val decided that over coffee she'd open up again. Surely it would work this time? Surely Betty felt confident enough now to confide in her?

She and Betty were searching the racks, but Val felt a wave of displeasure. Yes, the clothes were nice, of good quality, but nevertheless they weren't new. At one time she had shopped only in the best outlets, her clothes all bearing designer labels, but because of Mike Freeman, look what she'd come down to. Her wages were low, her car an old wreck, and she was forced to dress in clothes that other women had discarded.

Val's thoughts were cut off as Betty held up a busily flowered skirt, smiling with delight as she said, 'I like this one, Val.'

'Yes, it's pretty, but maybe something that isn't gathered so fully around the waist would be better. Something like this,' she suggested, holding out a fawn, linen skirt that would skim the hips to gently flare out at the hem.

Betty looked doubtful. 'Do you think so?'

'Why don't you try it on?'

'All right, but I'll try this one too,' she said, taking both skirts to the changing room.

Val waited outside and when Betty came out wearing the fawn skirt she was beaming. 'I've never worn this shape before, but I must admit it makes me look slimmer. My broad hips have always been a problem and, as you know, I usually wear full skirts to conceal them.'

'Yes, but to be honest, gathers or pleats make them look wider. That skirt looks wonderful and the length is perfect.'

'Do you know,' Betty said as she eyed herself in a full-length mirror, 'I think you're right. I can't afford both and won't bother to try the other one.'

The purchase made, they left the small shop, Betty chatting about what she could wear with the skirt. 'I've got a couple of blouses – when we get home, would you help me to choose one?'

'Yes, if you'd like me to.'

It didn't take long to drive to Battersea, and after parking they went into the flats. 'Treacle will need a walk as usual, but then I'll pop up.'

'All right. See you soon. And thanks for taking me to that shop, Val.'

'I'm glad you liked it,' she replied, saying goodbye before going inside. As usual Treacle went mad when he saw her, and after clipping on his lead Val was outside again and on her way to the park. She wasn't looking forward to talking about Mike Freeman again, but had to get Betty talking too – and sooner rather than later.

When Val returned, Betty opened her door with a flourish. 'Come on in. I've been sorting out a few blouses for you to look at.'

45

Treacle made straight for Betty and, seeing that the dog was panting, she hurried to get him a bowl of water. He lapped it up then headed for the rug where he settled down. 'He was thirsty. What would you like to drink, Val?'

'Something cold would be nice.'

'Lemonade?'

'Yes, lovely.'

Val looked at the blouses, but saw only one that might be suitable. When Betty returned holding two glasses, she pointed it out. 'That plain pale blue would go nicely with the skirt and I'm sure I've got some beads that would tone in nicely.'

'I can't take your beads,' Betty protested.

'They'd be no loss. I haven't worn them for ages.'

'If you're sure, then thank you very much. I noticed you didn't buy anything. Wasn't there anything you liked?'

'I saw a lovely dress, but with a couple of bills to pay this month I couldn't afford it.' Val sighed, 'My wages were a lot higher when I was a sales manager.'

'Why did you leave such a good job? Was it to do with that man you mentioned?'

The conversation was going as Val had hoped, but now her expression saddened. 'Yes . . . Yes, I'm afraid it was.'

'I'm sorry, Val. I've upset you and shouldn't have asked.'

46

'No, it's all right, and anyway, perhaps talking about it will help.' Val paused to take a sip of her lemonade, then saying, 'I've already told you how I met Mike Freeman so I'll go on from there. We met as often as we could and I found myself falling in love with him. I was so happy, Betty, and we actually began to plan a future together, but then my sales director announced his retirement. Applications were invited for the position and, as it was such a wonderful opportunity, along with a huge rise in salary, I decided to apply.'

'Oh dear, and I suppose Mike was against it?'

'No, it was nothing like that. As I said, Mike and I had become very close, and in the same industry we had a lot in common. Being a sales rep or manager can be a lonely life. With so much travelling, along with working long hours, it's difficult to maintain friendships. As Mike was in the same position he understood, becoming not just my lover, but my dearest friend.'

Betty's eyes widened and for a fleeting moment Val thought she saw an expression of disapproval. She should've guessed that Betty would be old-fashioned in her views and worried that she had put her foot in it by saying that Mike was her lover, she quickly continued, 'To gain the promotion, my application had to be dynamic, innovative, and through someone I knew, someone that risked their job to tell me, I got a whisper that their research company was very close to developing a ninety-six-well microplate for scientific assays and—'

'A what plate?'

'It doesn't matter, Betty; suffice to say that when it became available it would save laboratories a fortune on manpower. I knew that if our company wasn't to be left behind it would need to be first in offering to sell this technology. With Mike's help I drew up my proposal to gain an exclusive contract with the manufacturer, along with other ideas I had for growth and change.'

'It all sounds very impressive, Val.'

'I thought it was, and Mike did too. He promised to say nothing to his company about the new technology until I'd secured the position, and I thought my promotion was in the bag. Oh, Betty, I was such a fool, a complete and utter fool. I loved Mike, trusted him without realising the cost. I thought he loved me too, but instead he betrayed me.'

'What did he do?'

'He told his company about the new microplate, – who would be supplying it – and got the contract for his firm ahead of mine. Not only that, he was indiscreet and word got round that he got the information from me. When it reached my employer's ears, I was thrown out of my company. I lost my job, my career – and it was all down to Mike Freeman.'

'My God, if you ask me the man should be shot.'

'Yes, and I felt like shooting him too, especially

when he gained promotion whilst I couldn't get another decent job in the industry. I even applied to be a sales rep again but, as I said, word had got out that I wasn't to be trusted. That and the fact that I was now considered too old. At the time I was nearly forty-three. I'm forty-five now.'

'But that isn't old,' Betty protested.

'Yes, well, that's how I was seen within the industry. Mike Freeman destroyed my reputation, took away all that I had worked towards. I loved my job and was good at it, but it all counts for nothing now.'

'Huh, men. If you ask me, they're all the same.'

'Oh dear, have you been treated badly too?' Val asked, trying not to look too eager as she took another sip of lemonade.

'Yes, but I . . . I'm afraid I can't bear to talk about it.'

'Did it happen recently?'

'No, it was four years ago, but I still can't get over it.'

'I'm so sorry,' Val said, and seeing that Betty's eyes were full of tears she added, 'I can see that you don't want to talk about it, but if you ever change your mind and want to get it off your chest, I'll be a sympathetic ear.'

'Thanks, Val.'

Betty had clammed up, and hiding her disappointment, Val rose to her feet. 'Well, thanks for listening to me, Betty. It certainly helped, but it's time I did a bit of housework. If you aren't busy tomorrow, perhaps you'd like to join me for tea again.'

'I'd love to, and I could make a nice Victoria sponge.'

'Lovely,' Val said, waking Treacle from his snooze. She'd hoped that confiding in Betty would encourage her to do the same, but it hadn't worked, and her expression was now grim as she made her way downstairs. Talking about Mike Freeman had opened up the wounds, so once inside her flat she went straight to her drinks cabinet to pour a large glass of sherry. She would have to ring Paula and Cheryl to report her progress, but there was little to tell them. Val gulped down her drink then poured another, consoling herself with the thought that there was always tomorrow. Maybe with a little more urging, Betty would finally tell her story.

Betty awoke on Sunday morning to find that her thoughts immediately went to Val. It was wonderful to have a friend now, someone who trusted her enough to share a confidence. Betty's heart went out to Val. She'd been treated so badly, losing a job she loved, and her bitterness was obvious. She's as angry as me, Betty thought. Richard had ruined her life too, but she had never been able to talk about it – to confide in anyone. They would think her a complete fool, an idiot for allowing it, and her shame kept her silent. Yet now, as the memories returned to plague her, Betty found she wanted to get it off her chest, to unburden the pain that remained like a hard rock in her chest. Val had been betrayed too; she'd understand, and maybe, just maybe, if she could bring herself to talk about it, the pain would ease.

Once she'd towelled herself dry, Betty dressed, and after eating a light breakfast she set about making the Victoria sponge, pleased to see when she took it from the oven that the two halves had risen perfectly. The kitchenette was stifling and it had been daft to bake a cake, especially with the cost of the ingredients, but as she sandwiched the two halves together with jam and butter icing, just looking at it made her mouth water.

The rest of the day seemed to drag as Betty half-heartedly did a bit of dusting, but living alone and naturally tidy, there was little to keep her occupied. She read for a while, glad when at last it was time to get changed.

With the skirt on, Betty inspected the cut. It was simple, elegant, and would be easy to copy. If possible, she'd save a little money to buy some off-cuts of material and her old treadle sewing machine would come in useful yet again. With the blue blouse tucked in, Betty stood back, twisting this way and that as she looked in the mirror. Yes, it did look nice, and she was so grateful that Val had helped her to choose it. When she picked up her shoes, Betty frowned. They were scuffed, worn down at the heels and would spoil her appearance, but as they were the only pair that didn't have holes in the soles, she would have to wear them.

Cake in hand, Betty went downstairs and was pleased to see Val's smile of pleasure as she opened the door. 'Hello, Val. I hope I'm not too early.'

'Of course you aren't and it's lovely to see you. That sponge looks wonderful, and you do too. Come on in. I've been feeling a bit fed up so it's nice to have a bit of company.'

Betty stepped inside, balancing the cake as Treacle rushed over to jump up at her legs. 'Hello, boy,' she said, handing the sponge to Val before reaching down to pat him.

'Sit down, Betty. I've made some sandwiches and I've only got to fill the teapot.'

Betty sank onto the sofa and Treacle leapt up beside her to lay his head on her knee. She stroked him for a while, but then Val returned with the tray.

'He's certainly taken to you,' she said. 'Get down now, Treacle, there's a good boy.' Val was ignored, and she sighed. 'As you can see, there's little improvement in his behaviour. I'm sorry, Betty, he's probably creasing your skirt – and it looks so nice too.'

'It's all right, I don't mind.'

Val laid down the tray. 'You pour the tea while I find that necklace.'

Betty eased Treacle to one side, feeling relaxed and at home as she picked up the teapot. She had only just finished pouring when Val returned, holding a strand of blue and pale cream beads.

'Here, try them on,' she said.

Betty slipped them over her head. 'They're lovely, but are you sure you don't need them?'

'I haven't worn them for a long time and they look perfect on you.'

'Thanks, Val. I'll treasure them.'

Val took a seat and then held out a plate of ham sandwiches. 'Tuck in and then we can have a piece of your sponge.'

For a while they munched companionably and after eating a slice of cake each, Betty sat back, replete. Treacle remained beside her. Absent-mindedly stroking him again, Betty said, 'I've been thinking about what you told me yesterday, Val, and I still can't get over how badly you were treated.'

'I was an idiot, but thanks for listening.'

'You're not alone in that. I've been an idiot too.'

'You can't have been as daft as me.'

'Oh, I was. My marriage ended four years ago, but as it lays the foundation for what happened to me, I suppose I should tell you a little of my background. You see, I grew up in Surrey, on the outskirts of a small village. My father worked on a farm and we lived quietly in a tiny cottage. We never travelled, other than the occasional trip to our nearest market town, and I suppose compared to a sophisticated woman like you, I'm a country bumpkin.'

'Rubbish. You're a lovely woman, warm and generous, and there's nothing wrong with being brought up in the country.'

Now that she had started, Betty found herself unable to stop, the words so long held back, now pouring out. 'My father ruled the roost at home and my mother happy to let him. It was from her that I learned how to make do and mend. When I married Richard, I just followed in her footsteps and, though we weren't well off, I was happy. Richard eventually went off to fight in the war, but when it was over he came home with plans to start up his own business.'

'Really, doing what?'

'He wanted to open up a car showroom and repair shop. Every penny made was ploughed back into the business so we continued to live frugally. I had to take what little money he gave me for housekeeping and make it stretch. I never had a bank account or any money of my own, but I loved Richard and wanted him to succeed, so I never complained.'

'And did he make a success of the business?'

'Eventually, but I never saw the fruits of his success.'

'Didn't you? Why was that?'

The painful memories were too much and Betty found tears flooding her eyes. Unable to go on she gasped, 'I . . . I'm sorry.'

'Oh, please don't cry. Look, I'll make us a fresh pot of tea, and how about another slice of your lovely cake?'

Betty fought to pull herself together. She couldn't eat another slice of cake, it would choke her; but she dabbed her eyes and felt a little calmer when Val returned to pour out fresh cups of tea.

'You don't have to talk about it if you don't want to,' Val said softly as she poured.

However painful, Betty wanted to talk – to get it out of her system. 'It's all right, but I think I'll jump forward to when my children left home. I missed them so much, and with Richard so busy, I felt lost and lonely. Richard then told me we were moving and I was shocked when he took me to see the house he wanted to buy.'

'Oh dear, was it too small?'

'No, Val, it was huge with eight bedrooms, but it had been empty for some time and was in a bit of a state. It was even worse outside, with a massive garden that had gone to seed, with brambles, weeds and a knee-high lawn, let alone the shrubs that had grown out of all proportion.'

'With just the two of you, why on earth did your husband want to take on a house of that size?'

Betty's lips thinned. 'He said he'd been advised

that property was an investment, a way to build up assets for his retirement, but I didn't believe that. He wanted it because he's a social climber and during our marriage he went out of his way to make friends with the wealthy, well-connected families in the area. Richard wanted the house to impress, to keep up, but he took out a huge mortgage to buy it.'

'It sounds like it needed a lot of work too.'

'Richard paid builders to do the renovations, but after that he said money was tight and I'd have to manage without any help. It took me months to clean the house, and even longer to bring the garden up to scratch. In all, it took just over a year, but in that time I grew to love the garden, and the house.' Betty paused, the next part so painful, and taking a deep breath she struggled to continue. 'It wasn't long after that when Richard dropped his bombshell. He . . . he . . . told me. Oh God, I . . . I was such a blind fool.'

'You're not alone in that. I trusted Mike Freeman – and look what happened to me.'

Yes, despite all her worldly ways, Betty thought, Val had been betrayed too. She felt an affinity with her new friend and it gave her the courage to go on. 'Richard had been acting strangely for a while, going out in the evening with the flimsiest of excuses, but I still didn't see what was going on right under my nose. When he finally said there was someone else I was shocked to the core. It was his secretary, a girl who worked in the showroom office, and yes, I mean a girl. She was only in her late twenties, where of course I was then forty-seven. Like his used cars, Richard decided to trade me in for a newer model.'

'You must have been heartbroken. What a dreadful way to treat you. I hope he lives to regret it,' Val said quietly.

'Oh, so do I . . . so do I,' Betty sobbed, finding herself crying in earnest. She felt Val's arm around her shoulder, grateful that she wasn't at all like the aloof woman she had first taken her for, and for the comfort she was now offering.

'Have a good cry. It'll do you good,' Val said softly.

At last Betty was able to pull herself together, and said shakily, 'I'm sorry for breaking down like that.'

'Don't be silly: you've been through hell. No wonder you're upset.'

'You haven't heard it all yet, but to tell you the truth I've got a bit of a headache. I'll tell you the rest another day, but for now I think I'll go upstairs and take a couple of aspirin.'

'All right, but I hope talking about it has helped. Pop down any time; perhaps tomorrow evening if you aren't busy.'

'Yes, all right. Bye, Val, and thanks for listening.'

'Bye, my dear.'

Betty felt emotionally exhausted as she trod wearily upstairs. She hadn't known Val very long, but strangely it was beginning to feel as if she'd known her for years. There was a deep feeling of empathy, so much so that she had finally unburdened herself.

Yet there was more to tell – worse to tell. Val had been so kind, so sympathetic, but how would she feel about a woman who had been so weak, so stupid, that she had let her husband walk all over her?

Chapter Six

Val was disappointed. It was the weekend again but, despite seeing Betty for a couple of evenings, she hadn't mentioned her marriage again. So far her story had been all too familiar, one that she had often heard whilst working for Mr Warriner. Betty was angry about her divorce settlement, that was all, and Val now doubted that she'd want to join the group. There were lots of women who'd been hurt by divorce, by their husbands going off with a younger woman, but she hadn't heard of any who had hit back. Val heaved a sigh, yet maybe she shouldn't give up yet. Betty said there was more to her story, and it puzzled her that the woman had to live so frugally. From what Betty had said her husband owned a thriving business and they had lived in a very large house, so what had happened to her settlement?

The telephone rang at ten o'clock on Saturday morning and when she answered it, Val found Paula on the line. 'Hello dear. How are you?'

'I'm all right, but a bit fed up. Cheryl's on duty again so we can't meet up. Can I come round to your place?'

'Betty has clammed up, but I feel there's more she isn't telling me. I was going to pop upstairs to ask her if she'd like to go out for a walk, but to be honest, if she still won't talk, I'm stuck.'

'What about this afternoon? Can I come round then?'

'Make it about two o'clock and I'll make us some lunch.'

'Will I meet Betty?'

'No, I don't think so. Oh, but wait a minute,' Val said as she was struck by a thought, 'maybe if she hears your story it'll give her the confidence to open up again. I know I'm rushing it, but I really do want to get on with our plans.'

'Oh, Val, so do I, but I'm not sure about telling Betty,' Paula said, her voice reedy with doubt. Val could have kicked herself. Honestly, sometimes she was so thoughtless. Wanting to make amends, she said, 'Darling, I'm sorry, I spoke without thinking. Of course you don't want to talk about it again.'

There was a pause, but then Paula said, 'It's all right. If you think it will help, I'll give it a go.'

'Are you sure?'

'Yeah, but if I choke up you may have to take over.'

'That's fine.'

They said goodbye and, hoping that the ploy would work, Val waited a couple of hours before going upstairs to invite Betty to lunch.

'I was hoping to see my daughter, but so far there's no sign of her,' Betty said flatly. 'I doubt she'll turn up now, so yes, I'd love to join you for lunch.'

'I hope you don't mind, but a friend of mine will be joining us too – the young girl you saw waiting for me outside the flats a few weeks ago.'

'Err . . . no, of course not.'

'Right then, I'll see you in an hour.'

Val hurried back downstairs, and as she wanted to have everything ready for when they arrived, she hoped that the quick salad she knocked up would suffice. This was it – make or break time. Val liked Betty, felt sorry for her, but she couldn't afford to waste any more time on the woman. If hearing Paula's story didn't draw Betty out, she would have to find someone else to recruit.

Betty was the first to arrive, and Val was gratified to see that she was carrying a plate of buttered scones. 'I've only made salad, so you're a treasure.'

'I always enjoyed baking and it's nice to get my hand in again. I hope your friend likes them.'

'I'm sure she will,' Val said, and was just about to close the door when she saw Paula entering the block. 'There she is now.'

With both of them inside, Val could see that Betty was puzzled – and she understood why. Paula was young and pretty, but dressed like a nun in a threadbare long, dark skirt and high-necked blouse. She wore no make-up, her hair scraped back in an untidy ponytail, and with nails bitten down to the quick, she appeared a nervous wreck.

Val made the introductions, then said, 'Sit yourselves down. What would you like to drink?'

''Ave you got any gin?' Paula asked.

'Sorry, no, but I've got sherry. Will that do?'

'Yeah, I suppose so.'

Betty looked shocked, whilst Val went to her cabinet to pour the drinks. 'What about you, Betty? Will you join us in a sherry?'

'No, thanks, you know I don't drink,' she said, her face showing disapproval as, instead of sipping her sherry, Paula tipped up the small glass to swallow it in one gulp.

Not a good start, Val thought. Betty had no idea what Paula had been through, why she drank, but hopefully when she heard Paula's story there'd be understanding instead of disapproval. She poured Paula another sherry, and then asked, 'How's the new job going?'

'It ain't bad, and now that I've got the hang of it I'm left mostly on me own. The noise of the flippin' machinery cuts out much chance of chatting and that suits me fine.'

'Paula works in a print factory,' Val explained.

'Yeah, that's right. What do you do, Betty?'

'Oh, I'm just a cleaner-cum-housekeeper in a house in Kensington. I'm afraid I'm not trained for anything else.'

'I know how you feel. There was just me and Mum and we were hard up. When I was fifteen she couldn't wait for me to leave school and bring a few bob in. I've been stuck in one factory or another ever since.'

'Come on, you two, stop bringing yourselves down,' Val protested.

Betty smiled at last and, indicating the bowl of salad along with a plate of bread and butter, Val urged them to help themselves. They each filled a plate but the atmosphere was still a little strained until Treacle sat beside Betty, balancing on his rear legs to beg for some of her food.

'You won't want salad,' Betty laughed, 'but is it all right if I give him a piece of my bread and butter, Val?'

'Just a tiny bit. Honestly, he's like a dustbin.'

'I think he's lovely,' Paula said. 'I'd love a dog but I'm not allowed animals in my bedsit.'

'Don't you live at home?' Betty asked.

'No. When my mum got married again she moved out of London and her new bloke made it pretty obvious that I wasn't welcome.'

'But that's awful. How old were you?'

'Eighteen, but it wasn't a big deal. All me mates

were here so I didn't want to move out of London anyway.'

They continued to eat, and Val was pleased to see them looking more relaxed. When the meal was finished and the coffee made, they all sat on the sofas, Betty asking, 'How did you two meet?'

'Another long story I'm afraid,' Val said. 'I met Paula by chance about eighteen months ago. She had hurt her ankle and I took her to casualty . . . But I'll leave Paula to tell you the rest.'

Betty turned to look at Paula, but the girl had her head down.

'Paula, do you feel up to talking about it?' Val asked.

'Yeah, I fink so,' she said, but then took up her handbag. She removed a packet of cigarettes and, after opening them, offered one to Betty.

'No thanks, I don't smoke.'

'What about you, Val?'

'Yes please.'

Paula's hands shook as she lit the cigarettes, but then turning to Betty she said, 'I know it was a while ago, but it still haunts me. I can't face going out at night knowing that he's still out there – and even during the day I'm shit scared.'

Val could see that Betty disapproved of Paula's language, and as the girl paused, she quickly took over, saying gravely, 'Paula was raped, Betty.'

'Oh no! Oh God, how awful.'

When Paula began to cry, Betty moved along the sofa and, as though all her mothering instincts came to the fore, she wrapped the young woman in her arms. 'There . . . there,' she murmured.

For a while Paula cried, whilst Betty held her, but then with a juddering sob Paula finally stopped. She moved away from Betty to reach for her cigarettes again, hands trembling as she lit one up. 'Sorry Val,' she said in a voice barely above a murmur, 'do you want another one?'

'No, darling. I've managed to cut down to ten a day now.'

'I'm still on forty.'

'After what you've been through, I'm not sur prised but, like me, I think you should try to smoke less.'

'If he was in prison where he belongs, I know it would make all the difference, but you know he isn't, Val – he's still around and sometimes it feels like he's mocking me.'

'But why is he still around? How did he get away with it?' Betty cried.

'There were no witnesses, and it was Paula's word against his. After it happened she ran home, and it was twenty-four hours before she plucked up courage to go to the police.'

'It was awful,' Paula blurted out. 'There wasn't a policewoman at the station and the coppers who interviewed me made it obvious they thought it was my fault . . . that I had asked for it. I didn't, Betty, honestly I didn't. Just because I used to wear miniskirts and don't talk posh, they treated me like a tart. It ain't right.'

'Did they at least try to catch him?'

'It wasn't hard. He lives locally and, though I hadn't spoken to him, I'd seen him around. I knew his name, where he lives, and one night at a dance I let him take me home. That . . . that's when it happened. The cops said they'd bring him in for questioning, but it was a waste of time. He denied it, of course, and because there wasn't any evidence, the case didn't even get to court.' Once again Paula began to cry, this time spontaneously falling into Betty's arms.

Val had heard the story before, but it still touched her, angered her that Paula had to live like a virtual recluse. She went to work during the day, but never ventured out at night, her young life destroyed.

'It ain't right,' Paula cried, 'it isn't fair that he's still free. I just wish there was some way to make sure that he goes to prison where he belongs.'

'I agree,' Betty said, 'he should be locked up and the key thrown away.'

It was dreadful to see Paula in such a state again and, though it was necessary to recruit Betty, Val felt awful for putting her through such an ordeal. The girl moved from Betty's arms again to light yet another cigarette, her fingers stained brown from heavy smoking. When Paula finally stubbed it out, she stood up.

'I'm sorry, Val, but I don't like being out in the evenings and I've got a splitting headache.'

'Paula, I've got some aspirin. There's no need to leave yet. It won't be dark for ages and when you want to go I'll give you a lift home.'

Betty then rose to her feet, her smile soft and kind as she spoke to Paula. 'If you've got a headache, I think you need a bit of peace and quiet. I'll leave, but if you ever need anything . . .' Her voice trailed off.

'Fanks, Betty, and it was nice to meet you. I . . . I'm sorry I broke down.'

'Oh, sweetheart, there's no need to apologise.'

As Betty moved to the door, Val followed, saying quietly, 'You don't have to leave.'

'I know, but I think it's for the best. Bye, and I'll see you soon.'

When Val closed the door she turned to Paula. 'I'm so sorry. I should have realised that talking about it would be too much for you.'

'It . . . it's like reliving it all over again, but other than this rotten headache I'm all right now. I like Betty, she's nice.'

Val nodded in agreement. Yes, Betty was nice and had been so sympathetic, but would she understand what they wanted to do – and why? Not only that, unless she too had been badly hurt by more than a divorce settlement, Val still wasn't sure that she'd want to join them. Once again she felt a surge of impatience. How much longer was this going to take? Would she have to drop Betty? Oh, she hoped not.

Chapter Seven

On Sunday morning, Betty was thinking about Paula. She had been sickened by what she'd heard, her heart going out to the poor girl. Paula was a lot younger than her own daughter, with none of Anne's self-assurance. She was so tiny, only just over five feet tall, with dull blonde hair and baby blue eyes. Her clothes were dowdy, her face bare of make-up, hiding the fact, Betty was sure, that Paula was actually a pretty young woman.

When there was a knock on her door she hurried to open it, delighted to see her daughter. 'Anne, how lovely to see you – and on a Sunday for a change. Did you have a nice holiday? And what happened to my postcard? You've been back a week but it still hasn't arrived.'

'Hello, Mum. Sorry about the postcard, but I didn't get a chance to send any. Mel was taken ill and Dad was worried about her.'

'You didn't tell me that your father and Mel were going with you.'

'Didn't I?'

Betty was about to retort when there was another knock on the door. She opened it, her face lighting with joy. It had been so long since she had seen her son and his last visit had been to her previous flat. 'John, how wonderful to see you!'

'Hello, Mum,' he said, before leaning forward to kiss her swiftly on the cheek.

Betty stood aside to let him in, her voice high with excitement. 'Look, Anne, it's John.'

'Hello, sis,' he said. 'Mum told me you were going on holiday. Did you have a good time?'

'Yes, we had a week in Spain with Dad and Mel.'

Betty was pleased to see John's lips curling in derision, since she felt the same, but if they started to argue they'd leave and she didn't want that. 'It's marvellous that you've both turned up at the same time. Come on, now; don't stand there like a pair of combatants. Sit down and I'll get you something to drink.'

Anne flopped onto the sofa, whilst John took a chair, and as she hurried to the kitchenette, Betty could hear Anne talking to her brother.

'I'm glad you're here. I've got a bit of news and this way I can kill two birds with one stone.'

Wondering what this news could be, Betty hurriedly opened her small fridge, only to shake her head with annoyance. With so many other things on her mind she had forgotten to get any Cokes, and now could only offer Anne orange juice. She poured two glasses, saying as she took them into the living room, 'Sorry, this is the only cold drink I've got. If you'd prefer, I could make a pot of tea.'

'Orange juice is fine, Mum,' John said as he reached out to take a glass.

'It's too hot for tea and this will do,' Anne agreed.

'So, Anne, what's this news?' asked John.

Anne's eyes danced as she looked at her brother. 'When Mel wasn't well in Spain, we put it down to the food, but since returning she's been to see the doctor. You're not going to believe this. Dad said he didn't want any more children, but she's pregnant. Mel's pregnant.'

Betty felt herself going rigid with shock. 'Pr . . . pregnant?'

'Yes,' Anne said dismissively, as though unaware how her mother was feeling as she turned to her brother again, 'and John, that means we're going to have a new baby brother or sister.'

'Half-brother or -sister,' he retorted, 'and if you ask me, it's a bit sick. Bloody hell, Dad's old enough to be the child's grandfather.'

Betty's head was reeling. Somehow, deep down, she had always hoped that the marriage would end – that, as Richard aged, Mel would want a younger man. He was already twenty-five years her senior, and it sickened Betty that at fifty-eight years old he was about to start another family. 'How . . . how does your father feel about it?'

'He's really happy, cock-a-hoop and strutting about with his chest puffed out with pride.'

'I thought you said he didn't want any more children.'

'Yes, but Mel had other ideas. She's thirty-three now and I think felt the time was right if she was going to have children. She was feeling really broody so, without telling Dad, she stopped taking the pill.'

'Wasn't he angry?'

'No, I told you, he's full of it, and it seems to have knocked years off him. You should see him fussing over Melissa, even getting a cleaner to come in once a week.'

Betty's head was low. A cleaner – Melissa had a cleaner. Oh, not for her slaving to keep the house and garden up to scratch. Then, feeling a hand on her shoulder, she looked up to see John leaning over her, eyes full of concern.

'Are you all right, Mum?'

'Ye-yes, but I must admit it's come as a bit of a shock. Oh, it's awful,' she then blurted out, 'somehow I didn't expect the marriage to last, but . . . but now
. . . .'

'Mum, don't tell me that you still hold a torch for Dad?'

Betty stared up at her son, fighting to hide her

true feelings. She would never admit it to him, or anyone, but yes, she still held a torch for Richard. Despite what he had done, she still loved him, and felt she always would. 'Of course I don't,' she lied.

John's eyes narrowed in doubt, but Betty made a supreme effort to regain composure and change the subject. 'Come on, we've heard Anne's news, now what about you? It's been ages since I've seen you, so tell me, what've you been up to?'

'I'm sorry I haven't been round, but I ring you every week. It's work, Mum, I've been snowed under.'

'John, how's your love life?' Anne asked.

'I've got a new girlfriend and this one might be serious.'

'Really . . .' Anne drawled.

'Now then, there's no need for sarcasm,' he protested. 'Surely a man has a right to sow his oats before settling down.'

Doing her best to keep her mind away from Richard, Betty said, 'Tell me about this girl.'

'She's a cracker, Mum. Her name is Ulrika and she's from Sweden.'

'Goodness, how did you meet her?'

'My boss invited me round to dinner. She's their au pair.'

'How long have you been seeing her?' asked Anne.

'What's this, twenty questions? Still, if you must know, I've been seeing her for two months.'

Anne laughed. 'Two months – and you call it serious?'

'It is for me.'

John was so like his father in looks that Betty gulped. They were both tall, both dark and handsome. Their characters were similar, too, both of them charmers. 'You may be serious about this girl, but don't rush things. Make sure that she really is the one before you settle down.'

'Don't worry about me, I know what I'm doing,' he said, but then with a glance at his watch added, 'Sorry, but I've got to go.'

'John, you've only just got here.'

'I'm off too, Mum,' Anne said.

'I hardly see the pair of you,' Betty protested, 'yet when you do stir yourselves to visit me, you only stay for five minutes.'

'Don't exaggerate, we've been here for longer than that,' Anne protested.

Betty knew it was useless to argue. Like his sister, John still lived in Farnham, his job hectic and, with a wide circle of friends, his social life was full. With a sad sigh, she kissed them both on the cheek before saying goodbye. 'John, don't leave it so long next time. I really would like to see more of you. If you really are serious about this girl, perhaps you could bring her with you next time?'

'Yes, all right, Mum,' he called before he hurried downstairs, Anne close behind.

'Bye, Mum,' she too called.

Sadly Betty closed the door and then hurried to the window to watch them climb into their cars, both waving to each other before driving off. Anne might call again in a few weeks, but despite John's assurance, she doubted her son would do the same. She knew they had their own lives, but the room now felt empty without them. *She* felt empty, unlike Mel who was now having Richard's baby.

Betty's lower lip trembled. Yes, she still loved Richard, but he'd made a fool of her. She was miserable, whereas he was happy, and instead of the news helping her to move forward she felt a surge of bitterness – one that made her wish she could wipe the smile off his face.

At one o'clock, Val went upstairs to see Betty, but her smile dropped when she saw her friend's face. 'You look like you've been crying. What's the matter?'

'My son and daughter have been to see me, and . . . and . . .'

'Oh dear, did they bring bad news?'

'Not according to my daughter, but it's knocked me for six. They're going to have a baby.'

'You're upset because your daughter's pregnant?'

'No, not my daughter. It's Mel, my ex-husband's wife. She's the one who's having a baby.'

Val didn't know what to say. It wasn't unusual for

a second marriage to result in more children, but she didn't feel it would help to point this out to Betty. It was obvious that the ex-husband had moved forward, yet for Betty the wounds were still painful. 'Come and sit down,' she urged, 'and I'll make us both a cup of tea.'

'Thanks, Val.'

'Here, drink up,' Val said when she returned to see that Betty was still distressed, her hands wringing in her lap.

Betty took a sip of tea, but when she then spoke, her voice rang with bitterness. 'It just isn't fair. Richard is over the moon and, from what my daughter said, he's fussing over Mel like she's a china doll, even getting her a cleaner. He can afford it now, of course, whereas when I was married to him I had to work like a slave without an ounce of help.'

Val knew this was the ideal opportunity to probe, so said gently, 'How come he's comfortably off whilst you have to struggle?'

'I . . . I can't tell you. You'll think I'm mad.'

'I doubt it. Working for a solicitor I've seen and heard some terrible things and you'd be surprised how many women come out of a divorce with far less than they're entitled to.'

'Really?'

'Yes, really.'

'God, I thought it was only me. When I was married to Richard, he handled all our finances and I thought myself lucky that I had a husband who took care of everything whilst I was worry-free. I was living in my perfect little world, with my perfect marriage but, as I told you before, all that fell apart when Richard told me that there was someone else.'

'Yes, and it must have been a terrible shock.'

'It was, and when Richard told me about Mel, I didn't know what to do. I loved him so much and hoped it was just a passing fancy. I was wrong though, because shortly after he asked for a divorce. I couldn't believe it, wouldn't believe it. I begged, cried, pleaded with him not to leave me, but he was implacable. For nearly a year, I wouldn't accept it, refused to talk about it, but then, just when I thought that things couldn't get any worse, he . . . he moved his girlfriend in.'

'What! Into your home?'

'Yes, and Mel was so brazen, cuddling up to Richard in front of me.'

Val found it incredible, her voice high as she said, 'My God, what sort of woman would do that?'

Betty lowered her head. 'I don't know, but worse, I – I heard them having sex every night. In the mornings, Mel couldn't look me in the eye, but Richard didn't care. He was so cruel, fawning over Mel, showing me how triumphant he was about their sex life. It became unbearable to see them together, to hear them, and I felt an intruder in my own home.'

Val was secretly pleased that Betty now felt confident enough to talk to her about such a sensitive subject. 'What did you do?'

'In the end I couldn't stand it any more, and when Richard offered to find me somewhere else to live, I moved out.'

'I can understand how you felt, but maybe that wasn't the best thing to do. By making your life so unbearable that you moved out, Richard retained your home.'

'I know that now, but at the time I was at the end of my tether, my nerves all over the place. Richard rented me a flat in the next town, arranged a small allowance and advised me to see a solicitor to file for a divorce.'

'The bastard! Oh, pardon my language, Betty, but I can hardly believe what I'm hearing. You poor thing. What did you do?'

'I was in a terrible state, so at first I did nothing, but then Richard took the initiative and filed for divorce, using the grounds that I had deserted him.'

'But you didn't desert him. He more or less forced you out.'

'I know, but with no other choice I had to find my own solicitor.'

'Well, I hope he took Richard to the cleaners.'

'No, I'm afraid not. Our house was mortgaged to

the hilt, along with the business, and on paper Richard had little to show in assets. I felt sure that the business was doing well, that Richard had money, and my solicitor thought he might have hidden it in offshore accounts. The trouble was it would have taken years to unravel and I couldn't afford to retain a solicitor for that long. The children were grown up and had left home, so in the end all I got was a settlement.'

'It sounds like your husband was very clever.'

'Yes, but you probably think I'm a fool for letting it happen.'

'Of course I don't. You couldn't prove that your husband had money and if you ask me you were treated badly, but how did you end up in London?'

'After the break-up and then the divorce, I felt lost. My life had been centred round my home, my husband and children, but now I had no purpose. I couldn't bear to think about Richard and Mel, about all I'd lost, and sank into depression.'

'How awful for you.'

'Yes, it was, but my son, John, was supportive, cutting his father from his life, and, when he wanted to buy his own house, I knew he wouldn't go to Richard for help. I didn't want him taking on a huge mortgage, so stepped in to give him a large deposit. John didn't want to take it, but I insisted, and though it bit into what money I had, I didn't care. In fact, I didn't care about anything any more and just lived off my settlement for about two years. When I realised that the money was almost gone, I knew there was no choice. I'd have to pull myself together, get a job. It was then that I moved to London and, well, you know the rest.'

'Oh, Betty,' Val murmured.

'What's worse is that Richard is now living the life of Riley and Mel wants for nothing. Unlike me, she has every luxury, whereas I'm alone now and have to struggle to pay the rent every week.'

Val knew she still had to be careful, but took the opportunity to hint at revenge. 'It's so unfair and I wish there was some way to make him pay for what he did to you.'

'Me too, but there's nothing I can do.' She scrubbed at her face with a handkerchief and then sighed heavily. 'Compared to what happened to poor Paula, this all sounds rather pitiful, and I suppose it is really.'

Val's thoughts turned. Betty had been treated badly, so badly that – instead of harbouring doubts – she now felt a surge of glee that the woman could be recruited. She leaned forward, saying softly, 'We've both had a rotten time of it, but yes, I think Paula has suffered the most. She's coming round in an hour and I hope she's feeling better. It was lovely to see how she took to you. In fact, she thinks you're really nice.'

Betty's smile was faint, but she looked pleased. 'Does she?'

'Yes, and if you don't want to be on your own, why don't you join us?'

'You could bring her up here. I need something to take my mind off Richard and, as you made lunch yesterday, I'll do it today.'

'You're on, but I'd best pop downstairs just in case Paula arrives early.'

'Thanks for listening, Val – it really has helped.'

'I'm glad,' Val said, thinking about Betty's husband as she went downstairs. He had been so cruel; instead of living in comfort, he should suffer for what he'd done.

Betty fought to push thoughts of Richard away as she looked for something to make for lunch. Val hadn't been shocked; in fact she had been sympathetic and Betty was so grateful for her friendship.

There wasn't a great deal in her refrigerator, but enough eggs to knock up omelettes. She would wait until they arrived before cooking them, but they could be mixed in advance. That done, she then buttered some bread. Betty then hurried to the bathroom, appalled when she looked in the mirror to see that her eyes looked awful. She splashed her face with cold water, ran a comb through her hair, and hoped that a dash of face powder would make her look marginally better.

In what felt like no time there was a knock on her door. Forcing a smile, Betty opened it to let Val and Paula in.

'Oh, this is nice. It's cosy,' Paula said as her eyes swept the room.

'Compared to Val's flat, I'm afraid mine is rather old-fashioned.'

'Well I like it,' the young woman insisted.

'Sit down, the pair of you, and I'll get on with lunch. It won't take long, but would you like something to drink first?'

'Have you got any booze?' Paula asked eagerly.

'No, I'm afraid not.'

Paula looked disappointed, but Val said, 'Anything cold will do, Betty.'

'Yeah, for me too.'

Betty made them both a glass of orange squash and then returned to the kitchen. She could hear them chatting, the subject someone called Cheryl and plans to meet up with her the following weekend. It was strange really: she had thought Val lonely, but now friends seemed to be popping up from all over the place. Val and Paula's friendship was strange; the pair of them seemed like an unlikely couple, and Betty was intrigued about Cheryl. Would she be another one like Paula? Was Val the type who liked to help waifs and strays?

The omelettes were met with appreciation, Paula eating every scrap. 'Fanks for making lunch, Betty. It was great.'

'Yes, it was delicious,' Val agreed.

Betty smiled with pleasure as she began to stack

the plates. 'It's all right, dear, I can manage,' she protested as Paula took them through to the kitchen. 'Shall I make us all a drink?' she called.

'It's all right, I'll see to it.'

'Let her do it. She likes to muck in,' Val advised.

Betty nodded. 'All right, Paula, you can make the drinks and you'll find what you need in the cupboards. I've got some decent coffee now so Val might like that.'

'Yes please,' Val called and then patted the seat beside her. 'Come on, Betty, sit yourself down and tell me, are you feeling better?'

'Yes, a little. Having you two for lunch has kept my mind off things, but please, let's change the subject. I don't want to think about Richard.'

'Sorry, I shouldn't have brought it up. It's just that I'm worried about you.'

Betty lowered her eyes. Was this why Val had made overtures of friendship? Did she see her as another waif and stray to take under her wing? Oh stop it, she chided herself. Val had known nothing about her when they'd met in the park and, instead of going on the defensive, wondering why Val sought her company, she should just appreciate her new kind and caring friend. 'Thanks, Val, but I'm all right, honestly.'

Paula returned with the coffee, saying, 'I've washed up, but I didn't know where you keep your china and cutlery so I've left it all stacked up.'

'There was no need to do that, but thank you,'

Betty said, and as it had with Val, her heart warmed more and more towards Paula.

They drank their coffee, and when Paula asked her about her job, Betty described her duties, along with all the wonderful antique furniture and paintings in the house.

'It sounds nicer than working in a factory,' Paula mused.

'I'm on my own all day, and it can be a bit boring.'

'I wouldn't mind that.'

They went on to talk about Val's job, happy in each other's company now, but then, at four o'clock, Val said that Treacle would need a walk.

Paula rose to her feet too, and impulsively Betty hugged the girl, finding it returned as she said, 'We must do this again.'

'Yes, I'd like that,' Paula said.

Betty was sorry to see Paula and Val leave and remained in her doorway when they walked downstairs – but, unaware of this, they began talking about her, their voices drifting back up to her.

'I really like Betty, Val. Do you think she'll want to join us?'

'I hope so. The sooner we get started, the better,' Val replied, but then her voice went out of range as they reached the ground floor.

Betty closed her door, finding herself intrigued. Join them? Join them in what?

Chapter Eight

Paula nervously left her flat on Monday morning, constantly glancing behind her as she hurried to the bus stop on East Hill. As usual she was dressed dowdily. Before it happened, before Ian Parker had raped her, she'd been full of confidence, wearing the latest fashions, like most girls, proudly showing off her shapely legs in miniskirts. She had enjoyed a laugh, nights out, and her friends had likened her to the pop singer Lulu. Paula couldn't sing, but had to admit that there was a slight resemblance in their build and features.

When her mother remarried and moved out of London, she'd been glad to remain in the capital, finding a little bedsit close to Clapham Junction. She liked her independence, loved being able to hop on a bus over to the King's Road and Carnaby Street, but now the latest trends held no interest. A young man was walking towards her and Paula cringed, folding in on herself until he passed. At last she reached the bus stop to see one of the girls who worked at the factory already waiting.

'Watcha. Did you have a nice weekend?'

Paula just nodded, feeling nothing in common with the fashionably dressed girl of similar age.

'I went to a new shop that's opened in Kensington High Street. Biba, it's called and you should see it. The décor's all black, in the 1930s' style, with potted palms and loads of hat-stands festooned with feather boas. It was packed, especially in the communal changing room, but the clothes are fantastic. I got a great dress and wore it to the Hammersmith Palais on Saturday night.'

Paula eyes were fixed ahead, saved from answering as a bus drew up. She stood back to let the other girl get on first, relieved when she called, 'I'm going upstairs for a ciggie.'

Paula wanted to smoke too, but unwilling to chat to the young girl she stayed downstairs, relieved to find a seat next to an older woman. Her thoughts drifted to Betty, a woman she had liked, one who had held her, comforted her when she cried. Unlike her own mother, Betty had appeared warm and caring, her sympathy genuine. It had been six months since she'd seen her mother, but that wasn't unusual. On rare occasions she travelled to Essex to see her, but never felt welcome as her mother's life now revolved around her new husband.

Paula had no idea who her father was, and had

given up asking. From what she'd seen of her mother's life, the men who had come and gone, she doubted if her mother even knew which one had fathered her.

When the bus pulled up at a stop a passenger got on, taking a seat in front of her. Paula took one look at the back of his head and her heart stopped. He had red hair and that was enough to bring back the nightmare. She'd been so stupid, mad to be impressed that Ian Parker had a car. When he'd asked to take her home from the dance she had jumped at the chance, and he'd seemed so nice, with green eyes that crinkled at the corners when he smiled. Ian Parker was over six feet tall and she'd felt diminutive beside him as they walked to his car, but he hadn't driven home. Instead he'd taken her to Clapham Common, pulling up in a secluded side road. At first she hadn't been nervous, and had in fact felt excited when he pulled her into his arms. Even when he tried it on she hadn't panicked, used to boys' fumbling attempts and how to put an end to them. As soon as his hand went up her skirt, she had shoved it away, and when he immediately stopped, she felt safe, in control. He had then suggested getting out of the car, saying that as it was such a warm, clear night, they would be able to see the stars, something he professed an interest in. She'd agreed, but that moment, that one decision, had changed her life. Something had been taken away from her – something she could never get back.

Paula shivered, the scene playing over and over in her mind as her hands wrung in her lap. They had walked onto the common, Ian pointing out the Milky Way and other formations. She'd been impressed with his knowledge, trying her best to sound intelligent, but then shortly afterwards he struck. She'd been forced onto the grass, Ian's hands pushing up her skirt, pulling at her knickers, ignoring her kicks and screams of pain as he entered her. She'd been left broken, sobbing, whilst he just walked away, never once looking back.

'Are you all right, ducks?' the elderly woman sitting beside Paula asked.

It was only then that Paula became aware of the tears streaming down her cheeks. She fumbled for a handkerchief, wiped them away and managed to croak, 'Yes,' before rising swiftly to her feet, heading for the platform and willing the bus to stop.

It slowed on the approach to some traffic lights and Paula jumped off, relieved to find that it wasn't far to the factory. She clocked in, glad that she had managed to pull herself together as she entered the machine room. God, would she ever get over what Ian Parker had done to her? Would it always haunt her? And at the moment it wasn't her mother she longed for – it was the comfort of Betty Grayson's arms.

Chapter Nine

Cheryl Cutter vigorously washed her face and then frowned at her reflection in the mirror. She'd been complimented on her nice complexion, but secretly longed to look more glamorous. Her hair was short, wavy, naturally auburn, and her eyes were green. Instead of pale skin with a scattering of freckles across her nose, she'd prefer to have olive tones and mysterious, cat-shaped eyes like the film star Sophia Loren. With her head on one side, she tried a seductive pout, but then burst out laughing. There was no way she could look seductive and had once heard herself described as wholesome; something she had to admit was true.

With a sigh, Cheryl took a dress from her wardrobe. It was Friday evening and she was going to see Val, hoping to meet Betty, but in truth she was having serious doubts about Val's plans. When Val had first mentioned it, Cheryl had thought it could work, but as time passed, with lots of time to think, her nervousness had increased. The plan was fraught with risks, ones Cheryl felt sure could lead them all into deep trouble.

Cheryl slipped on a pair of white sandals and, after picking up her handbag, locked her door, still wondering if she should back out now before it was too late.

When she arrived at Val's flat, Cheryl was ushered inside, Val saying, 'If Betty doesn't come down, I'll take you upstairs to meet her. She knows my story and on Saturday she heard Paula's. I realise it was only six days ago, but we really do have to move things forward. If Betty can't be recruited, I'll have to find someone else. The trouble is that could take ages, so let's see how she reacts to what happened to you. Oh, and if you get the chance, it might intrigue her if you can somehow mention that I'm going to help you.'

'Yes, all right, but after hearing about Paula, my story will sound a bit tame.'

'Maybe, but nevertheless, you were swindled. If it hadn't been for that dealer, you wouldn't be stuck in nurses' quarters.'

Cheryl lowered her eyes, wondering how Val would react if she pulled out. Yes, she'd been cheated, but surely what Val wanted to do was a step too far? She'd been mad to agree, had been sucked in when she'd heard about what happened to Paula.

Poor Paula, and thinking about her Cheryl knew

she couldn't back out now. She was tied to this group, not only for Paula's sake, but her own too. If there was a chance of getting her money back she had to take it. Cheryl was snapped out of her thoughts when there was a sudden rap on the door.

Val opened it to admit a plump, middle-aged woman. 'Betty,' she said, 'I'm glad you've popped down. I've a friend here I'd like you to meet.'

As the woman stepped inside, she said hesitantly, 'Err . . . hello.'

Val made the introductions. 'Betty, this is Cheryl. Cheryl Cutter.'

'Hello, Betty, it's nice to meet you.'

'Cheryl's a nurse and has just finished a stint on nights,' Val explained.

'Oh dear, that can't be much fun. Do you enjoy nursing?' Betty asked as she took a seat.

'Yes, well, except for the shifts.'

'It doesn't help that Cheryl has to live in nurses' quarters, but after what happened to her, she has no choice.'

'Why, what happened?'

Cheryl found herself annoyed that Val had jumped in with both feet. She knew that Val was anxious to get started on their plans, but surely this was rushing things? Obviously impatient, it was Val who answered Betty's question.

'I'm sure Cheryl will tell you what happened to her, but I'll start by saying she was robbed.'

'Robbed! How awful. Were you hurt?'

Once again Val jumped in. 'Not physically, but financially and emotionally. Tell her what happened, Cheryl.'

Exhaling, Cheryl gathered her thoughts before starting at the beginning. 'I'm twenty-nine now, but tragically my parents were killed in a bombing raid when I was just a year old.'

'How awful for you.'

Betty sounded so sympathetic, her eyes kind, and it encouraged Cheryl to go on. 'To be honest, I was so young that I don't remember it, or being taken to live with my grandmother. She was a widow, living in Richmond, and it must have been hard for her, but she took me on. I grew up seeing her as my mother, and loved her dearly. When I left school I was drawn to nursing, qualified, and decided to make it my career, perhaps specialising in midwifery.'

'Oh, I'd have loved to do something like that, but I just got married and became a housewife and mother.'

'Betty, I've told you,' Val said. 'There's nothing wrong with that.'

'No, there isn't,' Cheryl agreed, 'but I had to put my career on hold when my grandmother became ill. I stayed at home to nurse her until . . . until she died.'

'I'm so sorry to hear that. You must have been devastated.'

'Yes, I was, and as my grandmother's house was rented, the landlord said I had to move out. I think he was going to turn it into flats, double his profit. I returned to nursing and, with no other choice, I applied for, and got, nurse's accommodation.'

'You're jumping the gun, Cheryl. Tell Betty about the dealer.'

'Yes, I was coming to that. I was in such a state, grieving for my grandmother, but the new place was furnished, and with no room for anything but a few ornaments, I had to have my grandmother's house cleared. All the furniture was old-fashioned, mostly junk really, but hoping there might be something of value, I invited a local dealer to see it. Two men came, but they didn't want any of it, saying there was nothing worth buying. I was so upset, but hearing my plight they were very kind and offered to clear it for me. There was a picture above the hearth, filthy from years of smoke damage, but obviously feeling sorry for me, one of the men said he might be able to sell it, and offered me twenty pounds.'

'Yes, twenty pounds,' Val said scornfully, 'and wait till you hear the rest.'

'I trusted them, Betty, but they took advantage of me in my grief. You see, about six months later, I happened to pass the dealer's shop. When I glanced in the window, I stopped in my tracks. It had been cleaned and was hardly recognisable as the picture that had hung over my grandmother's fireplace, but I had grown up seeing it and knew it was hers. It had a prominent place in the window, and the price tag was for two thousand pounds.'

'What?' Betty gasped. 'Oh my God, what did you do?'

'I was furious and went into the shop to confront the dealer – it was a waste of time and I got nowhere.'

'Yes, and that's how we met,' Val interrupted. 'Cheryl came to see my employer, but unfortunately she had signed a receipt saying "sold as seen". There was nothing Mr Warriner could do. In my eyes the dealer had cheated her, stolen from her, but he had the law on his side. Yes, I work for a solicitor, but sometimes I think the law is an ass.'

'It's dreadful,' said Betty.

'Yes, and Val was so kind,' Cheryl went on. 'She saw how upset I was and, as it was her lunch break, she invited me to join her for a coffee. I told her how the money would have given me security, the means to buy perhaps a small flat, but instead I'm forced to remain in nurses' quarters. It's awful, and my grandmother would turn in her grave if she knew I'd been cheated, but I still think it's nothing compared to what happened to Paula.'

Betty looked surprised. 'Oh, you've met her too.'

Cheryl felt colour flooding her cheeks, scrabbled around for an answer, and was glad when Val came to the rescue.

'Yes, Cheryl has met Paula, and in fact they've become friends. We're all meeting up in the park tomorrow, Betty, so why don't you join us?'

Obviously puzzled, Betty's eyes flicked between them, but then she said, 'All right, yes, I'd like that.'

'Good, and shall we say midday?'

'That's fine.'

'Right then, now, if you're ready to go, Cheryl, I'll run you home.'

'Thanks, Val. I don't know what I'd have done if I hadn't met you, and I know Paula feels the same. We know you'll be able to help us, and we're very grateful.'

Betty's brows were creased as she rose to her feet. 'Right, well, I'd best be off. Bye, Cheryl, it was nice to meet you, and . . . and I'll see you tomorrow.'

When Cheryl had said goodbye, Val showed Betty out, fingers crossed that her ploy had worked. When she closed the door she turned to Cheryl. 'Come on then, let's get you home.'

They climbed into her car, Val then saying, 'I think the timing was right. Betty has heard your story now and, after the hint you dropped, she must be intrigued.'

'Maybe, but when she hears what we plan to do, she'll probably run a mile. When are you going to tell her?'

'When we all meet up tomorrow.'

'That soon? Are you sure you're not rushing it?'

'Maybe, but I can't afford to waste any more time on Betty and I think it's worth the risk.'

'I spoke to Paula yesterday and I must say she seems rather taken with Betty.'

'Paula needs mothering and Betty seems to sense that. I'm afraid I'm not very demonstrative, but Betty thought nothing of holding Paula when she broke down.'

'That's nice, but I'm more like you. In my profession we have to grow an outer shell or the awful things we see would be too much to cope with.'

'I can understand that, but how you do it is beyond me. Just the sight of blood makes my stomach turn, let alone vomit and bedpans.'

'It has its rewards.'

'Not in the way of pay, that's for sure.'

'There's worse off than me, but back to Betty. Do you think she'll want to join us?'

'I'm not sure, Cheryl. She's a nice lady, but very bitter about what happened to her; she's rather meek and unworldly. She may find the whole idea too frightening.'

'I wouldn't blame her for that.'

Val frowned, sensing an undertone in Cheryl's voice. 'Are you changing your mind? Do you want to back out?'

'No, but what we intend to do *is* frightening.'

'As long as our planning is meticulous, with every last detail covered, nothing can go wrong.'

'I hope you're right, Val.'

'I am, so stop worrying.'

When she dropped Cheryl off outside her quarters, Val called goodbye, but drove home chewing worriedly on her bottom lip. Cheryl seemed to be getting nervous and she didn't want this fear to show in front of Betty. Maybe it was a mistake for them all to be there when she revealed their plans – perhaps it would be better if she told Betty in advance. Somehow she would have to broach the subject without putting herself, along with the others, in a bad light. And so for the rest of the journey, she worked out her strategy.

Chapter Ten

Betty was puzzled. She'd heard Cheryl's story and felt sorry for her, but why had Val seemed so eager that Cheryl recount it to someone who, let's face it, was a stranger? It had been the same with Paula, the girl talking about her terrible ordeal when they first met, and what did Cheryl mean about Val helping them? How was she supposed to do that? Betty felt there was something going on, strange undertones, something she couldn't put her finger on, but when Val said she was running Cheryl home, she knew it was her signal to leave.

It was only nine o'clock and a long evening stretched out in front of her with just a wireless for company. Though she was saving to buy a television, it would be a long time before she had enough money, and now that she was baking again, there was a lot less going into the kitty. When there was a knock on her door, Betty went to answer it, surprised yet pleased to see Val.

'I'm sorry, Betty, when I offered to drive Cheryl home it felt as if I was chasing you out. However, on the drive home I've been thinking, and if you're not busy, can we talk?'

'Yes, of course.'

Val took a seat, then pulling out her cigarettes said, 'Do you mind if I smoke?'

'No, go ahead,' Betty told her, fetching an old saucer that Val now used for an ashtray.

Val lit up and took a long pull on the cigarette, releasing a stream of smoke before she spoke. 'I wanted you to meet Cheryl, to hear her story, but I shouldn't have been evasive about the reason. It was wrong of me, and I'm sorry. I should have been open with you from the start and can only say in my defence that I have to be cautious.'

'I don't understand. Cautious about what?'

'You know what happened to me, Betty, how Mike Freeman ruined my life, my career. You've heard that Paula was raped, and how Cheryl was swindled, but you may not have noticed that we all have something in common.'

'We've all been badly hurt. Is that it?'

'Yes, but in every instance the men who hurt us got away with it. In my case, Mike's career has flourished, and the dealer who swindled Cheryl gained financially too. The man who raped Paula is still free, living his life without punishment – and there's always the risk that he might rape another poor young woman.'

'I know, and I thought the same. What happened to me was awful, but like Cheryl, I think it's nothing compared to Paula's ordeal.'

'I'd hardly call it nothing. Your husband cheated on you, and from what you've told me he's living the good life whilst you struggle financially.'

Betty heaved a sigh. 'Yes, that's true.'

'Wouldn't you like to pay him back? Wouldn't you like to see him suffer for what he did to you?'

'Yes, but I don't see how.'

Val leaned forward, her expression earnest. 'Betty, I think I can trust you so I'm going to tell you what Paula, Cheryl and I are going to do. If you want to join us, you'd be more than welcome, but if you'd rather not, can I have your promise that you'll keep what you're going to hear to yourself?'

'How can I promise that when I haven't got a clue what you're talking about?'

Val's smile was thin, but she nodded. 'Yes, I see your point, but we're friends and, as I said, I feel I can trust you. You see, Betty, we've all suffered, and as I mentioned, in each case the men responsible have got away with it. What we plan to do is to get our own back. We want revenge, because only then can we move forward. Take Paula, for instance. We want to see the man who raped her in jail. Instead of walking the streets, maybe stalking his next prey, we want to see him punished for what he did.'

'Yes, I can understand that, and it's no more than he deserves.'

'Then there's the man who cheated Cheryl. As far as I'm concerned, no matter what the law says, he's a criminal. We want him to pay for what he did too. As for me, I want Mike Freeman to be sacked, hopefully with his reputation in the industry ruined, like mine was.'

'Val, I know you're hurting, but what good would that do?'

'He stole my job, my life, my career – and I can't bear it.'

'Yes, maybe, but I don't see how you can get him sacked.'

'As a group we'll find a way, and, if you like, a plan to make your husband pay too.'

Betty lowered her eyes, thoughts racing. Only that morning she'd received an electric bill that would be a struggle to pay. Richard didn't struggle, though, or Mel with her cleaner to do all the dirty jobs. She had dreamed of reconciliation with Richard, that Mel would leave him, but knew it wouldn't happen now. Mel was pregnant and the thought still made her feel sick inside. Yes, she would love to pay Richard back, to see him, and Mel, suffer. But how? 'I don't see how I can get back at Richard.'

'That's the beauty of this, Betty. You won't be alone any more. With four of us working together, we're sure to come up with a plan. In fact, I already have something in mind for the man who raped Paula.'

'Have you?'

'Yes, and I'd like you to join us, Betty, but before you make a firm decision, I must tell you that to ensure that he goes to jail, we'll have to lie to the police.'

'Oh, no! I don't think I like the sound of that.'

'Hear me out first, and if you don't want to join us, there'll be no hard feelings.'

Betty listened to Val's plan, thinking that it could work, should work, and that maybe the end justified the means. Val explained that there were things to be ironed out, but if they were careful the risk of discovery would be minuscule. Even so, the thought of being involved with the police made her stomach lurch in fear.

'Well, Betty, what do you think?'

'Val, I'd be useless. I've never done anything like that in my life and the thought of lying to the police terrifies me. I'd be such a nervous wreck that it would give the game away.'

'I think you underestimate yourself, Betty, and remember, you won't be alone. We'll all be working together, and each of us will have our turn for revenge. When we implement the plan for Paula, she won't be involved, and in that way the police won't have any reason to be suspicious. The same goes for when it's your turn. We'll make the plans, but when we carry them out you won't be involved, so again no suspicion can fall on you. That's the beauty of this, Betty, and I'm sure you'll come to realise that.'

Betty shook her head. 'I'm sorry, but I still don't think I can do it.'

Val's smile was sympathetic. 'I know this must have come as a shock. It's a lot to take in and a big decision. I don't expect your answer now, so why don't you sleep on it?'

'Yes, all right,' Betty agreed, relieved when Val rose to leave. She showed her out, her mind reeling as she got ready for bed.

An hour later, Betty was still awake. They would have to lie to the police and the thought of prosecution if they were discovered had her trembling with fear. She scrunched her pillow, mind still churning. Her life had been ordinary, dull, and – since moving to London – lonely. Meeting Val had changed all that and it would be awful to lose her friendship. If she didn't join them, would Val drop her? Oh, and that meant she wouldn't see Paula again. She hardly saw her son, and Anne's infrequent visits were short, so much so that it felt like she'd lost them, that she was no longer needed in their lives.

In such a short time, Val and Paula had become almost a replacement family, Paula like another daughter: one who needed her; one who, unlike

Anne, craved affection. The thought of losing them, of being alone again, was unbearable.

Still Betty couldn't make up her mind. She went over Val's plan again and suddenly found that her trembles of fear turned to shivers of excitement. She tossed and turned, scared, yet wanting to join the others, wanting not only revenge for herself, but for them too. Could they do it? Could they really pull it off?

Finally, after another hour of agonising, Betty made a decision, at last drifting off to sleep.

Chapter Eleven

It was another glorious day, the sun a bright, golden orb in a blue sky. With rain forecast in the next few days, Cheryl was determined to make the most of her Saturday off, and for now pushed her worries about Val's plans to one side.

Paula was waiting at Clapham Junction, looking nervously in each direction until she spotted Cheryl striding towards her. A smile lit up her face and for a moment Cheryl saw a flash of her beauty, but as usual Paula was dressed in clothes that were far too old for her. Since they'd met ten months ago, Cheryl had become fond of Paula and was protective of her, as though she were an older sister.

'Hello, Paula, sorry I'm a bit late.'

'I've only been waiting for a couple of minutes.'

The two of them moved off, walking along Falcon Road, both beginning to perspire as the sun beat down on them. 'Maybe we should have caught a bus,' Paula complained.

'Yes, but we might as well carry on walking now. I'm looking forward to seeing Betty again. You're right, she's nice.'

'She's great,' Paula enthused. 'I wasn't sure at first, but once she invited us back to her flat for tea, I found her really kind.'

'Do you think she'll join us?'

'There's a good chance – and, anyway, you know how persuasive Val can be.'

'Yes, she can certainly win you round,' Cheryl agreed. When she'd first made an appointment to see a solicitor about the painting, she had been over-awed by his tall, sophisticated receptionist. Initially Val appeared coldly efficient, but Cheryl soon found out that it was just an outer shell – that underneath Val was a warm and caring woman. They had become friends, and she'd been introduced to Paula, soon after hearing about their plans. Cheryl realised then that Val had set out to recruit her, yet it hadn't stopped her from joining them. Now though, once again, doubts assailed her mind until Paula snapped her out of her reverie. 'Sod it: these shoes have given me a blister,' she complained.

'Hold on, I've got a packet of plasters in my bag.'

When Paula slipped off her shoe, Cheryl bent down to apply the plaster, and now Paula was able to walk comfortably again, they were soon on their way. At last the park gates came into view; as they entered, Cheryl's eyes quickly took in their surroundings. They passed a football pitch, and then after a while took a path that bordered the lake, where she saw rowing boats for hire by the hour, with several people already out on the water. The sun reflected on the surface in a dazzle of rippling lights that made Cheryl squint, but then they were approaching the tearooms. 'It looks packed. I hope we can get a table.'

'Maybe Val and Betty have already snagged one,' and Paula's comment proved to be right as they saw an arm waving to attract their attention.

'Hello, you two,' said Val as they reached the table. 'I didn't think you'd want to join the queue so I ordered your usual drinks.'

'Thanks,' Cheryl said as she took the proffered Cola from the tray, and passed sparkling orange to Paula.

'Thanks, Val,' Paula said as she sat down, immediately sucking on the straw.

It struck Cheryl that they looked an odd gathering. There was Paula, the youngest at twenty-two, her clothes as usual dowdy and dark. In complete contrast, Val was beautifully dressed in cream linen worn with amber beads. Beside her Betty looked old-fashioned in a plain navy skirt and prim white blouse, a cameo fastened at the neck, all topped by tight curly hair that was threaded with grey. Then there's me, Cheryl thought, Miss Wholesome, in her flowery summer dress and skin she knew would be turning an unflattering pink in the heat. Val suddenly leaned forward, saying quietly, 'Betty told me on the way here that she'd like to join us.'

'Blimey, that's great,' Paula enthused.

'I must admit it wasn't an easy decision. I tossed and turned all night.'

Cheryl nodded. 'I can understand that, and you do know the risks?'

'Yes, but as Val said, they're minimal.'

Val's eyes flicked to the other tables, and when she was satisfied that they couldn't be overheard, she said, 'Betty, you've heard what happened to us, but Cheryl and Paula don't know what you've been through.'

'Oh, I . . . I thought you'd have told them.'

'I wouldn't do that without your permission. Do you think you could talk about it again?'

Cheryl saw how Betty paled, her voice hesitant at first but gaining in confidence. As she listened, it sickened Cheryl that Betty's husband had been so cruel. All right, he might have fallen out of love with his wife and met someone else, but there was no excuse for moving his girlfriend into their home and forcing Betty out. Then, to make things worse, he had virtually robbed Betty, conniving to make sure that she came out of a marriage of over twenty years with hardly a penny.

When Betty stopped speaking, Paula was the first to respond. 'Blimey, what a bastard. Oops, sorry.'

'It's all right, Paula,' said Cheryl. 'I think that

hearing about Betty's husband is enough to make a saint swear.'

Val smiled. 'We're glad you've agreed to join us, Betty, but there's one proviso. Once we start, there's no pulling out. As I said, we'll take one case at a time, starting with Paula. Once we've pulled that one off, we'll have a talk to see who's next.'

Betty straightened her shoulders, her voice resolute. 'I won't pull out.'

'Right, then there's no reason why we shouldn't get started. We'll need to plan every last detail but, as we don't want it known that there's any connection between us, from now on we must make sure that we aren't seen together.'

'Val,' protested Betty, 'how are we supposed to do that when we live in the same block of flats?'

'You've been living in Ascot Court for a while, but we've only met recently. Have you met any of the other tenants?'

'No, I hardly see them.'

'Well then, as long as they don't see us going into each other's flats, and we stay apart when outside, it won't be a problem. Cheryl, until we're ready to put the plan into action, we'll talk mostly on the telephone.'

'What about me?' Paula asked.

'You'll have to stay away from all of us until it's over.'

'Oh, but—'

'No "buts", Paula. When we start on the next case, for instance, Cheryl's, you'll be involved, but she won't. If this is to work, we must stick to the rules.'

'Will . . . will I be able to talk to you all on the blower?'

'Yes, I should think that's safe, but make sure you don't discuss our plans if you can be overheard.'

'Val, I'm still not sure I can pull off my part,' Cheryl said. 'I mean, look at me. I hardly look the type that attracts men and I'm not sure that the police will believe me.'

'Of course they will. You look so innocent, and as a nurse they'll have no reason to doubt you, especially with Betty and me as witnesses.'

'What . . . what if they want to examine me?'

'You know what happened to Paula when she reported her rape. She was told that for an examination to be of any use it has to be done immediately, before any evidence is lost. The plan covers that and, as you're willing to have a few bruises, that should suffice.'

Cheryl lowered her eyes, doubts still flooding her mind. When it had just been talk, the planning hadn't really seemed real, but now the full force of what they intended to do made her stomach clench in fear. If the police found out she wasn't telling the truth, they were sure to prosecute, and her career would be in ruins. 'Oh, God, I don't know if I can do it.'

'Cheryl, there's no way the police will suspect that we've set Ian Parker up; after all, why should they? We'll appear three strangers, one a woman who has been raped, the other two witnesses who happened upon the scene.'

'But other than your door numbers, you'll both have the same address. Don't you think that'll look suspicious?'

Val frowned but, thinking on her feet, she said, 'We can say that it happened in the park, that Betty and I saw it from our windows.'

'Yes, good idea,' Betty enthused. 'We've both got a good view so it would be perfectly plausible. My goodness, I'm actually starting to enjoy this.'

'I'm glad somebody is,' Cheryl said. 'I just wish I could say the same.'

'You'll be fine – we'll all be fine and Ian Parker will be behind bars where he belongs.'

'I bleedin' well hope so,' said Paula. 'I don't think I'll rest until he is. Every time I leave my bedsit I'm terrified I'll see him.'

Cheryl looked at Paula, saw the distress in her eyes, along with the way her hands shook as she lit yet another cigarette. In the short time they'd been there she had already smoked two and her racking cough was worrying. Paula was drinking heavily too, and though Cheryl had tried to talk to her about it, she insisted it helped her to sleep. The rape haunted her, had turned her into a recluse, and with a sigh

Cheryl knew that she couldn't back out now. For Paula to have any chance of recovery, Ian Parker had to be punished. 'All right, I'm on, and I'm sorry for my last-minute nerves.'

'It's understandable,' Betty said. 'I know I said I'm excited, but I'm nervous too.'

Cheryl smiled gratefully, comforted to know that she wasn't alone in her feelings. 'What about you, Val? Are you nervous?'

'Of course I am. I'd be mad not to be; so much so that we must ensure that not one tiny thing can go wrong. To start with, when we make our accusation, we have to make sure that Ian Parker can't offer up an alibi.'

Cheryl felt reassured as she listened to Val. She was such a clever woman and, with input from all of them, the plan should be watertight. Cheryl just hoped that she'd be able to play her part convincingly. If she couldn't persuade the police that she'd been raped, the plan would fall at the first hurdle.

Paula's eyes darted from side to side, praying that Val and the others would succeed. Along with her fear of bumping into Ian Parker, there was hate too. She had seen the sort of life her mother had led, the succession of men who shared her bed. All through her childhood, no matter how many times they moved, it didn't take the neighbours long to discover that her mother was a tart. She'd heard the gossip, red-faced with shame, and had grown up determined to be different. She had dreamed of marriage, of walking down the aisle a virgin, of living in a nice house with a couple of kids. Their lives would be stable, with a mum and a dad – unlike her own childhood. She would shower them with love and cuddles, something that she had never known, and her life would be perfect.

Ian Parker had taken her virginity and destroyed her dreams. Along with that, he'd left her with a fear of men, a fear of ever being touched again. She would never forget the pain, the way she'd been left feeling used and dirty. Yes, she hated Ian Parker – but most of all she feared him.

'Are you all right, Paula?'

She turned to look at Betty, almost crumbling when she saw the sympathy in her eyes. If she could have chosen a mother it would have been somebody like Betty, and if they weren't sitting in the park she would run into her arms. Instead she lowered her head, just saying, 'Yeah, I'm fine. I . . . I'm just gonna miss you all.'

Betty scrabbled in her handbag and, pulling out a piece of paper, she wrote on it before handing it to Paula. 'Here's my phone number – you can ring me any time.'

'Fanks, it's good of you, but it won't be the same.'

'It won't be for long,' Val said. 'Once we make sure that everything is covered, that nothing can go wrong, I think we can make our move in about a month.'

'A month! But that's ages,' Paula gasped, horrified at the thought. She went to work all week and was stuck in every evening, with only her weekend meetings with them to look forward to.

'It'll soon pass,' Cheryl said, 'and it'll be worth it to see Ian Parker behind bars.'

Paula nodded, but was still unhappy. Since the rape she had stopped going out with her old friends, too afraid and too ashamed to tell them what had happened to her. Val, Cheryl, and now Betty had taken their place, and she would miss them something rotten. She had never expected to have friends like Val and Cheryl, both older than her and both so different. Val was the eldest, an upmarket sort of woman with a good heart, whilst Cheryl was a nurse, who she now saw as a sort of older sister. They had both taken her under their wings; and now there was Betty too – a kind, motherly sort, she felt, though she'd had little time to get to know her. Despite this, she felt safe with Betty, safe with the others, felt a bond, but now . . .

As though aware of her feelings, Betty reached across the table to pat the back of Paula's hand, saying gently, 'Never mind, love. As Cheryl said, the time will soon pass.'

'Yeah, I suppose so.'

Treacle began to whimper, straining at his lead, and with a small shake of her head, Val said, 'He wants a walk so I think it's time to break up. As I said, from now on we mustn't be seen together. When you get home, go over my plan again, and if you can think of anything that I've left out, give me a ring.' She then turned her head. 'Betty, we'll go home separately, but as long as none of the other tenants sees us, we can meet up either in my flat or yours.'

With a gulp, Paula managed a small smile as Val said goodbye, then shortly afterwards Betty stood up to leave, her smile kindly as she said, 'We'll meet up when this is all over, but until then, take care of yourself.' She then said goodbye to Cheryl, lifting a hand to wave as she walked away.

Cheryl touched Paula's hand. 'You were right, Betty's nice – but, come on, no matter what Val said, I don't think it'll do any harm if we walk home together.'

'It feels like we've only just got here and it's still early.'

'Yes it is, so let's go for a stroll around the park before we leave.'

'What if Val sees us?'

Cheryl grinned. 'If we go in the opposite direction, I don't think she'll spot us.'

'You're on,' said Paula, relishing the thought of a little more time outdoors before she returned to her poky bedsit. Four weeks, just four more weeks, and Ian Parker would be locked up – and with that would come her freedom.

Chapter Twelve

During the following weeks, Val and the others were so consumed with their plan that they seemed unaware of what was going on in the world around them. Cheryl was still worried about pulling off her part convincingly, of her lies being discovered, and was finding it hard to keep her mind on her work.

Val too was nervous. The plan was hers, the onus on her, and it had to be perfect. If anything went wrong she would never forgive herself. As she sat in reception now, typing a letter, Val cursed when she hit a wrong key. Tutting with impatience, she reached for the Tipp-Ex, knowing that any mistakes in her plan wouldn't be wiped out so easily.

Paula had taken to ringing Betty two or three times a week, but now on a Saturday in mid-August they were nearly ready, with one last thing to do. Betty was worried about Paula. It was going to be so hard for her, but Val insisted it was necessary and, in reality, she had to agree. When the telephone rang she went to answer it and wasn't surprised to hear Paula's voice.

'Hello, Betty.'

'Hello, sweetheart, and how are you feeling?'

'I'm all right, but nervous about tonight.'

'You won't be alone, sweetheart. We'll all be with you.'

'Yeah, I know.'

'Have you heard from your mum this week?'

'Nah, she hardly ever rings me.'

Betty asked the question that had been on her mind. 'Does your mother know about Ian Parker? What he did to you?'

'After it . . . it happened, I was in a state, and a couple of days later, I went to see her. I don't know why I bothered. She just said that I was a silly cow and should have kneed him in his bollocks.'

After hearing about Paula's upbringing, Betty wasn't surprised by the crude words she sometimes used, or her mother's callousness, but in this instance she had hoped that Paula would have been shown a little more support. 'Maybe your mother was shocked and that was all she could think of to say.'

'Yeah, and pigs might fly. It would take a lot more than that to shock my mum.'

The more Betty heard about Paula's mother, the less enamoured she felt. The woman had virtually abandoned her daughter when Paula was just eighteen and it broke Betty's heart that the girl seemed so alone.

They chatted for a while longer, Betty doing her best to again reassure Paula that everything would be fine that night, and then, saying goodbye, she replaced the receiver. She sighed heavily, hoping she was right. If Ian Parker spotted them, it could ruin everything, and all their careful plans would be in ruins.

An hour later there was a knock on her door, and Betty smiled with delight when she saw her daughter. 'Anne, it's about time. It's been a month since I've seen you.'

'Sorry, Mum,' Anne said as she stepped inside. 'I've been a bit busy, but I'm here now.'

'John hasn't been to see me either, but at least he rings me now and then.'

'I haven't heard from him. Is he still seeing the same girl?'

'Yes, and I think it really is serious this time.'

Anne snorted with derision as she sat down, but Betty ignored her, instead asking, 'And how are things with you?'

'To tell you the truth, I'm a bit fed up. I didn't get the promotion I was hoping for and I might look for another job.'

'But, Anne, you've been with that company for years. Do you really think it's wise to leave?'

'That's just it. I've been there for so long that they see me as part of the furniture. I'm taken for granted, but maybe if they think I'm leaving it'll make them sit up a bit.'

'I hope you're right,' Betty said as she went through to the kitchenette to find a bottle of Coke for her daughter.

When she returned, Anne had risen to her feet and was standing with her arms folded across her chest, shoulders hunched as she gazed out of the window. For the first time in ages, Betty could see a trace of vulnerability in her daughter, and impulsively she put a comforting arm around her. 'Don't let your job get you down, love. I'm sure it will all work out.'

'It isn't work that's upsetting me, it's Mel. The way she's been carrying on has been a bit of an eye-opener.'

'Why, what's she been doing?'

'Lately she's been behaving like an absolute bitch. Oh, I won't deny that I like her, but you'd think she was at death's door instead of pregnant. All right, she had a bit of morning sickness, but she's using the pregnancy as an excuse to do absolutely nothing. When I go to see Dad I end up like a servant, waiting on her hand and foot. I've tried to tell him that pregnancy isn't an illness, but he won't listen and still treats her like an invalid. Dad's so wrapped up in Mel that he hardly notices I'm there.'

So, Betty thought, her daughter was jealous. Her precious father was showing his wife more attention than her. Anne had always been a daddy's girl, but now felt she was coming second in his affections. 'I didn't have any help when I was carrying John, or you, and you're right, pregnancy isn't an illness.' Betty shrugged. 'Still, you never know, maybe there's a problem.'

'Dad did say something about her blood pressure being high, but she looks all right to me.'

Betty loved her daughter, but Anne had always shown a selfish streak. Yes, and I'm getting as bad, she thought, because in truth she was pleased that Anne was less enamoured with Mel. She'd been jealous of their relationship – jealous that they'd become friends. She too had had high blood pressure when carrying Anne, but there'd been no chance to rest. It hadn't done her any harm and Betty was sure it would be the same for Mel. She held out the glass. 'Here, Anne, drink your Coke.'

Anne took it, gulping it down and then saying, 'Right, I'm off.'

'But you've only just got here!'

'Oh, Mum, you always say that, but I need to buy a few things and I promised Tony I'd be back before two. We're going riding, and I'm trying out a new horse. I don't know how many times I've told you that I'd love to see more of you, but it takes up most of the morning just getting here and driving back.'

'Anne, don't exaggerate. I'm not that far away.'

'You are to me, Mum. I wish you hadn't moved away from Farnham.'

Betty felt a lump in her throat. Anne was making her feel that she'd abandoned her, just as Paula had been abandoned, but it just wasn't the same. Anne was a grown woman, already living away from home when she'd left the area; even when she had lived close by, Anne hadn't been a frequent visitor. 'I'm sorry I left, darling, but it's a good job and the pay is better in London. I do love you, you know that, and I'm always here if you need me.'

'Take no notice of me, Mum. I'm just a bit fed up, that's all.'

Betty kissed her daughter's cheek, pleased to find her kiss returned, and then Anne hurried out. Before she had met Val, her daughter's short visits were all she'd had to look forward to, but now Betty realised she only had herself to blame. Oh, but she really had been struggling to find well-paid work, her move to London easing the financial strain a little. She'd been lonely since moving away, her life mundane – just work, home and the occasional visit to the shops. She'd had nobody to talk to, but thankfully all that had changed. She now got up looking forward to each day, knowing that she had friends, their plans bringing meaning and excitement to her life. It was too late to change things now, too late to go back to the country; even if she did, would she really see more of Anne? Betty doubted it.

*   *   *

It was eight o'clock on Saturday evening, and in Battersea Bridge Road, all four women were sitting in Val's car. Betty was beside Paula and holding her hand, but the poor girl was still shaking from head to toe.

'Paula, I hate putting you through this,' said Val, 'but if we don't know what Ian Parker looks like, we won't be able to pick him out of an identity parade.'

'I . . . I know,' she said, her eyes fixed on the Ethelburga Estate. She wanted to bolt, to run a mile, as memories of the rape flooded her mind. Just the thought of having to look at him again made her stomach churn: his face, his hands, the way he had grabbed her. Bile rose in her throat and she almost choked, forcing it back down, her mouth filled with the bitter taste.

They were parked facing the most likely exit, but so far there had been no sign of Ian Parker. 'We've been sitting here for ages. What if he doesn't come out?' Cheryl complained.

'I . . . I don't think he'd stay in on a Saturday night,' Paula managed to say.

'All right, but what if he spots us, Val? Surely Paula's description is enough.'

'No, Cheryl, it isn't a chance I want to take.'

'If you ask me, this is riskier, and you were the one who said we shouldn't be seen together.'

'If there are similar men in the line-up, we could make a mistake. On this occasion I think it's worth the risk. As long as we keep our heads down, he won't spot us.'

'Is there still a gap in the park railings?' Cheryl asked, now changing the subject.

'Fortunately, yes. The park is locked at night and if the railings had been repaired, we'd have been forced to call it off. We're lucky the gap isn't highly visible or the park maintenance crew would have been on to it like a shot.'

'There he is,' Paula cried, pointing to Ian Parker before swiftly ducking down. Oh God, she was going to wet herself – she needed the toilet. 'Val, get me out of here!'

'It's all right, Paula – it's all right,' Val assured her. 'He isn't even looking our way and we'll be leaving soon.'

Though Val's words calmed her a little, Paula kept low, terrified that he'd spot her.

'Did you all get a good look at him?' Val asked.

'Yes,' Betty said.

'Me too,' said Cheryl.

'He's gone now, Paula, and he didn't even look in our direction as he drove off,' Val said as she started the engine.

Paula was so relieved that tears flooded her eyes, but she still kept her body low as the car moved away.

Betty reassured her, saying, 'It's all right, darling, you can come up now. Oh, don't cry. I know that seeing him must have brought it all back, but it's over now.

Paula sat up gingerly, unaware that Val was looking at her in the rear-view mirror, her eyes showing concern.

Val had heard the terror in Paula's voice and saw how pale she was. They'd set the date for the plot for the coming Thursday night, but she wondered now if Paula would have the strength to play her part. Val hadn't wanted to involve her at all, but when they'd hit a sticking point over Ian Parker's alibi, it was Paula who had come up with an idea. The problem was that she was the only one who could pull it off, and now Val asked, 'Paula, are you sure you'll be all right on Thursday night?'

'If it's too much for you, it isn't too late to back out,' said Cheryl.

Val shot Cheryl a look. Her tone sounded eager, almost as if she wanted Paula to pull out, but then Paula said, 'Don't worry. I . . . I'll be all right.'

'Right then,' Val said, 'we're all set. If it's all right with you, Paula, I'll drop you off at the end of your street.'

'Oh . . . do I have to go home?'

'I'm afraid so. We've already risked being seen together and must break up now.'

'Never mind, love,' Betty consoled, 'it won't be for much longer.'

Val glanced again in her rear-view mirror to see that Betty had an arm around Paula's shoulder. The two of them had taken to each other and though Val knew why, she wouldn't dream of voicing her opinion. She had come to know Betty well since their first meeting in the park, and had heard a lot about her two children. They were both grown up with thriving careers and neither seemed to need their mother. It was Paula's neediness that drew Betty – the girl's craving to be mothered; their relationship symbiotic. She felt a surge of envy, wishing that she were able to show Paula more affection, show her that she cared, but instead Betty had taken that role.

Soon they were close to Clapham Junction and at the end of Paula's street. Val pulled into the kerb, twisting round in her seat to smile at Paula, saying warmly, 'Bye, love, and I'll ring you tomorrow.'

'Yes, all right,' she said, her expression downcast as she said goodbye to the others. Paula climbed out of the car, her hand lifting in a desolate wave as she walked away.

They watched her for a moment, and then Val said, 'Right, I'll drop you off next, Cheryl, and we'll meet up at my place on Thursday night. Wait till it's dark and make sure you're not seen sneaking into the block.'

'That's going to be risky too.'

'It'll be fine,' Val said, but once again she was worried by the tone of Cheryl's voice. It wasn't Paula who was proving to be the weakest link, the one who would back out. If anything, it was Cheryl.

Chapter Thirteen

For once, the time passed too quickly for Paula. They had talked about the best night to carry out the plan, and she had suggested Thursday. It was the last night before pay-day, and with any luck Ian Parker would be short of money and likely to stay in.

Paula was now regretting her suggestion. She hated going to the Ethelburga Estate, was terrified of bumping into him, and scared out of her wits to walk the streets at night. It was only the thought of what Val and the others were risking for her sake that finally prised her out of the bedsit.

Thankfully Ian Parker lived in a different block from her friend Nicky, yet even so she shot into the entrance, running in fear to knock on her door.

'Come on in, Paula. Blimey, talk about long time no see. You could have knocked me down with a feather when you rang.'

Paula followed Nicky into her living room, relieved to be out of sight, and seeing a bloke lounging with his feet up on the coffee table, she forced a smile.

'That's Eddie, me boyfriend,' Nicky said.

'Watcha,' he nodded in greeting.

Paula nodded back then, turning to Nicky, held out a bag containing the silk designer shirt that she and the others had clubbed together to buy. 'Nicky, here's the gear I told you about.'

She pulled out the shirt to inspect it. 'Yeah, it's a nice bit of stuff.'

Paula continued with her well-rehearsed lies. 'If you can get a quid for it, you can keep half. The only thing is, I want you to offer it to Ian Parker.'

'What, that creepy git in the next block?'

'Yeah, that's right.'

'I'd still like to know how a single bloke got a council flat. I reckon it's a sublet and the council knows nothing about it.'

'Yeah, probably. Someone once offered me their council flat, but I couldn't afford the rent. They wanted twice what they pay the council.'

'Subletting sounds like a nice little scam,' Nicky agreed, 'but why do you want me to offer this gear to Ian Parker?'

''Cos he owes me ten bob and won't pay it back. I nicked the shirt so it cost me nothing, and it'll be doing you a favour at the same time.'

'It's good of you, Paula, but why don't you flog it to him yerself? You'd be ten bob up then.'

Paula knew her story was weak and was glad that Nicky wasn't all that bright. 'We fell out and if he knows it's my gear he won't buy it. You'd best keep it to yourself that it came from me.'

'If he doesn't want it, I know another geezer who might.'

'All right, but try Ian Parker first.'

Nicky gave her a hard stare, but then shrugged. 'All right, but I'm taking Eddie with me. You'll have to keep an eye on me nipper, but I'll be back soon.'

With her boyfriend in tow, they left the flat whilst Paula sank down beside the grubby-looking toddler asleep on the sofa. Her stomach churned as she waited, hand to her mouth as she nibbled stumpy nails. Nicky would keep her mouth shut, she was sure of it, and Ian Parker would have no reason to link the supposed knocked-off shirt to her. Not only that, he would never admit buying hooky gear to the police. Anyway, with the timing, there was no way he could use Nicky's visit as an alibi.

Paula continued to nibble her nails impatiently. She had one last thing to do and that was to ring Val as soon as she knew that Ian Parker was alone. If he was, the plan would go ahead, but if he had company! Oh, please, please let him be alone.

At last Nicky and her boyfriend returned, saying as she marched in, 'Bloody hell, Paula, it was like getting blood out of a stone. Still, in the end he could see it was really good gear and broke into his rent. I got a quid, so here's your share.'

Paula took the money, trying to sound offhand as she asked, 'Was he on his own?'

'Yeah, and I'm glad I took Eddie with me. I've heard he's a bit of a funny bugger so I didn't fancy going into his flat on my own.'

'Really? What have you heard about him?'

'Oh, nuffin' much, I suppose, but Jenny went out with him once and said he was a bit rough.'

Yes, he's rough all right, Paula thought, but Jenny was on the game so she wouldn't have fought him off. She'd have held out her hand for payment when he'd finished. Paula forced a smile, saying, 'Well thanks, Nicky, and I'll see you around.'

'It's me who should thank you. That's the easiest ten bob I've earned in ages. See you, Paula, and if any other stuff comes your way, let me know.'

Once again Paula forced a smile. She had hated seeing Nicky again; was glad to be away from her old circle of friends. When living with her mum, a life dependent on crime was all she'd known – some of her friends and her mother were always bringing home dodgy gear. They'd all lived for the moment, enjoying themselves when the pickings were good, but dodging the rent man during leaner times.

It was only after Ian Parker had raped her that she'd broken away from Nicky and the rest of her crowd, soon realising that if she hadn't, despite trying to deny it, they would have eventually sucked her into their way of life. She could remember a trip to Oxford Street with Nicky, the pair of them trawling the shops and Nicky laughing at her when she refused to nick anything. When they arrived home, Nicky proudly displaying her haul, Paula could remember feeling a surge of envy. She had to work in shitty factories to earn enough to buy cheap clothes from the market; whereas, in one morning, Nicky had bagged a smashing dress, blouse and skirt for nothing.

Ashamed now that she had been tempted to do the same, Paula left Nicky's block, but once outside, she was hit by nerves. Her eyes flicked around, and, though there was a telephone box right there, she was too scared to stop and use it. Instead she ran almost all the way home, breathless when she arrived, but felt safe to ring Val now. She fed coins into the box and after only two rings, Val answered.

'Val, it's Paula. He's on his own.'

'Well done. It means we can go ahead now. We won't be ringing the police until after midnight, so don't wait up. Try to get some sleep and I'll call you in the morning when it's all over.'

'Sleep, you must be kidding.'

'I know, but there's nothing more you can do. As I said, I'll ring you as soon as I can, but rather than disturbing the other tenants in your house, it won't be until morning.'

'Shit, I hate not having my own phone,' Paula wailed.

'I know, but goodbye for now – and please, do try to get some sleep.'

With that Val hung up, and Paula was left staring at the receiver. She slowly replaced it, going into her room with her heart thumping in her chest. It was happening – it was really happening! She sank onto the side of her bed. Please, please let it work, she begged, and please, keep them all safe.

Val too replaced the receiver and, turning to Betty, she said, 'We're on.'

'Thank goodness for that. I'll stay with you until Cheryl arrives if you like.'

'She won't be leaving her colleague's flat until eleven-fifteen, so I doubt she'll be here before eleven-thirty. I've booked the day off work tomorrow, but you haven't.'

'I'll be fine.'

'I can't believe how calm you are.'

Betty smiled. 'Do you know, neither can I, but to be honest, I'm only playing the part of a witness, so I've not got much to do.'

'This plan was mine, and it's down to me if it goes wrong.'

'Stop worrying. I'm sure it won't. Now for goodness' sake, sit down and try to relax.'

Val at last took a seat, going over the plan again

and again in her mind. It had to work, it just had to, and impatiently she looked at the clock. 'I'll make us a drink,' she said, rising to her feet again.

'Not for me, thanks. I feel like my stomach's swimming with tea.'

'What about a sherry?'

'You know I don't drink and I don't think you should have one either. We need to keep our heads clear.'

Val sighed. 'Yes, you're right, but one won't hurt me.'

'All right then, and at least it might calm your nerves.'

The time seemed to drag and their conversation was fitful. Unable to sit still, Val constantly went to the window, until at last she saw Cheryl approaching the flats. She opened the door, saying as soon as Cheryl was inside, 'We're on.'

Cheryl looked pale and tense as she flopped onto a chair. Concerned, Val asked, 'Are you all right?'

'Yes, yes, I suppose so.'

'Did your colleague think it was odd that you stayed so late?'

'No, it wasn't a problem. As I told you, she took up midwifery, leaving the hospital to work in the community. She acts as a district midwife for women who want to have their babies at home, and she loves it. I told her I might be interested in taking up midwifery too, and with so much to tell me, the time just flew past. God, listen to me, I'm gabbling. Oh, Val, I hung around outside my colleague's flat for ages, sick with nerves, with doubt. I . . . I'm not sure that I can go through with this.'

'Cheryl, you can't mean it. Don't say you're going to back out now?'

'I'm scared. What if it all goes wrong?'

'It won't. We've planned everything down to the last detail.'

'I know, but I still think there's the danger they'll want me examined.'

'We've been through this. When Paula was raped she was told an examination is pointless after a bath. They'll see your bruises, and with us as witnesses, that should be enough.'

'What if it isn't? When Paula went to the police she wasn't taken seriously and it's worrying me to death. It might be different for me, and if I have to have an examination, a doctor will be able to tell that I haven't been raped.'

'Val, she's right,' Betty said, her face now etched with concern. 'I thought we had everything covered, but now I'm having doubts too.'

'Let me think,' Val said as she began to pace the room. They couldn't pull out now, they just couldn't. She went over and over it, at last realising that there was still a chance, but felt her cheeks redden as she said, 'Cheryl, I'm sorry to ask, but are . . . are you a virgin?'

'No, I'm not.' Her eyes then flicked to Betty. 'Don't look so shocked. I've only been with a couple of men and that was some time ago.'

'I'm not shocked. How can I be when my own daughter is living with a man with no sign of them ever getting married?'

Val spoke again. 'Cheryl, as long as you aren't a virgin, if you made a fresh ... err ... penetration, do you think it would fool a doctor?'

Betty's eyes widened in shock as she spluttered, 'Val, how can you suggest that?'

Cheryl lowered her head whilst Val held her breath. Had she gone too far? Oh, please, don't let her back out now.

At last Cheryl looked up, her smile thin. 'It's all right, Betty. Done properly it should work, so yes, Val, I ... I'll do it.'

'Well, rather you than me,' said Betty, her expression showing her distaste.

Worried that Betty's attitude would make Cheryl change her mind, Val said brusquely, 'Betty, it's getting on for midnight so I think you'd better sneak back upstairs. I'll tell the police you saw what happened, and they'll probably come up to question you.'

'I'll be ready for them,' she assured her and, after a somewhat sheepish smile at Cheryl, she let Val poke her head outside to see if the stairs were clear before hurrying out.

Val closed the door, saying to Cheryl as she did so: 'Oh dear, I think I shocked her.'

'It would take more than that to shock me. As a nurse you wouldn't believe some of the things I've seen women do to themselves.'

'Such as?'

'I'll tell you some other time,' she said, smiling at last, 'but right now it's time to sort out my bruises.'

Val was surprised by the sudden change in Cheryl's attitude. It was as if all doubts had been cast aside, leaving her sounding brisk and efficient. 'What do you want me to do?'

'My skin is very pale and marks easily, but as I can't go to work with bruises on show, make sure they'll be covered by my uniform. Grip the tops of my arms, dig your fingers in, and that should suffice. After that you'll have to mark my thighs.'

Val hesitated, but Cheryl said, 'Come on, don't be squeamish.'

'It's all right for you, you're a nurse,' Val said, suddenly wondering if that was why Cheryl's demeanour had changed. It was almost as if she had put her nurse's hat on, becoming calm, controlled and in charge. 'Do you know, for a while there I thought you were going to back out.'

'I was scared of being caught out by a medical examination. Thanks to your idea, that's covered now, so come on, let's get this over with.' Cheryl

135

unbuttoned her blouse, showing no sign of embarrassment as she stood in just her brassiere.

'Ready?' Val asked, hesitant at first as she gripped Cheryl's arms, but told that she wasn't digging her fingers in hard enough, she increased the pressure.

'That should do it.' Val was amazed to see that marks were already forming on Cheryl's upper arms and, when Cheryl took over to scrape her own nails across her breasts, the lines flared a vivid red.

Cheryl then slipped off her skirt, once again unperturbed by her state of undress. Val though found her cheeks burning as she dug her fingers into Cheryl's inner thighs and was glad when it was over.

'Great, that should do it,' Cheryl said, then saying that she needed the privacy of the bathroom for the next bit.

As the door closed behind her, Val paced the room, trying not to think about what Cheryl was being forced to do to herself.

When at last Cheryl returned, her face even paler than usual, she said in a matter-of-fact manner, 'Right, all done, and I've managed to make it look rough.'

'Oh, Cheryl, I'm so sorry. I should never have asked you to do that.'

'I'm glad you did. I feel safer that my story will be believed now, and as far as I'm concerned, being a bit sore is worth it. Mind you,' she grinned, 'talk about pain without any pleasure.'

Val smiled back, feeling a little better now. 'I'll ring the police shortly – I doubt it'll be long before they arrive.'

While waiting they went over their stories again and, as predicted, it didn't take them long to turn up. Val hurried to answer the door, admitting two police officers. She led them to Cheryl, worried at first to see her shaking badly, but then realised that it actually helped to give credence to her story.

'Can you tell us what happened, miss?' asked one officer as he walked over to Cheryl.

She was hesitant, her voice quavering as she began to tell them what happened. 'I . . . I'm a nurse and I went to visit a colleague of mine who has taken up midwifery. You . . . you see I'm thinking of taking the course too. I didn't realise how late it was when I left, and missed the last bus home. I was on my way to Battersea Park Road, hoping to hail a taxi, when . . . when . . .' With a sob, Cheryl buried her face in her hands.

'It's all right, miss. Take your time,' the constable said, and Val was pleased to see that he looked sympathetic.

'A . . . a man grabbed me. He . . . he pulled me through some broken railings and dragged me into the park,' Cheryl continued, her voice cracking, 'and . . . and then he attacked me. I tried to fight him off, but I couldn't. Oh, God, he raped me!'

'Can you give us a description of him?'

'He . . . he was youngish, and I think he had red hair.'

Val could see that Cheryl was struggling now, so hastily broke in. 'I saw him, officer,' she said, relieved that both constables now turned to her. 'I couldn't sleep and got up to make myself a cup of cocoa when I heard what I thought was a scream. It's usually quiet around here at this time of night and I was concerned, so I went to look out of my window. I could see something going on in the park, some sort of struggle, but then nothing else.'

'I see, and what did you do?'

'Well, to be honest, nothing, though I did continue to look out of my window. I didn't hear another scream, but then a while later I saw a man coming through a gap in the railings and then running to a car that was parked just along the road.'

'Did you get a good look at him?'

'The car was parked close to a streetlight so yes, I did, and as I was a bit suspicious I also took note of the number plate.'

The officer turned a page in his note pad, taking down Val's description of the man, the car and the registration number, then saying, 'And what time did you say it was?'

Val was surprised at how calm she felt. It was as though going over the story so many times had set it so deep in her mind that it felt true. 'I didn't, but I think it was around midnight. I stayed at the window, wondering if there had been a fight or something, but then saw this poor young woman staggering out of the park. I didn't stop to think, but rushed outside in my dressing gown, and as she was in such a dreadful state I brought her into my flat. Oh yes, and I don't think I was the only one who saw something. A woman who lives above me appeared as I was bringing her in and offered to help. I told her I could manage so she went back upstairs to her flat.'

'Can you tell us her name, and what flat she lives in?'

'I don't know her name, but she lives in number six.'

'We'll have a word with her later, but for now,' he said, turning to Cheryl, 'I think you should come with us to the station. We'll get a doctor to take a look at you.'

Her eyes now wide with fear, Cheryl wailed, 'Oh, no . . . no, I don't want to.'

'Is there anyone you could call, someone to come with you?'

As Cheryl frantically shook her head, the constable moved Val to one side, saying quietly, 'She'll need to be examined for corroborative evidence. I know you've only just met, but would you mind coming with her?'

'Oh, for goodness' sake,' Val said imperiously, 'it's nearly one in the morning. I took the girl in, managed to calm her down, even let her take a bath, but if you don't mind, I'd like to get back to bed.'

'She had a bath? Bloody hell, that will have mucked up the evidence. You should have called us earlier.'

Val stretched her neck, feigning indignation. 'Please do not swear, constable, and as for calling you earlier, the girl was hysterical and it took ages to calm her down.'

'Pardon my language, miss.'

'Yes, well, I did the best I could. How was I supposed to know that she shouldn't bathe?'

He exhaled loudly, as though struggling to remain calm, then saying, 'She still needs to be looked at, so will you come with us? As a witness you'll need to give a statement and we can do that at the same time.'

'Oh, very well,' Val said huffily.

With a bit more persuasion they got Cheryl on her feet, her hand gripping Val's as they left the flat to go to the police station.

Once there, Val was asked to accompany the constable into a side room where he took down her statement. She doubted at this hour that they'd question Betty until morning and hoped she'd had the sense to go to bed. 'How much longer is this going to take?' she asked crossly as she signed the document.

'That's it, Miss Thorn. You can go now.'

'What about that poor young woman?'

'Once she's been examined she'll be driven home.'

Val rose to her feet, baulking at the thought of leaving Cheryl, but worried that it would look suspicious if she waited for her. 'And what about me? Surely you don't expect me to walk home at this hour?'

'If you'd like to wait at the desk, I'll see if I can find someone to drive you.'

'Well, don't take too long. Look at the time! If this is what happens when you try to help someone, I certainly won't be doing it again,' Val said indignantly before she stormed from the office. Shortly afterwards, she was told that someone would drive her home; with no sign of Cheryl, she left the station to climb into a police car. Her head was now thumping with worry. Would Cheryl crack? Would she fall apart when questioned again? And what about the medical examination? How was she coping with that?

With barely a thank you to the policeman who had driven her home, Val climbed out of the car and, going into her flat, almost fell onto the sofa. Oh, Cheryl, surely it's over. Please ring, she urged, looking at the telephone.

When there was a soft knock on her door she went to answer it. Betty scuttled in wearing a dressing gown and hairnet. 'The police haven't been up to question me and I saw you drive off. What happened?'

'They'll probably wait till morning now. You should go to bed.'

'I won't be able to sleep.'

'No, I suppose not. I just hope we hear from Cheryl soon.'

An hour passed, then another thirty minutes, with Betty dozing fitfully on the sofa, but knowing that she wouldn't be able to sleep until she heard from Cheryl, Val was drinking coffee when the telephone finally rang. She hurried to answer it, relieved to hear Cheryl's voice. 'Oh, God, what took so long?'

'I had to wait ages for the doctor, but don't worry, it all went well and I feel sure we've pulled it off.'

'I've been worried sick. Are you all right?'

'Yes, I'm fine,' Cheryl replied. 'After this, going to court will seem like a doddle.'

'Court, yes, the next stage. I'm not looking forward to it,' Val said worriedly.

'It'll be fine. You only have to repeat your statement, Betty too when she gives it, and then it's all over.'

Once again Val was surprised by how assured Cheryl sounded; again she was the strong one. 'Cheryl, you're absolutely marvellous, and well done for pulling it off so well.'

'Thanks. I didn't know I had it in me, but I must admit I feel totally worn out now.'

'Yes, I'm sure you are, and I think its only adrenaline that's been keeping me awake.'

'I'm glad I haven't got to report for duty tomorrow.'

'Today you mean,' Val said, 'but like you, I've got the day off.'

'When will you tell the others?'

'Betty's here, but I won't risk ringing Paula until later.'

'All right. Night, Val.'

'Night, Cheryl.'

'The telephone woke me. Is Cheryl all right?' said Betty, sleepily.

'Yes, she's fine and it all went well. You'd best get back to your flat and grab a little more sleep before the police turn up to question you.'

'I'm not looking forward to that.'

'You'll be fine,' Val said, and then yawned widely.

'I hope so, but go on, get yourself to bed too.'

It was only when Betty left that the realisation hit Val with a rush. They had done it – they had actually done it! Her plan had worked and at last she would be able to get some well-earned sleep.

Chapter Fourteen

Betty awoke to the noise of someone banging on her front door. Thrusting on her dressing gown, she hurried to open it, her eyes blinking blearily at the policemen. It had been the early hours of the morning before she'd got to bed, and now at nine-thirty the police were here. She felt exhausted from her broken night's sleep but, as the nerves kicked in, her mind cleared. With feigned horror, she cried, 'Oh, God, please don't tell me that something has happened to one of my children.'

'No, madam, we're only here to ask if you saw an incident in the park last night.'

'You'd better come in.'

As the two constables walked inside, she said, 'I saw a young woman being attacked, if that's what you mean.'

'Can I ask why you didn't report it?'

'Huh, I left it to that high-and-mighty woman who lives on the ground floor. It was she who went

144

to the young woman's rescue and, though I went down to offer my help, the woman insisted she was perfectly capable of handling it on her own. Honestly, I don't know who she thinks she is, but I assumed she'd ring you.'

'Yes, she did, but can you tell us what you saw?'

Betty told them her rehearsed story, described the man, and when finished one of the constables said, 'Thank you, and when the car drove off, did you take the registration number?'

'No, I'm sorry. I didn't think of that.'

'Would you be willing to come to the station to make a formal statement?'

As though giving the question consideration, Betty pursed her lips, then said, 'Well, I suppose so, but if you catch the man, does that mean I'll have to go to court?'

'Yes, I'm afraid so, but only to repeat what you saw.'

'Oh dear, I've never been in court before, but that poor young woman was in a dreadful state so I hope you catch him.'

'With the information we have, we'll get him, you can be sure of that.'

Betty agreed to go to the station later, and then showed them out, heaving a huge sigh of relief as the door closed behind them. She was already late for work, and so tired that she couldn't face going in. She rang her employers' country house and made her excuses to the butler; that done, she at last smiled.

When the police had questioned her it had been easier than expected and Betty was pleased with her performance. There'd been no sign of suspicion, no sign that she hadn't been believed. And now, once Ian Parker was arrested, there was just the court case to face.

Betty didn't feel any shadow of guilt for setting Ian Parker up. In fact, she just felt an enormous surge of pleasure to know that once he was behind bars, Paula's life could get back to normal.

Val opened the door to Betty then poked her head outside. 'If the other tenants saw the police, they're bound to be curious. We don't want to make our friendship obvious.'

'It's all right. There was no one around when I came down here.'

'Good, but I thought you'd be at work by now.'

'I took the day off.'

'How did it go when the police questioned you?'

'It was fine and I'm just off to the station to give a formal statement. Goodness, Val, you look exhausted.'

'I set my alarm for seven o'clock so I could ring Paula before she left for work. She's over the moon.'

'I'm glad, but it isn't over yet.'

'I know, but when it comes to court, I'm sure Ian Parker will be found guilty.'

'Have you spoken to Cheryl this morning?'

'No, not yet. She'll probably be up by now so I'll ring her shortly.'

'I'd best go, but I'll call in again when I get back from the station.'

Val closed the door, her eyes bleary from lack of sleep as she went to the telephone. When Cheryl answered she asked, 'Hello, how are you doing?'

'I'm fine, but wondering if they've got Ian Parker in custody yet.'

'I don't know, but as Betty's just gone to the station to give her statement, she might hear something. If she's got any news I'll ring you again. When are you back on duty?'

'I start night shift on Monday.'

'We won't be able to meet up, but I'll keep in touch.'

They spoke for a while longer, and then, saying goodbye, Val slumped onto her sofa, her eyes slowly closing until she fell asleep. She awoke an hour later with a start, realising that someone was knocking on the door. She went to answer it.

'They've got Ian Parker in custody,' Betty said as she hurried inside. 'There's going to be an identity parade later today, and they want me there. I should think they'll want you and Cheryl too.'

Val fought to clear her head. 'Right then, and if we meet up at the station, don't forget to act all huffy with me. We don't want to give them any inkling that we're friends.'

'Don't worry, I'll remember. Paula will be so much better when she hears that he's in custody.'

'He may get bail,' Val warned.

'Oh, no, I hadn't thought of that.'

'It's a serious crime, so let's just hope he gets remanded in custody. I'll give Cheryl another ring to let her know about the identity parade, and Betty, you had better go now. If the police call to ask me to attend the line-up, it might look a bit suspicious if they find you here.'

'All right, but let's hope it's the last we see of them until the case goes to court.'

'It should be, and once we're in the clear, we'll all meet up somewhere out of the borough for a celebratory drink. That should please Paula.'

'Yes, and I might even break the habit of a lifetime by having something alcoholic,' chuckled Betty.

They had all been called to the station at the same time, and now sat waiting for the identity parade. Betty was playing her part perfectly, her expression one of disdain when she looked at Val.

It was hard for Val not to laugh, and if this was anything to go by she felt Betty had missed her vocation – the woman perfect for the stage. It boded well for their future plans; ones she hoped would seem easy after this.

Cheryl was called in first, looking pale and nervous, but as she was supposed to be a rape victim, it didn't arouse any suspicion. In fact, she had been assigned a woman police officer, who was being very supportive and sympathetic as she led Cheryl into the room.

Next it was Val who, as she looked at the line-up, was pleased by her forethought. Two other men had red hair, one more vivid than the other, and had Paula not pointed out Ian Parker first, it would have been difficult to pick him out.

'Take your time, miss.'

Val made a show of studying all the men. 'Ask them to turn to the side.'

The instruction was given, and when they turned to the front again, Val shuddered as she looked at Ian Parker. This was the man who had raped Paula and he deserved everything he was going to get. 'Number three, that's the man.'

'Are you sure?'

'I'm not blind,' she snapped, keeping up her haughty manner. 'It was definitely him.'

Betty was next, and then they were told they could go. As she and Betty lived in the same block, and the police knew that, Val decided it would look odd if she didn't offer her a lift. 'Excuse me, but as we live in the same flats, perhaps you'd like a lift home?'

Betty feigned surprise, then said, 'Well, if you're sure.'

'What about you, my dear? Can I give you a lift home too?'

'It's a bit out of your way,' Cheryl said.

'It isn't a problem,' and then, her tone imperious again, Val added, 'Now do come on. I haven't got all day.'

Once again Val had to hide a smile when she saw Betty lifting an eyebrow to one of the constables, her expression one of '*Hark at her.*'

The man smiled as though in conspiracy, but then they walked out to climb into Val's car, only just managing to clear the station before bursting into laughter.

'Oh, Betty, you are a card,' Val gasped.

'It was the same policeman who came to question me. I had already described you as high and mighty, so your uppity manner played right into my hands. Honestly, Val, talk about wasted talent. You should be on the stage.'

'That's funny, I was thinking the same thing about you.'

'What about me?' asked Cheryl.

'Yes, you too,' Val said. 'Well done. You've been marvellous, your role the greatest, and I'm so proud of you.'

Cheryl's voice became sombre. 'I felt awful when I picked Ian Parker out. He looked so scared and for a moment I felt sorry for him. After all, he didn't do it and we're sending an innocent man to prison.'

'He may be innocent this time, but I just thought about what he'd done to Paula, and it was easy,' said Betty.

'Yes, I suppose you're right,' said Cheryl, but there was a trace of doubt in her voice.

'Cheryl, for goodness' sake,' Val snapped. 'You seem to have forgotten that he raped Paula, and he's getting no more than he deserves. We're putting him away, stopping him from doing it to some other poor young woman – so as far as I'm concerned, the end justifies the means.'

'My thoughts exactly,' said Betty.

'Yes . . . yes, I suppose you're right,' Cheryl murmured.

'Oh come on, cheer up. We should be celebrating.'

'Val's right, Cheryl, and I'm over the moon that we pulled it off.'

'I am too,' Val said, 'but we've still got a way to go yet and I hope it isn't long before the case goes to court. In the meantime, Betty, as I said earlier, I think we can risk meeting up out of the borough for a celebratory drink. Paula will love it, so who's going to give her the good news?'

'I will,' Betty offered.

'Right, let's make a date for Sunday afternoon. We'll all travel separately and perhaps meet up at Regent's Park?'

'Yes, all right,' said Cheryl, her voice still lack-lustre.

Betty agreed too, and after dropping Cheryl off at the nurses' quarters, she said, 'I suppose I can understand how Cheryl feels, but I still think we've done the right thing.'

'Me too.'

They were quiet again until Val pulled up at traffic lights, Betty then musing, 'I wonder which of us will be next?'

'I don't know, but we'll wait until Ian Parker's case goes to court before we make any plans. Not only that, I think we all need a break.'

'Yes, I suppose you're right, but it could be ages before his case comes up.'

Val caught the hint of disappointment in Betty's voice. 'It may not be too long,' she consoled, then concentrated on the road until they drew up outside the flats. 'I don't know about you, and it may be something to do with being at the police station, but somehow I feel a bit grubby and can't wait to have a bath.'

'Yes, I must admit I feel the same.'

She said goodbye to Betty, and once in her flat went to run a bath, climbing in to let the water splash over her shoulders. It wasn't over yet – there was still the court case to face – but Val felt such a huge sense of relief. She had hidden it from the others, but the plan had lain heavily on her mind.

It had been her idea, and so far it looked as if they'd pulled it off, but if it had gone wrong they could all have ended up in jail. How would she have felt then? Instead of relief, there would have been anguish. So from now on she was determined that any further plans they made would not involve the police.

When they all met up on Sunday, Betty saw that Paula was already looking better, even going so far as to wear a splash of lipstick. Her clothes were still dowdy, but her hair was down, framing her pretty face.

Paula flung herself into Betty's arms, and then gave Val and Cheryl a cuddle too, her eyes moist with tears. 'Thanks for what you've done,' she croaked, voice cracking with emotion.

Betty felt a surge of pleasure, so pleased now that she had agreed to join them. She had been a housewife, a mother, and was now just a housekeeper, but look how much she'd changed – how, thanks to Val, her confidence had grown. She'd found an inner strength, and of course, she thought with a smile, an acting ability that had been a hidden talent. It felt wonderful to be a part of something – to have achieved something. Looking at Paula, she felt it had all been so worthwhile.

'It isn't over yet,' Val cautioned, 'there's still court to face, but at least he's remanded in custody.'

'I know, but he'll go down, I'm sure of it,' Paula said.

'Yes, I am too. Now come on, this is supposed to be a celebration. Let's find somewhere quiet to have a drink.'

It was a lovely day, the sun bright as they headed for the nearest pub. Betty wasn't sure what to order, so when Paula recommended a Babycham she agreed to give it a try. The pale, golden liquid sparkled in the glass and she tentatively took a sip. 'Oh, it's lovely.'

'See, I told you,' said Paula, smiling happily.

Betty was glad to see Paula and Cheryl. With nothing else to concentrate on for the last couple of days, her mood had lowered, and she found her thoughts constantly turned to Richard. She didn't want to think about him, about Mel, the baby. What she needed was another distraction. 'I can't help wondering whose turn it'll be next.'

There was a gasp from Cheryl. 'How can you even think about the next plan when there's still the court case to face?'

'I know, but after all the planning, all the excitement, things seem a little flat now. Well, except for this,' she chuckled, holding up her glass of Babycham.

'Drink up and I'll get you another one,' Paula urged.

'Oh dear, I might get tipsy.'

'Go on, let your hair down for once.'

Betty finished her drink and then, taking their glasses, Paula went to the bar. 'The same again for the rest of you?' she chirped.

'Yes please,' Val and Cheryl chorused.

Betty did indeed get tipsy, but enjoyed the afternoon and was sad when it came to an end. It was hard to say goodbye to Paula, the young woman clinging to her like a limpet before she was finally able to say goodbye. Cheryl too looked sad when they parted, but until Ian Parker's case came up, they had no choice but to stay away from each other. Only she and Val would be able to meet when they sneaked to each other's flats. With only one flight of stairs separating them, and as long as they checked that no other tenants were in sight, it was easy to do. At least seeing Val offered some consolation, and, anyway, maybe she could persuade Val to think about their next plan.

Chapter Fifteen

Ian Parker had been on remand for over two weeks and now sat across from his brief, scowling at the man's words. All right, he might have been a bit naughty in the past, had been lucky to get away with it, but this time he was innocent and wasn't about to go down for something he hadn't done. 'There's no way I'm pleading guilty. I told you, I wasn't there. I was nowhere near Battersea flaming Park.'

'You were picked out in the identity parade by the victim and two other witnesses.'

'But it wasn't me!'

'It doesn't help that you haven't got an alibi.'

'I didn't leave me flat.'

'Yes, but as I said before, you haven't got anyone who can corroborate that. There's also the evidence that both witnesses saw you getting into your car and one took note of the number plate. How do you explain that?'

'For fuck's sake, you're supposed to be on my side.

They couldn't have seen me! It wasn't my car. They *must* have got it wrong.'

'I *am* on your side, but can't find anything to offer up in your defence. There's nothing wrong with either woman's eyesight. The victim is a nurse with an impeccable character, so again, nothing to make the jury doubt her story.'

'But I didn't do it!'

'Maybe not, but I can't prove that, whereas the prosecution seem to have a watertight case. If you plead guilty, you'll get a lesser sentence. However, if you insist on pleading your innocence, you could face ten years or more imprisonment.'

'Ten years! You must be fucking joking.'

'I'm afraid not. It was a serious assault – rape with bodily harm.'

Ian Parker slumped in his chair. Ten years! He couldn't face ten years in prison – he'd go out of his flaming mind. He didn't do it, hadn't been near the park, but nobody, not even his brief, believed him. None of this made sense. How had that nurse and two other witnesses picked him out? There had to be another bloke somewhere, his double; not only that, he must drive the same sort of car. 'Look, it wasn't me, I swear. There must be something you can do.'

'I can't find anything to break the prosecution's case. My advice is a guilty plea,' and, rising to his feet, he added, 'I'll leave you to think about it.'

Ian Parker shook his head with disgust. 'Forget it. I'm innocent.'

Only a moment later a guard came to take him back to his cell, and he cringed when the door slammed shut, the key turning in the lock. If his own brief was sure he'd go down, what chance did he have?

Paula returned from her break and climbed onto a stool to begin work again. She was miles away, in a world of her own, the clatter of machines and loud voices seeming distant. It felt like ages since she'd seen Cheryl, Val and Betty, but at least with Ian Parker in custody, she felt safer.

The last time they'd all met up, it had been funny to see Betty tipsy, and the memory made her smile. She missed them and prayed it wouldn't be long before the case came to court. She'd love to be there, love to sit in the gallery to see Ian Parker get his comeuppance, and surely . . . surely there was no doubt of that? Her heart thumped with fear at the thought that he might get away with it, that he might be set free, and her hands trembled as she picked up another sheet of paper to feed into the laminating machine.

'Are you all right, girl?'

Paula looked at the machine minder and nodded. Charlie Riley was a nice old bloke, due for retirement soon, and she didn't mind working on his machine. Unlike the younger machine minders, he didn't make dirty remarks, or flirt, and she was happy to chat to him when they had time. 'I'm fine, Charlie. Thanks for buying me a cup of tea in the canteen during our break.'

'You're welcome. Mind you, I don't know why you sit with an old geezer like me. What's wrong with the girls – and the young chaps, come to that?'

As she continued to feed paper, Paula said, 'I've got nothing in common with the other girls. All the young ones want to talk about is pop music and fashion, while the older ones are full of their husbands, kids and housework. As for the blokes, they drive me mad.'

'You're a funny girl but, despite the gossip, I reckon you've had a rough ride. Am I right?'

Paula took her eyes away from her work to look at Charlie, her hands still working automatically. She liked him, felt safe with him, but wasn't happy that he was now asking personal questions. With a shrug of her shoulders, she said dismissively, 'Yeah, maybe.'

'If you don't want to talk about it, that's fine and sorry I asked.'

'Fair enough, but what's been said about me?'

'Oh, nothing much, but like me, I think others have seen you having a crafty tipple.'

Paula reddened. Yes, she always carried a quarter bottle of gin in her handbag, but didn't realise that anyone had seen her having a snifter.

'It's not only that,' Charlie continued, 'you don't mix, love. You may have your reasons, but people think you're a bit stuck-up. They ain't a bad lot, and it wouldn't hurt to be a bit friendlier.'

'Yeah, maybe,' Paula said, thinking about Charlie's comments as he moved away. It was true, she did keep distant from the others, but once Ian Parker was sentenced and in prison, maybe she could make a fresh start.

Val was in the office, sorting out old files, flicking through them before putting them away. She didn't enjoy her job, felt it below her intellect, but one file caught her eye and she felt a surge of excitement as it sparked an idea. Yes, it might work . . . Taking it to her desk, she read it through. It sounded promising, but would need further investigation and would be something to keep her mind occupied whilst waiting for Ian Parker's case to come to court.

'What have you got there?' Mr Warriner asked as he came out of his office, his eyes on the file in her hand.

'It's just an old case that caught my interest.'

He leaned over her desk to scan the document. 'Yes, I remember it. The poor chap was innocent, but it was a sticky time for him. I'm glad to say he's still in business, and the last I heard he's doing well.'

'Is he still in Chelsea?'

'Yes, and if you're interested in buying that kind of thing, he's well worth a visit.'

Treacle had got out of his basket, rearing up to Mr Warriner's legs, and seeing this Val said sharply, 'Stop that, Treacle.'

'It's all right,' he said, bending over to make a fuss of the dog. 'What time is my next appointment, Val?'

'In an hour.'

'In that case I think I'll take this chap for a walk.'

Treacle must have picked out the one word that made his ears prick up, and Val smiled as she gave Mr Warriner his lead. 'He heard that.'

'Yes, you did, didn't you?' Mr Warriner said, speaking to Treacle as he clipped on his lead.

Val watched them as they went out, a smile on her face. She was lucky to have such a lovely boss, but now she returned to the file and her thoughts turned to a plan that was forming in her mind.

Cheryl too was deep in thought as she went about her work on the ward. She wasn't keen on Staff Nurse Trenton, and sometimes resented her orders. If she hadn't been forced to take a break in her career to nurse her grandmother, she too could have been a staff nurse by now. Once again Cheryl thought about her old colleague. She'd been to see her as an excuse for staying out late on the night of the alleged rape, but since then the thought of taking up midwifery, of working in the community, had become very compelling. Yet in truth there was something else she'd rather do, something Cheryl knew she'd find equally, if not more, rewarding.

Yet how could she even think about it with the court case pending? It hung over her head, keeping her awake at night, the thought of being in the witness box with a lawyer throwing questions at her, terrifying. On the night of the alleged rape and seeing Val's nerves, Cheryl had found herself taking over. She had felt assured, in control, but now that feeling had gone and once again her nerves were getting the better of her.

Cheryl took out the thermometer, but as she shook it, it flew out of her fingers, shattering into pieces on the floor.

'Oh dear,' the patient said.

'Nurse Cutter, what on earth are you doing?' Staff Nurse Trenton demanded as she hurried to her side.

'I'm sorry, it just sort of slipped.'

'Well, get a brush and clean it up. I don't know what's the matter with you lately, but your mind certainly isn't on your work.'

Feeling humiliated to be chastised in front of the elderly patients, Cheryl hurried down the ward, red-faced. Staff Nurse had made her feel like a naughty child, and once again resentment flared. It had been an accident, but no doubt she'd take great delight in telling the ward sister how clumsy she'd been.

Cheryl grabbed a dustpan and broom, unable to

miss the sympathetic glances of the patients as she passed their beds. Yet she knew that Staff Nurse Trenton was right. Her mind wasn't on her work, and her eyes were rimmed with tiredness. Oh, please, let it be over soon, she thought, wishing now that she had never met Val, or the others.

Betty too was nervous about the court case, dreading the thought of being called to the witness box, but at least she had Val to talk to, someone who always managed to alleviate her fears.

On Saturday she was worrying again, but when there was a knock on her door she opened it to see her son. Her eyes lit up.

'Oh, John, it's lovely to see you.'

'I'm sorry I haven't been to see you for a while, but I've been really busy.' His eyes then narrowed as they swept over her. 'Are you all right? You're a bit pale, and look to have lost weight.'

'Just a few pounds, but sit yourself down. What would you like to drink?'

'I can't stay long, so nothing thanks.'

'But I haven't seen you for ages!'

'I've come round to tell you that Ulrika and I are moving in together. I can't stay because I've got to pick up her stuff this afternoon.'

'Oh, not you too! Anne is living in sin and refuses to marry. Now you're going to do the same, and I haven't even met Ulrika.'

'Once we're settled I'll bring her round to meet you. She's lovely, Mum, and I know you'll like her. As for living together, well if you must know, I did ask her to marry me, but she wants to wait for a while.'

Betty sniffed. Why any girl would turn John down was beyond her – she didn't like the sound of this one at all. 'Ulrika must be mad to turn you down,' she observed.

'Yes, well, you can tell her that when you meet her. Have you seen anything of Anne?'

'She was here at the beginning of the month. It seems that your father is too worried about his wife to give Anne his usual attention and her nose is out of joint.'

'Worried. Why?'

'Oh, it's nothing, just high blood pressure. That isn't uncommon in pregnancy.'

'What about you, Mum? How are you doing? Have you got yourself a boyfriend yet?'

'I most certainly haven't,' Betty protested. 'Boyfriend indeed, at my age. No, I don't think so.'

'You're not *that* old, and it would be nice to see you with a chap, someone to look after you. It would be one in the eye for Dad, too.'

'Your father doesn't give two figs about me and wouldn't care if I met someone else. Not that I want to, of course. I'm perfectly capable of looking after myself, thank you.'

'I hate to think that you're lonely, Mum.'

Betty felt like telling her son that she'd be less lonely if he came to see her more often, but bit back the retort. 'I'm not lonely, at least not nowadays. I've made friends, one of them a woman who lives downstairs.'

'That's good, and what do you get up to?'

God, if you only knew, Betty thought. 'Oh, not much, just the occasional lunch, or a walk in the park, that sort of thing.'

'That's nice, but I really must be going, Mum.'

Betty sighed. As usual this was a flying visit, but Val would be expecting her shortly so she just kissed John on his cheek. 'See you soon, I hope, and don't forget to bring Ulrika to see me.'

'I won't, and I'll give you a ring to let you know when. Bye, Mum,' he said, returning the kiss before hurrying downstairs.

Betty sighed, wishing that at least one of her children would eventually get married. Yet on that thought she baulked. God, if she went to their wedding it would mean seeing Richard and Mel together. She'd be alone, the odd one out again. Betty didn't think she could face that.

Chapter Sixteen

It was almost six more weeks before Ian Parker's case came to court, and on the afternoon of Wednesday the first of October, all three women sat alone, waiting to be called, unaware – as yet – that there was going to be an unexpected anticlimax.

Though Paula had wanted to be there, to sit in the gallery and watch the man who raped her punished, Val had refused to allow it. If Ian Parker saw her, she'd said, he could make the connection and that was far too risky.

Val was pacing, unable to sit still, her nerves finally getting the better of her. She was so afraid of being tripped up when questioned by Ian Parker's lawyer, that she went over and over her story in her mind. She had seen him leave the park, had taken note of his number plate, and yes, he was the one she'd picked out in the identity parade. God, if she was nervous, how must Cheryl and Betty be feeling? Would Cheryl crack under questioning? Would she break down?

Val felt sick. If their lies were discovered, it wouldn't be Ian Parker who was sent to prison – it would be them!

Half an hour passed, but then, instead of being called into court, an usher told her that the prosecuting lawyer wanted to talk to her. She hurried to the corridor, finding Betty and Cheryl already there.

'What's going on?' Betty hissed.

Before Val could speak, the prosecuting lawyer approached, smiling as he said, 'Ian Parker pleaded guilty so you won't be called. You're all free to leave.'

'Guilty!' gasped Betty. 'But—'

'Thank you,' Val hastily interrupted. Hoping to draw the man out she added, 'I suppose he decided there was no other choice.'

'With the weight of evidence, his lawyer would have advised that a guilty plea might mean a lesser sentence. If the case had been fought and lost, he could well have faced a longer term in prison.'

'What . . . what was his sentence?' Cheryl asked.

'Five years, and with good behaviour he could be released in three.'

'Three years, but that's nothing,' Betty cried. 'Oh, I dread telling Paula.'

'Sorry, who?' the lawyer asked.

'Err . . . err she's just a friend,' Betty spluttered.

Val took over, her manner brusque. 'Well ladies, as we aren't needed, perhaps I could offer you a lift home?'

'Thank you,' Cheryl said.

They each then shook the lawyer's hand, saying goodbye, Betty almost tripping in her haste to leave the building. She said nothing until they were all in Val's car, her voice then contrite as she spoke. 'God, I nearly put my foot in it, didn't I?'

Val was so relieved that they hadn't been called. It was over, and she felt a surge of happiness. They had done it – all her fears about the police discovering their lies now gone. 'It doesn't matter, Betty. There was no harm done.'

'I can't believe he pleaded guilty,' said Cheryl.

'Neither can I,' Betty said. 'You could have knocked me down with a feather.'

'He obviously didn't think he had a leg to stand on.'

Cheryl's voice was high. 'But, Val, he didn't do it.'

Val couldn't believe the way Cheryl was reacting. What was the matter with her? Ian Parker was where he belonged, behind bars. Like her, Cheryl should be thrilled. 'I know he didn't do it, but he *did* rape Paula. As I've said before, he's only getting what he deserves.'

'I don't think she'll be happy with his sentence,' Betty said.

'We'll need to break it gently, and now the court case is over we can all meet up again. Maybe we should start a new plan and it will give Paula something else to think about.'

'I still can't believe that we didn't have to appear in court,' Cheryl said. 'When I was waiting to be called I was terrified.'

'Yes, I was the same,' Betty agreed.

'Me too, but thankfully it's over now.'

'We were lucky, Val; lucky to get off so lightly,' Cheryl insisted. 'I wonder now if I'd have broken down in court – if I could have pulled it off.'

'We'll never know, but I think you'd have been fine. I'd like to tell Paula what happened in person, so maybe we could go round to see her when she comes home from work.'

'Yes, good idea,' Betty said. 'What about you, Cheryl?'

'All right,' Cheryl answered quietly.

'I don't know about you two,' Val said, 'but I'm starving. Paula won't be home yet, and as we need to kill a bit of time, how about stopping off for something to eat?'

'Yes please. I was so wound up this morning that I couldn't touch breakfast or lunch, but now I'm hungry too,' said Betty.

'What about you, Cheryl? Do you fancy something to eat?'

'Yes, and I'd love a cup of tea.'

'How about the Nelson Café at Clapham Junction? They do a reasonably priced meal.'

Both Betty and Cheryl agreed so Val headed in that direction, pleased when they arrived to find a parking space. 'Goodness, I haven't been here for years, but it looks to have changed owners,' she said as they walked inside. 'It used to be run by a lovely Italian family.'

'That waiter looks more Greek than Italian,' Cheryl whispered as she pulled out a window seat.

'Instead of homely, it's now all Formica and chrome,' Val complained.

'Never mind, perhaps the food's good,' Cheryl said as she scanned the menu. 'I know it isn't Greek, but an egg and chips will do me. It's the cheapest thing on offer.'

'I'll have the same,' Betty said.

When the waiter arrived they gave their orders, and then began to discuss what had happened, all still shocked that Ian Parker had entered a guilty plea.

The man they were talking about was sitting in the court cells, waiting to be escorted to prison. Ian Parker's face was pinched with anger. Five fucking years for something he hadn't done. He'd wanted to scream at the judge, tell him he was innocent, and wished now that he'd fought the case. It was his shitty lawyer's fault, the man eventually persuading him that a guilty plea was his best option. He'd turned the man's advice over and over in his mind. He knew the git didn't believe he was innocent, and if his lawyer didn't believe him – who would? He didn't have an alibi, and with two witnesses swearing it was him they'd seen, what bloody chance did he have?

It wasn't him, couldn't have been him, so how had they picked him out? Nothing made any sense. If it had been that first time, he could have understood it. He'd picked up a girl he'd seen before in the area and taken her for a snog, parking up near Clapham Common. When she'd let him have a feel, he thought she was up for it, but when he shoved a hand up her skirt, the silly cow had protested. He was worked up, hard – and he was not about to be turned down. He'd got her onto the common on the pretext of pointing out stars, and the silly cow had fallen for it. Yeah, well, her mistake. It served her right for leading him on. Of course, she'd fought a bit, but since then he'd found they all did; and anyway, he enjoyed teaching them a lesson. You don't wind a bloke up and then back off – they all needed to learn that.

Mind you, with that first one, he'd been shit-scared afterwards. The girl knew him – could point him out, but though he'd been questioned, it had come to nothing. He'd got away with it, but it was a lesson learned, and since then he'd made sure that he couldn't be fingered again. *Yeah, but you were,* a small voice in the back of his mind mocked.

'Come on, Parker, the van's here.'

He scowled at the policeman. 'This ain't fucking right. I didn't do it.'

'Yeah, they all say that,' the man said offhandedly.

Parker was led outside and, as he climbed into the van, despair washed over him. All right, he hadn't been so innocent in the past, and maybe he was getting what he deserved, but five years still made him baulk.

He hadn't raped the girl, it had been some other lucky bugger, but he was paying the price.

Betty finished her meal and then sat back, replete. They'd gone over and over what had happened in court, still unable to believe how lucky they'd been. She was thrilled that they'd pulled it off, and proud of her part in it. Paula could get on with her life now. It was done with, finished, but she would miss the camaraderie, the thrills. She felt so close to the others now, part of their lives, and wanted to get on with the next plan.

'Come on, Val,' she said, 'let's talk about something else. You mentioned a new plan, so who's next?'

'If it's all right with you, Betty, I already have something in mind for Cheryl's dealer.'

'That's fine with me, but you never said anything to me about a plan.'

'I had to check out that it was plausible first, but I've done that now.'

'Why am I next? I'd rather it was you or Betty.'

'Well, to be honest,' Val said, 'I was sorting out

172

some old case files in the office and one of them caught my eye. It made me think about your dealer and a way to get your money back.'

'It doesn't involve the police, does it?' Cheryl asked anxiously.

'No, don't worry.'

'Let's hear it then,' Betty urged.

'Do you mind if we wait? It wouldn't be fair to discuss it without Paula. She'd be upset if she thought we'd started without her and for now we need to think about how she's going to react to Ian Parker's sentence.'

'Val's right, and anyway, there's no hurry to start on the next plan,' said Cheryl.

Val shook her head, 'Sorry, Cheryl, but I disagree. Paula might be upset about the sentence and, as I said before, a new plan will give her something else to think about. If she isn't doing anything this evening, maybe we could bring her back to my place and discuss it then.'

'Good idea,' Betty enthused.

'We've still got a bit of time to kill, so how about we pay the bill and then have a wander around the shops?'

Both women nodded, but they hardly looked at anything as they trawled Arding and Hobbs, glad when the time passed and they could make their way to Paula's.

It was only a short drive to her bedsit and, as they

climbed out of the car, Betty looked up at the tall, narrow house with a range of doorbells lining the wall by the front door.

Val pressed one, and a few minutes later the door opened, Paula's eyes widening when she saw them all on the step. 'Oh . . . Oh, what's wrong?'

It was Betty who answered, 'There's nothing wrong, sweetheart. We just thought you'd like to hear what happened in court today.'

'He . . . he didn't get off?'

'No, he was sentenced, but can we come in?'

Paula looked worried, but nodded, leading them up a flight of stairs to a small landing where she threw open one of the doors. 'As I said to Val when she first saw this dump, it ain't much.'

Betty was the first to step into the room, fighting to hide her feelings when she saw how cramped it was. There was just a lumpy single bed, a small wardrobe, and a scratched dresser, on top of which she saw a kettle. Paula moved to the bed, hastily picking up a crumpled sheet of newspaper that held a half-eaten portion of fish and chips. 'Sorry,' she said, 'I was just eating me dinner.'

'Haven't you got a kitchen?' Betty asked.

'There's a shared one on the ground floor, but it ain't fit for rats. I eat mostly from the chippie or have pie, mash and liquor, or occasionally jellied eels. Sorry, I've only got one chair, so the rest will have to sit on the bed.'

Val spoke then. 'It's all right, we won't be staying; but would you like to come to my flat?'

'Why? What's going on? You didn't lie to me, did you? Has he really gone to prison?'

'Yes,' Val assured her, 'but I . . . I'm afraid he pleaded guilty so only got a five-year sentence.'

'What? But that means with good behaviour he could be out in three.'

Betty placed an arm around Paula's shoulder, her voice echoing her sympathy. 'I know, darling, but at least he'll be in prison for a while.'

Cheryl stepped forward. 'I know you're disappointed and we are too. I'm so sorry.'

'It ain't your fault. You all did your best and at least he's out of the way for a few years.'

'Good girl,' Val said. 'Now finish your dinner, and when we get back to my place I'll tell you about a new plan I have in mind. Something for Cheryl's dealer.'

'Hearing about Ian Parker's sentence has put me off me dinner. Come on, let's go. I can't wait to hear about this plan.'

Betty heaved a sigh of relief. It had gone better than she had hoped, but once again her heart went out to Paula as she again took in the tiny room, one that since her rape had become a prison. Her mouth set into a grim line. Ian Parker had been sentenced to five years, but when he came out he could take up his life where he left off, yet for Paula it would still be many years, if ever, before she got over being raped.

When they got back to Val's flat, Val said, 'Oh, dear, Treacle's been cooped up for hours. I'll take him for a walk, and Betty, while I'm out, would you mind making a pot of tea? Help yourself to biscuits.'

The dog began to whine now, Betty urging, 'Just go, we'll be fine.'

Treacle strained at the leash as Val got outside, barely making it to the first tree before lifting his leg. In the park he raced off, returning with a small stick that she threw a few times before saying, 'Come on, boy, time to go.'

They were soon home and, after feeding Treacle, Val took a seat on the sofa whilst Betty poured her a cup of tea.

'I saw you coming so topped up the pot. It's nice and hot,' she said.

'Thanks, Betty.'

Treacle had wolfed down his food and now jumped up to squash himself between Betty and Val, laying his head on Val's lap.

'Are you ready to tell us about your idea now?' Betty asked.

'Yes, all right. As you know, I work for a solicitor, but Mr Warriner doesn't handle criminal cases now. He's getting close to retirement and mainly deals with conveyance work, or wills and such, so if anyone comes to the office regarding a criminal case, I have to turn them away.'

'So what's he got to do with the plan?' Paula asked.

'Nothing directly, but when I first went to work for Mr Warriner his files were in a dreadful state. Some were many years old, but I slowly began to sort them into a semblance of order. I was too busy to read them in depth so I just took a note of names and dates for my new filing system. However, there were a few that I left out to look at when I had time, and when I saw one again recently, it sparked off an idea. The file concerned a man who had been wrongly accused of selling a forged painting, and after a little digging I found that he's still at his old address in Chelsea. I went to see him, pretending that I might be interested in buying one. He didn't try to pass any off as genuine, instead telling me they're copies. It seems he makes a good living by selling them and taking the occasional commission.'

'Why would anyone want to commission a copy?' Cheryl asked.

'I should imagine that if you own the genuine article, the cost of insurance to have it on display would be astronomical, let alone the risk of robbery. It would be far safer to place it in a vault and just show a copy.'

'I get it,' Paula said. 'You think we should buy a fake and pass it off to Cheryl's dealer as genuine.'

'I don't think it would work,' Cheryl said. 'I can't see him being fooled by a copy.'

'I don't see why not,' said Val. 'He's an antique dealer, not an art specialist.'

'He knew enough to spot my grandmother's painting, despite the fact that it was so dirty you could hardly see a signature.'

'He may have just decided to take a chance. After all, he only gave you a pittance for everything, so even if he'd been wrong about the painting, he wouldn't have been out of pocket.'

'That's just it. He's hardly going to part with two thousand pounds unless he's *sure* the painting we offer him is genuine.'

'If he thinks it's worth a lot more, he might,' Val insisted.

Betty spoke for the first time. 'I think Cheryl's right. It wouldn't work.'

Val sighed. 'I still think it has possibilities, but admit it needs far more thought. Let's all mull it over and then talk again this weekend.'

The others all nodded in agreement and for a while they were quiet, but then Paula said, 'I still can't get over that bastard's sentence. Five years. It ain't bleedin' right.'

'I know, love,' Betty consoled, 'but at least he's out of the way for a good few years and you can get on with your life.'

'Yeah, I suppose so.'

'That's the ticket,' said Val. 'Try not to dwell on his sentence, and instead think about how we can get back at Cheryl's dealer.'

Betty yawned widely. 'Ooh sorry, but it's been a long day and I'm worn out.'

'Me too,' said Cheryl, 'and if you don't mind, Val, I think I'll go home.'

'I'll give you both a lift,' Val offered.

With obvious reluctance, Paula rose to her feet. 'When are we meeting up again?'

'Let's say here on Saturday morning, around eleven o'clock.'

'I'm on nights for a week after that,' Cheryl warned.

'Don't worry, if we haven't come up with anything by the weekend, we can still mull it over until you're free again.'

They left the flat, and in the hall Betty gave Paula a hug. 'See you soon, love.'

Val saw how they clung to each other and felt a stab of envy. She had grown fond of both of them, but found it hard to be spontaneously demonstrative. When a sales rep she'd been too busy to make friends and, other than Mike Freeman, she had never grown close to anyone.

They all chorused goodbye, but outside Val felt an autumn chill in the air. Intent on putting Ian Parker behind bars, the summer had flown by, but surely this next plan would be easier. They still had to refine her idea, but she was certain that between the four of them they would find a way.

Cheryl sat quietly on the drive home. She had tried to concentrate when Val spoke of her plan for the dealer, but, though trying to hide it, she was still swamped with guilt for setting up Ian Parker. His frightened face in the identity parade still haunted her, and though he deserved to go to prison for raping Paula, Cheryl felt sick to her stomach that on this occasion she'd sent an innocent man to prison.

Paula was obviously dwelling on it too as she said, 'Five years. I still can't get over it.'

'I know, dear,' Val said, 'but to be honest, we were all so relieved. None of us has been in court before, and were all worried about being called to the witness box.'

'Oh shit, I'm sorry. I sound ungrateful, but I ain't. It's just that, as I said before, in a few years, with good behaviour, he'll be back on the streets.'

Paula's right, Cheryl thought, and it was beginning to feel like setting him up had been a waste of time. She hoped his term in prison would serve as a warning – that he would never strike again: at least that would ease her conscience.

Cheryl was so deep in thought that before she knew it they were pulling up outside the house where Paula had a bedsit.

'Thanks, Val. Bye, Cheryl, and I'll see you both on Saturday.'

They said goodbye, and then watched as Paula unlocked the front door. Cheryl had thought her nursing quarters small, but it was luxury compared to the tiny, cramped room that Paula had to live in. Maybe she should count her blessings, forget about trying to get her money back from the dealer. She had a career and was still thinking about taking up midwifery. The pay would be better, her life a little more comfortable – and, after all, money wasn't everything.

'You're quiet, Cheryl. Are you all right?' Val asked as they continued their journey.

'I'm fine, but I must admit I'm wondering if it's worth going after the dealer.'

'We agreed that once we started, none of us would pull out. If we can get your money back you'll be able to buy a place of your own, and surely you'd prefer that to nurses' quarters?'

'After seeing Paula's tiny bedsit, my accommodation suddenly feels luxurious.'

'Yes, her room is awful and I feel so sorry for her. She's a nice girl, but so far hasn't had much of a life. If I had more room I'd be tempted to have her living with me.'

Val's words set off a train of thoughts that Cheryl found more and more compelling. If she got her money back from the dealer, Val was right: she *could* buy a flat, one big enough to offer Paula a decent place to live. She might have to take out a small mortgage, but rent from Paula would go towards the payments. It would be a real home, one they could share; and in another area, where she and Paula would be out of Ian Parker's way when he came out of prison.

Chapter Seventeen

Betty was tidying up on Saturday morning when there was a knock on her door. It wasn't yet ten o'clock and she was surprised to see her daughter on the doorstep. 'Well, hello stranger. I know we've spoken on the phone, but I haven't seen you for ages.'

'Now then, Mum, there's no need for sarcasm. I'm here now and as it's your birthday on Monday, I thought you might like to go shopping for a present.'

Betty was dumbstruck. This was the first time since moving into this flat that Anne had offered to take her out. She was supposed to meet up with Val and the others at eleven, but felt she couldn't say no to her daughter. 'Yes, I'd like that.'

'Come on then, get your glad rags on.'

Betty was smiling with pleasure as she went into her bedroom and, taking out the skirt from the second-hand shop, along with the blue blouse and beads, she hastily put them on. The warmth of the summer had passed, so she would need a jacket, but thankfully a pale blue and cream checked one that she'd had for years toned well with the colours. She would have to warn Val that she was going to be late, but could do that on the way out. 'Right, I'm ready.'

Anne's eyes widened. 'You look different, Mum. Have you lost weight?'

'John said the same, and yes, I've lost a few pounds.'

'It must be those clothes too. They make you look slimmer, younger.'

'Well, thank you. Now I just need to grab my handbag and . . .' Betty paused when there was another knock on her door. 'I wonder who that is. Oh, perhaps it's John.'

It wasn't her son, it was Paula, and Betty floundered. 'I . . . I'm sorry, love, I was just about to go out. Would you mind telling Val that I'll join you all later?'

'Yeah, all right. I'm a bit early and that's why I popped up here.'

'Who is it, Mum?' Anne called.

'It . . . it's a friend of mine.'

When Anne joined her at the door, Betty said, 'Anne, this is Paula.'

Paula grinned. 'Watcha, love.'

'Good morning,' Anne said brusquely. 'As my mother said, we're just going out.'

Betty cringed at her daughter's abrupt and rude tone. 'Sorry, but I'll see you at Val's later.'

'Yeah, bye for now,' Paula called as she ran lightly downstairs.

Anne spoke before Betty had barely closed the door. 'That girl hardly seems the type to be your friend.'

'Why not?'

'To start with she's a bit young – and she sounds common.'

Betty bristled. 'Anne, you sound like a snob and I don't like it.'

'All right, I'm sorry, but I still think it's an odd friendship.'

'There's nothing odd about it. Paula is a lovely girl and I've grown fond of her.' She picked up her handbag. 'Right, let's go.'

As Anne followed her downstairs, she asked, 'And who is this Val that Paula mentioned?'

'She's a very nice lady who lives on the ground floor. I met her in the park and she too has become a friend.'

Anne said no more and soon they were getting into her car. 'We'll go to a department store, maybe Debenhams if that's all right?'

'Yes, fine,' Betty said as she placed her handbag in the small well at her feet. It felt strange to be out with her daughter and that saddened her. It would be lovely to have a closer relationship, but it was even more difficult now they lived so far apart. 'How's Anthony?'

'Why do you always use his full name?'

'Because it's a nice name. Too nice to shorten.'

'He prefers to be called Tony and he's fine, but a bit fed up with going round to Dad's every Sunday.'

'Why go then? I thought you were unhappy with Mel.'

'Yes, well, I was wrong. Her blood pressure really is high and as she needs to rest, I offered to cook Sunday dinner every week.'

Betty felt annoyed. Anne was always too busy to visit her, yet she could find time to see Mel every Sunday. 'If you ask me she's making a fuss about nothing, and is probably just laying it on.'

'As usual, you haven't got a good word to say about Mel.'

'What do you expect – and anyway, what about horse riding? If you're going to your father's every Sunday to cook the dinner, it can't leave you much time.'

'I must admit it's one of the reasons why Tony's fed up, but I've told him to stop complaining. We manage to fit the odd ride in, and Dad is chuffed with me for helping Mel out.'

Betty pursed her lips but made no comment. Soon they were in the High Street, where Anne found a parking spot not far from the store. They climbed out of the car, Anne asking, 'How do you feel about John living with Ulrika?'

'I'm not happy about it, but it seems she doesn't want to get married.'

'Good for her, and before you start nagging me about marriage again, have you got any idea of what you'd like for your birthday?'

They entered the store, Betty's eyes on the cosmetics and perfume display. 'I'd love some make-up, perhaps eye-shadow and mascara.'

Anne's eyes widened. 'But you've never bothered before – well, other than a dash of lipstick.'

'I know, but I'd like to give it a try.'

They wandered over to a counter where Betty looked with dismay at the selection on offer, but as though aware of her dilemma, a sales assistant came forward. 'Can I help you, madam?'

'I'm looking for eye-shadow and mascara, though I'm not sure which colour would suit me.'

'I think a matt eye-shadow would be best . . . perhaps this blue,' she said, picking up a tiny flip-top container. 'If you'd like I could apply a sample, along with mascara.'

'Yes, please.'

Betty sat in a chair and with practised ease the make-up was applied. She was then handed a mirror and smiled with pleasure at her reflection. 'I like it. What do you think, Anne?'

'It looks all right. Do you want me to buy them for you?'

'Only if they aren't too expensive.'

With the purchase made, Anne said, 'That didn't take long. Would you like to go up to the cafeteria for coffee and perhaps a slice of cake?'

'Lovely,' Betty said, and soon they were on the escalator to the first floor.

When they had made their selection in the cafeteria, Betty got out her purse to pay, but Anne said, 'No, Mum, this is your birthday treat.'

'Oh, thank you, darling.'

Anne carried the tray across to a table and, after biting into her slice of fruit cake, Betty said, 'This is lovely, but have you ever tried tarte tatin?'

'No, what is it?'

'It's a French apple tart I tried when I went to a restaurant with Val.' Betty chuckled, 'I've since tried Babycham too, and it was lovely.'

Anne cocked her head to one side, her eyes narrowing. 'Mum, what's going on? You look different, you never used to drink and . . . well . . . you seem sort of happier.'

'I only tried Babycham once, but yes, I suppose I am happier nowadays.'

'I'm glad, Mum.'

Betty smiled at her daughter. 'I'd be even happier if I saw more of you and John.'

Anne shook her head in exasperation. 'Here we go again, the same old complaint. I told you, I'm at Dad's every Sunday, leaving only Saturday to do everything else. I just haven't had time to visit you.'

'I know, and I'm sorry for nagging,' Betty said, looking for a way to turn the conversation. 'It's only October, but did you see they're already putting up Christmas decorations?'

'Yes, I noticed, and talking about Christmas, have you anything planned?'

'Nothing special. I suppose you'll be going to your father's usual bash, assuming he's still putting it on.'

'He's already planning it, but as Mel won't be up to it this year, he's getting an outside caterer to provide the food. But no, I won't be going this time. Tony wants us to go to his parents, and as they live in Cornwall, we'll have to miss the party on Christmas Eve to drive down there.'

Betty sighed. If Anne was going to Cornwall, it meant she wouldn't see her over Christmas, but perhaps her son would call in – at least she hoped so. Oh, what was the matter with her? Christmas was well over two months away and she was supposed to be celebrating her birthday. Yet thinking of Richard's party and the influential people he'd invite, a nugget of an idea began to form, one interrupted when her daughter spoke.

'I'm sorry, Mum, but I'll have to take you home. I've got a stack of washing to do, plus ironing, and I promised Tony we'd go for a ride too.'

'All right, darling. It's been such a pleasure to see you and thanks for my lovely present.'

'It still seems strange to see you wearing make-up.

I'm sorry to dash off, but perhaps John will pop down either today or tomorrow.'

'I hope so,' Betty said as she rose to her feet. She wasn't unhappy that Anne had to rush off. She was meeting the others, mulling over the new plan, and was looking forward to it. She felt part of something now, a valuable part, and still thanked God for the day she had met Val.

Val saw the car when it drew up outside the flats. Betty climbed out, waved as it drove away, and then only a minute or two later she was knocking on the door.

Val let her in, Paula saying when she saw her, 'Blimey, look at your eyes, Betty. You look great.'

'Yes, you look really nice,' Cheryl remarked.

'That colour suits you,' Val said, 'and mascara too!'

'Yes, and they're both a present from my daughter.'

'Oh, is it your birthday?'

'Not until Monday. I'll be fifty-two – doesn't that sound old?'

'No, and anyway, you don't look it,' Val said, though in truth she had judged Betty to be in her middle fifties. 'I didn't expect you so soon, but I'm glad you're here. I've been mulling over my plan and I think I've found a way to make it work.'

'I'm glad you've come up with something. To be honest, I've been stumped.'

'Oh, sorry, Betty, I haven't offered you a drink. Can I get you anything?'

'No, I'm fine, thanks.'

When they sat down, Val said, 'When we talked yesterday, the stumbling block was that none of you thought a copy would fool the dealer.'

'Yes, and I still feel the same,' Cheryl said.

'I think it can work if we appeal to his greed.'

'How are we supposed to do that?'

'We've got to pitch it just right. It would be silly to buy a painting that, if genuine, would fetch a small fortune. Instead we should go for one that would sell for maybe six to eight thousand pounds. If we then offer it to him for two, he'll think he's getting a bargain.'

'Yeah, but he'll still want to give it the once over,' Paula said, 'and if he's any good, he'll spot it's a copy.'

Val then outlined a trap for the dealer that would make him anxious to buy the painting. They mulled it over, but when none of them made any comment, she said impatiently, 'It's the best I could come up with, and I think it's worth a try.'

'If he doesn't suspect anything, it might work,' Betty mused, 'but a lot would depend on how we set the scene. I wouldn't mind playing the part of the hard-up widow.'

'Yeah, let's give it a go,' Paula agreed, 'and anyway, if it doesn't work it ain't the end of the world and we can think of something else.'

'You're forgetting the cost of buying the copy,' Cheryl pointed out. 'How much would it be, Val?'

'Around fifty pounds.'

'Oh dear, I didn't realise it would be that much. If we don't pull it off I'll be considerably out of pocket.'

'I wouldn't want that,' Val said, 'and as the idea is mine again, I'd like to pay for the copy. I have a ring that belonged to my mother and I'm sure it would fetch enough.'

'No, Val, that wouldn't be fair,' Cheryl protested. 'I have a little in savings and would rather use that.'

'Does this mean you'd like us to give it a try?'

Cheryl's eyes swept over them, and then sighing she said, 'Yes, all right.'

'I'm not an expert,' Val said, 'but I love art and when I had any spare time I used to visit galleries. I've also read lots of books on the subject so, if you like, I could choose the painting.'

'That's fine with me.'

Paula chuckled. 'Rather you than me, Val. I ain't got a clue about art.'

'I'm just as bad,' said Cheryl. 'I had no idea that my grandmother's painting had value.'

'I should think there are many people who are prey to unscrupulous dealers,' Val said. 'Mind you, I'm sure there are lots of honest ones and you were just unlucky, Cheryl.'

'Yes, I'm sure you're right,' Cheryl said bitterly.

'I can't do anything about buying a painting until next Saturday. Until then, all we have to think about is setting the scene. Are you sure you don't mind playing the role, Betty?'

'I'd be happy to,' but then with a small cry Betty jumped to her feet. 'Oh, goodness, I've just seen my son passing the window. I'll have to go.'

Betty almost ran out and, waiting until the door had closed behind her, Val said, 'As it's her birthday on Monday, I must get her a little something. The shops will be closed tomorrow so it'll have to be today. Do you two fancy a little trip to the shops?'

'Yes, why not?' Cheryl said.

'I'll come too,' Paula agreed.

Treacle wasn't happy to be left but, as though he could understand every word, Val said, 'We won't be long, darling, and then I'll take you for a nice long walk.'

With that they all trooped out. Piling into Val's car they drove to Clapham Junction, where Val found a lovely scarf, Cheryl some gloves, whilst Paula picked up some beads, turning to Val to ask, 'Do you think Betty would like these?'

'Yes, I'm sure she would,' Val said, but then, seeing the price tag, she cautioned, 'They're a bit expensive.'

'I know, but Betty's worth it and I can just about afford them.'

When cards had been purchased, Paula said, 'I'll give my present to Betty on Monday evening.'

Val smiled with delight. Paula was going to visit them in the evening, which meant the girl was no longer a virtual recluse. It made everything they had done worthwhile. It had been right to seek revenge – right to make Ian Parker pay for what he'd done, and next it would be the turn of the antique dealer who had as good as robbed Cheryl.

While the others were out shopping, Betty was back in her flat and smiling at the very pretty girl with her son. Her hair was long, blonde, and her eyes were blue. She smiled back at her as John made the introductions.

'Mum, this is Ulrika.'

'Hello, and I'm pleased to meet you at last,' Betty said as she impulsively gave the girl a hug.

'Good morning, Mrs Grayson,' Ulrika said as she drew away. 'I am pleased to meet you too.'

The girl had a thick accent, yet her words were so correct. Betty held up her hands. 'Oh, please, not Mrs Grayson. Call me Betty.'

'Thank you.'

'Please, sit down,' she urged.

Ulrika chose the sofa, her eyes sweeping the room, but before John joined her, he held out a small package and a card. 'Happy Birthday for Monday.'

Betty opened the present, her eyes lighting up with pleasure when she saw an exquisite brooch. It was gold and shaped like a bouquet of flowers with tiny seed pearls along the stems.

'Oh, John, it's beautiful!'

'Ulrika chose it.'

'Thank you, my dear. I usually get a bunch of flowers from John – not that I'm complaining, but this is lovely.'

'I am glad that you like it,' she said, once again enunciating each word.

'I'll just open my card and then I'll make you both a drink,' Betty said. She read the message of love, her eyes moist with pleasure as she placed it on her sideboard before going to the kitchenette.

'Your mother's home is very different from your father's.'

'Shush,' John hissed.

Betty couldn't believe her ears and her mood changed instantly. She slammed down the kettle to march back into the living room. 'I'm not deaf. You've obviously taken Ulrika to meet your father. When was this?'

'Last week.'

'Oh, John, how could you?'

'Mum, please, sit down and I'll explain.'

Betty felt her eyes filling with tears. She'd waited ages to meet Ulrika, but now it seemed that Richard had had the privilege first. She couldn't believe it – couldn't believe that John had reconciled with his father.

'Ulrika made me look at things differently. She's away from her own family, living in a strange country, and she misses them. She wanted to meet both my parents, and how could I refuse? I know Dad treated you badly, but it was a long time ago, and Mum, no matter what, he's still my father. You told me when I last came to see you that you're happier now, so surely it's time to move on?'

'Does Ulrika know what he did to me?' Betty cried.

'Some of it. I know you came out of the divorce badly but, as Ulrika said, Dad couldn't help falling in love with someone else.'

'That didn't give him the right to force me from my home.'

'I know, Mum, it was wrong, but it's time to put it behind us.'

'Huh, just like that. Well, you might be able to forgive him, but I can't.'

'I hated him for ages for what he did to you, but as I said, he wasn't a bad father.'

'Now you sound like Anne, taking *his* side against me.'

'No, I'm not, but as Ulrika said, I shouldn't take anyone's side.'

'So, Ulrika said that, but I heard her comment about my home being different from your father's. A home that was once mine! But look at me now, living in a dump while your father and Mel live in luxury. How can you go there? How can you sit in his house, knowing it should have been mine?'

'John, this is my fault,' Ulrika wailed, her eyes too filling with tears. 'I didn't realise that your mother would overhear what I said.'

John threw his arm around her. 'It's all right, darling. It would've come out eventually. At least it's in the open now.'

'But I have upset your mother.'

'Mum, I think we'd better go.'

Betty just nodded, too upset to speak, and just watched as John drew Ulrika to her feet. The girl was pale, her voice cracking as she spoke. 'I am so sorry, Mrs Grayson . . . Betty.'

Once again Betty was only able to nod.

'Bye,' John said shortly, and whilst Betty stood rooted to the spot, he led Ulrika out, closing the door behind him.

With a sob, she flopped onto a chair. Tears came in earnest – tears she was unable to stop. Richard had it all now, his new wife, a new baby, and both his son and daughter. He was probably crowing with happiness, over the moon to have his son back in his life, whilst she . . . she had nothing!

Chapter Eighteen

Val had tried to see Betty again on Saturday evening, and on Sunday, but both times she'd been turned away. Betty looked low, said she had a chill, and obviously wanting to be left alone, Val had reluctantly left her to it.

It was now Monday evening, and as Val opened her door she said, 'Betty, I was just about to come up to see you. Are you feeling better?'

'To be honest, I didn't have a chill, but I was upset by my son's visit and wasn't in the mood to talk,' she said, going on to tell Val what had happened.

'I know it's dreadful, Betty, but if you don't somehow accept that John has reconciled with his father, you'll drive him away.'

'Yes, yes, I know you're right, but it's so hard, Val.'

'Never mind, you'll get a chance to get your own back on Richard. In the meantime, why don't you ring John? Tell him that you don't mind, that you're happy for him, even if the words feel like they're sticking in your throat.'

Betty nodded, looking a little happier as she said, 'You're right, and yes, I'll ring him this evening.'

'Good,' and turning to pick up a package, Val said, 'Here, I've got you something for your birthday.'

'Val, you shouldn't have.'

'Paula's coming round and should be here soon. I think it's wonderful that she's found the courage to make her way here in the evening, and it's thanks to your birthday.'

'Oh, bless her, but now Ian Parker's in prison she hasn't got anything to worry about.'

'I know, but after living in fear for so long, I think it's amazing that she's already found the nerve to make her way here alone at night. Oh, there she is now,' Val said as she went to open her door.

'Watcha, and Happy Birthday,' Paula said to Betty as she walked inside. 'This is from me, and that one's from Cheryl.'

Betty hugged Paula and then unwrapped her gifts. 'Thank you, thank you so much,' she enthused. 'I'll give Cheryl a ring tomorrow to thank her too.'

'You'd better wait until afternoon. After working all night she won't be up till then,' Paula warned.

'I don't know how she does it,' Val said. 'Now then, let's have a glass of sherry, to celebrate your birthday. I've still got some left.'

They toasted Betty's birthday, and then talked a

little about the plan, but they couldn't move forward until Val had purchased the painting. Val was pleased to see that Betty was looking happier now, the three of them chatting until at nine-thirty Paula rose to her feet.

'Sorry, but I think it's time I was off. I know it's daft, but I still don't like to be out late.'

'He can't hurt you now, love,' Betty said.

'Don't worry, Paula, stay for another half-hour and then I'll give you a lift home.'

'Thanks, Val,' she said, sitting down again.

Inevitably the conversation turned again to Val's plan, but then Paula said, 'I feel a bit useless. It's all down to you and Betty with nothing for me to do.'

'I'm a bit nervous about having to face the antiques dealer on my own. I'd feel better if you were there when he turns up. What do you think, Val?'

'It's a splendid idea. You could introduce Paula as your daughter.'

Paula looked delighted. 'Yeah I'd like that.'

Betty then said, 'I hope I can pull off my role, Val. What if I can't fool the dealer?'

'You'll be fine. You were marvellous last time, and as I said, you should have been an actress.'

'Maybe it would help if we did a sort of rehearsal.'

'All right, and I'll play the part of the dealer,' Val said.

There were a few giggles, but the role-playing helped and Betty's confidence grew until, at ten o'clock, Val said it was time to drive Paula home.

Once again Val watched as Betty hugged Paula, the two of them obviously growing closer and closer. Paula had been her first recruit and Val was so fond of the girl that she was unable to help feeling a surge of jealousy. Yet Betty had the motherly touch, something Val knew she lacked, so with Treacle trying to get between them she hid her feelings as she bent to scoop him up. 'Come on, you rascal. You can come with us for a ride.'

When they walked to the car, Val put Treacle on the back seat, warning him to stay there whilst Paula climbed in the front. It was a waste of time as the dog clambered over to sit on Paula's lap. 'You're a holy terror,' Val told him.

Paula held him, and as they drove away she said, 'I'm glad that Betty liked the necklace. She was dead chuffed with your scarf too. When's your birthday, Val?'

'Mine's been and gone, so it won't be until next June.'

'June! But you never said. That means I've missed it.'

'I didn't like to. Anyway, you haven't mentioned your birthday.'

'I know, but since . . . since the rape, I've never felt like celebrating it.'

'There's nothing to stop you now, so come on, when is it?'

'Not until Christmas Day.'

'Really – how lovely. A Christmas baby.'

'You must be kidding. My mum never stopped moaning about how going into labour ruined her Christmas booze-up, and I used to hate it that my present was always a joint one, if I got one at all.'

'Well yes, I can understand that.'

'When are you going to Richmond to see the dealer?'

'With any luck, after I've been to find a painting on Saturday.'

'Gawd, it'll be awful if it doesn't work and Cheryl loses her money.'

'I know and I must admit it's a bit worrying,' Val said as she drove into Paula's street.

'Then we'll just have to make sure it works.'

Val forced a smile as Paula climbed out of the car. They said goodbye, but as she drove away the thought of using Cheryl's money was heavy on her mind. Once again the plan had been her idea – and it would be her fault if they couldn't pull it off.

Chapter Nineteen

Val saw Betty a few times during the week, but now the weekend had come round again and on Saturday morning Val took a last look in the mirror before going out. She straightened her shoulders and turned this way and that, satisfied that she looked the part.

It was going to be a long day and she was grateful that Betty had offered to look after Treacle. 'Come on, boy,' Val now urged, the two of them going upstairs to Betty's flat.

'My goodness, you look the bee's knees,' Betty said when she opened her door. 'That suit looks a million dollars.'

'It's a Norman Hartnell, the man who designs for the Queen, and it would have cost the earth when it was new. It had just come in when I went to the second-hand shop so I was lucky to get it.'

'You look like an aristocrat.'

'Good, and as it's a bit out of fashion now, it's just the look I want to achieve.'

Treacle was jumping up at Betty's legs. 'Come on, you rascal, let's get you sorted out.'

'He's had his morning walk and been fed. I hope to be back by early afternoon.'

'He'll be fine.'

'Right, I'll see you later. Wish me luck.'

'Yes, good luck,' Betty said as she bent down to scoop Treacle into her arms.

It wasn't a long drive over the river to Chelsea. After parking close to the studio, Val took a deep breath and raised her chin as she went inside.

'Hello again,' the man said, his greeting warm.

'I know I looked at your work before,' Val said to him, 'but do you only have copies of works by master artists?'

'Yes. Is that a problem?'

'I'm looking for something by a minor artist, one who would sell for around six to eight thousand pounds.'

The man pursed his lips. 'I have one that might be suitable, but I hope you aren't going to try to resell it as genuine.'

'Oh no, of course not,' Val lied, thankful that her cover story was in place. As before, she had dressed to look and sound as if she were old money, now impoverished. 'It's for my fiancé, a birthday present. I'd love to buy him a genuine painting, but I'm afraid times aren't what they used to be and . . .' Val's voice trailed off for a moment. 'Oh, dear, I don't want to sound snobbish, but he's new money and hardly a connoisseur of art.'

'Ah, so you're hoping he'll think it's genuine.'

'Yes, I'm afraid I am, but he wouldn't be fooled if I presented him with something like a Rembrandt.'

'I'll show you the painting I have in mind. It's a good copy of a Dolchini, but I must insist that you sign a receipt acknowledging that it isn't genuine.'

'Of course,' Val said. When he found the painting, she studied it carefully but found it disappointing. 'Oh dear, it looks too new. Would it be possible to age it further and perhaps almost conceal the signature?'

'Yes, I can do that.'

'Wonderful,' Val enthused, 'and how much will it cost?'

'With the extra work, sixty-five pounds.'

'Goodness, that much?'

'It's a good copy and, with the added ageing, I doubt your fiancé will spot that it isn't genuine.'

'Very well, I'll buy it,' Val said impulsively, and after giving the man a deposit she left with her fingers crossed that Cheryl had enough saved to pay the rest. She should have waited until she'd spoken to Cheryl, but as the idea had been hers, if the worst came to the worst, she was prepared to pawn her mother's ring to top up any shortfall.

Val climbed into her car again. It was quite a drive to Richmond, but she felt it a necessary part of the plan. With this added element, the dealer's greed should be assured. When she arrived, Val looked at the area with appreciation. She had only been here on a few occasions, but had always liked it, especially the royal park with its herds of deer.

With Cheryl's directions, the antique shop wasn't too hard to find, and after parking, Val took in the quaintness of the building. She was surprised at how up-market it appeared and was relieved that once again she looked the part as she walked inside.

'Good morning, madam. Can I help you?'

Val looked at the man who had virtually robbed Cheryl. Instead of the ogre she was expecting, she was confronted by an amiable face and portly figure. She held her head up, chin tilted, her manner that of a woman who was used to service. With a slight sniff she moved around the shop, her eyes scanning the walls, and then said in an imperious deep tone, 'I was told you have a Dolchini.'

'Oh no, madam, I'm sorry, but maybe I can find you something else?'

'No, no,' she said impatiently, 'it has to be a Dolchini. My husband likes his work and wants to add to his collection.'

'Have you tried any other antique dealers or galleries?'

With an exasperated sigh, Val said, 'Of course I have. This is impossible. It's our anniversary in November and I'm running out of time.'

'Would you like me to make enquiries on your behalf?'

'Oh, very well,' and unclasping her leather handbag, Val took out an address book. 'I'll be away for the next few weeks, but if you find anything you can reach me through my London solicitor. Take this number, and tell him you've found a painting for Lady Margaret Parker Smythe. He'll know what to do.'

The man wrote down the number, and as she left he gave a small bow, which almost had Val bursting into laughter. The dealer had no idea. The card just gave the telephone number of her office, and when he rang, she'd be there to take the call. It was a shame the copy wasn't ready, but it was a chance in a million that he'd find a genuine Dolchini before then – and it was a chance they would just have to take.

Val strode back to her car, satisfied that she had done all she could to set things up, her hands relaxed on the steering wheel as she drove home.

Val wasn't surprised to find Paula in Betty's flat, and after flopping onto a chair she said, 'I've done it. I found a painting, but unfortunately it needs a bit of work. It won't be ready for about four weeks.'

'Did you go to see the dealer?' Betty asked.

'Yes, and I don't think he suspected a thing.

Fingers crossed that he doesn't put too much effort into finding a painting before ours is ready. He'd only get a finder's fee if he sourced one from someone else, so I doubt he'll try too hard.'

'Yes, fingers crossed,' Betty agreed and then chuckled. 'I'd have loved to have seen you playing the part of Lady Smythe.'

'He was so obsequious that I had a job not to laugh.'

'Blimey, Val, I've never heard of that word, "obse"-something. What does it mean?' Paula asked.

'It just means that he was servile, impressed by my title and eager to oblige.'

'But doesn't that mean he'll try really hard to find a painting?'

'Perhaps, but we'll just have to hope he isn't successful. I would hate to lose Cheryl's money. Talking of Cheryl, do you mind if I use your phone to ring her, Betty? I think I should tell her how much the copy is going to cost.'

'Go ahead.'

Val dialled Cheryl's number, and had a chat with her, bringing her up to date, then added, 'I'm afraid the painting will cost sixty-five pounds, but if you haven't got that much, I don't mind chipping in the extra.'

'I've just about got enough; but Val, I still think it's a bit risky.'

'I'm afraid I've already ordered the painting and

left a deposit, but if you're really worried, I suppose we could call it off.'

There was a pause, but then Cheryl said, 'No, it's all right. We've come this far so we might as well go ahead.'

'I know you've got to work tonight, but is it your last night shift?'

'Yes, thank goodness.'

'After you've had a sleep tomorrow morning, why don't you pop round?'

'Yes, I'll do that. Will the others be there?'

'Hold on, I'll find out,' Val said, getting an affirmative that she passed on to Cheryl. 'Shall we say two o'clock?'

Cheryl agreed and, after saying goodbye, Val replaced the receiver. She wouldn't admit it to the others, but she was still worried sick about losing Cheryl's savings. Stop it, she berated herself. The plan *would* work, it *had* to. However, she'd identified a snag in the plan on her way home and now discussed it with the others, hoping that they could come up with a solution to overcome it. 'Betty, you've offered to play the part of the widow wanting to sell the painting, but why would you invite a dealer from Richmond to look at it? Surely you'd use a local dealer? It's something he might find a bit odd.'

'Gawd, yeah, she's right,' said Paula. 'Here, why not just take it to his shop?'

'Yes, that could work, but it might give him too long to inspect it.'

'It'll be the same if he comes here,' Betty said. 'Unlike Cheryl, I won't be inviting him to buy everything in my flat, just one painting for two thousand pounds. I can't see him paying that without a proper inspection.'

'Don't forget, he'll be looking out for a Dolchini. With an assured buyer he'll know he can get at least three times that amount. All we need is a reason for inviting him here from Richmond. If we can sort that out, I still think his greed will make him buy it.'

They were all quiet then, all trying to come up with a plan. Betty suddenly sat up in her chair, speaking animatedly and, hearing her suggestion, Val grinned. 'Yes, Betty, that should work – well done. Thanks to you, all we have to do now is wait for the painting to be completed and then we can go ahead.'

Betty smiled at the praise, her face pink with pleasure. 'Until now, I didn't know I had such a devious mind.'

The onus for the rest of the plan now fell on Betty, but she didn't seem to mind. In fact Val could see a distinct change in her personality. Betty was more assured, no longer the shrinking violet she'd first encountered in the park. Val had started the group as a means to an end, but now wondered what would happen when all the plans had been carried out.

Would that be the last they all saw of each other? Val blinked as she realised again just how much Betty, Paula and Cheryl had come to mean to her. She couldn't imagine her life without them now. Would they remain friends? God, she hoped so.

Chapter Twenty

Ten days later, on a Tuesday morning, Cheryl clipped on her wide belt, straightened her starched hat, smoothed her apron and stifled a yawn as she made her way to the ward. She should be happy. So far the dealer hadn't called Val's office, the man so far obviously unable to find a Dolchini. Val would collect the copy in another couple of weeks and, if it fooled the dealer, there was a good chance she'd get her money back.

If only she could sleep, forget the part she'd played in putting Ian Parker behind bars. The others didn't seem to feel any remorse, so why her? Why couldn't she just be happy for Paula? It was lovely to see her confidence restored, her bubbly personality beginning to shine through; yet even this didn't ease Cheryl's guilt.

When she lay awake, haunted by what they'd done, the same thought had begun to plague her. If Paula had moved to another area, where there was no danger of seeing Ian Parker again, surely, eventually, she'd have recovered from her ordeal. Instead, a man who on this occasion had been innocent was now in prison.

Yes, she told herself, the man was in prison, but surely he deserved to be there? Yet his face haunted her, the tear she'd seen in his eyes, and with this came doubt. Had Paula exaggerated the rape? Had she led him on to the point where he'd been unable to stop?

Lost in her own thoughts as she hurried along the lengthy hospital corridor, strangely Cheryl found she felt no guilt about the antiques dealer. As far as she was concerned, the man had robbed her. He'd known the painting was valuable when he'd offered to clear the house and should have given her a fair price, one that would have left him a fair profit. If he'd been honest in the first place, none of what they intended to do would be necessary. If it worked, as far as she was concerned, the man would get no more than he deserved. At the end of the corridor, Cheryl threw open a door and walked into the ward, but hearing a voice she snapped to attention.

'Nurse Cutter, you're five minutes late for duty.'

Cheryl's face flushed. 'Sorry, Sister.'

'And why are you late?'

She felt like a naughty child in the face of the ward sister's annoyance and blustered, 'I . . . I overslept.'

'That's no excuse. Matron will be round shortly so check the ward. Make sure the beds are tidy, with unnecessary things on the top of patients' lockers stored away. After that you can clean the sluice room.'

'Yes, Sister,' Cheryl said as she scuttled off. She'd been given the tasks of a junior nurse, but knew better than to argue. This was her punishment for being late. As she walked along the ward, Cheryl saw that a new patient had been admitted, an elderly lady who was struggling to sit up. She looked awful, thin to the point of being almost emaciated, and one side of her face was badly bruised. 'Oh, dear, what happened to you?' Cheryl asked as she hurried to help the woman.

'I tripped on the edge of my rug and took a tumble.'

Cheryl made the patient comfortable and then looked at her notes. Edna Sands, aged eighty-two, had a fractured wrist and severe bruising. It was unusual to admit a patient with minor injuries, but her vital signs weren't good and Cheryl frowned as she read them.

'What a pretty girl you are,' Mrs Sands said. 'You may not believe it now, but I was once considered a bit of a looker.' Her rheumy eyes became bleak. 'It isn't much fun growing old, so take my advice and make the most of your life while you can. My son's married, busy, with little time to keep an eye on me. He wants me to go into a nursing home, but I've seen a few and can't face it.'

'He's probably worried about you.'

'Perhaps, but his wife treats me like a burden she can't wait to unload.'

'Nurse Cutter. Sluice room, please.'

Cheryl swung round at the sound of the ward sister's voice and, seeing the look of annoyance on her face, she said hurriedly, 'Sorry, I've got to go.'

In the sluice room, she set to work, but her mind kept drifting. Make the most of your life, Mrs Sands had said, and if the plan worked, Cheryl wanted to do just that. She would start looking for a flat, or even a house but, now that she had begun to have doubts about the truth of Paula's story, Cheryl didn't know if she could face offering her a home. Every time she looked at Paula it would bring back memories – bring back the doubts in her mind.

Paula too was at work, deep in thought as she fed paper into a laminating machine. Maybe it was the result of being in Cheryl's company, but whatever the reason there was a yearning to make changes in her life. She wanted to do something worth while that would make a difference, but knew she didn't have what it took to be a nurse. Like Val, the thought of looking after sick people, of dealing with blood and vomit, left her cold, but surely there was something she could do other than feeding flaming paper into a machine all day.

Paula felt there was something troubling Cheryl, but she couldn't put her finger on what it was. Though now enthusiastic about the plan to get her money back, at times Cheryl seemed distant, remote, as though her mind was elsewhere. Not only that, lately Cheryl had avoided looking her in the eye, but why? The ageing of the painting would take about another two weeks, and then, after rehearsing the plan again, they were all set. Maybe it was Cheryl's nerves, yet even as this thought crossed her mind, Paula felt it was doubtful. She'd been uptight for quite a while now; in fact, since they'd put Ian Parker behind bars. It couldn't be that – surely? – but, unable to find an answer, Paula sighed. She glanced up, saw that the machine minder, a bloke called Keith, was staring at her again. Throwing him a look of distaste she curled her lips into a sneer.

He just laughed, calling above the clatter, 'I know you love me really. If you play your cards right you can buy me a pint tonight.'

'Sod off!' Paula yelled.

Keith laughed again and shouted to the minder on the next machine, 'Did you hear that, Charlie? Miss nun face swore at me.'

'What?'

'The daft bugger's as deaf as a post,' Keith said, then shouted, 'Nothing, Charlie, just forget it.'

'He ain't daft or deaf,' Paula snapped.

'Oh, the nun speaks again. My, ain't I privileged?' Keith drawled.

Paula shook her head in disgust and, ignoring Keith, she looked across at old Charlie Riley. He was the only man in the factory she felt safe with and preferred working his machine to any of the others. When it was possible above the noise, he would talk to her about his son and how much he missed him since he'd emigrated to New Zealand. Charlie was obviously lonely and she knew he dreaded his retirement. As though aware of her scrutiny, he suddenly grinned, waving what looked like a letter. 'What's that?' Paula mouthed.

After working with the noise of the machines for many years, Charlie was practised in lip-reading but, even without the same skills, Paula understood when he mouthed back, 'Later.'

She smiled, but then hearing Keith's shout of anger as he turned off the machine, Paula snapped her attention back to her work.

'You soppy mare!' he yelled. 'You missed feeding in a sheet of paper.'

Paula grimaced. Because of her inattention, the huge chrome roller would now be coated in sticky laminate, and until Keith was able to clean it, production would halt.

'Look at the state of that,' he spat. 'Happy now, are you?'

Normally she'd apologise, but annoyed by his attitude, Paula just climbed off her stool, saying nothing as she headed for the cloakroom.

'Oi! Where are you going?'

Paula didn't turn, instead jabbing up two fingers at him. In the cloakroom she dived for her coat, pulling cigarettes out of the pocket. She quickly darted outside to light up, drawing in a lungful of smoke as though it were nectar, but had barely finished her cigarette when the door was flung open.

The forewoman stormed out, her face red with anger. 'You. Go to the office!'

Paula wasn't intimidated. After working in many factories, she knew the score, but in truth this wasn't a badly paid job and she didn't want to lose it. 'What's wrong?' she asked innocently.

'According to your machine minder, you deliberately caused production to stop, and I can see why,' she said, her eyes travelling pointedly to Paula's cigarette.

'It was a mistake; it wasn't deliberate. Anyway, I ain't the only one who misses the occasional paper feed.'

'I know that, but the other girls don't leave the machine room to have a cigarette without permission.'

'I don't see the harm. It's gonna take Keith a while to clean the roller.'

'I am *not* having this conversation in the cloakroom. Now go to the office.'

'All right, but I ain't talking to you without the union rep.'

'Oh, for goodness' sake, this is ridiculous.'

'I still want her there.'

'Very well, I'll put out a call for the mother of the chapel.'

Paula heaved a sigh. Why the union rep had such a silly title was beyond her, but she needed the woman on her side. She stubbed out her cigarette, head held up in defiance as she went to stand outside the office.

It was ten minutes before the mother of the chapel made an appearance, ten minutes in which Paula was left alone to ponder; but as soon as the woman turned up, she was straight on the case.

After a few words they walked into the office, the mother of the chapel saying, 'If this is a disciplinary action, I want the proper procedure followed.'

'Look, I don't know what all the fuss is about,' the forewoman said. 'I only called you because Paula insisted. I had a complaint from her machine minder, which I'm inclined to take with a pinch of salt. However, as Paula left the machine room without permission, my only intention is to reprimand her for that.'

It was only then that Paula realised that she'd overreacted. Since Ian Parker had raped her she had lost job after job – her defensive and surly attitude to male co-workers her downfall. Without thought she blurted out, 'Oh blimey, I'm sorry. I thought I was gonna get the sack.'

The forewoman smiled, the mother of the chapel sighed and, after a short reprimand, Paula was told to go back to her machine. She left the office pink-faced with embarrassment, which swiftly turned to red with anger when she saw Keith. The bastard had reported her and she felt nothing but loathing for him as she slipped back onto her stool. He held up a hand to indicate he was starting the machine and, head down, Paula once again began the mind-numbing task of paper feeding.

'Don't do that again,' Keith snapped as he came to her side. 'It took me ages to clean that soddin' roller.'

'It wasn't deliberate,' Paula retorted.

'If you hadn't been making eyes at Charlie it wouldn't have happened.'

'What!'

'You heard me. What is it? Are you one of those weird women who prefer older men? Or is it his money you're after? If it is you've picked the wrong bloke. Charlie ain't rich and he's only got his old-age pension to look forward to.'

'Fuck off.'

'Charming,' he said as he walked away, but then as an afterthought shouted, 'Instead of treating me like dirt, maybe it's time to show me a bit of respect.'

So that was it, Paula decided. She had wounded Keith's precious pride and reporting her had been his way of getting back at her. As she continued to feed paper, Paula's thoughts turned, and she slowly came to realise that it was no more than she deserved. Keith was all right really, always trying to make her laugh with his cheeky humour; but, instead of responding, she always gave him the cold shoulder. It had become almost habit to be standoffish, to remain distant from others, but now that Ian Parker was in jail, Paula knew it really was time to make changes. She doubted she could ever face a date again, but could at least be a little friendly. Taking a gulp of air, Paula called, 'Keith. Can I have a word?'

He looked surprised, and if anything a little nervous as he moved to her side. 'Yeah, what do you want?'

'I'm sorry,' she said sheepishly.

Keith wasn't much to look at, with a long face and thin lips, but his large brown eyes were nice. They widened now and with a grin he said, 'Blimey, does this mean the ice maiden is melting? Does this mean you're going to buy me that pint?'

Paula didn't want to go out with him, but if they were to remain on friendly terms she would have to let him down gently. 'Sorry, no offence, but I'm not looking for a date.'

'Who said anything about a date? Let me tell you

that birds flock to go out with me and my diary is full for at least the next few months. I may be able to fit you in after Christmas.'

Paula chuckled. 'Yeah, well, this is one bird that'd fly in the opposite direction, but thanks anyway.'

'Your loss,' he said, 'but if you change your mind, let me know.'

The rest of the morning passed quickly, and Paula found herself exchanging smiles with Keith as they worked. At lunch time he stopped the machine, saying, 'Are you sure you don't want to join me for a drink?'

'I'm sure,' Paula said as she slipped off her stool to see Charlie beckoning. 'See you later,' she called to Keith.

'Are you going to the canteen?' Charlie asked.

'Yeah, but what was that letter you were waving?'

'Let's get our grub and then I'll tell you.'

'I'm dying for a smoke, but I won't be long. You join the queue, and if you don't mind, can you grab me a cup of tea and a cheese sarnie?'

'All right, girl, no problem.'

By the time Paula finished her cigarette and made her way to the canteen, Charlie was sitting at a table.

'Why were you taken to the office?' he asked as soon as she sat opposite.

'It was nothing, just a bit of an ear-bashing for sneaking off to have a fag.' Paula took a gulp of tea, then asked, 'How much do I owe you?'

'I'm celebrating so it's my treat. The letter's from my son. When I retire he wants me to join him in New Zealand.'

'Oh Charlie, that's great.'

'Yeah, but it'll be a bit of a wrench leaving old Blighty. I'll have to give up my house – and I don't know what I'm gonna do with my budgie.'

'I'll have him,' Paula said impulsively.

'Are you sure?'

'Of course I am. It'd be nice to have a pet.'

'His name is Charlie too. Now don't laugh,' he added as Paula began to chuckle. 'It was my wife who named him after me.'

'Yeah, sorry . . . but don't worry, I'll take good care of him.'

'You're a nice girl and I can't tell you how much your offer means to me. I know you ain't popular but, as I've said before, I think you've been on a rough road. Am I right?'

Paula nodded and, seeing the kindness in the old man's eyes, she glanced around to make sure they couldn't be overheard before spilling it all out. Charlie didn't interrupt until she finished. 'So you see, it's made me all sort of bitter and twisted.'

'That ain't surprising, but don't judge all men by what that bastard did to you. Take Keith for instance. He's a bit of a cheeky bugger, but he's a good bloke.'

'I wasn't very nice to him, but I've apologised now.'

'That's a start. I can see that he likes you and you could do worse.'

'No, no, I don't want to go out with him.'

'Fair enough, but as I said, don't tar all men with the same brush.'

'I . . . I'll try not to, but it may take a bit of time.'

'Don't let it ruin the rest of your life. Now, to change the subject, I don't suppose you need any furniture, do you? My stuff is a bit old-fashioned, but it would do you a turn.'

'I only live in a bedsit and there isn't room to swing a cat.'

'Oh well, perhaps I can find someone else to pass it on to.'

'It would've been nice to have some stuff of my own, so thanks for the offer. When do you think you'll be off to New Zealand?'

'I retire in a month, and as my son is making all arrangements, I doubt it'll be long after that.'

'That soon? Blimey, I had no idea.'

Soon after they finished their sandwiches, and saying that she wanted another cigarette before going back to work, Paula left Charlie to make her way outside. Though it was cold she breathed in the fresh air as her thoughts turned. Charlie was right; she couldn't judge all men the same. Even so, she tensed when she saw three men walking through the factory gates. Swiftly she stubbed out her cigarette before bolting back inside.

'Hey, gorgeous, what's the matter?' a voice called.

Paula spun around and, seeing Keith, she heaved a sigh of relief. The men with him worked in the factory too, but blinded by panic she hadn't recognised any of them. 'Nothing's the matter,' she managed to reply. 'I was just on my way back to the machine room.'

'I know I'm irresistible and no doubt you're rushing back to see me, but I ain't there, love. I'm here, right behind you, if you fancy a cuddle,' Keith quipped.

'Dream on,' she called, but with a smile on her face as she went back to work.

Chapter Twenty-one

Trevor Riverton locked the door of his antiques shop. It was a Monday evening, the third of November. He made his way to his car, hoping he wasn't wasting his time. After making a few unsuccessful calls to source a Dolchini for Lady Smythe, he'd all but put the task out of his mind. In fact, as he would only receive a finder's fee, he hadn't made much of an effort. Now, though, he was on his way to Battersea and once again hoped it wasn't going to be a wasted journey. His wife had arranged a dinner party to celebrate their anniversary that evening, and if he was late she would make him suffer, but the telephone call he'd received on Saturday had piqued his interest. The woman said she had a painting by Drewer for sale, but her description of the work didn't tally with what he knew of the artist. In fact it sounded more like one he'd once seen catalogued as a Dolchini, but surely it was too good to be true? Despite his doubts, Trevor felt he should at least go to see it, but the woman had insisted on an evening appointment. This was his first free one, but he'd have to get a move on to be back in Richmond by eight.

Trevor puffed with annoyance. The timing was doubly a nuisance. Usually when he went to view a painting, or to a house clearance, he would take Marcus with him, who was an expert at spotting genuine art. If they managed to find a bargain they would split the profits, but Marcus was away until Friday night. Though Trevor had some knowledge, he didn't have Marcus's eye, but surely he knew enough to spot a genuine Dolchini. It was unlikely to be one of his works, but if it was, this could be a chance in a million and one he didn't want to miss.

When Trevor reached the address in Battersea and saw a small block of flats, he looked at the façade with disappointment. He'd expected a fine house: these dingy flats seemed unlikely to house a Dolchini. Still, he was here now, so he might as well take a look at the painting.

'Good evening, Mrs Grayson,' he said when a woman opened the door. 'My name is Trevor Riverton. You rang me on Saturday about a painting.'

'Yes, that's right. Please come in,' she said, then indicated a young blonde woman sitting on a sofa. 'This is my daughter.'

'Hello,' he said shortly before turning his attention back to the woman. 'You said you have a painting for sale.'

227

'Yes, that's right. It's over there,' she said, pointing to an alcove.

Trevor went to look at the painting; even though it was filthy, his heart leapt. He kept his expression composed, however, asking, 'What makes you think it's by Drewer?'

'I know it's dirty, but you can still see the D of his monogram.'

Trevor couldn't believe his luck. Yes, the artist used initials, but this wasn't one of his. He played along. 'I think you're right.'

'See, I told you,' the woman said as she turned to talk to her daughter, 'I told you Mr Riverton wouldn't be like that local dealer.'

'Local dealer?' Trevor queried.

'Yes, he said it wasn't a Drewer and offered me a pittance, so I doubt he was a specialist. I have a friend in Richmond and invited you to look at it on her recommendation.'

'May I lift it from the wall?'

'Yes, of course.'

Trevor took the painting down to look at it more closely, then turned it over to study the back. It looked genuine, but as the other dealer, specialist or not, hadn't spotted the woman's mistake, his eyes narrowed with suspicion. Surely it was too good to be true, and how had a Dolchini ended up here? He took in the woman's room, the shabby furniture, and asked, 'Did the other dealer ask how you came by this painting?'

'No, but if he had I'd have told him that my great aunt died recently and it was left to me in her will. She collected art and had more valuable pieces, but those, along with the house, went to my brother. Like me, he has little knowledge of art, and when probate was granted he said he'd bring in an expert to value the paintings for insurance. In the meantime he was happy for me to take the Drewer, and though I'd love to keep the painting, I . . . I'm afraid I need the money.'

Trevor studied the painting again. Was it possible? Had the silly woman taken the wrong painting and, if so, how long would it be before her mistake was discovered? He was still unsure, so said, 'I might be interested in buying it, but I'd like a friend of mine to look at it first. Could I make an appointment to come back with him next week?'

'Well, yes, I suppose so, but I should warn you that someone else is coming to see it tomorrow. If he offers me a fair price, I'll sell it.'

Damn, Trevor thought. If the man saw and heard the same things he did, he'd snap up the painting. It was a risk, but one that could net him a marvellous profit. Any doubts he had were now dispelled in his eagerness to buy it. 'How much are you asking for it?'

'I know its value and I want two thousand five hundred pounds.'

Trevor didn't want to give the game away by

appearing too eager, so once again he studied the painting. He knew that Lady Smythe would pay eight thousand pounds for this silly woman's mistake. 'Yes, I can see it's a Drewer,' he lied, 'but in this condition I'm afraid I can only offer two thousand.'

'Two thousand two fifty,' she bartered.

'No, I'm sorry, it needs extensive cleaning, so the most I can offer is two thousand one hundred.'

The woman bit on her lower lip as she considered his offer, but then with a small sigh she said, 'All right, you *were* recommended, so I'm sure it's a fair price. I'll take it.'

Trevor put the painting down to pull out his chequebook, thinking nothing of it when she asked for it to be made out to cash. He wrote it out with a flourish and then prepared a receipt. When the silly woman's mistake was discovered, he didn't want his purchase challenged, so as always he wrote *sold as seen* along the bottom. 'Would you sign this please, Mrs Grayson?'

'Yes, of course.'

Trevor smiled as she put her signature on the receipt, but hid the fact that it was one of triumph. This deal would bring him a tidy profit and, if he got a move on, he would just be in time for dinner. 'Thank you, Mrs Grayson,' he said, taking the carbon copy to tuck into his pocket. He then handed her the original and the cheque, anxious now to leave as he again picked up the painting.

'Thank you and goodbye, Mr Riverton,' the woman said as she walked across the room to open the door.

'Goodbye,' he said, nodding briefly to the woman's daughter as he left, and with the Dolchini clutched to his chest like treasure, he hurried downstairs. He'd ring Lady Smythe's solicitor first thing in the morning and, with an assured profit of six thousand pounds, he'd break out a bottle of champagne when he arrived home.

Trevor Riverton was unaware of two pairs of eyes watching him from a downstairs window as he drove off. Only minutes later there was a knock on Val's door. She hadn't missed the fact that the dealer had carried out the painting and relief almost made her knees give out as she hurried to fling it open.

'We did it!' Betty cried, flourishing a cheque.

'Well done,' Val enthused.

'Here, Cheryl,' Betty said as she walked across the room to hand her the cheque. 'He fell for it hook, line and sinker.'

'Oh, God, I don't know what to say. This is wonderful,' she said as tears flooded her eyes.

'We even got an extra one hundred,' said Betty proudly.

'Not we, it was you, Betty,' said Paula. 'I didn't do a thing and you were just brill.'

Cheryl dashed her cheeks with the back of her

hand. 'With the extra money I think we should do something to celebrate.'

'What a lovely idea,' said Val, 'but I don't think we should celebrate just yet. The cheque still has to clear.'

'I'll pay this in during my lunch break tomorrow, but I'm going to be on tenterhooks until it does,' Cheryl said.

'Val, I'm a bit worried,' Betty said. 'You briefed me well, and I know I said he fell for it hook, line and sinker, but I don't think he was fully convinced. He wanted to bring someone else to see it next week.'

'Did he?' Val said sharply. 'Who?'

'I don't know, maybe an expert. I managed to ad lib, saying that another dealer was coming to see it tomorrow, and I think that made him more eager to buy it.'

'Oh dear,' Cheryl cried. 'If an expert sees it, we're sunk.'

Val frowned. 'Let's hope he doesn't show it to him before the cheque clears. If he does, he's bound to put a stop on it.'

'Yes, but even if we do get the money, he's bound to come back when he discovers it's only a copy.'

'That's one thing we don't have to worry about, Betty. He made sure you signed a receipt saying "*sold as seen*", so for once he'll be getting a taste of his own medicine. Like Cheryl, he won't have a leg to stand on.'

'I still don't fancy facing him,' Betty said worriedly.

'Don't worry, he's no fool, and when he finds out his mistake I'm sure he'll know there's nothing he can do.'

'I hope you're right,' Betty said.

'Val, he'll want to tell Lady Smythe's supposed solicitor that he's found a Dolchini and will probably ring your office first thing in the morning. I still think there's a chance that he'll recognise your voice,' Cheryl warned.

'It was a risk I had to take. I could hardly give him a false number or that would have alerted him and he'd almost certainly stop the cheque. This way I can say that Mr Warriner is away until Friday and that will stall him long enough for it to clear. Not only that, I don't think he'll recognise my voice. I lowered the pitch, put on airs – my whole manner and diction was that of an upper-class lady.'

'Blimey, you already sound posh to me,' Paula said.

Cheryl's tone was derisive. 'Huh, anyone would sound posh compared to you.'

Paula looked instantly crushed, her head sinking down to her chest. Annoyed, Val said sharply, 'There's no need for that, Cheryl.'

'Oh God, I'm so sorry, Paula,' she said, looking ashamed.

Betty looked indignant too, her voice unusually sharp. 'I should think so too.'

'It . . . it's all right. I know I sound common. Please, don't fall out over me.'

Cheryl was red-faced. 'I shouldn't have said it. I don't know what came over me.'

Nor do I, Val thought, but thankfully Paula appeared mollified. The atmosphere still felt a little strained, so she said, 'Let's have a glass of sherry. I know it's a bit early to celebrate, but after playing her part so well, I think Betty deserves one.'

Val poured the drinks and then, holding up her glass, she said, 'Well done, Betty.'

After a sip of sherry, Betty let out a long sigh. 'At least my stomach has stopped churning. To tell you the truth, I was really nervous when Mr Riverton turned up. It helped having you there, Paula, gave me a bit of Dutch courage. I know you don't think you did anything, but honestly, love, on my own I'd have lost my nerve.'

Paula's expression was now one of pleasure. 'Thanks, but I didn't even open me mouth, sorry, *my* mouth.'

'There's no need to correct yourself,' Betty protested.

'No, there isn't, and once again I'm sorry,' Cheryl said. She then waved the cheque. 'I can't tell you what this money means to me. I'll be able to buy a flat, a place to call my own. Thank you, thank both of you, and you too, Val, for coming up with the plan.'

'If you need furniture, I know a bloke who wants to get rid of some. It ain't modern or anything, but he said it's in good nick.'

'Really? Oh, yes please.'

'Right, when I go to work in the morning, I'll have a word with Charlie. He's going to New Zealand to live with his son. I'm having his budgie and can't wait to take him on. It'll be lovely to have a pet of my own. I'd like a dog, or even a cat, but a bird is better than nothing and with any luck I'll get away with having it in me bedsit.'

'They can be a bit noisy,' Betty warned.

'Oh blimey, if he makes a racket someone might complain. What will I do then?'

'Don't worry. If you can't keep him, I'll take him on.'

'Thanks, Betty, but I hope it doesn't come to that.'

Cheryl was looking at the cheque again. 'I'm so thrilled with this, but until it clears, it somehow seems unreal.'

'Don't worry,' Val said. 'Everything went better than expected last time, and I'm sure it will this time too.'

Chapter Twenty-two

Paula lay awake for hours. Though she had hidden it from the others, she was still hurt by Cheryl's remark. Oh, she wasn't daft – she knew her voice sounded common, but Cheryl was the last person she'd expected to be judgemental.

Paula tossed and turned. She had grown close to Cheryl, had seen her as an older sister, and thought those feelings were returned. She'd been an idiot, a fool for seeing Cheryl and the others as a replacement family. How wrong she'd been, Paula decided, as with a groan she scrunched up her pillow, trying to fight the feelings of hurt and rejection that swamped her.

Oh Betty, her mind cried. *Are you going to turn on me too?* It had been lovely to play the part of Betty's daughter, if only for a short while, but now Paula's eyes filled with tears. Her own mother had rejected her, hadn't wanted her in her life, so why should Betty, a woman whose warmth and affection she craved, be any different? No, Betty wouldn't want her either, and even though she'd given up the gin, Betty wouldn't want someone so tainted and common in her life. Neither would Val, and once the last two plans had been carried out, it would be the last she saw of them. She'd be alone again, without friends or family, and somehow, some way, she'd have to stand on her own two feet.

With this thought, Paula felt a surge of determination. She would do it. Somehow she would do it. For a start, she'd be different at work – friendlier; maybe find a couple of mates. Then, when she had to say goodbye to Betty and the others, perhaps she wouldn't feel totally alone.

The man picked up a brick, threw it with force. A window shattered, setting off an alarm in the damp, dark street. Clang, clang, clang. Now the noise intruded on Paula's dream. It was her alarm clock, and groaning she reached out a hand, fumbling to turn it off. Bloody hell, she thought, as the dream receded, her memory of it fading as she threw back the blankets to get out of bed. She groggily put on her dressing gown, glad to find the bathroom free, and after having a wash she brushed her teeth before returning to her room to get ready for work.

A new day and a new start, Paula thought as she left her bedsit, determination in her stride as she headed for the bus stop. She didn't have long to wait, and twenty minutes later Paula was walking into the factory, forcing a smile on her face as she went to the cloakroom. 'Morning,' she said to a few young women who were already there, unable to miss that their eyes widened with astonishment.

'Err, yeah, good morning,' one said, and Paula recognised her as the girl she'd once talked to at the bus stop.

The other two said nothing as they brushed past her, but Paula ignored the slight and swallowed her nervousness to say, 'I think you live near me.'

'Yeah, I've seen you waiting for a bus. I live near the bottom of Lavender Hill.'

'I'm just around the corner from there.'

'Paula, ain't it? My name's Greta.'

'Yeah, that's right, and I don't know about you, Greta, but I fancy a fag before we start work. Have we got time?'

'Have one of mine,' Greta said, as they walked outside. 'I know it's only Tuesday, but roll on Friday.'

'I couldn't agree more. What are you up to this weekend?'

'My bloke's taking me dancing on Saturday night.'

'That's nice.'

It was time to start work and, as they stubbed out their cigarettes, Greta said, 'Right, we're off,' and together they walked into the machine room.

'I'm working with Keith this week.'

'You're lucky. I'm on machine four with Len and

he's a right miserable git. See you,' Greta called as she moved away.

'Yeah, see you,' she called back, pleased that she had broken the ice, at least with one girl.

Keith grinned when he saw her. 'Hello, sexy.'

For a moment Paula tensed, but then took a deep breath. 'Morning, Keith. Nice day, ain't it?'

'It is now I've seen you.'

'Yeah, and I bet you say that to all the girls,' Paula said as she slipped onto her stool.

'I only say it to the good-looking ones.'

Paula smiled. She didn't want to give Keith ideas – didn't want him to think she might be interested, but found that she enjoyed his friendly banter. 'Are you ready to start the machine?'

'Yes, boss,' he said, lifting his hand in salute, and then machine after machine along the room sprang to life, the clatter as usual deafening.

Paula just had time to wave to Charlie, and then it was time to start work, her hands busy as she fed sheet after sheet of paper into the rollers.

Cheryl's eyes widened when she walked into the ward and saw that Edna Sands's bed was empty. Her heart sank. Though her injuries had been minor, tests had shown high blood pressure along with angina. She had been further weakened by malnutrition, and now, fearing the worst, Cheryl went to talk to Staff Nurse Trenton.

'I see that Mrs Sands's bed is empty.'

'She died during the night,' she said brusquely. 'Now take over the trolley, please. Finish taking temperatures and blood pressures for these last three beds, and then prepare the ward for the doctor's rounds.'

Cheryl took over as the staff nurse walked away and planted a smile on her face as she approached a patient. She tried to concentrate, but found that half her mind was on the patient, whilst the other half remained on Mrs Sands. If the elderly woman hadn't been malnourished when admitted, if she'd had someone to care for her, she could have recovered from her fall.

For the rest of the morning Cheryl was so rushed off her feet that she didn't have further time to think. During her lunch break she went first to the bank to pay in the cheque, and then hurried back to the staff canteen to queue for a sandwich and a drink. After finding a table she sat down with relief, kicking off her black, lace-up shoes to rub the soles of her feet.

Her thoughts drifted as she munched on a ham sandwich, from hoping that the cheque would clear so she could buy a flat, then on to Paula and the offer of furniture from someone she worked with. She had been awful to Paula and was swamped with guilt, yet she was still unable to stop that little voice of doubt. Had Paula led Ian Parker on? Had they put an innocent man in prison?

* * *

Val had been tense all morning, waiting for the call. When it finally came, her hand tightened around the receiver.

'Good morning, I was given this number as Lady Parker Smythe's solicitor and I'd like to speak to him please,' said Trevor Riverton. Val glanced swiftly at Mr Warriner's door, glad to see it closed as she said, 'I'm afraid Mr Warriner won't be in the office until Friday.'

'I want to get in touch with Lady Margaret Parker Smythe. Can you give me her number?'

'I'm not allowed to give information on clients.'

'But Lady Smythe gave me this number. She told me to ring her solicitor if I sourced a painting by Dolchini.'

'I'm only the receptionist. If you ring again on Friday, I'm sure Mr Warriner will be able to help you.'

'Blast. All right, I'll ring him then.'

Val exhaled with relief as she replaced the receiver. So far so good, but there was still the risk that he'd show the painting to an expert before the cheque cleared. The wait was going to be nerve-racking, but even worse for Cheryl. Please let it clear, please, Val willed.

Betty too was thinking about Trevor Riverton as she went about her work, but worrying about him was giving her a headache. She did her best to push her thoughts away, but the house was quiet, with just the faint noise of traffic from outside as she walked through the hall. Betty found herself wishing for company, for someone to talk to – someone to take her mind off the dealer and the thought of him turning up at her door. It was all right for Val to say she didn't have anything to worry about, but it would still be an unpleasant confrontation and one she hoped she wouldn't have to face.

'Oh, for goodness' sake, woman,' she said, talking to herself. 'Pull yourself together.'

Betty smiled at last. It came to something when she had to talk to herself, but nevertheless it eased her tension. In truth she had to admit that having to face Trevor Riverton again was nothing compared to the lies she'd told the police, or her nerves when she'd sat at court waiting to be called.

She wished the time away, anxious for Friday, because if the cheque cleared it would be a cause for celebration. And after all this worry and waiting, she was looking forward to that.

Once again she noticed the silence of the house. She'd love to find another job, a place where she could work with others. If only she was trained to do something meaningful like Cheryl, or work in an office like Val. 'Stop dreaming,' she said, talking out loud again and then chuckling at her silliness.

For the rest of the day Betty worked steadily, and though she had managed to stop worrying about the dealer, her thoughts had turned to Richard. She had an idea, a plan to bring him low, but hadn't mentioned it to Val or the others yet. It had come to mind when talking to Anne about her plans for Christmas. She was sure it could work, but a lot would depend on either Paula or Cheryl. Not only that, she had no idea if they were going to work on her plan next. Val might want to go first. 'Oh,' she whispered, 'please let it be my turn.'

Chapter Twenty-three

The rest of the week was an anxious time, and on Friday morning Betty tapped on Val's door before she left for work. 'Val, I know Cheryl said the cheque hadn't cleared yesterday. Will you ring me at work as soon as you hear anything?'

'Yes, of course. Cheryl will ring me during her lunch break; but don't worry, if the dealer calls to speak to Mr Warriner this morning, it means he still thinks the painting is genuine.'

'Let's hope when we meet up this evening, it's to celebrate.'

'I'm sure it will be,' Val said, and then saying she'd better be off, Betty hurried away.

Val closed her door, and with twenty minutes to spare before she had to leave for the office, she poured herself another cup of tea. Once the dealer had spoken to Mr Warriner, he'd be on the alert, but surely it would be too late now to stop the cheque? It had to have cleared by now, Val thought as she finished her tea and left for work.

Half an hour later, Val was sitting at her desk, tense as she waited for Trevor Riverton's call. There were a few letters to type and she tried to concentrate on her work, but her eyes kept straying to the clock.

Val took two calls, neither of them from the dealer, but at eleven o'clock the telephone rang again and her stomach lurched when she recognised Trevor Riverton's voice.

'Good morning. I'd like to speak to Mr Warriner.'

'Who's calling, please?'

'Trevor Riverton.'

'Just a moment, I'll see if he's free.'

Val tapped in his extension, 'There's a call for you, a gentleman called Trevor Riverton.'

'All right, put him through.'

Val connected the call and then got up from her desk, sneaking to Mr Warriner's door. It was closed and at first she could hear little, but then his voice began to rise with obvious impatience.

'Now look, I've already told you, I've never heard of Lady Margaret Parker Smythe and she is *not* one of my clients.'

Val smiled as her employer's voice went up another octave. 'How should I know why you've been given my name and number?'

Oh, to be a fly on the wall and see Trevor Riverton's face, Val thought as she went back to her desk. Now he knew what it felt like to be swindled and it served him right. She had only just sat down again when Mr Warriner's door opened, her boss's face livid as he marched into reception.

'Val, if that man rings again, tell him I've no intention of taking his call.'

'Is something wrong?'

'He sounded like a madman. Went on and on about a Lady Parker Smythe and a painting he'd sourced for her. I kept telling him that she isn't my client, but the man had the gall to virtually call me a liar.'

'Perhaps he was given the wrong number?' Val suggested.

'Maybe, but as I said, if he rings again, don't put him through. If he has the nerve to turn up here, tell him I'm out,' and on that note Mr Warriner returned to his office.

On hearing his words, Val sat bolt upright in her chair. Oh God, she'd thought herself so clever, but there was one thing she hadn't factored in and that was the dealer turning up at the office. She hadn't given the man the address, but now realised that there was nothing to stop him finding it. All he had to do was to look up Mr Warriner's name in the telephone book.

Oh what a stupid, stupid mistake. Trevor Riverton had rung at eleven and his conversation with Mr Warriner must surely have alerted him to the fact that something was wrong. He must be going frantic and yes, there was a real danger of him turning up here to confront Mr Warriner. If that happened – if he saw her face, she was in deep trouble. There was only one thing to do – she had to take time off; say she was sick and stay away until the danger had passed.

Val waited fifteen minutes before tapping on Mr Warriner's door, and affecting a look of pain she placed a hand on the small of her back as she went in. 'I'm sorry, Mr Warriner, but do you mind if I go home?'

'Why? What's wrong, Val?'

'I was in the storeroom and balanced on a chair to put an old file onto the top shelf when I lost my footing. I managed to cling on, but I think I've pulled a muscle or something in my back.'

'Oh dear. Yes, go on home, and as my wife always advises when my back is playing me up, make sure you lie on a hard, flat surface. If it isn't any better tomorrow, perhaps you should see your doctor.'

'Yes, yes, I will,' Val said, bending slightly and still clutching her lower back as she walked out.

Val felt awful for lying to her boss. He was a lovely man and didn't deserve it, but there was no way she could risk being around if Trevor Riverton showed up.

Betty looked anxiously at her watch. Val still hadn't called. Had something gone wrong? But even if it had, she'd have let her know. If only she had Val's work number, but without it there was nothing she could do but wait.

At last the call came. 'Betty, sorry for the delay. Cheryl rang me at work and was told I'd had to go home, so then she rang me here and it's good news.'

'You're home, but why?'

Betty frowned as she listened. She was thrilled that the cheque had cleared, but unable to believe that none of them had spotted the flaw in Val's plan. Now Val was stuck at home and would have to remain there until she was in the clear. 'Will you get sick pay?'

'Yes, thank goodness.'

They said goodbye, but Betty was still a bit worried about the dealer coming back to her door. It was all right for Val, she could lie low, whereas she would have to face him.

For the rest of the afternoon, Betty pushed her worry to one side and now that Cheryl's plan had been completed, she turned her mind to Richard. The more she went over her idea, the more certain she felt it would work. Anne had briefly met Paula, so at first she discounted her for the role, but as her daughter was going to be in Cornwall, it would be safe to use her, or Cheryl, but it depended on who volunteered. She pictured them both in her mind, imagining them playing the part, and felt that Paula would be the better choice. But was she still too fragile? Would it be too much for her?

Whichever girl played the role, Betty smiled as she envisaged the scene in her mind. It would be the ruin of Richard's reputation – and with any luck it would bring about the end of his marriage too.

Chapter Twenty-four

Trevor Riverton had been annoyed when he spoke to Mr Warriner, but gradually calmed down. Lady Smythe had obviously made a mistake and given him the wrong details, but sure that he could find her, he started to make enquiries.

It was late afternoon when he slammed down the telephone. Lady Margaret Parker Smythe wasn't listed anywhere, and after making call after call to various acquaintances, none of whom had heard of her, he was beginning to feel that she didn't exist. Yet he had met her. She had been to his shop and he'd found the Dolchini that she was looking for. The find had been fortuitous, coming just at the right time, but now he couldn't find the bloody woman to sell it to her.

At that moment it was as though a lightbulb pinged on in his brain, illuminating the truth. It had been a scam: it had to be. Trevor felt sick as he snatched up the receiver again. Marcus might be back in Richmond by now and, dialling his number, he was relieved when he answered.

'Marcus, it's Trevor. I'm bringing a painting round for you to look at.'

'Hello, Trevor, I've only just got in the door. It was a good trip and I found several nice pieces you might be interested in.'

'Yes, yes, all right. I'll be there in fifteen minutes.'

Trevor locked the shop and, after carefully stowing the painting in the boot of his car, he drove to Marcus's place, his teeth clenched in anger. When he arrived he grabbed the painting and as soon as Marcus let him in, Trevor said bluntly, 'Take a look at that. Is it a Dolchini?'

The man's brow rose but he made no comment as he took the painting and, after studying it for some time, said, 'No, but it's a very good copy.'

'I knew it! I knew it,' Trevor barked.

'Where did you get it?'

Trevor took a great gulp of air and then started at the beginning, seeing Marcus's eyes narrowing in thought as he listened. When he had related the whole story, he said, 'So, as I now realise, it must have been a scam, and a very clever one.'

'Can you prove it?'

'Of course I bloody can't. I've been over and over it, but there's nothing. I was the only one who saw this supposed Lady Smythe, and now she's disappeared off the face of the earth.'

'What about the number she gave you? The solicitor.'

'I told you, he's never heard of her, and I'm certain he was telling the truth. It was probably a number she just picked out of the phone book.'

'What about the woman who sold you the painting? Is there any way of linking her to this Lady Smythe?'

Trevor exhaled with exasperation. 'The only way I can think of is to sit outside her flat in the hope that this supposed Lady Smythe turns up.'

'Well, old chap, you've got a business to run, and unless you're prepared to stake out her flat for an indefinite period of time, it looks as though you've been well and truly taken. If you ask me, you're just going to have to swallow your loss.'

'Yes, but not before I've given that bloody woman in Battersea a piece of my mind.'

'What good would that do? You shouldn't have bought the painting without my seeing it and it's a lesson learned. Anyway, let's face it, any scam is usually the other way round and we've done well over the years.'

'It's a lesson that's cost me over two thousand pounds.'

'A fair amount to lose, but don't worry, we'll soon make it up. Come and look at those pieces I told you about.'

Yes, Trevor thought, he was able to weather the

loss, and an opportunity to make up the money was sure to arrive. There were always people dying, houses to be cleared, and relatives who had no idea that some of the things they'd been left were valuable. Nevertheless, despite what Marcus said, he was still determined to see the bloody woman. It wouldn't get him his money back, but at least having it out with her would abate his anger.

He took a look at the antiques Marcus had acquired, ones that the man had got for peanuts and, cheering at the profit margin, he then left. A glance at his watch showed him that it wasn't too late to drive to Battersea; knowing that he'd been taken for a fool, he was determined to give the woman a piece of his mind.

Betty's eyes widened when she opened her door, the colour draining from her face. 'Y-you,' she stammered.

'Yes, Mrs Grayson, if indeed that's your name. Don't tell me you weren't expecting me.'

'What do you want?'

'Isn't it obvious? I want my money back.'

Betty floundered for a reply. 'I . . . I haven't got it.'

'Who has then? The supposed Lady Smythe?'

'I . . . I don't know what you're talking about.'

'Don't give me that. It was a scam, and I admit a good one, but don't take me for a fool. The painting you sold me was fake, a copy; as I said, I want my money back.'

Something welled up within Betty. This was the man who had swindled Cheryl. She had gone into his shop, like him, tried to get her money back, but he'd refused. How dare he come to her door? How dare he make demands? He might know it was a scam, but he couldn't prove it, and, knowing that, she lied confidently. 'I didn't know it was a fake. You bought it and wrote "sold as seen" on my receipt yourself. I don't have to give you your money back, and you know that.'

'Where is she? Where's this Lady Smythe? She was part of it, and don't bother trying to deny it.'

'I don't know anyone by that name. Now go away,' Betty demanded as she tried to shut the door, but his hand came out, holding it open.

'I'm going, but if I ever set eyes on you again, or the supposed Lady Smythe, you won't get off so lightly.'

Betty pushed harder on the door and was relieved when it closed. She rushed to the window, saw the man getting into his car and felt the air leaving her body in a huge sigh when he drove off. She'd done it; she'd faced him! Wait till she told Val, and on that thought, Betty hurried downstairs. 'Well done,' Val said when Betty recounted what had happened.

'I didn't know I had it in me.'

'I did – I don't think you realise how much you've

changed since we first met. Now come on, let's have a sherry. It's over with now and I don't think we'll have to worry about that dealer again.'

Betty felt a surge of pride. Yes, she had changed, grown in confidence, and once again thanked her lucky stars for the day she had met Val.

Chapter Twenty-five

It was four days later, Tuesday evening, and now that Trevor Riverton had been and gone, Val felt confident that they could all meet up again. She poured four glasses of sherry, saying, 'I'm glad you turned up with a bottle, Cheryl. Mine's nearly all gone.'

'With an extra hundred pounds, it's nothing, and as you always provide the sherry, it's only fair.'

'Yeah, I should buy you one too,' Paula said.

'And me come to that.' This from Betty.

Val handed out the drinks and then lifted her own glass. 'To us, and another plan successfully completed.'

'To us,' the others chorused.

'I think we're getting rather good at this,' Val said. 'Well, other than the fact that I didn't consider that the dealer might turn up at my office.'

'It was only one small thing and there's no harm done,' said Betty. 'Mind you, it wasn't pleasant when he turned up at my door.'

'Yes, but you handled him, and well. Here's to you, Betty.'

'Thanks,' she said, her face pink with pleasure.

'Cheryl,' said Paula, 'I know I rang you in the week about going to see Charlie's furniture. Are you still on for Saturday morning?'

'Yes, of course.'

'Right, so I'll see you outside the cinema in Northcote Road.'

'Thanks again, Paula.'

'Don't thank me, thank Charlie. He said I can pick up his budgie soon. He wants to know it's settled before he leaves.'

'When are you going to start looking for a flat?' Val asked.

'Very soon and I'll go to a few estate agents to see what they've got on offer. I still can't believe it. A place of my own,' she said, grinning from ear to ear.

'You're lucky,' Paula commented. 'I hate me bedsit, but this job is a bit better paid so I might start looking for a bigger room.'

'I wish I had two bedrooms,' Betty said. 'If I did, instead of living alone in a bedsit, I'd have you living with me.'

'Cor, bless you, Betty, but I'm a messy bugger and you wouldn't want to put up with me. Don't worry, I'm sure I'll find something and I won't be on me own any more. I'll have me budgie.'

Val frowned, wondering why Cheryl's face had

flushed, but then put it down to the sherry. 'Let's have another drink,' she suggested.

'Thanks,' Cheryl said, 'and how about making arrangements now to go out for a proper celebration?'

'Smashing,' said Betty.

They made arrangements for Saturday week; the venue, Val's favourite French restaurant in Chelsea.

'There's still this weekend. Once I've taken Cheryl to see Charlie's furniture, I ain't got anything else to do.'

'Why don't you both come here afterwards?'

'That's fine with me,' Cheryl agreed.

'I'll bake a cake,' Betty offered. 'I just wish I had the recipe for that tarte tatin they serve at the restaurant.'

As Betty went on to talk to the others about the wonderful food on offer, Val was hardly listening. She had spent so much time working out the first two plans that she'd hardly given any thought to Mike Freeman, and how she could get her revenge. They all needed a break from the planning, really, and with Cheryl looking for a flat and Paula a bedsit, it would give her plenty of breathing space. There was Betty's plan, too, but as she'd been the last recruit, surely she'd agree to wait her turn?

'Watcha,' Paula said on Saturday morning as she hurried to greet Cheryl outside the cinema. There was a cold wind blowing and she was glad of the woolly scarf thrown around her neck.

Cheryl looked cold too, her hands stuffed in her coat pockets. 'Hello, Paula. Is it far to this man's house?'

'No, it's just a few streets along.'

'Come on, let's go,' Cheryl urged.

They walked along Northcote Road, the market stalls on the opposite side busy with shoppers. It brought back childhood memories for Paula, of trailing behind her mother while she went from stall to stall, her mum flirting outrageously with the costermongers as she bartered for the cheapest vegetables.

'It's this one,' she said now as they turned a corner. Charlie's house, along with all the others in the row, was two storeys high, plain red brick and flat fronted. Number fourteen was about halfway along and, raising her hand, Paula rapped the door knocker.

'Come on in,' Charlie invited.

'Watcha, Charlie,' Paula said as they stepped inside. 'This is me mate, Cheryl.'

As Cheryl held out her hand, Charlie shook it, then led them along a narrow passage and into what was obviously his living room. He swept an arm around, indicating the furniture. 'Well, girl, it ain't much, but you're welcome to any of it. I've got some kitchen and bedroom furniture too.'

Paula took in the dark green three-piece suite that

was old but in good condition, along with an oak sideboard. There wasn't much else in the room, but hearing a chirp she made straight for a cage sitting on a small table. 'Hello, Charlie,' she said, smiling at the pretty budgie who sat on a perch, his head cocked to one side as his beady eyes surveyed her.

'I forgot to tell you that he can talk,' Charlie said as he came to her side.

'Can he? What does he say?'

'Who's a pretty boy, for one, and Charlie is me darling.'

Paula giggled with delight. 'Who taught him to say that?'

'Well it wasn't me, that's for sure. It was my old china. She spent hours talking to him.'

'He's lovely,' Paula said softly.

Charlie sniffed, his voice cracking with emotion. 'I'm just glad the little tyke's going to a good home.'

'Don't worry, I'll look after him.'

Charlie turned to Cheryl. 'What do you think? Is this stuff any good to you?'

'Oh yes, and thank you, I'd love it.'

'You'd best come upstairs to see the bedroom stuff, and there's a table and chairs in the kitchen, along with a gas cooker.'

Paula left them to it, remaining in the living room with the budgie. She was delighted when he scuttled along his perch to ring a little bell. 'Pretty boy,' she said. 'Go on, say it. Who's a pretty boy?'

The bird swung down to a lower perch and made for a length of millet seed, which he began to swiftly demolish, the shucks landing in the bottom of the cage. Paula knew she'd have many questions to ask Charlie about the budgie's care but in the meantime continued to talk to the bird as she waited for them to return.

Cheryl looked at the bedroom furniture and smiled with pleasure. She hadn't known what to expect, maybe plain utility pieces, but the large carved oak wardrobe and dressing table had come as a surprise. The bed looked solid, the headboard too, carved, and with a new mattress, perfect. 'I don't know what to say, Charlie. This is wonderful, but surely you could sell it? At least let me offer you something.'

'I'd rather do someone a good turn – and before you make me an offer, no, I won't take a penny. Now come on, I'll show you the kitchen stuff, and then if you want that too, I'll have to ask you when you can pick it all up. I'm off to New Zealand in just over two weeks so it'll have to be before then.'

'Two weeks? Oh, goodness.'

'As soon as I agreed to go, my son booked me a berth. Once the house is cleared I can always go into a hotel for a couple of days.'

Cheryl's thoughts raced. She hadn't even found a flat yet, but surely she could arrange storage. 'I'm buying a flat and can't tell you how wonderful this is. Yes, of course I'd love to have it and I'll make sure it's taken away as near as possible to your leaving date.'

'That's smashing.'

She followed Charlie downstairs, and seeing the table and chairs she agreed to take them too, along with a dresser and gas cooker. They went back to the living room but Charlie's next words had her reeling.

'To tell you the truth, love, you can have just about everything. Curtains, linen, cutlery, crockery – and anything else that you see.'

'Charlie, I don't know what to say,' Cheryl said, feeling overwhelmed by the man's generosity.

'Well, I can't take it with me so, as I said, it might as well do you a turn. Paula here told me that you're a nurse; seeing how your profession looked after my wife when she was in hospital, I'm just glad it's going to someone who needs and deserves it. I did offer it to Paula first, but it seems she lives in a bedsit and from the way she described it, there ain't room to swing a cat, let alone fit this stuff in.'

Charlie's description of Paula's room struck a chord, just as it had last night at Val's. She *could* buy a two-bedroom flat, or even a house, but still couldn't face offering Paula a home. Oh, why couldn't she cast her doubts about her to one side? It was thanks to Paula that she was getting all this furniture, that and the wonderful generosity of this kind old man.

'Charlie, can I still take the budgie next week?'

'Yeah, how about Friday?'

'Smashing, but you'll have to tell me how to look after him, what sort of seed to buy and things like that.'

'Don't worry, we'll sort that out, but first we've got to talk about all these bits and bobs, the china and such. If you want them, Cheryl, they'll have to be boxed up.'

'My nurses' quarters aren't far from here, so if it's all right with you, I can do that when I'm off-duty.'

'Yeah, and I can give her a hand,' Paula said.

'You'd better get started soon. There's loads of stuff to sort out.'

'Is tomorrow soon enough?' Cheryl asked, and grateful for Paula's offer she added, 'Are you free then, Paula?'

'Yeah, of course I am.'

'That suits me fine, girls. I'll pop down to the shops later to see if I can cadge some cardboard boxes.'

'Yes, and we'll try to find some too,' said Cheryl.

'Right then, if you're done, I'll see you both tomorrow.'

Paula went over to the budgie's cage, giving him one last look before she followed Charlie and Cheryl to the door. 'He didn't talk, Charlie, and I chatted to him for ages.'

'Give him time, love. He ain't used to you yet, but

once he gets started there's no stopping him. I chuck a cloth over his cage at night to shut him up.'

Cheryl smiled warmly at Charlie when she said goodbye. He was a lovely man, and she hoped he'd be happy with his fresh start in New Zealand. Impulsively she linked arms with Paula as they walked along the street and the girl smiled with pleasure. As they turned the corner they saw a bus pulling in at the stop and ran to catch it, both breathless as they sank onto a seat.

'Blimey, it's empty,' Paula said. 'Mind you, I expect everyone's upstairs having a smoke.'

'I prefer to sit down here,' said Cheryl.

'Yeah, well, I suppose I can do without a ciggie. I'm glad you're taking Charlie's stuff. As he said, it'll do you a turn.'

'The furniture and things are lovely and it's thanks to all of you that I've got the money to buy a place of my own. I still can hardly believe it.'

'I know how you feel. I felt the same when Ian Parker was put behind bars.'

Cheryl took a deep breath and at last voiced her concerns. 'Ian Parker's face still haunts me. When he was in the identity parade he looked so scared.'

'Huh, I'm glad. I was scared too, shit-scared when he raped me, and as far as I'm concerned he deserved all he got.'

'I just want to make sure we did the right thing.'

'Of course we did.'

'Paula, I hate to ask, but did . . . did you lead him on at all? I know that once men get . . . well . . . aroused, it's hard for them to stop.'

Paula's head shot round, her eyes popping as though on stalks. 'Lead him on? No, of course I didn't lead him on. When we was in his car we had a bit of a kiss and cuddle, but when his hands began to stray I told him to leave off.'

'Do you think it was wise to walk onto the common with him?'

'What is this, Cheryl? Why the questions? Don't you believe me . . . is that it?'

'Are you all right, ladies?' interrupted the conductor.

'Yes, we're fine,' Cheryl said, taking out her purse and paying both fares.

'Shit, the clippie probably heard every word I said.'

Cheryl ran a hand across her face. 'I'm sorry, Paula. I . . . I do believe you, of course I do, but if you hadn't gone onto the common with him, it might not have happened.'

'Oh, so now it's my fault!' Paula hissed.

'No, no, I'm not saying that.'

Paula glanced over her shoulder, her voice still low but emphatic. 'It sounds like you are to me. All right, I might have been a mug for getting out of the car with him, but that didn't give him the right to attack me! He said he'd point out stars to me, the Milky Way and that, and he sounded such a swot

that I trusted him. I wasn't kissing him or anything
. . . we were just looking up at the sky when he
pounced. He . . . he raped me, Cheryl. I tried to fight
him off, but I couldn't.'

Cheryl felt sick, her stomach churning with guilt.
She grabbed Paula's hand. 'I'm so sorry, really I am.
I shouldn't have doubted you and I know that now.'

Paula snatched her hand away. 'So this is why
you've been funny with me lately?'

'I was just feeling so guilty – sick that I might
have put an innocent man in prison.'

'Innocent! You must be joking. I ain't a liar, I told
the truth. I was the innocent one, but he took that
away from me. You're as bad as the police. You think
that just because I don't talk posh I must be a tart.'

'I don't think that, really I don't. Paula, please, I
said I'm sorry and I meant it. Forget I said anything.
Please, can't we put all this behind us?'

'Put it behind us! You've got to be kidding. Huh,
and I thought you liked me.'

'I do like you,' she cried and, knowing how deeply
she had hurt Paula, Cheryl knew she had to make
amends. 'In fact, I like you so much that when I find
a flat, I want you to share it with me.'

'Stick your bleedin' flat.'

'Oh, Paula, don't say that. You'd be out of that
poky bedsit and it'll be a proper home. Please say
you'll share it with me.'

'I dunno. I'll think about it.'

Paula sounded so young, so churlish, but Cheryl couldn't blame her. Maybe it would be better to say no more – to leave it for now until she'd had time to calm down. She sat quietly as they continued their journey. With Paula in this mood it was going to be an awkward evening and Cheryl now wished that she hadn't agreed to go to Val's flat.

Chapter Twenty-six

'Hello, Betty. Come on in,' Val invited. 'The others aren't here yet but, my goodness, that cake looks delicious.'

'It's only a chocolate sponge and easy to make,' Betty said, 'and to be honest I could only afford cooking chocolate. I was hoping the others hadn't arrived yet. I wanted to have a word with you first.'

'Is something wrong?'

'No,' Betty said as she put the cake on the table before sitting down, 'but I want to ask if it's going to be me next, or you.'

'I don't know yet, but I think we all need a break. It'll give Cheryl a chance to find a flat, and in the meantime maybe I can come up with a plan for Mike Freeman.'

'Oh, right.'

Val could sense her disappointment. 'What is it, Betty? Come on, don't be cagey. Have you thought of something for your husband? Is that it?'

'Well yes, but if we're going to take a break, it won't work.'

'If that's the case, tell me about it now.'

Betty nodded, looking eager as she said, 'As I've mentioned before, Richard is a social climber and his image is very important to him. With this plan, a lot will depend on Paula or Cheryl,' Betty said, going on to tell Val what she had in mind.

'Yes, it could work, but it won't help you financially.'

'It's too late to do anything about my settlement, but if this works it'll ruin Richard's reputation.'

'Would that be enough for you?'

'Oh yes, and with any luck it'll hit his pocket too. It's a lot to ask of either Paula or Cheryl. I'm not sure either of them will want to take it on.'

'We'll tell them what you have in mind and see what they have to say.'

'Are you sure? I know you said we need a break, but Richard always throws his party on Christmas Eve. I thought he might call it off this year, but it seems it's still on.'

'Call it off. Why?'

'According to my daughter, Mel has high blood pressure and needs to rest. I had high blood pressure when I was pregnant too, but I wasn't fussed over like Mel.'

'Isn't it dangerous?'

'It didn't do me any harm and lots of women have it.'

'How far along is she?'

'By Christmas, I think she'll be seven months, maybe a little more, but there's no need to worry. Richard has made sure that Mel won't have to do a thing – he's even getting the food from caterers.'

Val was quiet for a moment, but then said, 'I make it just over six weeks to the party.'

'Yes, but other than a bit of rehearsal, there isn't much to do.'

Val lowered her eyes. Betty was right. The plan was a simple one, the main onus on either Cheryl or Paula with little to do beforehand. Betty had everything worked out, leaving her free to think about Mike Freeman, and they could tackle him in the New Year. 'All right, Betty. I'm happy to go ahead with it, but, as I said, we'll have to wait to see what Cheryl and Paula have to say.'

'Are you sure, Val? You were the one who brought us all together, but now you'll be the last one to benefit.'

'I don't mind,' and hearing a knock on her door she said, 'That'll be the girls now.' Val's smile vanished when she saw the look on Paula's face. 'Come on in, but what's the matter?'

'Nuffin',' she said shortly, throwing herself next to Betty on the sofa.

Val raised her brow in enquiry to Cheryl, but she just shook her head before sitting down.

Val felt you could cut the atmosphere with a knife,

and Betty must have sensed it too as she asked, 'Have you two had a row?'

Paula snapped, 'Ask Cheryl.'

'We had a few words, but I've apologised.'

It might be the case of least said soonest mended, Val thought. 'I'll make us a drink and we'll have a slice of that lovely chocolate cake.'

'What was the furniture like?' Betty asked.

'It's nice, and not only that, Charlie said I can have everything. China, cutlery – in fact, the lot.'

'That's wonderful, and once you've found a flat, you'll be all set up.'

'I'll have to store it for now, but yes, thanks to Charlie, I'll hardly have to buy a thing.'

Val made the drinks, sliced the cake, but handing it out she could still feel a strain in the atmosphere. It was time to give them something else to think about. 'I had thought we'd take a break before our next plan, but Betty has come up with an idea for her husband and it's a good one. I'll leave her to tell you all about it.'

Betty told them what she had in mind, then adding, 'Of course a lot will depend on either you, Cheryl, or Paula. One of you will have to play the role and I know it's a lot to ask.'

Paula shrugged. 'I'll do it. As everyone seems to think I'm a tart, it's only fitting.'

'What are you talking about? We don't think you're a tart,' Betty protested.

'Yeah, well, maybe you ain't as narrow-minded as some people I could mention.'

'Paula, please, I said I'm sorry,' Cheryl said.

'Look, what on earth is this about?' Val asked impatiently.

'Ask her,' Paula snapped.

'It's my fault. I've been feeling guilty about sending Ian Parker to prison, and I was stupid enough to ask Paula if she led him on.'

'You what?' said Betty, her voice loud in indignation. 'Of course Paula didn't lead him on. How could you think that?'

'I don't now. It was silly to doubt her story and I've said I'm sorry.'

'I should think so too,' Betty snapped.

Cheryl looked stricken as she jumped to her feet. 'I'd better go.'

Val shook her head as she laid a staying hand on Cheryl's arm. 'No, don't go.' She then turned, her tone soft and persuasive. 'Paula, surely you don't want our little group to break up? Cheryl has said she's sorry. Can't you forgive her?'

'It's all right for you to say that, but I was really hurt. I thought we were friends, that Cheryl liked me, but now . . .'

'We *are* friends. When I find a flat, I've asked you to move in with me. Do you really think I'd do that if I didn't like you?'

Paula sniffed, and then said grudgingly, 'Well, no, I suppose not.'

'You've offered Paula a home. Betty, don't you think that's wonderful?' Val cried, expecting Betty to agree, but instead saw that she looked less than happy.

'Well . . . yes.'

Val knew that Betty had grown fond of Paula, seeing her as a second daughter, and felt that her reaction was jealousy. Gently cajoling she said, 'It'll be lovely for them. There's only a staircase between us, Betty, and just like us, they'll be close together.'

Betty managed a smile. 'Yes, you're right, but I hope they won't be too far away.'

'Paula hasn't agreed to move in with me yet,' Cheryl said.

'Paula, surely you won't turn down the offer?' Val exclaimed.

'I dunno. I'm still thinking about it.'

Val heaved a sigh. 'All right, but will you at least accept Cheryl's apology?'

There was a pause, but then she said, 'Yeah, all right.'

'Good girl,' said Val and, deciding that they needed to focus on something else, she suggested, 'Perhaps we can get back to Betty's plan now?'

With a look of relief, Cheryl sat down again.

'Thanks, Paula, and as for you playing the role, I don't mind doing it.'

'No, it's my turn,' Paula said, 'but there's one thing, Betty. What about your daughter? She might recognise me.'

'Don't worry. Anne won't be at the party.'

'That's good 'cos I really want to do it and can't wait to see the look on your ex-hubby's face.'

'I wish I could see it too,' said Betty.

The tension had eased, and for the next hour they went over the plan, but as most of the onus lay on Paula, the others had little part to play.

'Paula, I'll tell you everything I can about Richard. In that way, if you're asked questions, you'll be able to give credible answers. Other than that it's just a matter of Val driving you to Farnham.'

'Betty, unlike in my case, this plan won't make you any better off financially,' Cheryl pointed out.

'I know, Val said the same,' Betty admitted, 'but it's too late to get a new settlement and I've accepted that.'

'Right then, I think we've covered everything,' Val said. 'It's just a matter of drumming as much information into Paula as possible over the next six weeks and then waiting for the night of the party.'

'I'm afraid I can't meet up with you tomorrow. I told Charlie that I'd start packing his things.'

'Yeah, and I'm giving her a hand.'

Cheryl's eyes widened. 'You're still coming?'

'If I'm moving in with you, it's only fair.'

'You're moving in?'

'That's what I said, didn't I?'

They grinned at each other, Cheryl saying, 'That's wonderful.'

Val smiled too, then said, 'Cheryl, as you won't have a role to play in Betty's plan, I don't see why you can't concentrate on finding a flat.'

'Are you sure?'

'Yes, and I'm sure I can get my boss to give you a discount if you want to use him for the conveyance work.'

'That'd be great. Thanks, Val.'

With the atmosphere now a happy one, Val relaxed. One by one she looked at their faces; like Betty, she hoped that Cheryl would stay in the area. Once again she realised that these three women had become like a family to her, one that she didn't want to lose. It was something she had never expected, hadn't planned on, but the feelings she felt for them had crept up on her until she couldn't imagine her life without them in it.

Chapter Twenty-seven

When the group broke up on Saturday, Val had driven them home, but both Cheryl and Paula had forgotten about getting boxes to take to Charlie's. They were at his house by ten on Sunday morning, apologetic, and making do with what he had managed to rustle up.

'You youngsters,' Charlie commented with a good-natured smile, 'and judging by the way you're wrapping that china, we'll run out of newspaper too.'

'It's so pretty and I don't want to risk any breakages,' Cheryl said as she carefully removed another piece of the dinner service from the sideboard.

'Yeah, my Nora liked nice things. Mind you, that set only came out on high days and holidays.'

'I'll take good care of it, Charlie, but I still think you could sell it.'

'Maybe, but as I said before, I'd rather it did you a turn.'

'It won't just be me. When I find a flat I've asked Paula to move in with me.'

'Well, ain't that nice? I bet Paula's dead chuffed.'

'Did I hear my name?' Paula said as she walked into the room.

'I was just telling Charlie about us living together.'

'Yeah, and it'll be great to get out of me bedsit.'

'Have you finished in the kitchen?' Cheryl asked.

'You must be joking. I've made a fair old dent in it, but I've run out of boxes and newspaper.'

'I've run out of paper too. It's only one o'clock, but I suppose we'll have to call it a day.'

'I'll see if I can scrounge up more tomorrow,' Charlie said.

'We'll do the same, and if it's all right with you, come back tomorrow evening.'

'Yeah, that's fine.'

Paula was now by the budgie's cage, one finger poked through the bars, but the bird scuttled along to the far side of his perch. 'Leave it out, you silly sod. I ain't gonna hurt you,' she said softly, but as though struck by a thought, her head shot round. 'Cheryl, can I still have Charlie?'

'Yes, of course you can.'

Paula smiled with relief as she turned back to the budgie. It had knocked her for six that Cheryl had doubted her, and in truth it still rankled a bit. She'd spent hours lying awake last night, going over and over it, wondering if her impulsive decision to move in with Cheryl had been a mistake. Finally, in the early hours, her mind had stopped racing. Cheryl *had* apologised, and she'd hardly offer her a home if she didn't mean it. They still had a lot to talk about, not least how much rent Cheryl would want, but now Paula's ears pricked up as Charlie asked, 'What sort of gaff are you looking for, Cheryl?'

'As long as it's got two decent-sized bedrooms and doesn't need a lot of work, I don't really mind. I was thinking about a flat, but if I could find a small house with a garden it would be a bonus.'

'I've always fancied a bit of gardening, but this council house has only got a yard. Mind you, my son reckons he's got a big spread so maybe I can get me hand in when I get out there.'

'I'm sure you will, but as there's nothing more we can do today, I think we'll be off, Charlie.'

'Yeah, all right,' he said, then glanced at the clock, 'and I'll just have time for a pint before me local closes.'

Paula took one last look at the budgie and then followed Cheryl to the door. 'Bye, Charlie.'

'Yeah, see you at work in the morning.'

'We didn't get a lot done,' Paula said as they walked away from the house.

'I know, but we don't want to leave Charlie with nothing to use, so we can take our time.'

'Cheryl, it's good of you to offer me a place, but how much rent are we talking about?'

'How about the same as you're paying now?'

'No, no, that wouldn't be fair. I was talking about finding a bigger room and can manage an extra ten bob, or maybe even a quid.'

'If you're sure, the extra ten shillings would be fine.'

'What's the set-up going to be, Cheryl? At the moment I get use of the bathroom and kitchen, but other than that I stick to me room.'

'No, no, it won't be like that. We'll each have a bedroom, but as for the rest of the flat, we'll share it. We'll have a living room we can both use and, as Charlie has given me all those wonderful things, I might even be able to stretch to a television.'

'Blimey, that sounds great, but when you've got a feller coming round, tip me the wink and I'll stay out of the way.'

'I don't think that's likely, but the same goes for you.'

'Huh, no thanks. I ain't interested in blokes.'

'I know that's how you feel now, but things might change, Paula.'

'I doubt it.'

They paused at the end of Charlie's road. 'What have you got planned for the rest of the day?' Cheryl asked.

'I thought we'd be longer at Charlie's, so nothing really.'

'Me too, but it's too cold to stay outdoors. I think

I'll go back to my quarters and catch up on a bit of ironing.'

'Yeah, I should do the same,' Paula said, though in truth she dreaded the thought of going back to her poky bedsit.

'Tomorrow we'll meet up around seven at Charlie's, if that's all right with you?'

'Yeah, that's fine.'

'See you then,' Cheryl said, waving as she walked away.

'See you,' Paula called, but then seeing a telephone box she hurried towards it. If Betty wasn't busy, she could pop round to see her, maybe Val too.

At the same time, Betty was doing her best to hide her feelings as John sat holding Ulrika's hand, his face animated with happiness. 'I can't believe she said yes this time.'

'Have you set a date for the wedding?'

'Not a definite one, but we thought sometime in spring next year.'

'That's nice,' Betty said, trying her best to sound sincere whilst her thoughts raced. The one thing she dreaded was happening. A wedding, one she'd have to attend, where she'd be forced to face Richard and Mel. There was still the plan, though, and she was cheered by the thought. If it worked, and surely it would, Mel might be long gone before the wedding.

'I am sorry that I upset you the last time we were

here,' Ulrika said, her accent still evident as she enunciated each word.

'No, my dear, it's me who should apologise. I overreacted and I'm sorry. Now come on, tell me what you have planned so far. Is it to be a church wedding?'

'Yes it is.'

'That's good and far nicer than a registry office,' Betty said, but then the phone rang and she rose to answer it, finding Paula on the line. 'I'm sorry, love,' she said on hearing that Paula wanted to come round, 'but my son is here with his girlfriend. I think Val's in, so why don't you give her a ring and maybe I'll see you later.'

'Who was that?' John asked when Betty sat down again.

'Oh, just a friend of mine.'

'You didn't have to turn her away. We'll be off soon.'

'At least stay for another half an hour.'

'Sorry, Mum, we can't this time. I rang Dad to give him the news and he insisted on laying on a bit of a celebration.'

'If you'd rung me first, I could have done the same,' Betty said huffily. 'I suppose your sister will be there too.'

'Yes, I think so,' John said as he rose to his feet. 'Come on, Ulrika, we'd better make a move.'

Betty made a supreme effort to hide her unhappiness at her feelings of exclusion. 'I'm happy for you both,' she said, moving to kiss Ulrika on the cheek.

'Thank you,' she said, returning the kiss.

'Bye, Mum,' John said.

'Don't leave it so long before you both come to see me again.'

'We won't,' he said, bending to give her a swift hug.

Betty walked with them to the door, still managing to keep a smile plastered on her face as she showed them out – one that dropped as soon as she closed the door. They'd only been with her for an hour, but were now off to Richard's where no doubt he'd break out the champagne. She could picture it: Richard, along with Mel, Anne and Anthony, all toasting the happy couple whilst she had to remain on the outside. Excluded from it all – from the family that she had given so many years to and the house she had grown to love.

Chapter Twenty-eight

'Betty's kids are just leaving,' Paula said as she turned away from the window. 'I expect she'll be down soon.'

'You said she knows you're here, so I'm sure she will.'

Paula plonked herself on the sofa, 'Cor, Val, it's gonna be great. When I move in with Cheryl, I won't be stuck in me room. She said we're sharing the whole flat.'

'It sounds wonderful, and a proper home.'

'Yeah, and to think I nearly turned her down. She even talked about buying a telly and—'

A knock on the door interrupted Paula, and when Val opened it she said, 'Hello, come on in.'

'Hello, Paula,' Betty said as she walked into the room.

Treacle ran over to her; after scooping him up, she sat next to Paula. 'My son has just told me that he's getting married. I should be happy, but John is on his way to his father's to celebrate the news and I feel left out, like an outsider.'

'I'm sure he doesn't want you to feel like that,' Val consoled. 'You're his mother, an important part of his life.'

'He's got Ulrika now, and though he rings me once a week, I hardly see him.'

'Did you see more of him before he met Ulrika?'

Betty's brow creased in thought. 'No, I suppose not. Oh, it isn't Ulrika. It's the thought of him being all pally with his father and Mel.'

Paula hated to see Betty unhappy and reached out to clasp her hand. Her own life had changed for the better now. Ian Parker was behind bars, she was making friends at work, and now, to top it all, she was going to live in a real home again. Deep down, she wished it was Betty she was going to share a flat with, but living with Cheryl was next best, and better than being stuck alone in a bedsit. 'I'm sorry, Betty,' she said.

'Oh, take no notice of me,' she said as her hand tightened in reassurance around Paula's. 'Now come on, let's talk about something else. How did you get on this morning? Is everything packed?'

'We forgot to take any boxes, or newspaper, so there's loads left. We're going back tomorrow night, but it means I can't come round to rehearse your plan.'

'Don't worry, there's plenty of time for that.'

'Will your son be at the Christmas party?'

'I don't know, but I'm sure his father will invite him.'

'Let's hope he is – and when he hears what I've got to say, he's sure to turn against him again.'

Betty's eyes lit up. 'Yes, you're right.'

Pleased that she'd managed to cheer Betty up, Paula now said, 'Here, and talking about Christmas, it's nice to think that me and Cheryl will be together in a flat.'

'Paula,' Val cautioned, 'even if Cheryl finds a flat quickly, you can't bank on the sale going through by Christmas. With vacant possession it can be done in weeks, but more often than not, it takes a couple of months.'

'Oh blimey, that means I'll still be stuck in me bedsit.'

'No, Paula, I insist you spend Christmas Day with me, especially as I know it'll be your birthday.'

'Your birthday?' Betty cried. 'Oh, that's lovely. I was going to suggest that we all spend Christmas together and just hope that Cheryl isn't on duty. I'd love to cook dinner – and if you don't mind sleeping on my sofa, Paula, you're welcome to stay.'

'Mind! Of course I don't mind,' Paula cried. Life was certainly on the up and the thought of spending Christmas with Betty, Val and Cheryl made her happiness complete. It was strange, really. Before Betty had come onto the scene, she'd seen quite a bit of Cheryl and Val. They'd been friends and she'd grown fond of them, but Betty had added something to the mix – a feeling that they were now a family.

Cheryl wasn't feeling the same as she finished the last piece of ironing. She no longer regretted offering Paula a home, and now her doubts had been dispelled she was in fact looking forward to it. The only thing was she wanted to move out of the area, to be long gone before Ian Parker came out of prison. There was a fear that she couldn't dispel – that when released he'd come looking for the woman who'd falsely accused him of rape.

Not only that, she wasn't happy with Betty's plan. Yes, she'd been hurt, had suffered financially, but her plan had nothing to do with getting a better settlement.

Cheryl hung her ironing in the closet, still thinking, still worrying. The plan for Paula had made sense. The man who raped her had got away with it and deserved to be punished. It had enabled Paula to move forward, to stop living like a hermit, afraid to go out at night for fear of bumping into him. Likewise, the plan for the dealer who had cheated her made sense. She had got her money back and now had the means to buy a place of her own. Justice had been served. Betty though just wanted to see her husband brought low, and as for Val, even if she could ensure that the man who ruined her career lost his job, it wouldn't make any difference. It wouldn't get her the job back. It was too late for that. In fact, if they both got the revenge they sought, what good would it do? Other than perhaps a sense of satisfaction, it wouldn't make any difference to their lives. Neither of them would be any better off.

Cheryl shook her head with impatience. Betty and Val were living in the past, eaten up by unhappy memories. Surely it would be better to let it all go, to move forward with their lives? She had listened to Betty's plan, annoyed with herself for not speaking up, telling them how she felt. At least this time she didn't have a part to play, but doubted she'd get off so lightly when it came to Val's plan.

Her mood low, Cheryl now sat on the side of her bed. She just wanted it to be over, to be able to get on with her own life again, to plan for the future in a new area and, with any luck, a new job. If she took up midwifery she'd be more or less her own boss, but was it what she really wanted? The money she now had offered her choices, and something that had been at the back of her mind now forced its way to the front. It would be so worthwhile, but would she be able to raise the money? Could she do it? Yes, maybe, but one thing was sure, she couldn't do it alone.

Chapter Twenty-nine

Cheryl had arranged storage for the furniture, and over the next ten days occasionally met Paula at Charlie's to pack it all up. It was mid-November, but at last they were finished and, sighing with relief, Cheryl said, 'That's it, Charlie, all done, but your house looks so spartan now.'

'Don't worry about it. You've left me enough to get by on until Saturday.'

'The storage company van will be here at eleven. Is that still all right?'

'Yeah, that's fine. I've found a bed for the night with a mate, so that just leaves me budgie.' He then turned to Paula. 'When Keith ran me home with more boxes, I told him you were taking the budgie. He said it'd be a bit of a job lugging his cage on a bus, so offered to give you a lift.'

'Keith? What, Keith at work?'

'Yeah, and it was good of him to offer.'

'But you shouldn't have done that, Charlie! I'd have sorted something out.'

'Well there's no need now. He's gonna drop us off here, and then take you on to your place with Charlie.'

'But . . . but that means I'll be alone with him in his car!'

Paula's fear was palpable, and Cheryl wished she could help. 'I'm so sorry, Paula, but I've already agreed to stand in for one of our nurses until eleven.'

'Paula's got nothing to worry about. Keith might be a bit mouthy, but he's a nice bloke.'

'But, Charlie, he's always trying to chat me up and . . . and he might try it on.'

'I'm sorry, girl. After what you told me I should've realised you'd be a bit skittish.' He scratched his head. 'Don't worry, I'll come on to your place with you.'

'Oh, thanks, Charlie.'

Cheryl glanced at her watch and seeing it was nearly ten she said, 'Paula, I think we should go now.'

They both put on their coats, but then Cheryl took a small package from her handbag, holding it out to Charlie. 'Thank you so much for giving me all your lovely things. I know you don't want anything, but well, I've got you a little present.'

'Blimey, girl, you shouldn't have done that,' Charlie said as he took the package. With gnarled fingers he opened it, and seeing the gold cufflinks his voice croaked, 'They're smashing. Thanks very much.'

'I don't suppose I'll see you now before you go, so goodbye, Charlie. Good luck and have a safe journey.'

'Me mates are throwing a bit of a party for me in the Railway Arms on Saturday night. If you can make it, you'd be more than welcome. You too, Paula.'

'I'm afraid I can't, but thanks for the invite.'

'Me neither,' Paula said, as they walked to the door, 'but I'll see you at work in the morning.'

'Bye, Charlie,' they both chorused, and as he closed the door behind them, they hurried along the street.

'It was nice of Charlie to invite us, but a pub on a Saturday night ain't my cup of tea.'

'I felt the same,' agreed Cheryl. 'Come on, I'll walk you to the bus stop.'

'There's no need. I'll be fine.'

'You always say that, but as usual I'll ignore you.'

'Well this time, don't hang around until a bus turns up.'

'We'll see, but I'm glad the packing is out of the way. I can concentrate on finding a house now.'

Paula grinned as she linked her arm through Cheryl's. 'Oh, a house now is it?'

'Yes, if I can get a mortgage, but as a professional with a huge deposit, I don't think it'll be a problem. Look, there's a bus and if we run you should be able to catch it,' Cheryl urged, glad as they dashed along Northcote Road that it brought an end to the conversation. She wasn't ready to reveal what she had in mind yet. There was so much to think about, so much to find out before she'd know if it was really viable.

At the same time in Val's flat, Betty yawned. 'I think it's bed for me.'

'Would you like a cup of cocoa first?'

'Oh, go on then. I won't say no.'

When Val returned with the drinks, she found Betty dozing. 'Wake up, sleepy head.'

'I was only resting my eyes.'

'Yes, you always say that, but you can fall asleep at the drop of a hat.'

Betty absent-mindedly stroked the dog's head. 'Work again tomorrow . . . I must admit that these days the job is getting me down.'

'Really? Why?'

'It's being on my own all the time, that and the endless round of cleaning.'

'Why don't you look for something else?'

'Like what? It'd just be another cleaning job, and at least where I am now I'm more or less my own boss.'

'You could try for a job in a shop.'

Betty looked thoughtful for a moment. 'Yes, I suppose I could, but I've no experience.'

'How much experience do you need to work behind a counter? It's just a matter of serving people and taking the money.'

'I've never used a till.'

'You'd soon learn.'

'Yes, I think I could. After the things I've done lately, learning how to use a till should be a doddle. Oh, dear, I seem to be picking up some of Paula's words – what I meant was, it should be easy.' Betty chuckled, then picking up her cup of cocoa she drank it down, smacking her lips with appreciation. 'That was lovely, but if I don't go now I really will fall asleep.'

'All right. I'll see you tomorrow.'

Val showed Betty out, washed the cups, and then took Treacle for his last walk. On her return she went to bed, the dog jumping up to claim his spot beside her. Val threw an arm around him, thoughts drifting. Like Betty, she too was dissatisfied with her job. The filing system was all but complete, and after that she had no idea how she was going to fill her days. What little typing there was didn't take long, and other than answering the telephone, she'd be left twiddling her thumbs. Oh, if only she was still in sales, even as a rep, but thanks to Mike Freeman there was no chance of that. Once again she thought about ways of getting revenge, but as usual she came up with nothing. The frustration was driving her mad.

Val finally gave up and, hugging Treacle closer, she finally drifted off to sleep, but in the night her torturous body betrayed her. Treacle moved away as Val thrashed and turned, dreaming that she was in Mike Freeman's arms, their love-making passionate.

Paula was struggling to fall asleep too. She couldn't stop thinking about Keith. He'd have no idea why she was frightened to be alone with him in his car; would wonder why Charlie was coming with them, but she wasn't about to tell him the truth. She and Charlie would have to work out an excuse. But what?

Finally, giving up, Paula impatiently threw back the blankets. She shrugged on her dressing gown, and then went down to the communal kitchen. Her nose wrinkled as she opened the fridge, frowning at the sight of mouldy cheese, and the fact that her bottle of milk was half empty. Some rotten sod had nicked some again, but fed up with trying to catch the culprit she just poured what was left into a saucepan and set it on the filthy gas cooker. As she waited for it to boil, her thoughts drifted to Betty and all the information about her husband she had to remember. It felt that her mind was saturated, that she wouldn't be able to take anything else in, but there was no stopping Betty from trying to drum in even more.

When the hot drink was made, Paula rinsed out the saucepan but, unable to bear the thought of sitting in the dirty kitchen, she carried the mug of milk up to her room. At least she wouldn't be in this stinking house for much longer, and the thought cheered her as she sat on her bed. But in the meantime there was still the problem of Keith and her unwillingness to be alone with him in his car.

When her drink was finished, Paula scrambled under the blankets again, deciding that the problem would have to wait until morning. She'd have a word with Charlie and maybe he'd come up with something. If she could have chosen a father, it would be someone like Charlie, and Paula knew she was going to miss him.

Behind closed lids, unbidden, the image of Keith now arose again. He wasn't good looking, but she liked his cheeky smile, the way he made her laugh, along with his pointless chat-up lines. If she could ever face going out with a bloke again, it would be someone like Keith, someone who could make her laugh, Paula mused as she slowly drifted off to sleep. Her last conscious thought was that, even though Keith was nice, it would be years before she could face a date again.

Chapter Thirty

Betty shivered as she stepped outside on Friday morning. Her thoughts drifted as she walked to the bus stop, hands in pockets. Cheryl and Paula had finished the packing on Wednesday but, as Paula was going to pick up her budgie tonight, she had telephoned to say she wouldn't be round. Cheryl had rung Val, saying that she was going to be busy looking for a house this weekend, but hoped to see them one evening during the following week. After that Cheryl was on nights again, but as she wasn't needed for the plan, Val had assured her that it didn't matter.

Betty still couldn't help comparing her life now to how it had been before she had met Val and the others. She'd been a sad, lonely woman with only Anne and John's visits to look forward to, but now look what she'd achieved. She had helped to put Ian Parker behind bars. Cheryl had her money back, and soon it would be Richard's turn. Betty shivered again, but this time with anticipation.

However, when Betty arrived at her employer's house half an hour later, her mood immediately lowered. Another day on her own, without a soul to talk to, but her conversation with Val last night had inspired her. She *would* look for another job, something different, but she'd wait until Richard had had his comeuppance. There was a little over five weeks to go, but then it would be over. Not long after that it would be the start of a new year. The perfect time for a fresh start.

Paula was working on Charlie's machine. It was his last day at work, and she'd been told that a small party was planned for him at the end of the day. It would mean a delay in going to get the budgie, but hopefully not a long one. She couldn't see anyone wanting to hang around on a Friday. For a start the married women would want to get home to see to their husbands and kids.

When Charlie walked to her side, she asked, 'Is Keith still giving us a lift later?'

'Yeah, but you've no need to worry. I told him the budgie might be a bit nervous in the car so, when he drives you home, I'd best come along to keep him calm.'

'He fell for that?'

'Why wouldn't he, especially as it ain't far from

the truth? That bird hasn't been out of the house since the day we bought him. He's bound to find it a bit upsetting.'

'Blimey, we should have thought of that before. I'm glad you're coming. Hearing your voice is bound to help.'

Charlie's expression saddened. 'People don't think birds have feelings, but when my wife died, Charlie went quiet for days. He missed hearing her voice, I'm sure of it. When you get him home he's gonna be in strange surroundings, so he might well do the same. Just keep talking to him and I'm sure he'll come round.'

'He's going to miss you too.'

Charlie's voice was gruff with emotion. 'I know, but I can't take him to New Zealand. I know it sounds daft, he's only a budgie, but my wife loved him and he's been hard to part with. I'm just glad that you're going to look after him.'

'I won't only look after him, I'll spoil him rotten.'

Charlie sniffed, then pulled out a large handkerchief as he walked away, hiding his emotions as he fiddled with something on the machine.

Paula worked steadily until lunchtime and was glad for the break. She rushed outside to smoke a cigarette, finding Greta and a few other girls already huddled in a group.

'Watcha, Paula,' Greta greeted. 'We was just saying that it's a bit of a pain having to hang around later for Charlie's presentation.'

'Yeah,' Doreen agreed. 'I've got a date tonight so I ain't staying long.'

'Me neither,' said another.

Paula took a long drag on her cigarette. 'Keith is giving us a lift back to Charlie's place, so I've got to wait until they leave.'

Greta's eyebrows shot up. 'You and Keith? When did this happen?'

'No, no, it's nothing like that. He's only taking me to pick up Charlie's budgie. That's all.'

'Oh yeah, but knowing Keith, I should think it's you he wants to pick up.'

'He ain't got a hope in hell,' Paula snapped.

'If 1 didn't already have a bloke, I wouldn't say no. It'd be nice to have a feller with a car.'

Doreen grimaced. 'With his looks it'd take more than a car to tempt me.'

'He ain't that bad,' Greta protested.

'Yeah, in the dark.'

Paula smiled at the banter, but then dropped her cigarette to grind it underfoot. 'I'm off to grab something to eat.'

'Yeah, me too,' Greta said.

They all went to the canteen in a small group and Paula caught Charlie's smile of approval at seeing her with the other girls. Things had changed since she'd made an effort to make friends, and though she didn't see the girls outside of work, she enjoyed their company during breaks. At first she'd felt a bit guilty for not joining Charlie at his table, but he didn't seem to mind, and had, in fact, encouraged her to sit with the girls.

They lined up to buy a sandwich, then found a table, Doreen asking, 'What have you got planned for the weekend, Paula?'

'Nothing much. I'm just seeing some friends.'

'If you fancy joining me, I'm going to a dance at Battersea Town Hall on Saturday night.'

Paula shuddered at the memory of the last time she'd been to a dance. 'I'm busy,' she said, unaware that her tone was terse.

'Please yourself,' and obviously in a huff, Doreen turned to talk to one of the other girls. 'What about you, Mandy? Do you want to come?'

'Yeah, I'm game.'

Greta leaned closer to Paula, hissing, 'You were a bit sharp with Doreen.'

'Was I? Sorry, Doreen, I didn't mean to sound rude. It's just that I really am busy.'

Mollified, she said, 'That's all right. Maybe some other time.'

'Well, to tell you the truth, I ain't keen on dancing.'

'Yeah, right,' Doreen said sarcastically before taking another bite of her sandwich.

Paula lowered her eyes. She knew that her excuse sounded lame, and with her appetite now gone she rose to her feet. 'I'm off for another fag.'

Outside Paula quickly lit a cigarette. She hated her fear, hated being different from the other girls and wished she still had their assurance, their enjoyment of life. They went dancing regularly, kept up with all the latest pop music and, though she tried, she felt out of it, distant from them and their interests. Ian Parker had not only robbed her of her virginity, he had destroyed her confidence. She just hoped he was suffering for it now.

Paula found her mood low for the rest of the day, and when the machines were finally turned off, her shoulders drooped, arms folded defensively as she followed everyone to Charlie's presentation. She stood apart, but then sensed someone beside her.

'Look at Charlie's face. He's dreading the presentation,' Keith said.

Paula just shrugged, and then the boss was giving a speech, thanking Charlie for all his loyal years with the company. When it came to an end he motioned Charlie forward and, shaking his hand, gave him a package.

Charlie opened it, smiling as he drawled, 'A clock, just what I need.'

Keith chuckled. 'I hope the boss caught the sarcasm in Charlie's voice. Bloody hell, a clock. How daft is that? Come on: let's grab a drink and a bite to eat.'

'No, thanks. You go, I'm fine.'

Keith just raised an eyebrow before walking away, whilst Paula leaned against the wall, watching Charlie as he was surrounded by people, men shaking his hand and women kissing him on the cheek. He looked bemused, and when a glass was shoved into his hand he downed the drink in one go which was soon followed by another. Paula wanted a cigarette and headed outside. She didn't hurry back, remaining to smoke not one cigarette but two. She then went to the ladies' room, afterwards washing her hands and at the same time staring at her reflection in the mirror. She'd been a bit late getting up; her face was devoid of make-up and hair lank. What did it matter? Yet, even as this thought crossed her mind, Paula went to get her handbag, applying a bit of lipstick and powder. Why had she bothered? Paula knew the answer, but refused to acknowledge it as she went back to the party, her eyes searching for Keith.

It wasn't Keith she saw first; instead it was Charlie, his face red and eyes bleary as he walked up to her. She could smell the whisky on his breath, but had to smile when he spoke.

'Can you find Keith? I think I've had a few too many and if I don't go home now, I'll fall flat on me face.'

'All right, stay there. I'll be back as soon as I can.'

Paula searched the room, finally spotting Keith standing in a corner with a few of his mates. She hurried up to him, saying, 'Charlie's a bit under the weather. He wants to go home.'

'I ain't surprised. He must have had at least six whiskies in under an hour. Come on; let's get him out of here.'

Keith said goodbye to his mates, but when they walked across the room to find Charlie, he had yet another drink in his hand.

'Charlie, you've had enough,' Paula protested. 'You said you wanted to go home.'

'I do,' he said, gulping the drink. He raised his arm to wave, calling, 'Bye everyone, and thanks for the party.'

There was a chorus of goodbyes, shouts for him to enjoy his retirement, and hands thumping his back as they led him outside. Keith helped him into the car, whilst Paula scrambled into the back, and then they were off, Keith saying, 'Blimey, Charlie, you should've eaten something to soak it up.'

'I didn't get a chance, mate. As soon as I finished one drink, another was shoved in me hand. Gawd, me head's spinning.'

'Oh blimey, don't throw up in my car.'

'I'll be all right. Just get me home.'

Paula saw that Keith kept glancing worriedly at Charlie, but at last they were pulling up outside his house. She got out of the car, Keith running round to help Charlie, and after he managed to find Charlie's door key in his pocket, they took an arm each to guide him inside. Charlie managed to make it, but his legs were wobbly as they led him to a chair. Paula glanced around. The room looked bleak, piled with boxes ready for the storage firm to pick up in the morning, but Charlie hardly seemed aware of it as he slumped down.

'I feel rough.'

'If you ask me, the best place for you is bed,' Keith said.

'Yeah, I think you're right.'

'What about the budgie?' Paula asked.

'If I have to get back in that car I'll throw up. Take him, love, and don't worry, you'll be all right with Keith.'

'Charlie,' Paula wailed, mortified.

'What's he on about? Why wouldn't you be all right with me?'

'She's a bit nervous of men and I ain't surprised. Do you know what happened to the poor—'

'No, Charlie,' Paula quickly warned.

'Sorry, girl. It's the drink, it's loosened me tongue, but every time I see you and Keith together, you remind me of me and my Nora. You could do a lot worse, love,' and with that Charlie closed his eyes, groaning softly.

Paula's face flamed, but Keith just grinned, saying, 'Come on, Charlie, let's get you up to bed.'

He didn't resist as Keith pulled him up, but then weaved his way over to the budgie's cage, unsteady

303

on his feet as he leaned forward to peer at the bird. 'Bye, old feller.' He then managed to focus watery eyes on Paula. 'There's a bag of seed and such, so make sure you take it with you.'

Paula nodded, but then found tears filling her eyes. She ran forward to throw her arms around the old man. 'Thanks for giving him to me, and . . . and bye, Charlie. Have a safe journey.'

As she removed her arms, Charlie staggered and his voice slurred as he said, 'Take care of him, and . . . and yerself.'

Keith took his arm, leading him from the room, whilst Paula fought the hammering in her chest at the thought of getting into Keith's car. Stop it, she told herself, stop being silly. As Charlie said, she'd be all right. She covered the bird's cage with the cloth, then found a bag containing a box of seed, millet and a new cuttlefish.

It was a while before Keith returned, shaking his head as he walked into the room. 'I had to undress the silly sod, but if you're ready, we can go.'

'I'm ready,' she said and, taking the cage whilst Keith picked up the bag, she gently carried it outside.

Keith held the front passenger door open, but tensing she said, 'I'll sit in the back. Instead of balancing the cage on me lap, it can go beside me on the seat.' Without waiting, Paula climbed in, relieved that she'd found a way to avoid sitting beside Keith.

He went round to the driver's side, saying as he

got behind the wheel, 'Charlie's gonna have a sore head in the morning.'

'I hope he'll be all right.'

'Don't worry. I'll pop round to check on him.'

Her eyes widened. It was nice of Keith to do that, but now as he spoke again, her ears pricked.

'Did Charlie tell you there's another party tomorrow night?'

'Yes, he invited me.'

'Are you going?'

'No, I'm busy,' she lied.

'I'll be there, but if he gets in the same state, I dread to think what he'll be like when he boards ship on Sunday. It's a shame you're not coming to the party though.'

Keith was looking at her in the driving mirror, and she said churlishly, 'Don't you think you should keep your eyes on the road?'

'Yeah,' he said, glancing at her in the mirror again, 'but I'd rather look at you.'

Flushing, she looked away, lifting the cloth a little to check the budgie. He was sitting on the floor of the cage, his feathers looking ruffled. 'I hope Charlie's going to be all right.'

'He'll be fine; as I told you, I'll check on him in the morning.'

'Not that Charlie. I'm talking about the budgie.'

'Oh right,' Keith said, and then laughed. 'Daft name for a bird – no wonder I got confused.'

Paula smiled, but shortly after they were pulling up outside her house. She quickly grabbed the cage to scramble from the car. Blast, Keith was getting out too.

'I'll carry him if you like,' he offered, 'while you bring his bag of stuff.'

'No, no, it's all right, I can manage. Just hook the bag over my arm.'

'Are you sure?'

'Yes, and thanks for the lift.'

'You're welcome, but are you sure you can't make it to Charlie's party?'

'I told you, I'm busy.'

'Fair enough,' he said, but then moved closer, leaning over as though to kiss her.

She reared back, the cage swaying and rattling, her eyes frantically looking round. There was no one in sight, no one to help her – the street empty, dark and foreboding. 'Get away from me. If you come any closer, I'll scream.'

'Leave it out, Paula, I ain't gonna touch you. Charlie said you'd be safe with me, and you are.'

There was reassurance in Keith's voice, along with a sympathetic look in his eyes and, horrified, Paula said, 'He told you. Charlie told you.'

'He didn't tell me anything, but from your reaction it doesn't take a genius to work it out. Somebody scared you, maybe hurt you, and if I get my hands on him I'll ring his bleedin' neck.'

'Oh, Keith . . .'

'Go on, go indoors. I'll stay here until you're safely inside.'

'Th-thanks.'

'You're welcome. And Paula, not all men are monsters.'

Paula nodded, and then turning she went to her front door, putting the cage down while finding her key. With trembling hands she opened the lock, managed to give Keith a small wave, then picked up the cage again before stepping indoors.

She heard the car door close, the engine start, and then slowly went upstairs. Keith had been nice, kind, but after what she'd been through was it any surprise that she'd overreacted? If she'd allowed him to kiss her, it wouldn't have stopped there. Like Ian Parker, he'd have wanted more, and at that thought she shivered with fear.

In her room, Paula set the cage on a small table before lifting the cloth. She bent to look through the bars and, as though he could understand every word, she spoke gently to Charlie, reassuring both the bird and herself. 'There, you're safe now. I'm safe too.'

The budgie remained on the bottom of the cage and, worried, Paula hurried to fill his seed and water containers. She spoke to him the whole time, until at last, though he still didn't make a sound, he at least climbed the bars to sit on his perch.

Paula grinned with relief. 'There, that's better. I know you'll miss Charlie, and I will too, but I'll look after you. You'll be fine. We'll be fine,' and with a chuckle she added, 'Anyway, you should consider yourself lucky. You're the only male that's ever gonna get into me bedroom.'

Chapter Thirty-one

Nothing went as expected for the next two weeks. Cheryl's plans to find a house and sort out a mortgage went on hold as she went down with a severe bout of flu. Betty had succumbed too and, though she protested, Val insisted on looking after her, calling in before she went to work and again every evening.

When Anne rang to say she was coming over, Betty had to tell her to stay away. She was already fearful that she'd infect Val; the fewer people she came into contact with, the better. God, she felt awful. Every muscle, every bone in her body seemed to ache, and when she tried to sit up in bed, her head swam. Her temperature fluctuated from feeling cold and shivery to hot and sweaty, and the last thing she could face was food. Val cajoled her to eat soup, and she managed a few spoonfuls, but alone all day, she mostly slept.

Slowly Betty recovered, and at last she was up in the living room when Val came to her flat on Sunday.

'Paula's been on the telephone this morning. She's worried about you.'

'I still feel a bit weak, but I'm a lot better now. Have you heard from Cheryl?'

'Yes and, like you, she's over the worst of it.'

'That's good, and thank goodness you didn't catch it.'

'I'm fine, but to be on the safe side I've told Paula to stay away until next weekend.'

'Oh, Val, we're so behind with the plan now. It's already the end of November.'

'Don't worry. There's little to do. Paula might need a few reminders, but with the delay it'll be fresh in her mind.'

'I hope you're right.'

'Have you heard from your son?'

'Yes, he's coming to see me next weekend, as is Anne.'

'In that case we'll have to make sure we keep Paula out of sight.'

'They never stay long, so as long as she comes over in the afternoon we'll be in the clear. I've missed her, and Cheryl.'

'Yes, me too, but no doubt once Cheryl is fully recovered, she'll be busy looking for a house.'

Betty found she was struggling to keep her eyes open. 'Yes, I suppose so,' she said tiredly.

'I think you should go back to bed.'

'But I've only been up for a couple of hours.'

'I think it's enough for one day. Go on, have a lie down. I'll pop up again later.'

Too tired to argue, Betty nodded. This bout of flu had drained her of any energy and, though over the worst of it, she felt like an old, old lady as she climbed into bed. She was aware of Val leaving, but that was all before her eyes closed in sleep.

Cheryl was feeling mean as she tried to read the local paper. Paula had rung to see how she was; as she had done with Val, Cheryl had told her a little white lie. She had indeed gone down with the flu, but unlike Betty had recovered earlier. It was just that she wanted a break from all of them, a chance to gather her thoughts, ones that despite the flu had gone around and around in her head.

After going to the bank, she'd been delighted to find that there wouldn't be any problem in getting a mortgage. She'd been worried that they'd turn down a single woman's application, but was told that as more and more professional women were being granted loans, it wouldn't be a problem. Once again Cheryl's eyes scanned the newspaper. She had yet to find the right property, but that wasn't the only thing that was worrying her. How was Paula going to react to her change of plans? She would still offer her a home, but it would be totally unlike the one she'd portrayed. Would Paula come on board? Would she want to help? It wouldn't be easy;

they'd be living in a totally different environment and not everyone was suited to the task.

Cheryl flung the paper aside. She had two houses to view after work tomorrow, one in Streatham, the other Wimbledon, both of them out of the borough. The first sounded promising, the price good, but it would need a lot of work. The other had more bedrooms, was more viable, but needed work too. The price was on the steep side, and though able to get a mortgage, until it was established, would she be able to keep up the payments? Cheryl picked up her pad, again going over her figures. Maybe she was mad in trying to set this up, but once the idea had taken root it had refused to go away. She would be her own boss, doing something she loved and knew she was good at.

Val wrapped a thick scarf around her neck. It was freezing outside, but Treacle needed a walk, so pulling on leather gloves she braved the outdoors. The park looked bleak, yet there was still beauty to be found. Many trees had dropped their leaves, yet some still clung in varying shades of brown and gold, some tinged deep red. Children were playing, gathering heaps of fallen leaves into piles before jumping into them, their giggles making Val smile too. Treacle ran to join them, yapping with excitement as leaves flew into the air for him to chase.

It was too cold to sit and linger, so after a while

Val called Treacle, her pace brisk as she walked the paths. Betty's plan was a relatively simple one, with little for her to think about, so Val had begun to concentrate on Mike Freeman. She wanted to discredit him, to see him thrown out of the industry, and, like her, to find no way back. Every plan she'd come up with so far needed someone on the inside, but she had lost contact with all old colleagues. Val grimaced. Even if she had still been in touch with them, it wouldn't help. None would risk their jobs and she couldn't blame them for that.

Val cursed her lack of forethought. She should have come up with her own plan before recruiting. If she'd done that, she might have found someone who had the necessary qualifications to gain a job within the industry. It was too late now. Finding another recruit could take forever, especially one with qualifications and the same need for revenge. She'd have to find another way, another plan. After Betty's plan had been completed, she'd get them all on to it and, surely, between them, they'd come up with something. In the meantime she'd have to be patient: celebrate Christmas and Paula's birthday. It would be a wonderful day, and Betty would be over the moon that she had managed to bring her husband down at last.

By Saturday, Betty had recovered all but her appetite, and was looking forward to seeing Anne and John. It was already December, and in just over two weeks

Richard would be holding his annual party. Anne would be in Cornwall, but Betty still didn't know if John and Ulrika would be there. When she'd spoken to her son on the telephone, his reply had been evasive, so today would be her chance to ask him face to face.

Anne was the first to arrive, her expression anxious as Betty opened the door. 'Are you all right now, Mum?'

'Yes, I'm fine.'

'At your age you have to be careful. I was worried it would turn into pneumonia.'

'I'm not *that* old,' Betty protested. 'Come on, sit by the fire and I'll make us both a drink. I've missed you.'

'Mum, I wanted to come to see you, but you wouldn't have it,' Anne pointed out as she took a seat. 'You sounded really rough, and I was relieved to hear you had someone to keep an eye on you.'

'Val has been a good friend.'

'Is that the woman who lives downstairs?'

'Yes, and I don't know what I'd have done without her.' Betty was about to go into the kitchen when there was another knock on the door. 'That'll be John,' she said, her smile wide as she let her son in.

'Hello, Mum.'

'Hello, darling, and where's Ulrika?'

'I wasn't sure you'd be completely over the flu. Rather than risk her catching it, I left her at home.'

'Hello,' Anne said as he flopped onto the sofa. 'How are the wedding plans progressing?'

'Please, not you too. I'm sick of hearing about the wedding – it's driving me mad. Even when we go to see Dad, it's all she and Mel talk about. Yap, yap, yap – from what shade to choose for brides-maids' dresses, to what colour Mel should wear so she won't clash with them. It's the same when she rings you. I wish I hadn't agreed to a big wedding now. It would have been much simpler to pop into a registry office.'

'Leave it out, John. It isn't that bad . . . Anyway, all girls want their wedding day to be perfect.'

Betty listened to this exchange and felt a flare of anger. Ulrika had never rung her to discuss wedding plans or to ask her opinion on anything. It seemed that privilege had gone to Mel. Once again she felt excluded. Oh, it wasn't fair, it really wasn't. John was *her* son – *she* was the groom's mother – not Mel! She marched into the kitchen, filled the kettle and then slammed it on the cooker.

'What's up, Mum?'

Betty spun round to see John in the kitchen doorway. 'Doesn't it occur to you, *or* Ulrika, that *I* am your mother?'

'What's that supposed to mean?'

'How come it's Mel that's helping Ulrika with the arrangements? As I said, *I'm* your mother so why hasn't she come to me?'

A look of understanding crossed John's face. 'Oh, I see. You're feeling left out.'

'Of course I am, and can you blame me?'

'Look, Mum, we didn't mean to upset you. It's just that with Anne and Mel being younger, I think Ulrika finds them on the same wavelength, that's all.'

Betty huffed, turning her back on John as she spooned tea leaves into the pot. Only moments later she felt his arms around her waist, his voice in her ear.

'Come on, don't be like this. In future, I promise Ulrika will keep you up to date on any arrangements.'

'Don't bother. It's a bit late now and, anyway, I'm not even sure I'll come to the wedding.'

'What! But why?'

'It seems I won't be needed,' Betty snapped, as she pulled away from John's arms. Once started she found herself unable to stop, her words pouring out in a tirade of pent-up emotions. 'It's obvious that I've been relegated, with Mel playing my part. *She'll* be in the front pew with your father, so what about me? As the cast-off wife, will I have to sit at the back of the church? And what about photographs? No doubt I'll be on the sidelines, with Mel and your father by your side in family shots. Then there's the reception. Instead of sitting at the head table with you and Ulrika, once again Mel and your father will take those seats while I'm tucked away somewhere out of sight.'

'Stop it, Mum. This is silly. Of course you won't be hidden away. You're my mother and I want you there.'

Betty remained rigid with anger, but then Anne appeared.

'I heard every word and, like John, I think you're overreacting, Mum.'

It was too much for Betty. Pushing past them she fled the kitchenette to run to her bedroom. With a sob she threw herself onto the bed. Yes, she was being unreasonable and she'd upset John, but hadn't been able to stop the words that tumbled from her mouth. How could they understand that to her this was the final straw? Mel already had her husband and her house – and now she felt the woman had stolen the only thing she had left. Her children.

'Please, I can't bear to see you like this,' John begged as he sat on the side of the bed.

'Come on, Mum, don't cry,' Anne urged.

Betty fought to pull herself together, but her emotions were all over the place. Maybe the flu had weakened her more than she realised, but she was unable to stop sobbing. 'I . . . I'm sorry,' she gasped.

John gathered her into his arms. 'It's all right, Mum. I should've realised you'd be feeling left out but, as I said, it won't happen again.'

Betty clung to her son, finding strength in his arms. He was no longer her little boy, the one who needed protecting. He was a man now – had grown away from her, but if she carried on like this, she'd lose him completely. She'd behaved like a child and a wave of shame washed over her. Betty pulled away from her son, somehow managing a watery smile. 'Oh dear, it was silly to get so upset. I don't know what came over me. I'm fine now. Come on, let's go back to the living room.'

'Are you sure?' Anne asked worriedly.

'Yes,' Betty insisted as she swung her legs over the side of the bed, only to be struck by a wave of dizziness.

'Anne, quick, give me a hand!'

John's voice sounded distant and Betty was vaguely aware of being pushed gently back onto the pillows.

'What's wrong with her?'

'I don't know, John, but perhaps she isn't completely over the flu. Look at her, she's lost more weight. I bet she hasn't been eating properly.'

Betty's head had cleared, and opening her eyes she managed to say weakly, 'I'm not deaf you know.'

'Oh, Mum, you gave us a fright,' Anne said. 'Maybe we should call a doctor.'

'No, no, don't do that. I'm fine, really I am, but you're right, I haven't been eating much lately.'

'Well, you're going to eat now,' Anne said, her bossy nature coming to the fore as she added, 'Stay there, and don't get up. I'm going to make you something.'

Feeling better, Betty smiled ruefully. 'Oops, John, now I really do feel like a naughty child. Darling, don't look so worried. The flu took away my appetite, that's all.'

'In that case you need building up again, but to be on the safe side, maybe it wouldn't hurt to have a checkup.'

'There's no need. I'll be fine.'

It seemed her reassurances didn't satisfy John and he continued to nag, but was thankfully interrupted when Anne came back to the bedroom.

'I've made you a sandwich and a cup of tea.'

With the tray laid across her lap, Betty managed to eat half the sandwich. 'Thank you, darling, that was lovely.'

'You can manage more than that. Come on, eat the other half,' John urged.

With both of them looking so concerned, Betty knew she'd have to try, and managed to force down the rest of the sandwich. 'There, are you satisfied?'

'Yes,' Anne said, 'but drink your tea.'

Betty did as she was told, then laid her cup down. 'You can take the tray away. I feel fine now and I'm getting up.'

'You don't look fine to me. You're as thin as a rake,' Anne protested.

'I wish. I may have lost a few pounds but, let's face it, I had them to spare.'

John at last smiled, whilst Anne glanced at her

319

watch. 'I'm supposed to be meeting Tony, but I don't like leaving you like this.'

'I'm not an invalid, dear. I had the flu, that's all. There's no need to stay.'

'Well, if you're sure.'

'I am. Now off you go,' Betty urged.

'Promise you'll eat more.'

'I promise, but don't blame me if I pile the weight back on.'

'I can stay for another half-hour,' John said, 'but then I'll have to dash off too.'

Betty didn't mind – in fact for the first time she was anxious for them to leave. Paula would be waiting downstairs and with so much to remind her about Richard, time was running short. Anne bent over the bed to kiss her goodbye, once again urging her to look after herself, and then with a wave she was gone.

Betty leaned back on the pillows, raising the subject at last. 'John, I'm spending Christmas with friends. Have you anything planned?'

'Nothing much. With this wedding costing an arm and a leg, our Christmas will be a quiet one.'

'Are you going to your father's annual party?'

With his head down, he mumbled, 'Err . . . err, I'm not sure.'

'You should go. Ulrika would enjoy it.'

He looked up now, eyes rounded with surprise. 'Wouldn't it upset you?'

'Why should it? You've let bygones be bygones with your father now, and I've accepted that.'

'You were upset enough about being left out of the wedding plans.'

'I don't know what came over me. I overreacted, and I'm sorry.'

'Once I've spoken to Ulrika, like me, you'll be sick of hearing about the blasted wedding.'

'I'm sure I won't,' Betty said, then urging, 'Go to your father's party, darling, but if you get the chance, do pop over to see me at some point during the Christmas holidays.'

'All right, I'll go to Dad's on Christmas Eve, and how about we come to see you on Boxing Day?'

'Lovely,' Betty said, then yawning to feign tiredness, 'It's been lovely to see you, darling.'

Taking the hint, he said, 'Why don't you have a little nap, Mum? I know you said you're over the flu, but it's taken a lot out of you.'

'I won't argue with that.'

John leaned forward, giving her another kiss on the cheek. 'Bye for now, but I'll ring you later to see how you are.'

'Bye, darling.'

When Betty heard the front door close behind her son, she sighed with relief. It was just as she hoped. John was going to his father's party, and once he heard what Paula had to say, it would change everything.

Chapter Thirty-two

'Morning, Paula, how's things?' Keith asked as she walked up to his machine.

'Fine thanks.'

'How's the budgie?'

Paula smiled. Since Keith had given her a lift home weeks ago, he'd never mentioned what happened, but always asked after the bird. 'He's fine, but a noisy bugger now that he's settled. He's even worse if I play music – I reckon he tries to join in.'

'Are you sure he's not a canary?'

'I'm sure. He's blue, not yellow.'

'I know, I'm only joking. Have you heard from Charlie yet?'

'No, but I expect he's still on board.'

'Yeah, and after the skinful of booze he had at the going-away party, he's probably still suffering. You should've come, Paula. It was a right laugh.'

'Pubs ain't my scene.'

'So you said. But if you don't like pubs, dancing,

or anything else by the sound of it, what *do* you get up to in your spare time?'

With a shrug, Paula said, 'I meet me mates, listen to music, things like that . . . And before you ask me yet again, I ain't going out with you.'

'Don't worry, I've given up now. Anyway, I rather like the look of that new girl on Pete's machine.'

'Good luck, but I don't fancy your chances,' she told him whilst refusing to acknowledge a twinge of jealousy.

'Why not?'

'You'll find out,' and grinning from ear to ear she climbed onto her stool.

Keith started the machine and once again the daily grind began. With so much to occupy her mind, Paula was hardly aware of the noise as once again she tried to assimilate all the stuff Betty had tried to drum into her about her husband. Paula knew that if she couldn't convince them, if she slipped up, Betty's plan would fail, and with only eight days to go the responsibility hung over her head like a dark cloud. When it came to putting Ian Parker away, they had all risked so much for her. She'd had little part to play in Cheryl's plan, but this time the major role was hers. What if it all went wrong? What if she couldn't pull it off?

'Here, Paula, what makes you think I won't have a chance with that new girl?'

'What? Sorry, I was miles away.'

Keith's smile was wide. 'Dreaming about me, were you?'

'No I sodding well wasn't. Now bugger off and leave me in peace.'

'All right, all right,' he said, holding both hands up in surrender. 'I'll go and chat up Lucy then.'

With her train of thought now lost, Paula continued to feed paper into the rollers, but was unable to resist glancing at Keith as he walked up to the new girl. She couldn't hear what they were saying, but soon the look on Keith's face was a picture. When he marched away, Paula bit on her lower lip, trying not to roar with laughter, yet unable to hold back a chortle.

'Yeah, go on, but instead of having a good laugh, you could have warned me,' Keith said indignantly.

'Warned you about what?'

'That she prefers women and makes no secret of it.' He scratched his head, perplexed, as once again he glanced at the pretty, dark-haired woman. 'Bloody hell, what a waste. You'd stand more chance with her than I do.'

'Never mind, Keith, you can't win 'em all.'

'Here, come to think of it, I've seen you sitting with her in the canteen. Is that it? Are you another one like her? Is that why you keep turning me down?'

The smile left Paula's face. She knew he was only joking, and she liked Keith, but this was a joke too far. 'Who I sit with, and why, is none of your flaming business. I like Lucy a lot, so stick that in your pipe and smoke it.'

'Huh, I should have guessed. I was daft enough to think you were off men because you've been given a bad time. What an idiot I've been,' Keith growled, shaking his head as he stormed off.

Paula was livid. She wasn't a lesbian, but as far as she was concerned, Keith could think what he damn well liked. Yeah, in fact it would ensure that he left her alone, and that suited her just fine.

Betty was getting excited. Eight days to go before Richard got his comeuppance and she couldn't wait. She'd been back at work for over a week now, and between jobs had written copious lists of extra things to tell Paula. Of course most would probably be a waste of time, but she wanted to ensure that every question thrown, every attempt to trip Paula up, would fail.

If everything worked to plan it would be perfect, and once it was over she could start thinking about her wedding outfit. True to his word, John had made sure she was now kept up to date with the arrangements. Ulrika had rung twice, and they had begun to speak easily, but a final colour had yet to be decided for the bridesmaids' dresses, though the leading contender so far was her own suggestion of pale apricot.

Betty stopped to look at herself in the hall mirror, determined not to put weight back on. She wanted to find an outfit that was stylish, sophisticated, and one that would be guaranteed to turn Richard's head. Val was sure to help, and there'd be no more perms. Instead she was going for a younger-looking cut and even a rinse to cover her grey. With make-up, a manicure and the perfect hat, Richard would see a new woman. Oh, she couldn't wait to see his face.

The house was, as usual, silent, and Betty was surprised that her employer hadn't returned to London for the winter season. There'd been no instructions to prepare the house, no need to remove dust covers, or to air the beds, and it was like working in a ghost house. If her employer stopped coming to London, would he keep the house on? Would she still have a job or would she be obsolete? Oh, what did it matter? She had already decided to make changes in the New Year, and once she'd found another job, she would hand in her notice.

Val too was at work, but as she listened to Mr Warriner her face took on a stunned expression. 'You're going to retire?' she parroted.

'Yes, Val, but don't worry, it won't be until the end of January so this will give you plenty of time to find another position. I will, of course, give you a glowing reference.'

'Oh . . . oh dear, this has come as a bit of a shock. You . . . you don't seem old enough to retire.'

'I'm not far off sixty, and it's something my wife and I have been discussing for some time. We'd like to travel, to see a bit of the world before we become too decrepit to manage it.'

Val saw that his face had saddened and she blurted out, 'You're not ill, are you?'

'I'm fine, but my wife has rheumatoid arthritis. At the moment she's still mobile, but there'll come a time when she won't be fit to travel.'

'I'm so sorry. I didn't know.'

'Yes, well, as I was saying, I'll be closing the business at the end of January. I've been in touch with some of my clients, and for the others I've drafted a letter to recommend another solicitor. Will you get them typed and posted as soon as possible?'

'Yes, of course.'

'Oh, and Val, I'm happy for you to take time off to attend interviews.'

'Thank you.'

Mr Warriner returned to his office. Taking up the draft letter, Val found that the words blurred before her eyes. She'd been dissatisfied with her job and was often bored but, now that she was losing it, Val knew it was unlikely that she'd find another boss as nice as Mr Warriner. It wasn't the best-paid job in the world, her earnings a fraction of what they used to be, but she doubted she'd find anything better.

Yes, and that was thanks to Mike Freeman. Oh, he'd suffer, she'd make sure he suffered, and then he'd know how it felt to have his qualifications and ideas count for nothing.

Cheryl's mind was elsewhere as she went about her work on the ward. She'd found the perfect property, but that was only the start. Her mortgage application was in, along with her business plan, and they were just awaiting approval. The bank manager hadn't foreseen a problem, so once they were cleared she'd be able to go ahead with the next stage. It had been hard to fob off Paula, to say that she was still looking for a house, but Cheryl didn't want to reveal her plans until everything was in place. Her stomach lurched at the enormity of what she was about to do, but along with that came a shiver of excitement. The list of things to do was endless. She'd need help, but finding just the right people wasn't going to be easy. Cheryl hoped that Paula would be one of them, but even if she wasn't interested, with the basement flat she could still offer her a home, and one that was nicer than her poky bedsit.

At last Cheryl's shift was over and she went back to her quarters on weary feet. She felt on the brink of a new life, a fresh start, but was still tied to Betty and Val. Thankfully she wasn't involved in Betty's plan, but there was still Val's and she dreaded the thought of playing a part.

With a heavy sigh Cheryl knew she couldn't go back on her promise. She *was* involved, would have to stay that way until Betty and Val's plans were complete. It was thanks to the others that she had her money back, with the opportunity now to fulfil her dream. There'd be no such opportunity for Betty. She might gain some satisfaction from seeing her husband suffer, but there'd be no financial gain. It would be the same for Val, and deep down Cheryl still wished they'd let the past go instead of being intent on revenge.

Paula had spent the evening with Betty, but was now glad to be home, poky bedsit or not. Her head was aching from so much information, most of which she felt unnecessary. When Val came up to Betty's flat, Paula had been sad to hear she was going to lose her job, and with the need to take her mind off it, Val was given the task of asking her questions about Betty's husband. Paula managed a smile now. She had answered most of them without hesitation, and had received high praise, but now all she wanted to do was to climb into bed and forget about Richard Grayson for a while.

- With her nightdress on she went over to the budgie, the bird cocking his head as he looked at her. 'Time for bed, Charlie,' she told him, placing a cover over the cage. She'd become so fond of him, his cheerful chirps greeting her when she came home every day, and had taken to letting him out every evening, gratified that he was now happy to perch on her outstretched finger.

Yawning widely, Paula got into bed. As she laid her head on the pillow, her thoughts returned to Val. It was rotten that she had to find a new job, but at least she'd find a decent one. Unlike me, Paula thought. All she'd known was one factory after another, one mindless job after another, and all had bored her to tears. With another wide yawn, she closed her eyes, soon fast asleep.

When the alarm sounded, Paula fumbled to switch if off, unable to believe it was morning. It felt as if she'd only just gone to sleep before it was time to get up again and she blinked blearily as she threw back the blankets. It was still dark outside and, shivering, she threw on a dressing gown before hurrying along the landing to the bathroom. Another day at work. Another day of feeding sheet after sheet of paper into a machine. Gawd, what a life, Paula thought as she cleaned her teeth. Still, at least she had the occasional laugh now, if not with Keith then with the other girls, and it helped to break up the day.

Paula returned to her room, dressed, and then went over to the cage, pulling off the cover. 'Mornin', Charlie.'

No! No! Oh God, he was on the bottom of the cage and even as she frantically opened the little door to reach for him, Paula knew he was dead. Her hands closed round his tiny form. 'Oh, Charlie, Charlie,' she cried, tears now rolling down her cheeks as she held his fragile little body in the palm of her hand.

Chapter Thirty-three

Paula's eyes were red-rimmed from crying as she walked up to Keith's machine.

'Watcha, love,' he said cheerily, but then his eyes narrowed. 'You're late. What's up?'

She hadn't wanted to come to work, had sat on her bed for ages, the budgie still in the palm of her hand whilst her fingers stroked his stiff little body. It was only the thought of remaining on her own all day that had forced her out, and after gently placing Charlie in a small box, she had fled her room.

With watery eyes she looked at Keith. 'It's Charlie. He . . . he's dead.'

'What? Oh blimey, the poor old sod. No wonder you look upset,' and as Paula began to cry in earnest he frantically scanned the room until he saw the person he was looking for. 'Joyce!' he yelled.

The forewoman came bustling over and, taking one look at Paula, she said, 'Oh, dear, what's the matter?'

It was Keith who answered. 'She's just heard that Charlie's dead. I think you should get her out of here for a while.'

Joyce's hand clutched her heart. 'No, not Charlie! I can't believe it. When did it happen, Paula?'

'It . . . it must have been during the night. I found him dead this morning.'

Joyce frowned. 'But I thought he was on his way to New Zealand.'

'No, no, I'm talking about his budgie.'

'Oh for fuck's sake, Paula,' Keith exploded.

'There's no need for that language,' Joyce protested, but then there was a titter and soon both she and Keith were doubled over with mirth. 'A budgie!' Joyce gasped. 'And like me, you thought Paula was talking about Charlie Riley.'

'Yeah, well, he's called Charlie too, and with the state she's in, it's no surprise I made a mistake. Paula, you're a right dozy dollop. You really had me going for a minute.'

Paula turned and fled, bursting through the machine-room doors, on through the loading bay and out into the fresh air. It was freezing, but she was unaware of the cold as tears rained down her cheeks. He wasn't *just* a budgie. He was Charlie's budgie and she'd promised to take care of him. A hand touched her shoulder and she turned to find the forewoman by her side.

'Paula, I need you on the machine. We can't stop

production for a budgie. I'm sorry we laughed at you, but if you can't do your work you'll have to go home and forfeit a day's pay.'

Paula hunched her shoulders. She didn't want to go back to the machine room, didn't want to face Keith's mirth, yet couldn't really afford to lose a day's pay. 'All right, I'm going back,' she said, brushing tears from her cheeks. With a sniff, and head held high now, she walked back inside, finding to her surprise that Keith was looking shamefaced.

'Sorry, munchkin. I shouldn't have laughed, but you've got to admit it was funny.'

'Not to me,' she snapped, climbing onto her stool.

'How about I make amends by taking you out tonight?'

'Sod off.'

'Charming, but as you're upset I'll let it pass. Now, are you ready to start work?'

'Yes,' she said, voice clipped, and for the rest of the morning she kept her head down, mindlessly feeding paper into the machine whilst Keith gave her a wide berth.

At lunch time, Paula was feeling a little better as she hurried outside to smoke a cigarette. When she was greeted by titters, it was obvious that the forewoman had told the story.

'Blimey, Paula, when Joyce told me, I cracked up,' Doreen said.

'Yeah, talk about funny,' Greta agreed. 'Keith's face must have been a picture. There he was, trying to console you about Charlie Riley, and all the time you were talking about his budgie.'

'I'm glad you all find it funny, but *I* don't.'

'If it'd been a cat or a dog, I'd have understood,' said Doreen. 'We were upset when our spaniel had to be put down. But a *budgie*!'

Paula ground her cigarette underfoot, saying nothing as she spun round to head for the canteen, only to be greeted with laughter, this time from the men. She stood in the queue, flushed with embarrassment.

'Take no notice of them,' Lucy said as she stepped up behind Paula. 'They're all pigs.'

'I suppose you've heard the story too?'

'I have, but my dad keeps budgies so I can see why you were upset. If you want a replacement, I'm sure I can get you one.'

'Thanks, but I don't think I could face it. Charlie was special and really tame. I thought I was doing all right, that I was looking after him, but I must have done something wrong and now he's dead.'

'How old was he?'

'I . . . I dunno.'

'I doubt you did anything wrong. If he was passed on to you, he was probably old, that's all.'

'Do you think so?'

'Yes, now come on, it's your turn to order.'

Paula felt marginally better as she ordered a sandwich. If Lucy was right, Charlie hadn't died from lack of care, but from old age. She paid for her food along with a cup of tea and then sat down at a vacant table. It was all right for people to laugh, but she'd grown fond of Charlie, would miss his chirpy greeting when she went home. Still, at least she wouldn't be stuck in her bedsit for much longer, and she brightened as another thought now struck her. If Cheryl found a place with a garden they could get another pet, maybe a kitten.

Lucy pulled out a chair. 'Mind if I join you?'

'No, of course not.'

'Aren't you afraid of getting tarred with the same brush?'

'People can think what they like, and that includes Keith.'

Lucy's eyebrows rose. 'Oh, so he's been making comments?'

'Yes, but I don't care. I wouldn't touch him or any other bloke with a bargepole.'

'Leave it out, Paula. I know you're straight, so why the attitude? Have you been hurt? Is that it?'

Paula shrugged, saying dismissively, 'Maybe.'

'There's plenty more fish in the sea. Take Keith, for instance. I can see he fancies you and, despite what you say, he seems a nice bloke.'

'I'm not interested,' Paula said, and annoyed that

Lucy sounded just like Charlie Riley, she deflected the attention from herself by asking, 'What about you? Ain't you ever fancied men?'

'No, but it doesn't stop them trying. When I started work here, for the first time I decided to be upfront. I thought it would be the easiest way to keep the blokes at bay, but I'm regretting it now. It backfired, and all the women give me a wide berth.'

'I don't.'

'You're the only one who doesn't and I'm wondering why.'

'All the other girls talk about is men – who they fancy or their latest boyfriend – and it gets on my nerves. If they give you the cold shoulder, it's their problem. I think it's up to you how you live your life. You ain't hurting anyone, so what's the problem?'

'I think I scare them. Take that ugly cow, Doreen. I wouldn't fancy her in a million years, but she's obviously terrified I'll try it on. She must be kidding. I don't fancy every woman I see, just as you don't fancy every man; and anyway, I'm in a steady relationship. You should give it a try, Paula; dip your toe in the water again. As I said, Keith obviously fancies you.'

'I don't want a boyfriend, least of all him.'

'That's a shame, because I think you're meant to be together.'

'Leave it out! What makes you think that?'

'I don't know, it's just a feeling. When you're

337

together I see these strange little lights bouncing between you.'

'Now you sound weird,' Paula protested.

'I've been told I'm a bit psychic,' Lucy said, but then grinned widely.

'You daft cow. You had me going there for a bit,' Paula chuckled. She finished her sandwich and gulped her tea before saying, 'If all you're going to talk about is Keith, I'm going outside for another fag. See you later.'

'Yeah, see you,' Lucy called.

With a smile still on her face, Paula walked outside to light a cigarette. Huh, lights bouncing between her and Keith. What a load of rubbish. First Charlie Riley, and now Lucy, both waxing lyrical about Keith, trying to matchmake. Why? He wasn't that special. He wasn't even good looking, and as for Lucy saying that they were meant to be together: bloody hell, she must be out of her mind.

Betty was waiting for Paula to arrive, and spread her arms to hug her when she opened the door. 'Oh, love, when you rang me, I was so sorry to hear about your budgie.'

Paula returned her embrace before saying sadly, 'I made a right fool of myself at work. Everyone had a good laugh and I felt a proper twit.'

'Why, what happened?'

When Paula told her, Betty too had to fight

laughter, but managed to stay composed. 'Never mind. I suppose I can see why they thought you were talking about Charlie Riley, but I'm sure it'll all be forgotten by tomorrow.'

'I hope so,' Paula said, sniffing as she moved away from Betty's arms.

'Take your coat off and settle yourself down. Val will be up in a minute, but if you like we'll forget about my husband this evening.'

'No, I'm all right. There's only a week to go and I want to make sure I remember everything you've told me.'

'I'm sure you'll be fine. Oh, that must be Val,' Betty added as she went to open her door.

'Hello,' Val said as she stepped inside. She smiled sympathetically when she saw Paula. 'I'm sorry to hear that you lost Charlie.'

'It was a bit of a shock, but I feel silly now for making such a fuss.'

'Val, any luck on the job front?' Betty asked.

'I don't think there's much point in looking until after Christmas. Most businesses, other than shops, will probably close at the weekend. I'll make a start in the New Year.'

'Talking about Christmas, Val, is Cheryl joining us?'

'Yes, for dinner, but I'm not sure about overnight.'

'Paula, are you still sleeping over?' Betty asked.

'Yeah, I'd love to.'

'That's good. I've started to get a few bits in: a box of Turkish delight, some dates, and I've made a fruitcake. It just needs icing.'

'I'll bring a few things. What else do you need?'

'Val's getting the chicken, so how about the vegetables?'

'All right. Give me a list of what you want.'

'It's a shame Cheryl hasn't found a flat or house yet,' Val said.

'She's been to see loads of places,' Paula complained, 'but just keeps saying that none of them are right.'

Betty held her tongue. Whenever she spoke to Cheryl about her search, she found her vague, almost standoffish, and wondered if there'd been a change of heart about offering Paula a home. Secretly it was what Betty wanted, her ideal solution. There was nothing to stop her moving – nothing to stop her from finding a two-bedroom flat and, if Paula contributed towards the rent, it would be ideal for both of them.

'Are you all right, Betty? You look miles away.'

'Sorry, Val, I was thinking about Richard,' Betty blustered, feeling her face turning pink at the lie. 'I'll make us all a drink and then we'll make a start.'

Betty hurried to the kitchen. She would miss Val if she moved and so far hadn't mentioned her idea. Of course, the ideal answer would be that they all

340

lived together, all shared a home, but would Val agree? Oh stop it, she told herself. Cheryl might not have changed her mind – in fact, why should she? Yet deep down, Betty prayed that she would.

Chapter Thirty-four

Betty found that the week leading up to Christmas Eve was agonisingly slow. She had saved a little, had been to Clapham Junction for her shopping, but once she'd found presents for John and Anne, along with their partners, there hadn't been a great deal of money left. Northcote Road market hadn't been far away, and ambling along she'd found a solution on the stalls; one of them perfect for Paula. She was used to this, used to making money stretch, and hunting for the gifts had filled a little more of her time.

It was her last day at work now and she locked the house, hoping once again that in the New Year she'd be able to find another job. Val had suggested a shop; though it would be nicer than cleaning, it wasn't really what she wanted. Yet what else could she do? Nothing much – nothing that would be rewarding and give her a sense of purpose.

When Betty arrived at the flats she knocked on Val's door to tell her that she was expecting her children to call, but if they didn't stay long, she'd be down to see her later. She then hurried upstairs to tidy up before grabbing a bite to eat.

By eight o'clock, Betty was hovering at her window, her face lighting up when she saw John's car. Ulrika was with him, and with a swift look in the mirror Betty patted her hair before going to the door. 'Hello, darling,' she cried as they appeared. 'Hello, Ulrika.'

On the threshold, John bent to kiss her cheek, and Betty was gratified when Ulrika did the same. 'Come on in. It's lovely to see you. Sit yourselves down, and how about a glass of sherry?'

John's eyes widened. 'Well, that's a first. I thought you were teetotal, Mum.'

'I was, but nowadays I enjoy the occasional glass of sherry.'

'Well, in that case, yes please.'

'What about you, Ulrika?' Betty asked.

'Yes please.'

Betty poured the drinks and was just about to hand them out when there was a tap on the door. 'That'll be Anne,' she said, smiling as she let her daughter in. 'Hello, sweetheart. We were just about to have a glass of sherry. Would you like one?'

'Hi you two, and no thanks, Mum. It's too sweet for me.'

'Hello, sis,' said John. 'Are you still off to Cornwall in the morning?'

343

'Yes, but I wish I hadn't agreed to go now. It's a long journey and a rotten way to spend Christmas Eve.'

Betty sipped her sherry. It was lovely to see her children, to have them here, but it wasn't the same as sharing Christmas Day. She could remember times past, when she and Richard had crept upstairs to put presents by the children's beds, and the joy on their faces when they opened them in the morning. Then later they would all sit down to the dinner she had loved to prepare, pulling crackers and laughing at the silly jokes. As she thought about the happy times they shared, Betty wished she could turn the clock back, but then felt a surge of bitterness. It was all right for Richard, he was having another child, a chance to do it all again, but for her . . .

'Mum, you're miles away. Are you all right?'

Betty forced a smile. 'I'm fine.'

'We've brought your present,' he said, 'but no opening it until Christmas Day.'

Betty took the large squashy parcel. 'Thank you, darling, thank you both,' and going to the tree she laid it down before picking up two prettily wrapped boxes. 'One for you and one for Ulrika, and the same goes for you. Don't open them until Christmas morning.'

'Thanks, Mum, and don't worry, we won't. Oh, and as you know, we've been invited to my boss's house for Christmas dinner. He's now suggested that we stay the night, and though I said we'd call round on Boxing Day, I'm not sure I can guarantee it now.'

'It doesn't matter, darling. I'm spending Christmas with friends, so though it would be lovely to see you, if you can't make it, don't worry.'

'That's a relief, but we'll do our best to get here.'

'Here, Mum,' said Anne as she pulled a small package out of her handbag.

'Thank you, darling,' Betty said, and as she had with John's present she laid it under the tree before finding two more packages, one for Anne and one for Tony.

Anne thanked her, and then turned to Ulrika. 'Did you try that dressmaker I told you about?'

'Yes, and she was very kind. I have made up my mind now, and will have apricot for the bridesmaids. She is going to make a start on them in the New Year.'

Betty smiled at Ulrika's so correct, but stilted pronunciation, saying warmly, 'I'm glad. I know when we spoke last you favoured that colour, and it's so pretty.'

'Oh, please, not the wedding again,' John appealed. 'Can't we at least give it a rest until after Christmas?'

They all laughed at his petulant expression, which didn't stop them from going on to discuss Ulrika's dress, veil and bouquet. Despite John's protest, a happy hour passed, but then Anne said, 'Sorry, I must go.'

'All right, darling. Have a lovely time in Cornwall, but drive carefully.'

'The wilds of Cornwall in winter aren't my idea of fun. It's a lovely place in the summer, but at this time of the year, Bodmin Moor will be bleak.'

'We'd better go too,' John said.

Betty gave all three of them a hug, sad to see them leave. 'Bye, and see you soon, I hope.'

'Bye, Mum,' John said. 'I'll ring you before we leave for my boss's house on Christmas Day.'

'Thank you, dear, and have a lovely time at your father's party tomorrow night.'

Betty remained standing at the open door as they went downstairs and, though out of sight now, Anne's voice carried upwards.

'What's come over Mum? I still can't believe she doesn't mind you going to Dad's party.'

Betty didn't hear her son's reply, but she had a smile on her face as she closed the door. Oh, she didn't mind John going to his father's party. In fact it was just what she wanted. But of course, neither of her children knew why.

One more night to go, Betty thought as she washed the sherry glasses before going downstairs to spend the rest of the evening with Val. One more night before Richard's party – how she wished she could be a fly on the wall to see their faces when Paula turned up.

* * *

346

Paula found that, just as Betty predicted, it hadn't been too bad at work. There were just a few titters here and there which had, as the week progressed, died out altogether. She had been put on another machine so saw little of Keith, but found that she missed his comical banter.

It was now Christmas Eve and the factory closed for the holidays, but at eight o'clock that evening, when Val drove her to Farnham, Paula was shaking with nerves. She was hardly aware of the journey as she went over and over all that Betty had told her, praying that she wouldn't slip up.

'Don't worry, you'll be fine,' Val assured her. 'I know Betty drummed a load of information into you, but to be honest, I doubt you'll be asked many questions, if any. All you have to do is say your piece, add a bit of personal stuff to make it convincing, and then leave.'

'If I let her down it'll be awful.'

'I'm sure you won't. It'll soon be over and, as you're staying over with Betty tonight, we'll wake up to a wonderful Christmas Day. It'll be your birthday too, and something else to celebrate.'

Paula knew that Val was trying to calm her, but still she trembled. 'What if they don't believe me?'

'It might help if you step away from yourself. You aren't Paula; you're someone else, like an actress playing a role in a play or film. I did that when the police questioned me about Cheryl's supposed rape.

I took on another persona, pretended that I was a haughty, standoffish woman.'

'All right, I'll try,' Paula said. She had to do this. The others had done so much for her and this was for Betty – lovely, kind, caring Betty who had come to mean so much to her.

By the time they reached Farnham and Val drew into the kerb at the end of a very posh-looking cul-de-sac, Paula felt that her advice had done the trick. She did feel better now, ready to play her new role. 'Right, what's the time?'

'It's just coming up to nine o'clock. All the guests should be there so it's perfect.'

Paula opened the door. 'I'm off.'

'Good luck,' Val called.

Paula walked along the tree-lined cul-de-sac, looking for the house that Betty had described. They were all large, all set back, some gated with long drives, but at last, on the curve, Paula found the one she was looking for. For a moment she just stared at it, unable to picture the Betty she knew living in such a grand place.

The grounds were well lit, the gates open and, as Paula walked down the drive, she skirted some very expensive cars. She faltered. Blimey, the place was probably full of toffs. She felt out of place, out of her depth, and for a moment wanted to turn and flee. Come on, come on, she urged, moving forward on shaky legs. The house seemed to loom over her now, bright lights shining through leaded windows as she forced herself back into the persona she'd invented.

Paula straightened her shoulders, and with what now felt like righteous indignation, she lifted a large, black metal knocker on the heavily studded oak door. When opened by a well-dressed woman, Paula had no idea who she was. She wasn't pregnant so it couldn't be Mel, but nothing was going to stop her now. She strode forcefully in without invitation, and in the spacious hall demanded, 'I'd like to see Richard Grayson.'

The woman looked bemused, but before she could respond Paula heard the buzz of voices and headed towards the sound.

'Wait,' the woman called as she hurried behind her, but Paula was already through the open double doors of a large room, seeking the face of the man that Betty had shown her in photographs.

He was there, by the hearth, standing by a roaring fire and talking to a group of men. Paula drew in a huge breath, stretched her neck, head held high as she brushed past guests to confront him.

Standing rigid in front of Richard Grayson now, arms akimbo, Paula yelled, 'You bastard!'

The man's eyes widened and his tone of voice echoed his shock. 'I beg your pardon?'

'You heard me! You didn't tell me you're married.'

The room fell silent, all eyes on the scene now as

he said, 'I don't know what you're talking about. Who are you? And how did you get into my house?'

'Don't give me that. You know who I am all right.'

'Richard, what's going on?'

Paula spun round to see a heavily pregnant woman, and guessed it was Mel. 'Huh, you must be his wife, but don't bother to ask him. He'll only lie, just like he lied to me.'

Mel looked confused and, ignoring Paula, she asked, 'Richard, who is she?'

'How the hell do I know? I've never seen her in my life before.'

'See, I told you, *lies*,' Paula spat, and turning to look the man in the eye again, she added, 'and I ain't going anywhere until your *wife* hears what I've got to say.'

'Richard . . .' Mel wailed.

'It's all right, leave this to me,' Richard Grayson said, and grabbing Paula's arm he tried to drag her from the room. 'I *don't* know who you are, *or* what your game is, but I want you out of my house – *now!*'

'Get off me,' Paula yelled, and wrenching her arm from his grasp she once again rounded on Mel. 'He knows me all right, but I didn't know I was his bit on the side, honest I didn't. When one of my mates told me he's married, I nearly had a fit.'

'No, no, I don't believe you,' Mel cried.

Paula felt a stab of pity, but forced it from her

mind. This was the woman who had stolen Betty's husband – the woman who had driven her from this lovely house. 'You should believe me, because other than the satisfaction of having it out with that cheating bastard, I've got nothing to gain from coming here.'

'Shut up! You must be mad – out of your mind!' Richard Grayson roared.

'Yeah, I was mad to believe your lies,' Paula retorted. She felt everyone's eyes on her and nearly wavered, but then taking another deep breath she fought to remain in role. She was on stage and the guests were her audience as she spat out her next lines. 'You said you were a widower . . . that your wife died years ago. I only slept with you because you promised we'd get engaged.'

'No . . . no,' Mel cried, swaying as she held a hand to her head.

Richard Grayson moved swiftly, taking her arm. 'John, give me a hand,' he called. 'I think Mel's going to faint.'

Paula saw the young man step forward, his voice a low growl. 'Is it true, Dad?'

'What? Of course it isn't. Look at her. She's younger than your sister.'

'Huh, that didn't stop him,' Paula snapped as she met John's eyes. 'Yeah, I must have been mad, but after some of the young twerps I've been out with, it was nice being an old man's darling.'

John's face twisted with disgust. 'You're as bad as him.'

'Shut up, John! Can't you see she's lying?'

Paula's tone was scathing, 'Oh yeah, well if I ain't telling the truth, how come I know about the scar on your leg? You know, Richard, the one at the top of your thigh.'

John's eyes narrowed with suspicion as he looked at his father. 'Yes, Dad, how *does* she know about your scar?'

Before he could answer, Paula said, 'That's not all, is it, Richard? I've seen every part of you – for instance that mole on your back . . . And if that's not enough, what about your feet? It's not everyone who has six toes!'

Mel gave a cry of anguish, pulling herself away from Richard, but as she fled her legs seemed to go from under her and she crashed to the floor.

'Mel!' Richard Grayson yelled as he crouched by her side. He then looked up, his eyes frantic. 'John, please, help to get her up.'

John stood unmoving, his jaws working in anger, but a young woman who'd been standing by his side rushed forward, followed by two men.

'Ulrika, no. Come on, we're leaving,' John ordered.

She shook her head, refusing to leave Mel's side, and soon after she came round. She groaned as they helped her up and moved her towards a sofa, whilst

Richard asked worriedly, 'Mel, are you all right? Do you want me to call the doctor?'

'No, get away from me. Don't touch me.'

'I think it would be best if I got everyone to leave,' one of the men said.

'Yes, yes, thanks,' Richard agreed, his face now as white as Mel's as she sank onto the sofa.

Paula saw the disdain on the guests' faces as they looked at her, but she was also pleased to see that many also threw Richard Grayson a look of disgust as they left.

'Mel, come on, let's get you upstairs,' Richard urged.

'No, no, leave me alone. I hate you! I hate you!' she cried, her voice stronger now, bordering on hysteria.

Richard Grayson rounded on Paula, his voice a roar. 'You did this! You and your lies. I'm calling the police. You should be locked up.'

At the threat of the police turning up, Paula baulked, but knew she didn't dare show fear. 'Call them, I don't care. I haven't done anything wrong. It's you who should be locked up . . . you who were sleeping with me while your poor wife is pregnant.'

On that note, Paula turned to march from the room, her heart thumping in her chest. She hurried along the hall and out of the front door, brushing past a young woman who was just coming in. Paula hardly noticed her, or the puzzled look the woman gave her, her sole focus to get away from the house. Guests were still leaving, climbing into cars, but outside now, Paula felt a surge of relief. She'd got some of what Betty had told her in first and, judging by Mel's reaction, it had been enough.

Betty couldn't sit still. She went to look out of the window for what felt like the hundredth time, but so far there was no sign of Val's car. Had it worked? Had Paula pulled it off? Oh, come on, come on, she urged, her eyes once again on the road outside.

At last Val's car pulled up and Betty strained to see their faces as they climbed out, but they had their heads down as they hurried into the flats. She ran to her door, flinging it open, and when they appeared on the staircase, both grinning widely, she cried, 'You did it! I can see by your faces that you did it!'

'Yeah, it went like a dream,' Paula said as she and Val walked inside.

'What did he say? Oh come on, Paula, tell me all about it.'

'I could do with a cup of tea,' Val said, 'but I can see you're too excited to make one. I'll do it while Paula tells you what happened.'

Betty nodded, hardly aware of Val, her eyes on Paula as the girl flopped onto the sofa. She sat opposite, leaning forward eagerly as Paula spoke.

'I marched in, found Richard, and you should have seen his face . . .'

As the story unfolded, Betty grew more and more excited. John had been there, had heard every word. But when Paula got to the part about Mel collapsing she frowned, interrupting Paula to ask, 'Was she all right?'

'Yeah, I think so. She fainted, but soon came round, and then she wouldn't let Richard near her.'

'Do you think it was an act, or did Mel really pass out?'

'I dunno. She seemed all right when I left.'

'Thank goodness for that, and as she wouldn't let Richard near her, she must have believed you.'

'I'm sure she did; your son too.'

The air left Betty's body in a huge sigh. It had worked, her plan had worked, but would Mel leave Richard? Oh surely she would. 'Paula, I don't know how to thank you.'

'There's no need. Anyway, it was nothing compared to what you all did for me.'

Val came in now, carrying a tray, her smile wry. 'Did Paula tell you that he also threatened to call the police?'

'Did he? Oh dear.'

'Don't worry, Betty, I left before he got the chance,' Paula assured her.

Val laid the tray down. 'We've got nothing to worry about. They have no idea who Paula is, or where she came from. Now that it's over, tea hardly seems appropriate. We should be having a toast, but to be honest I'm so dry and tea will be the only thing to quench my thirst.'

The telephone rang and Betty rose to answer it. 'Hello, Cheryl. Yes, they're back and it went like a dream.'

She listened, and then turned to speak to Val and Paula. 'Cheryl says well done, and she'll see us in the morning.'

Val nodded and, after a few more words, Betty replaced the receiver, saying as she walked across the room to sit beside Paula, 'It was nice of her to ring.'

'It would have been nicer if she'd been here,' Val said.

'I know, but she didn't finish work until six o'clock and then had to view another house.'

Val pursed her lips. 'I'm surprised she got an appointment on Christmas Eve.'

'I was, too – but never mind, she'll be here in the morning. And talking of the morning, look at the time. It's gone eleven and in less than an hour it'll be Christmas Day.' Betty felt a surge of joy and clapped her hands with glee. 'Oh, I still can't believe the plan worked. For me it's going to be the best Christmas in years. Richard will never be able to hold his head up again after this. Once an adulterer might have been forgivable, but *twice!* Even if his male business acquaintances and friends turn a blind eye, I'm sure their wives won't. He'll be ostracised and it serves him right. But best of all, my son heard and saw it all! He'll never forgive his father this time – and wait until Anne hears about it. Surely this will knock her father off his pedestal?'

'Yes, I'm sure it will,' Val agreed. She yawned widely. 'Oh, sorry, but I'm worn out and think it's time for bed. Goodnight, you two, and I'll see you in the morning.'

As Val stood up, Betty rose too, impulsively throwing her arms around her friend. 'Val, you've been wonderful and meeting you made all this possible. Thank you – thank you so much.'

For a moment, Val remained stiff in her arms, but then she seemed to relax and returned Betty's hug. 'Three down and one to go,' she said, a smile on her face as she pulled away. 'Goodnight, and sleep well.'

'Oh I will,' Betty enthused.

'Night, Val, see you in the morning,' Paula called.

'Goodnight, and once again, well done, Paula.'

'Thanks,' she said, smiling with pleasure.

Betty closed the door behind Val, then asked, 'What about you, Paula, are you ready for bed?'

'I think so. I was a bit wound up on the drive home, expecting to hear police sirens.'

'As Val said, nobody knows who you are, or where you live, and anyway, you didn't break the law. Come on, let's make your bed up. I just hope you'll be comfortable on the sofa.'

'I'll be fine.'

It didn't take long, and now Betty kissed Paula on the cheek. 'Goodnight, love, sleep tight.'

'Night, Betty,' Paula called as she began to undress.

Betty threw her one last warm smile, and soon she too was climbing into bed. She pulled the blankets up to her chin, trying to picture the scene when Paula had confronted Richard. Oh, to have seen his face, Betty thought, unaware that she was still smiling as she finally drifted off to sleep.

In Farnham, Richard returned to the drawing room to see John sitting, elbows on knees, his face buried in his hands, whilst Ulrika remained quietly by his side.

It was midnight and so much had been said. The doctor had left now, but John was still there, an anguished expression on his face as he looked up to ask, 'Why, Dad?'

'John, I've had enough for one night, and all I care about at the moment is Mel. The doctor's worried, so much so that if she isn't any better by morning, he thinks she'll need to go into hospital. He'll be round again first thing – it's good of him to turn out on Christmas Day.'

'Is she asleep?' Ulrika asked.

'Yes, and thank God for that. Her blood pressure rocketed with all the stress and I just hope it's gone down by morning.'

'Come on, Ulrika, let's go home,' John said as he rose to his feet.

'What are you going to do, John?'

'What do you think, Dad? This is unforgivable.'

With his face set in anger, John then took Ulrika's arm and almost dragged her from the room.

'John!'

Richard was ignored, and soon he heard the front door slam. Yes, it was unforgivable and his son understandably upset, but for now, as he had told John, all he cared about was Mel.

Chapter Thirty-five

Betty awoke early, and her first thought was Richard. Had Mel left him? She hoped so. In fact she hoped he was very alone, as alone as she'd been every Christmas since their marriage ended. But not this year. This year would be spent with friends – ones with whom she'd shared so much; ones who had become a substitute family.

With a smile on her face, Betty threw back the blankets and, after putting on her thick, warm dressing gown, she tied the belt firmly around her waist. It wasn't just Christmas Day, it was Paula's birthday, so softly opening her bedroom door she crept into the living room, only to find that Paula was already awake. 'Oh, you're up. Was it uncomfortable on the sofa?'

'A bit,' she admitted, 'but it's lovely to be here and tons better than waking up in my bedsit.'

'Well then, Happy Birthday,' Betty beamed, bending down to give her a kiss before she hurried to light the fire.

Paula grinned. 'Thanks, and while you're doing that, I'll make us a drink.'

'Smashing,' Betty said, whilst hoping that John would ring soon. She could anticipate what he'd have to say, but of course she would have to feign surprise, and of course, disgust. There'd be no more spending time with his father now and, when Anne heard about it, surely she'd feel the same?

Betty sat by the lit fire, appreciating its warmth. Paula returned with drinks on a tray, and she smiled with pleasure. Oh, this was so different from last year when she had only seen Anne and John for a couple of hours, the rest of the time spent alone with only her radio for company.

'Lovely,' Betty said when Paula handed her a cup of tea, 'and once I've had this, I'll make our breakfast.'

'A bit of toast will do me,' Paula said. She looked at the Christmas tree and the small pile of packages at the base. 'When are we going to open our presents?'

'Val and I decided that we'd celebrate your birthday first. We'll open our Christmas presents later.'

With wide-eyed wonder Paula said, 'Really? Blimey, that's great.'

Paula looked so pretty now, fresh-faced, happy, and so different from the pale shadow of a girl that Betty had first met. There were still traces of nerves, but she was smoking less, drinking less, her eyes bright and clear. 'Paula, what about your mum? Didn't she invite you to spend Christmas with her?'

'You must be joking. Her bloke has made it plain that he doesn't want me around and Mum ain't about to upset him. She did send me a card, though, with a ten-bob note in it.'

'It's Christmas morning and surely it wouldn't hurt to ring her?'

Paula frowned, small teeth biting into her lower lip. 'Yeah, I suppose I could do that.'

'I'll leave you to it,' Betty said as she went to the kitchenette.

She tried not to listen, but couldn't help over-hearing when Paula's voice rose in anger.

'Why should I buy him a Christmas present?' she yelled. 'Alfie ain't me dad! In fact, I don't know who is.'

'No, I ain't apologising, and you seem to forget that Alfie didn't want anything to do with me.'

Betty walked into the room to see Paula staring at the receiver and, replacing it, she said, 'That was a waste of time. She hung up on me. I got her a nice scarf, the best I could afford, but she's got the hump because I didn't send Alfie a present.'

'Yes, I gathered that,' Betty said, smiling wryly. Yet she felt there was more to this than met the eye and said gently, 'It must have been hard for you when she first met him, and perhaps you were a bit resentful. Maybe Alfie found you difficult, or sulky, something like that.'

Paula's eyes narrowed in thought. 'I suppose there could be something in that, but to be honest, men came and went with my mum and I soon cottoned on that it was daft to look for a dad in any of them. They never stayed long, so mostly I just kept out of their way. When Mum met Alfie, I thought he'd go the same route, so you could have knocked me down with a feather when they got married.'

'How did you react?'

'I wasn't funny with him. We just didn't gel. All he wanted was me mum, and I was just someone who was in the way, someone who stopped him getting her full attention.'

'What a shame. She should have put her foot down, told him that if he wanted her, he'd have to accept you too.'

'Leave it out, Betty. My mum was never the maternal type, and she ain't gonna change now. I'm not naïve enough to believe that we'll ever play happy families. She's found a mug who'll look after her, and if they want me out of the picture, that's fine with me.'

'But . . .'

'Please, can we change the subject?'

Betty accepted defeat. It seemed that nothing could change Paula's relationship with her mother.

'Eat your toast and then we'd best get dressed. There won't be any buses running, and I know Val's picking Cheryl up at ten.'

When there was a knock on the door at ten-thirty, they were washed, dressed and ready. 'That'll be Val and Cheryl. Let them in, love.'

Paula jumped up to open the door, finding Val laden down with parcels, all balanced precariously up to her chin. 'Gawd, let me give you a hand,' she offered.

'Put them under the tree with the others,' Betty urged.

'Happy Christmas everyone,' Cheryl said as she crouched beside Paula to lay her presents alongside the others. She then stood up, one still in her hand. 'Happy Birthday, Paula.'

'Cor, thanks. Can I open it now?'

'Yes, of course you can.'

Val handed her another one, whilst Betty reached down beside her chair. 'And here's mine.'

Paula's face was pink with pleasure as she sat down, opening them one by one. There was a bottle of Tweed perfume from Val, a make-up bag and lipstick from Cheryl. Paula thanked them profusely, but when she came to Betty's present, her face positively beamed. 'Oh, they're lovely.'

Since finding off-cuts of material on a market stall, Betty had been busy on her sewing machine. She'd made Paula a matching skirt and bolero in a pretty blue woollen material. 'I'm glad you like them, but if they don't fit I can make alterations.'

Paula jumped to her feet. 'I'm gonna try them on,' she said, lightly running from the room.

When Paula came back, Betty smiled with delight. The outfit looked lovely, the skirt sitting two inches above her knees. 'If it's too long, I can take it up,' she offered.

'No, I don't wear miniskirts now and this is perfect,' she said, then giving a little twirl. 'This is my best birthday ever.'

The next hour was a happy one, with them all mucking in to prepare the vegetables for dinner. They then decided to open the Christmas presents. Paula was on her knees by the tree, handing them out, when there was a thump on the door.

'Goodness, I wonder who that is,' Betty said as she went to open it. 'Anne!'

'How could you! How could you do such a thing?' Anne yelled as she pushed past Betty to storm into the room.

Paula was still on her knees, a package clutched in her hand as Anne marched up to her, eyes blazing. 'You bitch! I knew it! I knew it was you.'

'Anne, what are you doing here?' Betty cried. 'I thought you were in Cornwall.'

'That would have suited you fine, wouldn't it!' Anne cried as she turned to her mother. 'But we had problems with the car and had to turn back. If it wasn't for that, your sick, rotten scheme might have worked. But I was there, Mum, and turned up at Dad's just in time to see *her* leaving.'

'No . . . no,' Betty cried, shrinking away from the look of anger and disgust on her daughter's face.

'Why, Mum? Why did you do it?'

'You know why,' she cried in defence. 'You know what your father did to me.'

'Not again! How many times have we been over this? Yes, Dad found someone else. Yes, he had to virtually force you to leave, but you left him no choice.'

'No choice! I gave my life to your father, but then he moved that . . . that woman into my home.'

'Shut up! That woman, as you often call Mel, was admitted to hospital early this morning. Her blood pressure has rocketed and it's touch and go whether she loses the baby. Her own life is at risk too, and if they die, Mum, what does that make you?'

Betty stared at her daughter in horror. She had wanted to bring Richard low – even to break up the marriage, but this . . . 'No, no, I didn't want to hurt the baby, or Mel.'

'And I'm supposed to believe that! You knew Mel had high blood pressure, but it didn't stop you, did it! Oh, I've had enough of this. John and Dad are at the hospital and I'm going back to see if there's any news. I'm sure they'll love to hear that – while Mel is fighting for her life, for her baby's life – you, your friends, and that . . . that evil bitch over there are having a lovely time celebrating Christmas.'

'John . . . John's there?'

'Yes, Mum. Your precious son has at last heard Dad's side of the story. He wouldn't listen to either of us before, but thanks to your little plan, he's now seen you for what you are.'

Betty was now frozen with shock, her feet unable to move beneath her as Anne stormed out. She managed to hold out a hand in appeal, but then the room grew dim. She heard a distant voice, saw pinpricks of light floating before her eyes; then, unaware of anything else, she crashed to the floor and into oblivion.

'Betty,' Cheryl cried, and was the first to rush to her side. Like the others she'd said nothing whilst Betty's daughter had confronted her. She had stood in shock, feeling helpless, but though she was kneeling by Betty now, she was sickened by what she'd heard. Betty had known that Mel had high blood pressure. As a woman who had borne two children, she knew the risks of upsetting her, yet during the planning she hadn't even mentioned it. Why? No, no, surely she hadn't wanted this to happen? Surely she hadn't wanted to put Mel and the baby at risk?

Val and Paula were by Cheryl's side now, both trying to help, but Betty remained unconscious and Cheryl frowned worriedly. 'I don't like the look of this.'

'What's the matter with her? Why won't she wake up?' Paula appealed.

'I don't know. Help me to roll her onto her side, and Val, call an ambulance.'

'But why? Surely she just fainted?'

'I think there's more to it than that. To be on the safe side I think she should go to casualty.'

'Oh God,' Val choked, rising swiftly to run to the telephone.

'Betty! Betty! Wake up, please wake up,' Paula begged, but to no avail.

Cheryl could see that Paula was shaking and sent her to find a cold cloth, anything to keep her occupied while they waited. Val looked frantic too, but at least she remained controlled, yet Cheryl sighed with relief when the ambulance arrived.

Betty was loaded into the back, Cheryl climbing in too, and after shouting to Val and Paula that she'd see them in casualty, the doors closed. Taking a seat she looked at Betty's ashen face, feeling sick inside, fearing the worst as the ambulance sped off.

Chapter Thirty-six

Anne's voice was ringing with hostility. 'I don't know why I bothered to go, John. As usual Mum just went on about how she gave her life to Dad.'

'That girl was so convincing. If you hadn't turned up when you did, I'd have fallen for her story hook, line and sinker. Poor Dad. Until we let everyone know, his name will be mud, and I dread to think how it's going to affect his business.'

'I think that's the least of his worries at the moment. Hasn't there been *any* news?'

'No, not yet. Dad's still in with Mel.'

'I hope she's all right, that the baby's all right,' Anne said worriedly.

The door opened, and both rose swiftly as their father walked in. He looked exhausted, his face etched with fatigue, but then he smiled. 'Mel's out of danger now, the baby too.'

'Oh, Dad,' Anne cried, throwing herself into her

369

father's arms. 'What about the Caesarean? Have they called it off?'

'Yes, but they're keeping her in for the time being.'

'Can I see her?'

'Sorry, darling, she's asleep now, but we can come back this evening.'

John stood to one side, still reeling with shock at what his mother had done. He too had wanted to confront her, had intended to drive to Battersea that morning, but then a frantic call from his father had stayed his hand. Anne had been so incensed that there'd been no stopping her, but feeling he couldn't leave his father on his own, he'd chosen to remain at the hospital. After listening to his father's side of the story last night, sometimes embarrassed by how frank he'd been, John couldn't reconcile the woman he'd described as his mother. If it hadn't been for Anne turning up at the party, nothing would have convinced him that his father's words were true. Yet if Mel had died, if the baby had died, it would have been his mother's fault. He felt sick at the thought, the urge to confront her gone now. In fact, at the moment, he didn't feel that he'd ever want to see her again.

'John, you had best get home to Ulrika. She's probably waiting for news, and the same goes for you, Anne.'

'No, Dad,' Anne protested. 'I'll give Tony a ring and tell him to meet me at your place.'

'There's no need. Now I know that Mel and the baby are going to be all right, I'll be fine on my own.'

'Dad, your place still looks like a bomb's hit it. There's still the aftermath of the party to clear up, and Mel won't want to face that when she arrives home.'

'All right, darling, I won't argue.'

'I'll get Ulrika and we'll give you a hand,' John offered.

'Thanks, and I'm sorry your Christmas has been ruined.'

John shook his head. 'You've got nothing to apologise for, Dad. This was all down to Mum.'

'I know I wasn't blameless, and of course she was badly hurt, but I never thought your mother would resort to this. It was a long time ago and I thought she'd be over it, so why now?'

'She's been bitter and twisted for years,' Anne said, 'always harping on about how hard up she is because you robbed her of a decent settlement.'

'You know that isn't true.'

'Yes, of course I do, but nothing can convince Mum. Maybe I should've seen this coming, but lately I thought she'd moved forward. She's made new friends and seemed happy.'

'It might be my fault,' John said. 'She was dreadfully upset about the wedding and felt we were leaving her out.'

'That's no excuse,' Anne snapped. 'Ulrika has been in touch with her every week since then, and she's been included in all the plans.'

'Now hold on, you two. Neither of you are to blame. If anyone should take responsibility for this, it's me.'

'You're not to blame either,' John insisted. 'All right, you fell in love with someone else, but now I know how unhappy you were, I can understand why.'

'Come on, Dad, enough of this for now,' Anne insisted as she took his arm. 'You look worn out. It's two-thirty and I think you should try to get a couple of hours' sleep before we come back this evening.'

'I won't argue with that.'

John suddenly noticed how old his father looked, the usually tall, handsome, and distinguished man appearing bent with fatigue as they walked out of the waiting room. After what had happened last night, followed by his fear for Mel that morning, it wasn't surprising – and he was also anxious that his father got some rest. The urge to confront his mother resurfaced, but there would be time enough later. For now all he cared about was his father, and he felt a surge of guilt that he'd so badly misjudged him. Why didn't I listen before? he asked himself. But there was no answer to this question as they walked out of the hospital and to their cars.

* * *

Anne was the first to receive the news. Tony was waiting for her when she walked into their flat, his face grave.

'Anne, it's your mum. She's in hospital. They think she's had a slight stroke.'

'Who's they?'

'A friend of your mum's rang from casualty. A woman called Valerie Thorn.'

'I only saw Mum a couple of hours ago and she was all right when I left.'

'Yes, well, just after that she collapsed.'

'A slight stroke doesn't sound much to worry about. After what she did, it's no more than she deserves,' Anne retorted, still too upset about what her mother had done to care.

'How can you say that? She's still your mother.'

'As far as I'm concerned she can rot in hell.'

'Anne, surely you're going to see her?'

'No I'm not!'

'You don't mean that.'

'Oh yes I do. I've listened to her moaning and carping for years, and though I've tried so many times to get her to see Dad's point of view, she just wouldn't listen. Now this. Because of her, Mel nearly died, along with my new baby brother or sister. What my mother did is unforgivable and I never want to see her again.'

'Does John feel the same?'

'Yes, he does. She poisoned his mind for years,

but he's seen the light at last. God, Tony, if I hadn't turned up, John and Mel would have believed that bitch's story.'

Tony ran a hand through his hair. 'What a mess. What a Christmas. First the car played up on the way to Cornwall and we were lucky to make it back, let alone having to placate my parents. Then there was that scene at your father's last night, followed by Mel being rushed to hospital this morning. How is she?'

'It's about time you asked. She's fine, the baby's fine, they're both out of danger.'

'That's good, but now your mother's in hospital too and I still think you should go to see her.'

'I said no. Now come on, we're going to my father's. I want to get the place cleared up before Mel comes home.'

'What if your mother has another stroke? What if she dies? How will you feel then?'

'Shut up, Tony. I know what you're trying to do, but it won't work. Now are you coming with me or not?'

'I'm coming, and are you going to tell your dad that your mother's in hospital?'

'Yes, and I'm looking forward to it. Like me, he'll see it as just punishment,' Anne said maliciously.

Richard stared at his daughter, horrified by the smug expression on her face. She looked gleeful that her mother was in hospital, whereas when he glanced at John, he could see his son was deeply upset. 'Anne, that's enough! You may find what your mother did unforgivable, but I wouldn't wish a stroke on her, or anyone.'

'But, Dad . . .'

'I said that's enough! I hurt your mother, badly, and I'm not proud of myself. I hoped she'd get over it, that she'd eventually see my point of view. It's obvious now that she hasn't been able to, and I suspect her pain has been festering for years. I'm not happy about what she did, but I can at least show some understanding.'

'You wouldn't be saying that if Mel and the baby had died.'

'Maybe not, but they didn't. Your mother may still be in danger though.'

John rose to his feet. 'Sorry, Dad, but I must go to see her.'

'I understand, son. In fact, I'm coming with you.'

'What!' Anne cried. 'But you can't. What about Mel?'

'It's over three hours to visiting time, and with little traffic on the roads, we'll make it back to Surrey in time. If your mother is up to it, I think it's time we had a good, long talk. Maybe she's ready to listen at last.'

'Well I'm not going.'

'That's up to you, Anne, but can I give her a message?'

'Yes. Tell her to go to hell.'

'Anne, Anne,' Richard muttered as he left the room with his son. He wasn't looking forward to seeing Betty again, but this hate, this venom, had to be thrashed out. If it wasn't, there was always the danger that she would try something else and he'd be living on tenterhooks. Of course she might be too ill to receive visitors, or unable to talk. If that was the case he'd have to try again when she recovered. *If she recovers,* a small inward voice warned.

Chapter Thirty-seven

'Blimey, you gave us a fright, Betty,' said Paula.

'I'm just relieved that you're all right,' Val murmured.

'Me too,' agreed Cheryl. 'I call myself a nurse, but when you passed out with shock and then didn't come round, I thought you'd had a stroke. I didn't spot that you'd bumped your head badly, and it's lucky you weren't concussed.'

Betty said nothing, her eyes turned away from them. She didn't want to talk, didn't want to think. Thinking only brought pain. She had lost John, lost Anne. They would never forgive her. Never! Oh, God, if Mel died – if the baby died!

'You can get dressed now, Mrs Grayson,' a nurse said. 'Doctor said you can go home.'

As the others left to wait outside, she rose to her feet. Why hadn't it been a stroke? Why hadn't she died? Because at this moment she wanted just that, to sink back into oblivion – to never have to think again. Never have to face what she had done.

'Come on, let's get you home,' Val said.

Betty found herself being gently led forward, one step following another until they reached Val's car. She was aware that they were driving home, but her brain still felt foggy. She didn't mind that. If she couldn't die, then all she wanted was to escape into sleep.

When they arrived at the flats, Val said, 'We'll all come upstairs with you. I'm sure you need to talk.'

'No, Val,' she managed to protest. 'I . . . I just want to lie down.'

'But we can't leave you like this.'

'Please, Val.'

'Oh, all right, but we'll pop up to see you later.'

Paula moved forward to give her a cuddle, which Betty was just able to return, and then she walked upstairs to her flat. Inside she closed the door behind her, and momentarily looked at the unwrapped presents. She would never be able to face Christmas again – never be able to forget what she had done. Desolate, she went to her bedroom and, lying fully clothed on her bed, closed her eyes. Yet haunted by what had happened, her mind twisting and turning, she was unable to sleep.

'I should have said something. I should have spoken up,' Cheryl said as they walked into Val's flat.

'Me too,' Paula agreed. 'Betty's daughter called me a bitch and instead of giving her a piece of my mind, I stayed on me knees like a dummy.'

'I'm not talking about Betty's daughter. I'm talking about the plan.'

'We couldn't have known that Anne would turn up at the party,' Val pointed out.

'No, you don't understand. What I'm trying to say is, we should never have agreed to it in the first place.'

'Sit down, you too, Paula,' Val urged, and once seated she said, 'Right, Cheryl, what was wrong with Betty's plan?'

'With the plan, nothing, but I've been over and over this in my mind, and as I said, I wish I'd spoken up. Betty should have let go of the past, moved forward. She had nothing to gain financially. It was all about revenge.'

'You can't blame her for that,' Val protested. 'After what her husband put her through—'

'Val, for God's sake,' Cheryl interrupted. 'From what her daughter said, there's another side to the story, but worse, Betty knew that Mel had high blood pressure. And don't tell me she didn't know the risks. If Mel dies, or the baby dies . . . oh, oh . . .' she choked, her voice trailing off.

'No, no, she didn't know the risks,' Val protested. 'When Betty was having a baby, she had high blood pressure too, and because she was all right, had no idea it was dangerous. Neither did I, or I wouldn't have agreed to the plan. Unlike you, Cheryl, we aren't nurses.'

'Mel will be all right, won't she?' Paula appealed.

Cheryl shook her head. 'I . . . I don't know.'

'Oh blimey! What 'ave we done?'

Val stood up and moved to the sideboard. Her hands shook as she poured three glasses of sherry. 'Here,' she said, handing out the glasses, and instead of sipping her own drink as usual, she swallowed it in one gulp.

'If something happens to Mel, or the baby, despite what you say, I don't think Betty's children will ever forgive her,' Cheryl said.

Paula blanched. 'If . . . if anything does happen, you . . . you don't think they'll go to the police, do you?'

'I don't know, though I doubt it. But come on, let's not get ahead of ourselves,' Val urged. 'I'm sure Mel and the baby will be fine.'

'I hope you're right,' Cheryl murmured.

'I am,' Val said, trying to convey a more positive attitude than she felt. 'For now, Betty should be our main concern. She's in a terrible state and I'm worried about her. I think we'll give her an hour and then go upstairs.'

Both Paula and Cheryl nodded, their mood sombre as Val poured them all another drink.

* * *

Richard and John were leaving the casualty department of the hospital in Battersea. 'If your mother's been released, she must be fine.'

'Yes, and we might as well go home.'

'No, John, I'd still like to talk to her.'

'All right, I'll direct you to where she lives, but I'm not coming in.'

Richard started the car and followed his son's instructions until they pulled up outside a small block of flats. He asked John which one she lived in, and then before getting out of the car said, 'Are you sure you won't come in?'

'I'm sure, but don't be long, Dad. We've still got to drive back to Farnham and Mel will be expecting you at visiting time.'

'I'm well aware of that, son,' Richard said as he closed the door. Yes, Mel was his main concern, but he'd never be able to relax until he'd sorted things out with Betty. He climbed the stairs, heaving in a deep breath before knocking on her door.

'Richard! What . . . what are you doing here?' Betty stammered. 'Oh, no, don't tell me something's happened to Mel and the baby.'

He took in Betty's horrified expression, her rumpled clothes and hair and, instead of anger, found he felt only pity. 'They're both out of danger.'

She seemed to slump before him and, hastily stepping inside, Richard took her arm. 'Are you all right?'

'Yes, yes, I was just a bit dizzy for a moment.'

'Betty, if you're up to it, I'd like to talk to you.'

'Richard, please, I'm sorry. I didn't mean to harm Mel or the baby. It was you I wanted to punish.'

'I don't doubt that,' Richard said gently, 'but we still need to talk.'

She nodded and, indicating a chair said, 'You'd better sit down.'

He took a seat, waiting until Betty sat opposite. 'I thought you'd be over our divorce by now, but from what Anne tells me, you're always harping on about it.'

Her head shot up. 'What do you expect?'

'Please, can't you see my side of the story?'

'You moved Mel in, forced . . . forced me out of my home.'

'I know, but you left me no choice.'

'You left me almost penniless.'

'I gave you all I could and it was a good amount,' and seeing that she was about to protest, he held up his hand. 'I think it's time you heard a few home truths, and after the stunt you just pulled, you at least owe me that.'

Once again she seemed to slump, her head bowed as she nodded.

'I'm a man, Betty, with a man's needs, but after the children were born you shut me out. Sex became a dirty word to you. All you cared about was the home and our children. No, no, please don't interrupt,' he urged. 'My frustration was thrown into the business, and I worked hard, making enough money to ensure that both John and Anne had private educations.'

'I . . . I helped. I was thrifty with money.'

'Yes, I won't deny you were good at handling the housekeeping money, leaving most of the profits to plough back into the business. You were good with the children, too, but Betty, you were never a wife, not even in a social sense. I was trying to gain contacts, but you wouldn't even entertain my business colleagues and friends.'

'I tried, but they made me feel uncomfortable, with the wives all looking down on me.'

'No, it was you who made *them* feel uncomfortable, as if coming into your home was an intrusion.'

'I didn't have their gadgets or their fancy clothes. I was worn out with looking after you and the children. You didn't care about that; all you seemed to care about was . . . was sex.'

'You make it sound like a dirty word.'

'I . . . I gave you two children, wasn't that enough?'

'There's more to marriage than children. As I said before, a man still has his needs.'

'And I suppose you got your so-called needs fulfilled by Mel.'

'It wasn't like that. When Mel came to work for me, I wasn't looking for an affair. It just sort of happened. I fought the attraction, Mel did too, but we couldn't help falling in love.'

'Love! You call sex, love?'

'No, but it's a part of it. If you had ever truly loved me, you'd know that.'

'I did love you! Do love you,' Betty blurted out, her face flooding with colour.

Richard shook his head. 'No, Betty, you loved the idea of marriage, of a house, children, but once you had filled what you saw as your role, you had no further use for me.'

'That isn't true. It was *you* who had no further use for me. You swapped me for a younger model and I was thrown out of my home.'

'Oh please, it wasn't like that and you know it. I told you about Mel, asked for a divorce, but you just wouldn't accept it. For months and months I tried, but you just wouldn't listen. In the end I couldn't stand it any more. I knew I'd have to do something drastic, and moving Mel in seemed the only way. She argued against it, refused at first, but I eventually persuaded her. Mel felt awful, uncomfortable, especially when I showed her any affection. She wanted to leave, but I wouldn't let her, and then when I found you a flat, you *agreed* to move out.'

'Don't give me that. Moving Mel in wasn't the only way. *You* could have left, found yourself a love nest, but instead it was me who had to go.'

Richard lowered his eyes. Yes, what Betty said was true, but he'd worked like a dog to buy the new house, to pay the mortgage, and had put all his capital into renovating it. The thought of giving it up had sickened him, so he'd reconciled his actions by deciding that he was the one paying for it and that Betty had done nothing, except playing the part of a housekeeper rather than a wife. He met her eyes, saying regretfully, 'I know, and I'm not proud of my actions.'

'You filed for divorce, said I'd abandoned you, and then did me out of a decent settlement.'

'I took my solicitor's advice, but I *did* give you a good settlement, even remortgaging the business, risking everything I had built up to make sure you got a decent amount.'

'If that's the case, how come I have to take on a cleaning job to survive?'

'Betty, if you had invested wisely, you wouldn't have to work. Instead, John told me that you gave him a very large deposit to buy a house, and I'm not pleased that he accepted money from you.'

'I wanted to see him settled, and he'll pay it back one day.'

'I hope so, but it seems you also became a spend-thrift. If that's the case, it's not my fault you're hard up now.'

'After our divorce, I suffered from depression. I had scrimped and scraped for years on the pittance you gave me for housekeeping, but then for the first time I had money. I was so unhappy, and I . . . I suppose buying things became a sort of compensation.'

Richard glanced at his watch. Worried about the time, he said, 'I'm sorry, Betty, sorry you suffered depression, but this is getting us nowhere. Can't you see that there were faults on both sides? Surely it's time to put this all behind us?'

Tears filled Betty's eyes as she considered his words, but then at last she said, 'Yes, it is. I was so hurt, so full of bitterness that I could only see my side of the story and I still think it was wrong of you to force me out. I worked so hard to make the house and garden lovely, and the thought of Mel living there in luxury now, drove me mad. I feel awful about pulling that stunt and about using a good friend to do it. If anything had happened to Mel and the baby, I would never have been able to forgive myself.'

'I doubt I could have forgiven you either, but thankfully Mel's all right. As for living in luxury, we aren't rich. I still have a large mortgage to pay and I've had to work my socks off to build up capital again. I bought the house on financial advice, as an investment towards my retirement, yet you're right, I did force you out. If you really are hard up, I'll see what I can do to help you.'

'No, I don't want your money.'

'Then I'll talk to John about paying back the money you gave him.'

'Don't do that. He's getting married and will need every penny.'

'Very well, but he can pay you some time in the future. Talking of John,' Richard said as he stood up, 'I'd better go. He's waiting in the car and we've got to get back to Farnham.'

'John! John's downstairs?' Betty cried as she jumped to her feet.

'Yes, but I'm afraid he doesn't want to see you.'

Betty ran to the window, shaking with emotion as she looked down on the car.

Richard didn't know what to do, and hesitantly put an arm around her shoulders. 'Please,' he murmured, 'don't cry.'

'You . . . you've won. You've got them both now.'

'It was never a contest, Betty. John doesn't want to see you, or Anne, but give it time. I'll work on them and I'm sure they'll come to forgive you.'

'Perhaps I should go down? Talk to him?'

'Leave it for now. He's in no mood to listen and it might make things worse.'

'Why? Why did I do it? John will never forgive me. Never!' Betty sobbed.

As Betty continued to cry, Richard felt awful. He wasn't happy with the stunt she'd pulled, yet could understand why she felt driven to do it. He felt callous, but all he wanted now was to leave, to get back to Farnham, and Mel. 'John *will* come round, you'll see, but I'm sorry, I really do have to go now.'

She sniffed, nodded, her eyes still on the car, and

after muttering goodbye, Richard left, the tension in his body easing as he went downstairs.

John turned his head to look at his father as Richard got behind the wheel, but said nothing, his face set like stone. With a sigh, Richard started the engine. 'Your mother is sorry, really sorry. We had a good talk and she's agreed to put the past behind us.'

Still John said nothing, his eyes now fixed straight ahead. Deciding to leave it for the time being, Richard's thoughts turned to Mel. With any luck she'd be able to come home soon, perhaps even tomorrow.

It had been a dreadful time, but it was over now. In January their baby would be born, and what a wonderful way that would be to celebrate the New Year.

Paula was standing by the window when she saw a man leave the flats, but didn't see his face until he walked round to the driver's side of the car. She stiffened with shock, and as he drove off found her voice, exclaiming, 'Oh no, that was Betty's husband!'

They all scrambled for the door and rushed upstairs, Val's voice echoing her anxiety. 'Betty, has something happened to Mel and the baby?'

Cheryl stood in the background, tense, dreading what she'd hear. Betty looked desolate as she wiped a handkerchief across her eyes. 'It's all right. They're both fine.'

'Oh, thank God for that,' Cheryl blurted out.

Paula asked, 'Did he come to have a go at you?'

'I expected him to, it's what I deserve, but he just wanted to talk. He . . . He's made me see sense at last.'

Paula placed an arm around Betty's shoulder. 'Come on, come and sit down.'

'John . . . John wouldn't come up to see me. I've lost him now, and Anne. They'll never forgive me.'

'Don't cry. They'll come round, you'll see.'

'That . . . that's what Richard said.'

Cheryl sat quietly. She'd benefited from their plans, as had Paula, but for Betty, revenge hadn't paid. She had tried to turn her son against his father, but instead the reverse had happened. If only Betty had left things alone, if only she'd let the past go, been happy for her son that he had both parents in his life. Now she had lost him, lost Anne, and she was utterly devastated. It was awful to see her in such a state, and leaning forward she urged, 'You could write them a letter, explain why you did it – try to make them understand.'

'It's a good idea,' Val said.

Betty nodded, and with a juddering sob, at last stopped crying. 'I . . . I'll do that. If I tell them how wrong I was, and . . . and say how sorry I am, it might work.'

'It's sure to,' Val said, 'but what's this about your husband making you see sense at last?'

Betty bowed her head, avoiding their eyes as she

relayed her conversation with Richard. She held nothing back, ending with, 'So you see, Richard made me see his side of things. I realise now that I was cold – that I drove him into having an affair.'

'He still shouldn't have forced you out of your house,' Paula protested.

'He agrees it was wrong to do that, but in truth, he did give me a very good settlement.'

'But you said it was small,' Val protested.

Betty told them about her depression, how she had spent the money like water and had given her son a large deposit on a house. 'Richard's right. If I had invested the money wisely, I wouldn't be so hard up now.'

Cheryl's jaws tensed. When Val recruited Betty, she'd told her side of the story and they all felt so sorry for her. Now though there was a different point of view, and it made Cheryl feel worse, angry at herself for going along with Betty's plan. The fact that she'd known about Mel's high blood pressure, yet failed to mention it, still rankled – even if Betty hadn't realised the risks. Thankfully Mel and the baby were all right, but Cheryl had had enough of these schemes, and if Val wanted to carry on, taking her revenge on Mike Freeman, she wanted nothing to do with it.

'Betty,' Val said, 'we had a couple of drinks downstairs, but I don't think another one would hurt. I know you've got a bottle of sherry, do you mind if I open it?'

'No, go ahead.'

'Not for me thanks,' Cheryl said. In truth, all she wanted was to leave, but was stuck until Val was ready to give her a lift home. She could walk, and though it would be a long one, it would be better than staying here. The day had been a disaster. The presents remained unopened, the Christmas dinner uncooked and, realising this, Cheryl's stomach growled. Val had made them a snack, but other than breakfast it was all they'd eaten that day. 'Oh, I'm sorry,' she said as her stomach growled again.

'It sounds like you're hungry, and I am too,' Val said. 'What about you, Betty? Along with a drink, I could make some sandwiches.'

'I . . . I'm not hungry, but there's a tin of red salmon in the cupboard, and . . . and the Christmas cake.'

'I'll give you a hand,' Cheryl offered. Yes, she could walk home, but doubted Val would let her, and anyway, she didn't have a good excuse for leaving.

In the kitchenette the vegetables they'd prepared that morning sat in water, the chicken dressed and ready to go into the oven. Val shook her head sadly. She put the chicken in the fridge, but decided to discard the vegetables, saying, 'What a waste, but it's too late to cook them now.'

They then made a plate of sandwiches, unaware that in Farnham, another tragedy was about to unfold.

Chapter Thirty-eight

Richard was fighting exhaustion. After a bad night's sleep, then Mel being admitted to hospital that morning, it had been mad to drive to London to see Betty. Yet despite his tiredness, he felt it had been worth it. He didn't want Mel worrying, didn't want her living on tenterhooks, and could now tell her that it was all over, that his ex-wife was prepared to put the past behind her at last.

When Richard dropped John off at his mews cottage, his son said he'd freshen up and then see him at the hospital but, feeling he had no time to do the same, Richard drove straight on to see Mel. When he arrived, he walked into the main reception area and for the first time noticed the Christmas tree. There were fewer staff than usual, but as it was still Christmas Day it wasn't surprising. Thanks to this hospital, Mel had survived, his unborn child had survived, and he felt a surge of gratitude for the doctors, nurses and other staff who had given up their Christmas to the care of patients. He guessed that Mel would have been moved to one of the wards by now as she was out of danger so, after asking the young lady on reception where to go, he headed for the lift.

As he got out on the second floor, Richard was smiling. He was anticipating taking Mel home today, or maybe tomorrow, but instead when told by a nurse where his wife was, he walked in to chaos. 'What's going on?' he cried.

'Oh Richard. Richard,' Mel sobbed. 'They can't hear the baby's heart.'

'What!'

'I'm sorry, Mr Grayson,' the doctor said, 'we're just about to take your wife down to theatre for a Caesarean. She has pre-eclampsia, and though we managed to stabilise her blood pressure this morning, it has now become dangerously high. We can't afford to wait,' he said abruptly, all his focus on Mel.

Richard was only able to briefly clutch Mel's hand as she was wheeled away and, feeling helpless, he paced the corridor until told to sit in the waiting room. His stomach lurched, his emotions on a roller coaster. So much had happened in such a short time. First Mel had been in danger, and then out of it, and now they couldn't hear the baby's heartbeat.

With a groan Richard rubbed both hands over his face. He hadn't wanted more children, but from the moment Mel had told him she was pregnant, his feelings had changed in an instant. He'd watched her blooming, seen how happy she was, and it felt like a second chance. When John and Anne were children, he'd been so wrapped up in making a success of the business that he'd given them little time. He'd missed so much, but this time was determined to be different, to play a larger role in this baby's upbringing.

No heartbeat! They couldn't find a heartbeat, he thought, his panic growing as he realised the implications of this. Oh please, he prayed inwardly, please let the baby be all right, please let Mel be all right. Mel . . . Mel . . . if anything happened to her he'd go mad. He'd given up on happiness, on love, but then Mel came along to change all that. At first he'd feared the age gap, but found it didn't matter. Mel kept him young, and the prospect of having a new baby had given him a new lease of life.

Richard's eyes watched the clock, waiting for news, willing time to pass. Half an hour later, John arrived, asking as he walked into the waiting room, 'What's going on, Dad? A nurse told me I'd find you in here. Where's Mel?'

'In theatre, having a Caesarean,' but then feeling his eyes welling with tears, Richard once again held his hands over his face.

'Why, Dad? I thought they'd managed to bring her blood pressure down.'

'So did I, but the doctor said it's dangerously high again and . . . and they couldn't hear the baby's heart.'

John sat down, placed a hand on his father's arm. 'Don't worry, Dad, they'll be fine.'

'I hope so, son. I hope so,' Richard croaked.

They sat then in silence, but then Anne turned up, she too looking worried 'Dad, what's going on?'

Richard repeated what he'd told John, his daughter taking a seat on the other side of him. She reached out to clutch his hand, her expression earnest. 'They'll be all right, Dad, I know they will.'

He tried to draw comfort from both John and Anne's words, until at last a nurse came into the room.

'Mr Grayson.'

'Yes,' he said, leaping to his feet.

'Come with me, please. Doctor Jackson would like to speak to you.'

'Is my wife all right? Is the baby all right?'

She didn't answer the question, only saying as John and Anne walked to his side, 'I'm sorry, but just Mr Grayson.'

Richard found his heart thumping in his chest and anxious thoughts swimming round his head as he was shown into a small office. The doctor was there, his face etched with sympathy as he told Richard to sit down.

'No, no, please, just tell me,' Richard urged.

'Your wife is fine, Mr Grayson, but I'm afraid we were unable to save the baby.'

Richard clutched the back of a chair. Mel was all right! Relief flooded through him, only to be followed by a surge of grief. 'Oh God, no,' he gasped.

The doctor was talking, medical jargon, something about the baby, but his voice sounded distant to Richard's ears. A hand came out, holding a glass of water.

'Please, sit down,' the nurse said in a kindly voice, 'drink this.'

Richard found his throat constricted, but managed to swallow the water, then asked, 'Can I see my wife?'

'Yes,' the doctor said, 'though due to the hypertension we had to administer a general anaesthetic.'

Richard was only able to nod, and turning he followed the nurse again, this time to see Mel.

After nearly an hour, John rose swiftly when his father at last returned to the waiting room. 'Dad, is Mel all right?'

'Yes,' he said, obviously fighting tears, 'but she . . . she lost the baby.'

'Oh no, no,' Anne cried, 'she must be heartbroken. Can I see her?'

He shook his head. 'Sorry, but she's not up to visitors yet.'

'Then when?'

'I don't know, tomorrow maybe.'

'But . . .'

'Mel's still feeling the effects of the anaesthetic and was hardly aware I was there. I was told to leave now, to come back tomorrow, so please, let's just go.'

'This is down to Mum,' Anne cried. 'If it hadn't been for her, Mel wouldn't have lost the baby. I'll never forgive her. Never!'

'Please, not now,' Richard appealed.

John felt a surge of anger. His sister was right. Mel had been fine until that girl had turned up, shouting her accusations, ones that he'd been ready to believe until Anne arrived. No wonder Mel had collapsed and her blood pressure had rocketed. He looked at his father, saw that he was close to breaking point, and managed to swallow his feelings enough to say, 'Come on, Dad, let's get you home.'

When they got to the car park, Anne said, 'Dad, I don't want to leave you on your own. Would you like me to stay at your place?'

'There's no need. I'll go to bed as soon as I get home, and then come back to the hospital in the morning.'

'If you're sure, but I'll see you here first thing tomorrow,' she said, eyes moist as she gave him a swift hug before going to her car.

John was also worried about his father. 'Dad, you look worn out. Leave your car here and I'll take you home.'

'No, son, it's only a ten-minute drive. I'll be fine.'

'But, Dad . . .'

'I appreciate the offer, son, but just go, will you? I've had enough for one day and just want a bit of time to myself. Mel has just lost our baby, our son, and I need some space,' he begged, his voice cracking with emotion.

'A boy? Oh Dad.'

John saw his father break down then, sobs racking his shoulders, and in the dim light of the car park, for the first time, he held his father in his arms. There had never been any great displays of affection between them, but as John's arms tightened around his father his feelings were of sorrow, pity and love. Yes, he loved this man, but thanks to his mother he'd cut him from his life, believing all that she had told him. There were faults on both sides, John knew that now, but his father didn't deserve this – Mel didn't deserve this. His mother needed to know, to *hear* what she had done, and he'd make sure that he was the one to tell her.

Chapter Thirty-nine

Paula awoke on Boxing Day, her body stiff from sleeping on the sofa, but she'd insisted on staying. Val had driven Cheryl home, but Paula hadn't wanted to leave. Betty was still upset, even though with their help she'd spent a long time composing a letter to her children.

Post was suspended until after the holidays, so it would be a while before Betty found out if it would do any good, but surely they'd understand? Surely they'd realise what a wonderful mother Betty was and, if they didn't, they must be mad. All right, she hadn't tried to see her husband's point of view, may have been a bit cold, but as far as Paula was concerned it didn't excuse what he'd done. He could've had a bit on the side if he was that frustrated – what was it with men and sex anyway? That thought brought back memories of her rape and she shuddered, but forced a cheerful note into her voice as Betty appeared.

'Morning, love,' Paula said brightly.

'Did you manage to sleep?' Betty asked, her voice sounding lacklustre.

'Yeah, and as you're up, how about I make us a nice cup of tea?'

'I'll do it. I need some Alka-Seltzer too. I drank too much sherry on an empty stomach and I still feel a bit queasy.'

'You ain't used to it, that's the trouble.'

'Before I knew Val I never drank at all. Oh Paula, I can't help wishing I'd never met her now. Despite the sherry, I've been awake half the night thinking about it. If I hadn't got involved with Val, none of this would have happened.'

'Don't say that, Betty. It was just bad luck your plan went wrong and you can't blame Val for that. She was just trying to help us, to help all of us, and I'll never forget what she did for me.'

'I know, I know,' she said tiredly. 'I don't know what's wrong with me. I'm trying to use Val as a scapegoat and that isn't fair.' Betty then looked at the letters lying on the table, stamped and ready to post. 'Do you think they'll ever forgive me?'

'Of course they will,' Paula said, hoping she was right but not voicing her fears. Then there was a knock on the door.

'It's a bit early, but I expect that's Val,' Betty said as she went to open it.

'She's probably worried about you,' said Paula, but then trailed off, her mouth gaping in surprise.

'John!' Betty exclaimed.

He brushed past his mother and, seeing Paula, yelled, 'You! I might have guessed you'd be here.'

Paula jumped to her feet, and in the face of his anger her eyes flicked around, desperately looking for escape. She dashed to Betty's bedroom, but there was no drowning out his voice.

'Yes, it's just as well she ran, Mum. It's thanks to you both that Mel lost the baby.'

'What? No! Your father said they're out of danger.'

'They were, but Mel's blood pressure shot up again. She had to have an emergency Caesarean. It was a boy, Mum, my half-brother, but they couldn't save him.'

'John, I'm so sorry, really I am. I had no idea that blood pressure was dangerous, that the baby was at risk.'

'The fact that she was heavily pregnant should have been enough to stop you from pulling that stunt! But no, you had to have your revenge, didn't you? Well Dad's in a terrible state now so I hope you're happy. You make me sick! For years I kept away from Dad, listened to your poison, but no more. I'm finished with you. Don't try to ring me, or see me. Just stay out of my life!'

Paula heard a door slam, followed by Betty's cry of anguish. She rushed back to the living room but, finding her inconsolable, sobbing, and frightened, ran downstairs to bang on Val's door. 'Val, Val, you've got to come. Betty's in a terrible state and I can't get her to stop crying.'

'What happened?'

'Her son came round. It was awful. Mel lost the baby and—'

'No, no,' Val cried, and together they dashed upstairs.

It took a long time, but at last Betty stopped crying, her face blotched, eyes red rimmed as she gasped, 'Val, Val, what have I done? The baby, the poor innocent baby . . .'

'I know, it's awful, but it wasn't your fault.'

'My son thinks it was, and when I tried to make a feeble excuse, I realised he's right. I *did* know that Mel had high blood pressure, should have asked Cheryl if there were risks. But I didn't. All I cared about was revenge, and . . . Maybe, deep down, I wanted this to happen.'

'Of course you didn't.'

'But Mel was having Richard's baby, and I was sick with jealousy.'

'Stop this,' Val urged. 'I know you're distraught, but I know you better than that.'

Betty clutched Paula's hand, fighting tears again, and then groaned, 'Oh, my head is splitting.'

'Why don't you go back to bed? Paula can come downstairs with me and we'll pop up to see how you are in a couple of hours.'

Betty didn't argue and released Paula's hand as

she rose to her feet, bent like an old woman as she went through to her bedroom.

'Val, I don't like leaving her like this,' Paula protested.

'With a headache like that, sleep is the best thing for her. We won't be far away if she needs us.'

Doubtfully Paula followed Val out, worried about Betty's state of mind. 'Maybe we should call Cheryl.'

'If she's no better in a couple of hours, we'll do just that,' Val assured her.

Paula wasn't happy, but thinking that Val probably knew best, she said no more.

Richard was at the hospital. Mel looked awful, her face, hands and feet grotesquely swollen with oedema, but it was the desolation in her eyes that worried him the most. He did his best to comfort her, and when Anne arrived, he left her with Mel while he went to find a nurse. She led him to the ward sister's office, where he voiced his concerns.

'The fluid retention will reduce, Mr Grayson, and once her sutures have been removed, your wife will be allowed home.'

'I'm worried about her state of mind. She won't talk.'

'It's to be expected. She's grieving, Mr Grayson, and it takes us all in different ways.'

'I don't know what to do, how to comfort her.'

'Just give her time.'

Richard thanked her, but still felt helpless as he returned to Mel's room.

'She's asleep,' Anne said. 'I'll go to the tea machine. Can I get you anything?'

'No thanks,' he murmured and, as his daughter left, he sat beside Mel, took her hand, but felt no return pressure. Anne had thought her asleep, but Richard knew better. 'I've spoken to the ward sister. She said you can come home soon.'

Still she said nothing, her eyes closed. 'Mel, Mel, I know it's awful, but we can try again. We can have another baby.'

It was as though a dam burst. Mel cried out in anguish, tears flooding her eyes and rolling down her cheeks. 'No, no, I'm not fit to be a mother. It was my fault. I lost him. I lost my son . . . our son. They wouldn't let me see him. They said he . . . he had something called . . . called anencephaly.'

'I know, darling, but it wasn't your fault,' Richard said as he continued to hold Mel's limp hand. He remembered going to the doctor's office, grief clouding the man's words, the medical jargon only sinking in when he arrived home. He had cried for his son, for a baby who never had a chance of survival.

'It was. It was my fault,' Mel sobbed. 'It must have been something I took. You've heard about thalidomide, what that did to unborn babies.'

'That was in the late fifties and early sixties. It's

404

been withdrawn now. You didn't take that; in fact, I can't remember you taking anything.'

'I once took an aspirin when I had a headache.'

'Oh, Mel, Mel, that wouldn't have done any harm.'

'You can't be sure of that. It *was* my fault. It must have been,' she wailed.

'Dad, can I come in?'

He swung around. 'Not now, Anne.'

As the door closed, Richard turned back to Mel. She was sobbing and he wanted to hold her, to drag her into his arms, but feared hurting her wound. Nothing he'd said helped, and he was seriously worried now. 'Mel, I'm going to find the doctor. Maybe he can make you see sense.'

'Richard, don't tell Anne about the baby. She . . . she'll hate me.'

'Mel, it wasn't your fault.'

'It was . . . it was. Don't tell her. Don't tell anyone, please, Richard, please!'

'All right, darling, I won't say a word for now, but you've got to calm down.'

'I . . . I can't.'

'I'll get the doctor.'

Richard found Anne hovering in the corridor. 'Oh, Dad, I only got a glimpse of Mel, but she looked awful. Can I go in again?'

'Not yet. She needs to see a doctor.'

He hurried to the ward, lucky to find one just

finishing his rounds. He listened to Richard, then went straight to Mel's room.

'Now then, Mrs Grayson, what's this your husband's been telling me? You can't blame yourself, you know. Anencephaly is a neural tube disorder and I can assure you it doesn't occur as a result of taking aspirin.'

'A . . . a neural tube disorder. I . . . I don't understand.'

'It's a disorder that involves an incomplete development of the skull, sometimes also the spinal cord, or other protective coverings.'

Mel's eyes were swimming with tears. 'If it wasn't the aspirin, then why? Why did it happen?'

'Research is being carried out, but at the moment we don't have a definitive answer. We know it occurs because the neural tube fails to close, usually early in pregnancy.'

'So it *is* my fault. There's something wrong with me,' Mel wailed.

The doctor tried to reassure her, but Mel was becoming hysterical again, hands now tearing at her hair. 'Mel, Mel, don't,' Richard begged.

'I'm going to give you a mild sedative, Mrs Grayson. We'll talk again later.'

A nurse ushered Richard from the room. 'Your wife will sleep now, Mr Grayson. You might as well go home, but you can come back this evening.'

'I can't leave her like that!'

'There's nothing you can do. She's in good hands and, as you heard, when she wakes up the doctor will speak to her again.'

Anne ran to his side again. 'Dad, what's going on?'

'The doctor's giving Mel something to calm her down.'

'Can't I see her?'

'Not now, but maybe she'll be up to it this evening.'

Richard reluctantly left the hospital saying, 'I expected to see John.'

'He's gone to see Mum, to tell her what she's done. Like me, he'll never forgive her.'

'No, no, it wasn't your mother's fault.'

'Yes it was,' Anne retorted. 'Mel was fine until that . . . that bitch Mum sent turned up.'

He had to bite back his words. Mel didn't want anyone to know the baby had anencephaly, had been hysterical about it, and until Mel was ready to accept she hadn't caused it, he'd have to remain silent. He was sure it wouldn't be for long, and once they knew the truth, despite the stunt she had pulled, the children would reconcile with their mother. For now, though, Mel's state of mind had to come first.

Chapter Forty

'Betty, please, it's been over a week now. If you don't go back to work you could lose your job. What will you do for money then?'

When as usual there was no response, Val tried again. 'At least see a doctor to get a medical certificate and then you'll get sick pay.'

There was still no answer from Betty and, with a heavy sigh, Val had to give up. It was all right for Cheryl to say that Betty had depression, but how much longer could this go on? It was becoming more and more difficult to get her to open the door; so much so that Val had surreptitiously taken a key. She'd have to leave for work soon, but hated leaving Betty like this. 'I'll make you a cup of tea before I go,' she said, feeling that she was again talking to herself, 'and how about getting up today? I hate to say this, Betty, but you really do need a wash.'

'Leave me alone.'

'Oh, she speaks! Well that's an improvement.'

Betty closed her eyes, turned on her side, and pulled the blankets up to her chin. With a shake of her head, Val went to Betty's kitchenette, and after making a cup of tea along with a sandwich, she placed it by the bed. 'I've made you a drink and something to eat. Now don't let me find it untouched when I come back after work.'

Betty said nothing, not a word; with her worry mounting, Val decided that she'd have to call the doctor. It was as much as she could do to get Betty to take a few spoonfuls of soup and, like yesterday, she would probably come back to find the sandwich uneaten. This couldn't go on any longer, and hoping that Mr Warriner would understand, she rang him to say that she'd have to take the day off.

'It's all right, Val. All my clients know that I'm retiring now, so there's little for you to do. Take as long as you need.'

Val replaced the receiver, grateful that her employer had been understanding. She hadn't appreciated her job, but now dreaded Mr Warriner's retirement. So far she'd done hardly anything about finding another job, but knew it was time to start looking in earnest. For now, though, her main concern was Betty.

Once again guilt swamped Val. She had dragged Betty in, recruited her, and though the first two plans had gone well, the third had been a disaster. Not only had Betty's children disowned her, but a baby

had died, and like Betty, Val held herself account-
able. She had wanted revenge on Mike Freeman,
and to this end had set about gathering in the others,
but now in the face of this tragedy, all angst had left
her. Revenge wasn't sweet. She could see that now.
Too late though – too late to save an innocent baby's
life.

'What's up, Paula?' Keith asked.

'Nothing,' she said shortly.

'Did you go out last night to see in the New Year?'

'No.'

'You should have come down to my local. We had
a right laugh. Mind you, it was rotten getting up for
work this morning. I reckon they should make New
Year's Day a bank holiday.'

She just shrugged, but not ready to give up on
her yet, Keith said, 'Come on, I can see you're upset
about something. You've been the same since we
came back to work on Monday. It ain't that bleedin'
budgie, is it? Surely you've got over that by now.'

'I told you, I'm fine. I've got a bit of a headache,
that's all.'

'Oh, so you had a few bevvies too?'

'I had a couple of glasses of sherry, that's all.'

'Sherry! Blimey, that sounds a bit posh. Now my
old mum likes a port and lemon, so do her mates,
but sherry! I can't see her asking for that in our
local.'

Paula's hands fumbled as she picked up the next sheet of paper, and after just managing to feed it into the machine, she snapped, 'If you don't want the roller mucked up, I suggest you bugger off.'

'All right, there's no need to bite me head off,' Keith retorted as he walked off, fed up with her stroppy ways. He'd chat to the second girl working on his machine. When each sheet of paper had been laminated, it passed through the roller, and it was her job to separate each one with a knife. Maureen was new to the job and looked flustered, so smiling kindly he said, 'Don't worry, you're doing all right.'

Though intent on her task, Maureen managed to return his smile. He lifted the pile of newly cut sheets from the trough in front of her, taking them to his table and knocking them into shape. He usually preferred it when there was one girl feeding on the machine, the sheets left uncut and winding into a large roll that was lifted off to be separated later. His job was easier then, but with Paula in one of her moods, at least he had the new girl to chat to.

Maureen wasn't a patch on Paula in looks, and her figure wasn't as good but, as he couldn't make any headway with Paula, maybe it was time to give up. It was a shame, though, because he really did like her, and before the Christmas break he'd thought that maybe, just maybe, he was getting somewhere. Mind you, she'd been terrified when she thought he was going to kiss her, so scared that he'd guessed she'd been hurt in some way, and badly. His anger at the thought had come as a surprise, but Paula was so tiny, so fragile looking, that she aroused his protective instincts.

Keith looked at Paula now and, as though aware of his scrutiny, she met his eyes. He winked, but got a scowl in return. Sod it, he thought as he returned to his work. Maybe he'd been wasting his time, particularly as – let's face it – he was no oil painting. When Paula *was* ready to dip her toe in the water again, she could do a lot better than him.

When Keith got the chance he spent the rest of the morning chatting to the new girl. Maureen was easy to talk to, not bad looking really, and hearing that she was footloose and fancy free, he decided to take the plunge. 'Here, Maureen,' he said after shutting down for the lunch break, 'do you fancy taking me out tonight?'

She grinned, revealing a row of perfect teeth. '*Me* take *you* out! You cheeky sod,' but then with another grin she said, 'Yeah, why not?'

Paula heard the exchange and was surprised at the lurch of jealousy she felt. What was wrong with her? What did she care if Keith was taking the new girl out? Yet even as the question crossed her mind, Paula knew the answer. She really liked Keith, more than she'd been prepared to admit, but was still too afraid to date anyone. Ian Parker might be in prison, but he had still won. He would come out of the nick and take up his life again, whereas she would always have to live with what he'd done to her – her sentence for life.

'Why the long face?'

Paula had avoided the other girls who popped outside for a smoke, hiding herself away around the corner of the building, but Lucy had found her. In other factories she'd worked in, smoking was allowed in the canteen, but with the amount of paper and chemical inflammables in this one, it was banned. 'There's nothing wrong. I'm fine.'

'Then why are you hiding?'

'I'm not. I just don't feel like chatting, that's all.'

Lucy didn't take the hint. 'I saw Keith getting cosy with that new girl.'

Paula just shrugged. 'So what?'

'Are you jealous? Is that why you're skulking here?'

'I couldn't care less,' Paula retorted, but then, to her chagrin, tears filled her eyes.

'Blimey, I didn't mean to upset you.'

Paula tried to blink the tears away. It wasn't just Keith, it was Betty's plan. Cheryl was right, they shouldn't have done it, and now a baby was dead.

'I've seen the way Keith looks at you. Just give him the wink and he'll jump at the chance to take you out,' Lucy urged.

Unable to tell Lucy what was really upsetting her, Paula blurted out, 'I . . . I've been raped.'

'What? Are you all right? No of course you're not,'

Lucy babbled. 'You should go home. I'll get the forewoman.'

'No, no, wait! It . . . it happened ages ago.'

Lucy paused, her eyes narrowed in thought. 'Of course, it all makes sense now. I thought you were off men because you'd been dumped, or something like that. But rape. Oh, you poor cow. Mind, if it happened ages ago, you can't let it ruin the rest of your life. If you do, the bastard who did it has won.'

'He . . . he already has.'

'No, you shouldn't think like that,' Lucy insisted.

'Who's gonna want me now? I'm not a virgin, and if a bloke finds out, he'll think I'm a tart. Men don't marry tarts.'

'It wasn't your fault – and anyway, with the way things are going nowadays, I doubt there are many girls who walk down the aisle as virgins.'

'I wanted to. It was my dream.'

'Blimey, Paula, if you ask me it was a bit unrealistic. Most men want to get into your knickers well before the wedding. Look, I know I'm not interested in men, but I ain't a bad judge of character. Keith likes you, and I reckon he's one of the decent ones, a bloke you'd be safe with.'

'No, no, I don't want to go out with him, or anyone.'

'So you're going to let the bloke who raped you win?'

Paula took a last drag on her cigarette. Lucy was right: by letting Ian Parker ruin her life she *was* letting him win and the thought sickened her. She felt a surge of anger, and ground her cigarette underfoot, wishing it was his face. 'No, I'm not going to let him beat me, and thanks, Lucy, thanks for making me see sense. I will try going out on a date again, but not with Keith. He ain't my type,' she lied.

'If you say so. Now I don't know about you, but I'm off to the canteen. I didn't have any breakfast and now my stomach feels like my throat has been cut.'

'I'll be along in a minute,' Paula said. Unlike Lucy, she wasn't hungry. She had spent last evening with Val, both of them trying to snap Betty out of her awful depression. Nothing seemed to work, and when Cheryl had joined them, her attempts had also failed. Cheryl said not to worry, that, given time, Betty was sure to snap out of it. There was another thing too. Once again Cheryl had avoided talking about her attempts to find a house. But why? And what was taking her so long? There was something funny going on – something Paula couldn't put her finger on. If anything Cheryl seemed secretive. But secretive about what?

Paula didn't go to the canteen. Instead she stayed outside until the lunch break was over, her thoughts turning to Betty again, wanting to be with her, to somehow comfort her. Yet how? When she returned to her machine, it was to see Keith chatting to Maureen, the two of them intent on each other.

'Right, we're off,' Keith called.

The routine began again, and when Keith saw that everything was up and running without any problems, he went to talk to Maureen again. A few minutes later he moved to Paula's side.

'Here, guess what? I'm taking Maureen out tonight.'

'I'm pleased for you,' she snapped, 'and now perhaps you'll leave me in peace.'

'Don't worry, I will,' he bit off in reply.

She kept her head down, yet aware that Keith was now laughing as he chatted to Maureen again. She couldn't hear what he was saying, but maybe he was talking about her, telling Maureen what an awkward bitch she was. Keith had been nice, sweet really, but she'd treated him like dirt.

'Keith,' she called now.

He came to her side, saying shortly, 'What?'

'I'm sorry, I didn't mean to be nasty,' said Paula. 'I . . . I've got a lot on my mind, but I shouldn't have taken it out on you.'

'Oh, right. Well, thanks for that.'

'So you like Maureen then?'

'Yeah, she's all right and a bit of a laugh.'

Paula swallowed, wanting to tell Keith how she felt, but the words stuck in her throat. She couldn't do it – couldn't find the courage, and instead said, 'Well then, it sounds like you'll enjoy your date.'

'Yeah, I will,' he agreed and, hearing a noise from the roller, he went off to investigate.

When the machine was finally turned off for the day, Paula hurried to the cloakroom. She wondered where Keith would take Maureen, and if he'd want to see her again. Maybe they wouldn't get on. Stop it, stop it, she told herself. What did it matter anyway? Sod Keith. She'd grab a bag of chips on the way home, have a quick wash and then go to see Betty.

Chapter Forty-one

Cheryl was taking a patient's blood pressure, but her mind was elsewhere. After working all weekend, she had three days off, and with the sale complete, would collect the house keys in the morning. Instead of using Val's solicitor, she'd chosen a local one so she didn't have far to go, and she should have been spinning with happiness. Instead Cheryl was worried sick. What she had taken on was such a huge responsibility. To start with there were builders to sort out, the renovations sure to take at least a month, and then she had to face local authority inspections. Her notice was already written and would soon be handed in to Matron, but the risk of what she was going to do now felt enormous.

'Do you think I might be able to go home tomorrow?' the patient asked.

'I'm sorry, I don't know. The doctor will be able to tell you when he does his rounds in the morning.'

'Well, I bleedin' well hope so. My old man's missing me cooking,' she joked.

Cheryl wrote the readings on the patient's chart, and then forced a smile as she moved on to the next bed. This patient wasn't so chirpy, and for a moment Cheryl felt a pang of compassion. The unhappy woman reminded her of Betty, but it was probably the after-affects of the anaesthesia, unlike Betty's black depression.

At first Cheryl had felt only anger at what Betty's plan had caused, but gradually this feeling had left her to be replaced by pity. Betty was a lovely woman and it had been madness to think that she had wanted Mel's baby to die. Revenge had spurred Betty on, and made her thoughtless of what could be the outcome. So much tragedy, so much pain, and if Val still wanted to exact her revenge on Mike Freeman, Cheryl would have to tell her that she wanted no part of it.

With Betty so close to Paula, and too fragile at the moment, Cheryl hadn't told them about the house, either; where it was, or what her plans were. Of course there was no guarantee that Paula would want to make such a huge change in her life, but for Cheryl, the thought of starting out without at least one friend to help, was a lonely and frightening one.

In Farnham, after suffering an infection, Mel had been allowed home, but she was still in deep grief.

She'd finally accepted that she wasn't to blame for the baby's medical condition, but still refused to let Richard tell anyone that anencephaly had been the cause of their son's death. Richard had no idea why, but because it upset her so much when he tried to argue, he went along with her decision.

It was Sunday, and Richard knew that Anne and John would call in, but guilty that Betty was still being blamed for the baby's loss, Richard wasn't looking forward to seeing them. 'Mel,' he said, 'I've had an idea. How about a holiday, somewhere warm and sunny? It might be just what you need.'

'I'm not up to it yet.'

'Of course you are. It doesn't have to be strenuous, perhaps even a cruise.'

'I'd get seasick.'

'Then we'll fly somewhere.'

'No, I don't need a holiday.'

Mel looked tired, too eaten up with grief to muster enthusiasm for anything, but gently cajoling, Richard urged, 'Darling, it might help.'

'I'll never get over losing my baby.'

When the doorbell rang, Richard went to answer it, and as he'd expected it was Anne. 'Hello, darling, come on in,' he said.

'How's Mel?'

'She's still down in the dumps, but it's early days yet. I suggested a holiday, but she doesn't want to go.'

'I'm not surprised. It's too soon, Dad.'

'I thought it might help,' Richard said as Anne followed him through to the living room.

'Hello, Mel. I hear that dad's been a bit crass and suggested a holiday.'

'Yes, he did, and I told him no. Now what can I get you to drink?'

'Coffee would be nice.'

'I'll get it,' Richard offered.

'Will you stop treating me like an invalid?' Mel snapped as she walked out of the room.

Richard smiled ruefully at his daughter. 'I can't do anything right.'

'You need to stop wrapping Mel in cotton wool.'

'Anne, she's had surgery followed by an infection, and I think she needs to rest.'

'Making a coffee won't hurt. You're stifling her, Dad. You haven't gone back to work, and hardly let her out of your sight. I think she needs things to get back to normality. Not only that, she's probably angry because you haven't done anything about sorting out the bitch that Mum sent here – or Mum herself, come to that. Have you even asked Mel how she feels about it?'

'No, I haven't, but do you seriously think I should try to prosecute your mother? What if she was sent to prison? Surely you don't want that?'

'No, no, of course I don't. It just seems awful that she's got away with it.'

'Anne, we need to let this go. Before Mel lost the baby, your mother agreed we should put the past behind us; despite what happened, we need to do just that.'

'*You* might be able to forgive her, but *I* can't.'

Mel walked in and, holding out a cup of coffee, she gave it to Anne, saying, 'I'm sorry. I've got a dreadful headache and think I need to lie down.'

'Are you all right, Mel?' Richard asked worriedly.

'Oh, for goodness' sake, I said I've got a headache, that's all.'

Mel walked out of the room, glad to get away from Richard, Anne, and talk of his first wife. When she and Richard had fallen in love, she'd argued against moving into this house and had never forgiven herself for letting him persuade her. Yes, they had wanted to be together, but to force Betty out had been wrong. It had lain heavily on her mind, but no more, not now. She would never forget that young woman turning up on Christmas Eve, could remember word for word the accusations made in front of their friends; but worse, she'd believed them. When she fainted, and was then rushed to hospital the following morning, her blood pressure at a dangerous level, it was down to Betty and her hateful scheme. The blood pressure had put the baby in danger, caused a lack of oxygen in her womb, her baby dead before he was born. Yes, he had anencephaly, yet some babies survived.

Mel ground her teeth. Because of Betty, her baby hadn't been given a chance of survival. She would never forgive her, never, and to that end was determined that Anne and John would never know about the baby's medical condition. Like her, they blamed their mother, but if they found out about the anencephaly it would put doubt in their minds. Mel didn't want that. She didn't want them to ever forgive their mother.

Holding her empty stomach, Mel lay on the bed. Yes, she had lost her baby, but there was a crumb of comfort in knowing that Betty had lost her children too.

Val held out a glass of water. 'Time to take your pill, Betty.'

Lacklustre, her eyes glazed, Betty did as she was told; but Val hated this – hated how the medication made Betty unfocused and distant. It was what the doctor had prescribed, and at least she was now getting sick pay, but Val still tried to arouse her interest. 'Paula is sure to be here soon. Cheryl's busy so she can't make it, but we might see her this evening. Talking of work, I haven't had any luck finding another job. I've only got until the end of this month, but it isn't looking good. Still,' she joked, 'there's always the dole.'

'Yes, I suppose so,' Betty replied, but her voice lacked interest.

'That must be Paula now,' Val said, going to let her in.

'Blimey, it's freezing out there. Me gas heater's broken, so my room's like a fridge.'

'Have you told the landlord?'

'Yeah, but he can't do anything until tomorrow.'

'Well until then, you can't stay there without heat. I'm sure Betty won't mind putting you up, or you can have my sofa if you like.'

'I was hoping you'd say that,' Paula said as she held up a brown paper carrier bag. 'I brought me nightclothes.'

'What do you think, Betty? Your place or mine?' Val asked.

'I don't mind.'

'It's your choice then, Paula.'

'No offence, Val, but I think I'll take Betty's sofa. I just wish Cheryl would settle on a flat or a house, but she seems to be taking forever to find something.'

'I know, but she's sensible not to rush.'

'Yeah, but every time we mention it, she goes all cagey.'

Val had to agree. Cheryl was being evasive, but, like them, she'd been deeply upset about Mel's baby. Maybe she'd decided to break away from them, to go it alone, and if she did, Val couldn't blame her. It would be awful for Paula, her chance to live in a decent home gone, and now Val felt the weight of responsibility for another devastating effect caused by her plans.

'I think Betty's gone to sleep,' Paula said.

'It's the pills. She's just taken one and they make her drowsy.'

Paula kept her voice low. 'Val, do you think we're safe now?'

She kept her voice equally soft. 'If you're talking about the police, then yes. If Betty's husband was going to lodge a complaint, I feel sure he'd have done it by now.'

'I hope you're right, but I've hardly slept since it happened. I still feel so guilty.'

'We all do, and if I could turn the clock back, I would.'

'Me too.'

Val couldn't bear talking about it any more. It had happened, a baby had died, and there was nothing they could do to make amends for the pain and suffering they'd caused – that *she* had caused by her hateful need for revenge. Yes, Mike Freeman had stolen her career, but she knew now it was her own fault for trusting him, for telling him things about her company that had given him the ammunition he needed. She wasn't a child, knew how cut-throat the business world could be, and should have been circumspect. When she'd failed to find another job within the industry, she blamed him – it had been easier that way. In truth, she'd been disheartened, full of resentment, and hadn't presented herself in the best light.

'I'm thinking about looking for another job,' said Paula, suddenly.

Val was startled out of her thoughts. 'Are you? What brought this on?'

'I just fancy a change.'

'I'm still looking, but I haven't had any luck yet.'

'At least you can get a job in an office.'

'It's funny really,' Val mused. 'Before all this happened, Betty was going to look for another job too. She's fed up with housekeeping and I suggested a job in a shop.'

'So, when she gets better – hopefully soon, we'll be looking for jobs at the same time. It's a strange coincidence, and I hope we all find something. You in an office, Betty in a shop, and, though I'd like to do something else, no doubt I'll be stuck in another soddin' factory.'

Chapter Forty-two

The builders had been wonderful, completing the work on schedule in mid-February, and now Cheryl took a final look around. The bedrooms looked nice, with pretty wallpaper and room for a few choice pieces of furniture that would add familiarity, a way to give a feeling of home. The authorities had completed their inspection; they were happy with the facilities, her qualifications and standards. She'd have to employ another nurse, mainly for the night shifts, but now the necessary paperwork allowing her to open was in place.

It had been hard to keep it from Paula, to fob her off, but whilst waiting for the work to be completed Cheryl had come up with another idea, one she hoped would solve *all* their problems.

She wandered downstairs to the comfortable sitting room with adequate seating for everyone, and then on to the room that had been converted. Perfect, everything was perfect – well, not quite. So far the house was empty. Would she be able to fill it? The thought made Cheryl's stomach churn. She was committed now, her mortgage large and payments to be made on time every month. Come on, she chided herself, you've come this far and there's no turning back now. She would tell them tonight and, if they agreed, everything would indeed be perfect.

Paula couldn't stand it any more. She was so jealous, but it was her own fault. She should have told Keith how she felt, but fear had held her back. It was too late now. Keith and Maureen were an obvious pair and had been courting for what felt like ages. During the lunch break, Paula sat with Lucy in the canteen, her mind made up. 'I'm giving me notice in on Friday.'

'Are you? What for? This ain't a bad job and the pay's good.'

'I just feel like a change,' she said, her eyes inadvertently moving to where Keith and Maureen were sitting.

'Oh, I get it,' Lucy said as she followed her gaze. 'It's the lovebirds, ain't it?'

'No, why should it be?'

''Cos no matter what you say, you fancy Keith, and it's got up your nose that he's with someone else.'

Paula cocked an eyebrow. 'As usual, you don't mince your words.'

'I speak as I find, but yes, I know I'm a bit blunt. I take after my mother. Speak the truth and shame the devil was one of her favourite sayings. And as for those two,' she said, nodding in their direction, 'they won't last.'

She doubted that Lucy was right. If anything, Keith and Maureen were getting closer by the day. 'It makes no difference to me.'

'If you say so, but I still think you're mad to leave. Oh sod it, there's the bell. It's time to go back to work.'

'I'm sneaking outside for another fag first.'

'You ain't got long.'

'Enough for a few drags. See you later,' Paula said as she hurried out, brushing past Keith's table, head down, and uncaring if she got into trouble with the forewoman as she stepped outside to light up. She was leaving anyway, so what did it matter?

Her thoughts turned to Betty; though still down in the dumps, she now seemed a little better. Cheryl hadn't been there last evening, but she'd rung to say she was coming tonight and had something to tell them. Had she found a house at last? Oh, she hoped so. It would be a fresh start, a new home along with a new job.

With reluctance, Richard had gone back to work. Mel still wasn't right, but at least there was some improvement. He'd given up trying to talk about

429

the baby's medical condition. Every time he mentioned the subject, Mel became almost hysterical and remained adamant that nobody else was told. John and Anne still blamed Betty – still refused to talk to their mother – but with Mel his sole concern, Richard had found justification in keeping the truth from them. If Betty's madcap scheme had worked it would have ruined his marriage, his reputation – in fact, his life. John had been ready to believe the accusations, but as his mother had been poisoning his mind since the divorce, was it any wonder? If Anne hadn't turned up in time to recognise the girl, she'd have heard the story second-hand and he'd have lost her too, just as he'd lost his son for so many years. Yes, he thought now, he was justified in thinking that it was time for Betty to find out just how painful it was to be estranged from her children.

He looked at Mel that evening as she picked at her dinner. She was still grieving, but as the doctor had told him when he'd voiced his concerns, it was early days yet. His voice gently cajoling, Richard said, 'You've got to eat, darling.'

'I'm not hungry.'

Richard still felt that a change of scenery might help. His staff had managed competently during his absence, and he was confident they could manage again. 'I know you said a month ago that you didn't want a holiday, but how about now? We could go somewhere quiet. I could rent a villa for just the two of us, somewhere warm and secluded.'

Mel said nothing at first, pushing her food around on her plate until at last she looked up. 'Yes, all right.'

He smiled with relief. 'I'll pop down to see the travel agent first thing in the morning.'

When he'd cleared his plate, Richard rose to his feet, and taking Mel's almost full one from in front of her, took them through to the kitchen. There were a few things to sort out at the showrooms before they could leave, and with business slow at this time of year, he'd have to find a holiday that wasn't going to cost an arm and a leg. He scraped Mel's food into the bin and was just about to start washing up when she came into the room.

'Leave it, Richard, I'll do it.'

He opened his mouth to protest, but the look on her face stilled him. He was treating Mel like an invalid again and knew she hated it. 'All right, darling, while you're clearing up, I'll give the kids a ring to let them know that we're off on holiday.' He glanced at his watch. 'It's seven o'clock so they should be home from work.'

'You . . . you won't invite them to join us, will you?'

'No, of course not,' and leaving the room he went to the telephone.

'Hello, Dad,' John said, 'how's things?'

'Mel's just agreed to a holiday. I'm hoping the change will do her the world of good.'

'When are you going?'

'I don't know yet. I'm off to the travel agent's in the morning.'

'Dad, don't forget I'm getting married in about six weeks.'

'Don't worry. I want to get away as soon as possible, and we'll be back well before the twenty-eighth of March.'

'Right-o, but I doubt you'll be off before Sunday, so we'll see you then.'

'Yes, but do me a favour, John. Don't talk about your mother. I think it upsets Mel and she doesn't need the constant reminder of what happened.'

'Sorry, Dad, I should have realised that before.'

They spoke for a few moments longer, and then, saying goodbye, Richard hung up. He dialled Anne's number, giving her the same news.

His daughter wasn't so happy. 'I still think it's a bit too soon, Dad.'

'Well I don't, and anyway, Mel's agreed.'

'Maybe we should come with you, though I'd have to check if I can get time off work, Tony too.'

'Sorry, darling, but this holiday is for just the two of us.'

'I see. See you on Sunday then.'

'Yes, but as I told John, please don't talk about your mother. I know you're both bitter, but going over and over it isn't helping Mel. Why don't you talk about the wedding instead? It might arouse

Mel's interest, give her something else to think about.'

'Mel's just as angry as us, and can you blame her? She seemed pleased when we told her that we'd hung up on Mum when she rang us – and anyway, maybe talking about it helps to get it off her chest.'

Anne sounded a bit miffed, but Richard said firmly, 'I think enough has been said on the subject, and no, I don't think it helps Mel. Now, I'll see you on Sunday, and I don't want to hear another word about your mother.'

'What if Mel brings it up?'

'Then divert the conversation to something else.'

Anne reluctantly agreed and, relieved, Richard said goodbye. The sooner he got Mel away from all the angst the better, and with any luck they'd be able to get away in just over a week.

At the same time that evening, Val and Paula were in Betty's flat, but she wished they'd leave. She didn't want to think or to talk, but since her medication had been cut in half a lot of the fogginess had cleared. Betty preferred it when her thoughts were cushioned in cotton wool. They were chatting, but she didn't join in, only listened; unable, now that her head had cleared, to cut out the sound of their voices.

'Do you think Cheryl's found a house?' Paula asked.

'Yes, probably.'

'Oh, I can't wait. It'll be great to get out of my bedsit. Not only that, I've definitely decided to find another job. I'm giving a week's notice on Friday.'

'It might be better to find another one first. I haven't had any luck, just a job typing all day that would drive me mad. It was lovely of Mr Warriner to give me a cushion of three months' salary when he retired, so at least I'm not pushed to take just anything.'

Betty closed her eyes. There'd been a time when she too wanted to find another job, to do something other than cleaning, but the will had left her now. In reality she dreaded going back to work, and if the doctor stopped her medication completely the silence of her employer's house would give her nothing but time to think. No, she didn't want to think, didn't want to feel. When the fogginess in her mind had first lifted, she had tried to ring Anne and John when Val wasn't around. It had broken her heart when they refused to take her call, both hanging up as soon as they heard her voice. Val had told her to give them time, that eventually they'd come round, but in her heart of hearts, Betty doubted it.

'There's Cheryl,' Paula now said as she moved from her post at the window. 'Oh, Val, I hope it's good news.'

It didn't take long for Cheryl to climb the stairs, and before she had even knocked on the door, Val was letting her in. She said hello, but then almost immediately walked across the room to crouch in front of Betty. 'How are you doing?' she asked gently.

Betty heard her soft voice, saw the concern in her eyes, and felt a surge of sadness that brought tears to her eyes. No, no, she didn't want this, didn't want to feel again. 'I . . . I need another pill.'

'Yes, your medication is due,' Val said.

'Wait, Val, don't give it to her yet. I need to tell you all something, and need Betty to be alert for a little while longer.'

'No . . . no, I want my pill.'

'I know, darling, I know, but just give me five minutes, that's all,' Cheryl urged, as she rose to her feet.

'Have you found a house?' Paula asked eagerly.

'Yes, but sit down.'

There was a moment's silence until they were all settled and then, taking a deep breath, Cheryl said, 'I'd better start at the beginning, but I've put a lot of thought into what I'm going to suggest and I think it's the perfect answer for all of us.'

'All of us? What do you mean?' Val asked.

'I've always dreamed of opening my own residential home, but never thought it possible and had settled on midwifery. However, when I put the idea to the bank manager, to my amazement, he actually agreed to my business plan, and the mortgage.'

'A residential home. What's that?' Paula asked.

'It's a sort of nursing home, not for physical illness, but for elderly people who can no longer care for themselves.'

'But . . . but I thought we were going to share a house.'

'We still can, but not in quite the same way.'

'How then?'

'Let me tell you about the house first. With two bedrooms, we can live in the basement flat. I've converted the ground floor, making another two, an office and sitting room. Upstairs, there's another six.'

'Ten bedrooms! Where is this house?' Val asked.

'In Wimbledon.'

'Wimbledon,' Paula exclaimed. 'Blimey, that's miles away.'

'It's not that far, but please, let me finish. I'll need help, Paula, lots of it, and with this in mind, if you want it, I'd like to offer you a job.'

'Doing what?'

'To start with, I'll need auxiliaries and I think you'd be perfect.'

'What's an auxiliary?'

'A nursing aide. You'll be trained to look after the residents' general needs, seeing that they're comfortable, eating properly, changing the linen, things like that.'

'I dunno, Cheryl. It's a bit different from working in a factory.'

'I know, but I'm sure you'd be good at it. I want

the residents cared for in the best possible way. It's awful for the elderly when they're shunted off somewhere because they can no longer look after themselves and feel that they have become a burden. When they come to us I'd like them to feel that they're part of a family, loved, with a few of their own things around them.'

'If they can't look after themselves, I don't think I'd have the stomach for some of the things I'd have to do. I ain't like you, Cheryl, I'm squeamish.'

'It might be hard at first, but honestly, you'd become used to it. One thing though, until we're established, I won't be able to offer you much in the way of pay, but you won't have to give me anything for your keep.'

'Well, Paula, you wanted a change,' said Val, 'and this would certainly be one.'

'Val, have you found another job yet?' Cheryl asked.

'No, I'm afraid not.'

'Oh good, because I'd like to offer you a job too.'

'Me! But I'd be a useless auxiliary.'

'No, no, I'd like you to handle all the administration. I'm hopeless at paperwork, accounts and such. With two bedrooms on the ground floor, you could live in too. Like Paula, I can't offer you much in the way of wages, but you'd be living rent free.'

Betty felt her eyes welling up again. If they accepted Cheryl's offer it would be more than she could stand. They'd become like a family to her, and now she had lost her children, Paula, Cheryl and Val were all she had left. Unbidden, a sob escaped her lips.

'Oh, Betty, Betty, don't. I'm so sorry. I should have spoken to you first. There's a job and home for you too. I know you're a wonderful cook, and I'm sure the residents wouldn't fail to eat if you provided their meals. If you don't fancy that, then you too could be an auxiliary.'

Betty began to cry in earnest now, and Val jumped to her feet, saying, 'I think she's had enough, Cheryl. I'm going to give her a pill.'

'Yes, all right, but please, all of you, give my offer some thought. I know it's been a bit of a shock, but it could be perfect. We'd all be together, like a family, like the residents' family. Look, I know you need time to think about it. I'll go now and we'll talk again tomorrow.'

Betty found that she didn't want to take the pill. She wanted to be alert, to be aware of Val and Paula's decision. If they accepted Cheryl's offer, then she would too, the thought of life without her friends unbearable.

Chapter Forty-three

It was Paula's last day at work. She was on Keith's machine, unable as she fed paper to resist stealing glances at him. There was no getting away from the fact that he was nothing to look at, or that the attraction had been physical, but now Paula longed to know how it felt to be held in his arms. What an idiot she'd been, what a fool to miss what had been right under her nose. She had feared dating; feared being alone with a man, of what he might try, but knew now that she'd have felt safe with Keith. He was a cheeky bugger, but there was kindness, caring in his nature too, and if she'd had the courage to tell him why she'd been afraid to go out with him, surely he'd have understood.

He wandered up to Paula now, but there was no cheeky remark, just sadness in his tone. 'So, this is your last day. I'm sorry you're leaving, Paula.'

'I should think you'll be glad to see the back of me.'

'You might have given me a hard time now and then, but it was a laugh sparring with you.'

'I see Maureen isn't in today. Is she off sick?'

'Yeah, bit of a tummy upset.'

'Tell her goodbye for me.'

'I'll do that,' he said, but as the bell sounded for lunch break, he moved to switch off the machine.

Paula climbed from her stool, finding it hard to hide her feelings as she headed outside. A few of the girls were already there, Greta saying, 'In case I don't see you later, I'll say goodbye now. Good luck, Paula, and I hope your new job works out.'

'Yuk, I wouldn't fancy wiping old men's bottoms,' Doreen said, 'but like Greta, I wish you luck.'

Paula grimaced. She didn't fancy wiping anyone's bottom either, and hoped the task wasn't going to be part of the job. Maybe she'd been mad in agreeing to take it on, but anything was better than seeing Keith with Maureen every day. Not only that, she really was sick of working in factories. She'd wanted to do something worthwhile, and caring for elderly people gave her the opportunity to do just that. All right, a few things might make her feel queasy, but as Cheryl had said, she'd harden to that. Earlier that week, Cheryl had taken her to see the house and she'd been amazed at how spacious it was. Her bedroom in the basement was much larger than the bedsit she had now. Even better, it was only a room to sleep in!

'Hello, Paula.'

'Watcha, Lucy. If you're going to the canteen I'll join you.'

'I'm just off.'

Paula stubbed out her cigarette, impervious to the looks from the other girls as they walked away. She knew how they felt about Lucy, but refused to join in their gossip and suspected that she was also a part of it now If they wanted to think that she too was a lesbian, so what? They were a narrow-minded lot, giving Lucy a hard time just because of her preferences, and Paula was glad that she was leaving – glad to be away from the lot of them.

'So, it's your last afternoon,' Lucy said when they were sitting at a table.

'*And* the last night in me bedsit. I'm moving into the nursing home tomorrow.'

'I'll miss you. It's been nice having your company during lunch breaks, and I can't see anyone else joining me.'

'Do you know what? I'll miss you too.'

'Wow, are you flirting with me? If you are, let me tell you I'm already spoken for.'

Paula giggled. 'Shut up, you silly cow.'

Lucy pretended to pout unhappily. 'I think you'll miss Keith more than me.'

'No I won't, and anyway, he's well happy with Maureen now.'

'Joking aside, Paula, I'd like to stay in touch. It'd

be nice to hear how you're getting on with your new job. Have you got an address?'

'I can't remember it off the top of my head, but I've got it in my handbag. Remind me to pass it on before I leave at the end of the shift.'

'Will do,' Lucy agreed.

By eight that evening, Mel and Richard were all packed. John was taking them to the dockside in the morning. Richard knew he'd been a bit extravagant when he chose a last-minute cruise. At first Mel protested, saying she didn't fancy being on board a ship full of other passengers, but he'd convinced her that it would be fine, that there'd be plenty of places where they could secrete themselves away. He was a little unsure about whether he might have misled her; but anyway, even if seclusion were difficult, surely meeting new people and seeing new places was just what Mel needed?

He watched as she now closed the suitcase, hoping that it wouldn't be much longer before she could also bring closure to the past. As soon as she was ready, they could try for another baby, and maybe this holiday would see a resumption of their sex life. When the telephone rang, Richard hurried downstairs to answer it, finding his daughter on the line.

'Hello, Dad, I've just called to wish you and Mel bon voyage.'

'Thanks, darling. I'll give her a shout.'

442

'Wait, Dad, there's something else. I've had a letter from Mum. I haven't opened it, in fact it's in the bin, but I wondered if she'd written to you too.'

'No, she hasn't, and before you speak to Mel, I'd rather you didn't mention it to her. She seems a little better and the last thing she needs is another reminder of your mother.'

'All right, I won't say anything.'

'Good girl. I'll give Mel a call now, and see you when we get back.'

'You'll only just be in time for John's wedding.'

'Don't exaggerate, darling. We dock in Southampton four days before the event.'

'I'm still surprised you can afford a cruise, especially as you said business is slow.'

'I got a last-minute deal and, anyway, after what we've been through, I think Mel and I deserve a break.'

'Oh, I'm sorry, Dad, of course you do. It's just that I'm going to miss you both.'

'You'll be busy helping Ulrika with last-minute wedding plans – the time will pass in a blink of an eye.'

'Yes, I suppose you're right. She's already starting to panic.'

'You'll be able to calm her down, but bye now, sweetheart. I'll fetch Mel to talk to you.'

'Don't get seasick.'

Richard called Mel, and then left her to speak to

Anne. No doubt Betty had sent John a letter too, one probably full of apologies and excuses. Unlike Anne, perhaps John would read it, but Richard doubted it would make any difference. Oh, what did it matter? All he wanted now was to get Mel away from everything, and maybe, just maybe, make a fresh start. In fact, if he never heard another word about Betty, it would suit him just fine.

'Are you all done?' Val asked as she looked at Betty's empty wardrobe.

'Yes, I'm ready. Instead of ringing them, I wrote to John and Anne. They have my new address now, but I doubt they'll get in touch.'

'Given time, I'm sure they will,' Val said, her advice always the same.

'I can't believe we'll all be living in the same house.'

'I know, but I'm sure we made the right decision.'

'I hope my cooking will be up to scratch.'

'You'll be fine, we'll all be fine,' Val said. 'Well, except for Treacle. He's going to find it a bit strange.'

'He'll probably lick all the residents to death. Oh, dear, that didn't come out right. I don't mean death, but you know what I mean.'

Val smiled. It was lovely to see Betty a little more like her old self. She still had some way to go and still took medication, but the awful depression was lifting. Val hoped she was right, that given time both John and Anne would forgive their mother. In the meantime, she had the three of them, and with a new home, along with a new job, there'd be plenty of other things to fill her mind.

They had all been to see the residential home, impressed not only by the size of the house, but by the area too. Wimbledon Common was a short walk away, perfect for Treacle, but the house also had a large, mature garden for him to explore. Paula would be sleeping in the basement along with Betty, and Val knew they were both thrilled with that. She and Cheryl had bedrooms on the ground floor, and they would all share the communal areas. It was going to take a lot of adjustment and, as she had found it difficult to give up the privacy of her own flat, Val hoped it would work out.

'Do you know, I once thought it would be lovely if we could all share a house, but it's taken Cheryl to make it possible,' Betty now said.

'You should have mentioned it.'

'Maybe, but it wouldn't have included new jobs for all of us.'

'That's true, but the pay's rubbish,' Val quipped, a grin taking any sting out of her words.

'Yes, but with no rent and food thrown in, I'm sure we'll manage. What time is the removal van coming in the morning?'

'I told you, nine o'clock.'

'I'm glad we can take our things with us.'

'Yes, and it makes you realise how the residents

will feel. Cheryl's right, it'll be nice for them to have a few of their own bits and pieces around them.'

'So we're all set?'

'We are, but come on, let's finish the last of the sherry. I think after all this packing, we deserve it.'

'Val, you know I can't drink while I'm on medication.'

'Well then, how about doing without your pill? We should share a toast. A new home, new job, and a fresh start for all of us.'

'Right, you're on,' Betty said, and for the first time in ages, she seemed to have a genuine smile on her face.

Chapter Forty four

What followed were months of hard work. When she had first taken on the job and seen the expenses, Val had feared that Cheryl would fail – that the costs of running the home would outweigh any profits. Thankfully she'd been proved wrong, and for the first time in six months the residential home was showing a profit. Cheryl would never be rich, but Val knew that money wasn't her goal.

Val closed the account book and sat back in her chair. This office had become her sanctuary, a place where she could sit alone, undisturbed for most of the day. Any capable residents were free to use the sitting room, the conservatory, or to wander in the garden, but by eight in the evening Cheryl insisted they were in their rooms.

At first, Val thought this a bit harsh, but with a few pieces of their own furniture, and a television in each room, she'd soon come to appreciate why this rule was in place. With a nurse employed to cover the night shift, her job would have been impossible if the residents weren't settled, and when she came on duty, the rest of them would finish work to gather in the small basement sitting room.

Val and the others had their weekends free too, with staff employed to cover their shifts. It had surprised her how well they all got on, staff and residents, and though a couple of the old folks were proving to be a little difficult, Cheryl had a marvellous way with them that was rubbing off on Paula.

Betty had proved herself a godsend in her ability to make cheap yet nourishing meals – as did the weekend cook – and this went a long way to counterbalance the other costs. Betty had stopped taking any medication now, but still wasn't her old self. It hadn't helped that before her son's wedding she had sent another letter, along with a present, only to be devastated when it had been returned unopened.

When the wedding day arrived, Betty had fretted dreadfully, wanting to be there, yet afraid of wrath and rejection if she turned up. They had done all they could to keep her mind off it, trying to keep her occupied, but nothing had worked.

That had been in March, but it was now July, the summer day warm as Val rose to throw open a window. A couple of residents were sitting in the garden, Paula bending to talk to them. The change in her since becoming a trained auxiliary was amazing. She had blossomed, and the residents seemed to love her chirpy nature. Treacle had become a firm favourite too, spending most of his time being fussed over by the residents, with Val beginning to wonder who he belonged to. Look at him now, the little rascal, sitting on the bench between Elizabeth and Alicia, getting attention from both of them.

Paula wasn't immune to his charms either, and her laugh reached Val's ears, but then as her office door opened, Val turned to see who was coming in.

'Sorry to disturb you,' Cheryl said, 'but can we have a word?'

'Yes of course. I just opened my window to see Paula in the garden with a couple of residents. She's certainly got a way with them.'

'Despite her fears, she took to the job like a duck to water. I only wish the other day-shift auxiliary I took on was doing such a good job. I know she doesn't live in, and the pay isn't great, but I've seen how she leaves most of the unpleasant tasks to Paula. She'll have to go, Val, but I'm not looking forward to sacking her.'

'Leave it to me. I'll do it.'

'Will you? Oh, thanks, Val. I don't know what I'd do without you, and now you'll have to advertise for a replacement too.'

'No problem. Was that what you wanted to talk to me about? Or is there something else?'

Cheryl sat down. 'Yes, there is. I wanted a word

about Betty. I'm worried about her, Val. She's a marvellous cook, but she spends all her time in the basement, only mixing with us. We need to think of a way to draw her out, encourage her to become more a part of the residential home.'

Val had to agree, and then struck by an idea she said, 'Unless we find an immediate replacement, we're going to be short of an auxiliary. Paula will be rushed off her feet, and if this is pointed out to Betty, maybe we can persuade her to help with serving the meals.'

'Val, she has to cook the meals; she certainly doesn't have time to serve them too.'

'You have a point, but once the food has been dished up, Betty only has to wait until the plates are returned to the kitchen.'

'She hasn't got Paula's young legs, and it's a bit much to ask of her. Oh, but wait, once the meals have been served, they're followed by cups of tea. If we could get Betty to take that on, she'd come into contact with the residents.'

'Good idea. It would only be until we find another auxiliary, yet maybe it will be enough time for her to get to know them and come out of her shell a bit.'

'All right, we'll give it a try.' She rose to her feet. 'I must go. As you know, Alicia's son rang to say he's coming to visit her today and I want to pass on the good news.'

'It's about time. He hasn't been for over a month.'

'I know, but last time he came she barely recognised him. Her dementia is getting worse, but as Doctor Harman said when I last asked him to call in, there isn't much we can do. See you later, Val.'

Yes, Doctor Harman, Val thought. He was a nice man, around Cheryl's age, and he always came quickly when called out. He and Cheryl got on well, both showing great concern for the residents. Taking care of the elderly was something they had in common. Val smiled inwardly, wondering if anything would come of it – if Cheryl and Doctor Harman realised they were the perfect match.

An hour later, in the basement, Betty tested the lemon jelly, pleased to find that it had set. When Paula ran lightly down the stairs, she forced a smile, saying, 'Just in time. Lunch is ready.'

'I can't find Tina. Have you seen her?'

'No, love.'

'Well she'd better turn up soon. I'm sick of the way she disappears every time there's work to be done.'

'You should have a word with Cheryl.'

'Yeah, I think I will.'

Betty changed the subject. 'I see you got a letter this morning.'

'It's from Lucy, a girl I used to work with in the laminating factory.'

'That's nice.'

'I didn't know the telephone number here then, so could only give her the address. It's been ages since I left the factory and I'd given up on hearing from her. Now she's written to say she'd like to see me, asking when I'm free.'

'That's nice,' Betty said again as she dished up, then placed a food cover over the plates. She yearned for the postman to bring her a letter too, and it was a struggle to hide her feelings. It was all right for Val and the others to say that, given time, John and Anne would come round, but repeated letters to them remained unanswered. Her son had been married for nearly four months now, but she hadn't even seen a photograph of the wedding. In one of her letters she'd begged John to send her at least one, but yet again, he hadn't responded. Oh, it was cruel, unkind, yet Betty couldn't blame him. He wanted nothing more to do with her, and once again she thought it no more than she deserved.

Paula picked up a laden tray, saying as she walked out, 'If Tina thinks I'm going to serve this lot on my own, she's got another think coming. They'll want tea too, but I've only got one pair of hands.'

Moments later, Betty could hear Paula yelling Tina's name, and wished her luck. She was right, Tina was lazy, and it was unfair that the greatest share of the work fell to Paula.

At last, five minutes later, Tina appeared, a scowl

on her face as she said, 'Thanks to that bitch I got a rollicking from Cheryl.'

Betty bristled. 'If you're referring to Paula, I won't have you calling her that. She works twice as hard as you. If you ask me, you deserve a ticking off.'

'I didn't ask you. What would be the point? You always take Paula's side.'

'Sides have nothing to do with it. I speak as I find.'

'Leave it out. Miss Goody Two Shoes can do no wrong in your eyes.'

'That's enough! Now I suggest you get on with your work. That tray is waiting to go upstairs.'

Tina's face flushed with annoyance. 'Who are you to give me orders? I'm an experienced auxiliary, but you're just the cook and a right miserable old cow too.'

'How dare you speak to Betty like that?' Val spat, neither of them aware until then that both she and Paula had walked into the kitchen. 'Get out, Tina. You're fired.'

'That suits me fine, but I'm not going anywhere until I get my wages.'

'You'll get what's due to you, and your cards, in the post. Now go!'

Tina ripped off her overall, hurled it on the floor, grabbed her handbag, then flung open the basement door, pausing to shout, 'I was going to tell you to stick the job anyway.'

The door slammed, reverberating in the room, followed by a short silence before Betty said, 'Oh, Val, you've done it now.'

'I know, but she was going to be given notice anyway.'

'I can't say I'm not glad to see the back of her, but until you find someone else, how is Paula going to cope?'

Val's temper had flared when she heard the way Tina had spoken to Betty and she had sacked her without thought. It may have been the wrong thing to do, but at least she could make the most of this opportunity. 'Oh dear, I don't know,' she said, feigning worry. 'I'm sorry, Betty. I suppose I can give you a hand with the rest of the trays, but that's about all. I've got someone coming in half an hour to view the home. There's one place left and I know Cheryl needs to fill it. She's busy too . . . Oh,' she cried, 'I really have put my foot in it, haven't I?'

'Calm down,' Betty urged. 'It's not like you to get in a state. Don't worry, we'll think of something.'

'Like what?'

Betty pursed her lips. 'I'll just have to give Paula a hand for now. If you help with the trays, I'll follow on with the tea.'

'I can't ask you to do that. You've got enough to do down here and you'll be worn out.'

'It won't be for long, and if we all muck in until you find another auxiliary, I'll be fine.'

'Are you sure?'

'Yes,' Betty said as she prepared another tray. 'There, one each. That'll be three served and only leaves two more. I'll get them ready for you, and then follow on with the tea.'

'Betty, you're an absolute treasure,' Val said, smiling with delight.

'It takes one to know one,' she quipped. 'Now come on, get moving.'

'Yes, sir,' said Paula, jokingly offering up a salute before picking up the tray and hurrying out.

Betty had to smile, but it was brief. She had offered to help out, but was now regretting it. The basement was a hideaway, a place where she didn't have to put on a front. It was hard to give up the reins when Janet came in to do the cooking at weekends, but by then she was worn out and needed a break. They would walk Treacle on the common, or take a drive to explore the area, but Anne and John were never far from her mind. It had been six months now, six months since she had seen them, and their estrangement still tore her apart. Sometimes she longed for the cushion of medication again, but knew it would make her incapable of doing her work. At least she now felt needed, a part of a team, and though she was without her children, she wasn't alone any more.

Chapter Forty-five

It was the start of a new chapter for Betty. As they did Paula, the residents loved her, and to her surprise she found enjoyment in chatting to them. She'd expected them to be miserable, echoing her own feelings, but instead found that, for the most part, they were a lovely bunch. Three were more stoic than the others, accepting they could no longer care for themselves, but the latest resident was finding it difficult to settle in.

'Here you are, Mrs Wilson, a nice cup of tea,' Betty said.

'Thank you, my dear. Do you know if my daughter has rung to say she's coming to see me?'

'No, I'm afraid not,' Betty said, sad to see the hope dying in Mrs Wilson's eyes. 'Maybe she'll come tomorrow.'

'I wish that were true, but I doubt it. I . . . I upset her, you see, and I don't think she'll ever forgive me.' Mrs Wilson pulled out a lace-edged handkerchief from her cardigan sleeve to dab at her eyes.

Betty placed the cup of tea by the side of the bed before sitting on the edge. So far Mrs Wilson had refused to get up and had remained isolated. She must be lonely, but perhaps with a bit of persuasion Betty could get her to socialise with other residents. The woman was estranged from her daughter too, and Betty felt a sense of affinity as she gently said, 'Give her time, she's sure to come round.'

They were words that had been said to her so many times, but Betty had all but given up hope. Now that she was involved with the residents, with their care, she had begun to feel a sense of self-worth again, but still longed to see her children.

'I wouldn't accept my grandchildren – shunned them, and now it's too late to make amends. When I couldn't look after myself, my son hoped my daughter would help, but . . . but she refused. He was being transferred abroad, so had to make arrangements for me to come here.'

'I'm so sorry,' Betty said, wondering why Mrs Wilson had rejected her grandchildren. 'I know it must have been hard for you to give up your home, but I'm sure if you give it a try, you'll be happy here. The other residents are lovely, and really, we're all like one big happy family. How about getting up after lunch? There's usually a game of cards or a puzzle in progress in the sitting room, or, if you fancy a stroll, the garden is lovely. Two of our residents have taken to looking after the shrubs, and they make all the lovely flower arrangements you'll see dotted around the house. I'm sure they'd love your help.'

'No, no, they're all strangers.'

'You won't feel like that once you get to know them.'

'Perhaps I will get up. I . . . I'll think about it, and Betty, why don't you call me Louise?'

'Thank you, I'll do that,' Betty said, relieved that the ice had been broken. Louise Wilson was such a dainty little thing, what you'd call a proper lady, but at least she had confided in her, happy at last to drop the formalities.

'How is Mrs Wilson doing?' Cheryl asked as she came upstairs.

'She's a little better. I'm hoping she'll get up after lunch.'

'It's been weeks since she arrived, so I'm glad to hear it. I knew that if anyone could break through her reserve, it would be you.'

'Thanks, but while I've got a bit of time, I'd better pop down to the kitchen. The new cook is doing all right, but still needs a bit of help with the menus.'

'Betty, are you sure you don't regret the change of roles?'

'Not really. I love cooking, but this is so much more rewarding.'

'That's good,' Cheryl said, 'but is it too much for you?'

'I've been doing it for a month, so why ask now? Don't you think I'm up to it?' Betty asked worriedly. 'I might not be a spring chicken, but this is no harder than my last job.'

'Of course I think you're up to it. In fact, you do more than is asked of you.'

'We all muck in, you too, and what about Val? I never thought I'd see the day, but she took over from Paula to feed Alicia yesterday.'

'Yes, it's wonderful, isn't it? She's got the administration work so organised now that it gives her a bit of spare time.'

'Talking about time, I'd better get a move on.'

Betty went downstairs, whilst Cheryl gave a short rap on Mrs Wilson's door before going in to see her. The room looked nice, cosy, with the elderly woman's own chintz curtains and bedspread in place, along with a few pieces of furniture. 'Hello, I've just popped in to check your blood pressure; Betty tells me that you might get up today.'

'Yes, perhaps.'

'That's good,' Cheryl said as she wrapped the band around Mrs Wilson's stick-like arm. The reading was a little high, but not enough to cause concern. Cheryl's voice was gently cajoling as she now said,

'I see you've finished your tea. Would you like to get dressed? Betty and Paula are a bit busy, but I can give you a hand. We could go downstairs together.'

Mrs Wilson hesitated, but then with a small sigh she said, 'Yes, all right.'

'As it's such a lovely day, we should make the most of it. Perhaps take a stroll in the garden?'

'Oh no. I'm rather unsteady on my legs and if I hadn't had a fall, my son wouldn't have put me in this . . . this place.'

Mrs Wilson made her admittance to the home sound like punishment, but it was the usual initial reaction. It was hard for the residents to give up their homes, to lose their independence, and that was why she'd been determined to make her nursing home special. 'You'll be perfectly safe. I'll be with you, and the paths are smooth, but if you'd rather go to the sitting room, that's fine.'

It took some time, but at last Mrs Wilson was dressed, and, after taking her cane, she clung on to Cheryl with her other arm. Slowly they descended the stairs, and as they reached the hall, Betty appeared, obviously pleased to see that Mrs Wilson was up.

She hurried forward, saying, 'Louise, how lovely. Let me take you to the sitting room.'

Cheryl smiled. So for Betty it was Louise now, and it was wonderful that she'd broken through Mrs

Wilson's reserve. Whilst waiting to find a suitable replacement for Tina, it hadn't taken long to see that someone like Betty would be perfect. Though at first her kind and cheery manner might have been false, the residents hadn't noticed, all responding well to her. In just a short time, Betty had taken them under her wing, surprising Cheryl when one day she'd asked to be an auxiliary. A replacement cook had been found, one almost as good as Betty, and the nursing home now ran on well-oiled wheels.

Cheryl crossed her fingers, hoping that nothing would happen to change it. If things carried on like this, she would at last be able to relax, safe in the knowledge that her nursing home was the success she'd hoped for.

On Friday night, Paula went to meet Lucy. She loved her job, but it was nice to have a change of scene, to meet up with someone nearer her own age. Cheryl was lovely, but still older, and though they were close they had little in common really. Cheryl's world was the home, the residents, and though Paula had grown fond of them too, she liked a break now and then. Not only that, Lucy still worked at the laminating factory and she loved to hear the latest gossip.

They would meet as usual in a coffee bar in Putney, one they had found was easy for them both to get to by bus; as she walked in, Paula saw that

Lucy was already there. The jukebox was playing, but above the sound of Mungo Jerry singing 'In the Summertime', Paula said, 'Watcha, Lucy, how's it going?'

'Hi, Paula.'

'I'll just grab an espresso. Do you want another one?'

'Yes please.'

There were a few blokes sitting at tables, one of them giving a soft wolf whistle as Paula went up to the counter. She tensed, but ignored them, and after getting the drinks took a seat opposite Lucy.

'Still off men I see,' Lucy drawled.

'Don't start. Now tell me, what's the latest news on Greta?'

'Word must have got around and some of the older women have gone a bit sniffy with her. Bitches.'

'So you were right. She is pregnant.'

'Yes, poor cow, but I hope her bloke does the right thing and marries her.'

Paula took a sip of her coffee, wanting to ask, but wondering how to make it sound as though she wasn't really that interested. She tried to sound nonchalant, tacking the important question onto the end. 'Any other news? How's Doreen, and what about the lovebirds?'

'There's nothing new. As far as I can tell, Doreen's fine, but as you know, she keeps well out of my way.'

Lucy picked up her cup, whilst Paula inwardly

462

fumed. No mention of Keith and Maureen, but she didn't want to give the game away by asking again.

'Oh, Paula, you should see your face.'

'I dunno what you mean.'

'Blimey, girl, you must think I'm a right mug. It's Keith and Maureen you want to hear about, not Doreen or anyone else,' Lucy teased.

'No it isn't.'

'All right, so you don't want to hear that things aren't going so smoothly now?'

'Since when?' Paula squeaked, then kicked herself for giving away her interest.

'See, I knew you liked him.'

Paula slumped. 'All right, you've got me. I don't suppose there's any harm in admitting it now.'

'Well then, from what I've seen, I reckon he's gonna be footloose and fancy free again soon.'

'What makes you think that?'

''Cos Maureen has got her eye on someone else and is making it a bit obvious.'

'Really! Who?'

'A new bloke who started a couple of weeks ago. He ain't bad looking, and seems interested in her too. If he asks her out, I reckon she'll chuck Keith. When that happens, I'll tip you the wink and you could sort of accidentally bump into him, if you know what I mean.'

'No, I wouldn't have the nerve to do that, and

anyway, if Maureen chucks him he'll be gutted. Even if he did ask me out, he'd only be on the rebound.'

'So, you're just gonna let him go?'

'Keith's in the past now. I've moved on,' Paula lied. 'And as you once said, there're plenty more fish in the sea.'

'Yeah, well, he ain't much of a catch, that's for sure. I don't know what you saw in the ugly git anyway.'

Paula's neck stretched with indignation. 'He might not be much to look at, but he's a lovely bloke. Looks ain't everything, you know.'

'Whoa, I was only saying.'

'Oh, sorry, Lucy. I didn't mean to get on my high horse.'

'That's all right, now come on, let's talk about something else. Tell me more about the nursing home. Has the new lady settled in yet? And how are the other patients?'

'They're not patients, they're residents,' Paula corrected her.

'They're all unable to take care of themselves; some ain't in the best of health, so why not call them patients?'

Paula frowned. 'Yes, I see your point, but Cheryl prefers to call them residents. She reckons it makes them feel less helpless, more capable.'

'I like the sound of Cheryl more and more. Is she straight?'

Paula laughed. 'You're impossible, and yes, as far as I know, she's straight. Anyway, from what you've told me, Myra would go potty if she could hear you.'

Lucy's expression suddenly turned to one of sadness. 'I . . . I think she's gonna leave me.'

'Oh no. Lucy, I'm so sorry, but what makes you think that?'

'It's been coming on for a while. All the signs are there, and I think it's someone she met at art classes on Friday nights. She . . . she's probably with her now.'

'But you've been together for three years. Surely you're mistaken?'

'I hope so, but if I'm right and she leaves me, I . . . I dunno what I'd do.'

Paula had never seen Lucy showing vulnerability before. She was usually so hard faced, her feelings never on show. 'Why don't you have it out? Talk to her?'

'I'm too scared to do that. I'm hoping that if I say nothing it'll all pass, that it'll all go away.'

'I wish there was something I could do to help.'

'Thanks, love, you're a nice girl,' but as though she regretted showing her vulnerability, she forced a cheeky smile. 'In fact, it's a shame you prefer men.'

Paula went along with her. 'Even if I didn't, what makes you think I'd fancy you?'

'What, with these looks! How could you resist me?'

'Well, yes, you do bear a passing resemblance to Julie Andrews.'

'What, her who played Mary Poppins?'

'Yes, but I can't see you in that role.'

'Me neither, and anyway, I ain't got the voice. The looks, yes, but not the voice. Mind you, I'd be great playing the chimney sweep and I could do a better cockney twang than that American geezer who took the part.'

'I can't argue with that.'

Lucy leaned forward. 'Paula, I know you're trying to cheer me up, and thanks, but if it's all right with you, I think I'll go home.'

'Of course it's all right with me, but will I see you next week?'

'It depends on how things go with me and Myra. I'll give you a ring.'

'It'll be fine, I'm sure it will.'

'I hope so, love, I really do hope so.'

Together they left the café, Lucy to walk to a bus stop in one direction, Paula in the other. It saddened Paula to see Lucy so unhappy but, unbeknown to her, despite her own troubles, Lucy was thinking about Paula too, and an idea she had in mind.

Chapter Forty six

In August, Richard took a call from his son.

'Dad, I've got a bit of news,' John said, 'but I'm not sure how Mel will take it.'

Richard balanced the receiver on his shoulder, signed the letter that had been put in front of him and, as his secretary left the room, he concentrated on the call. 'Why, what is this news?'

'We've put off saying anything but, at four months, Ulrika is really starting to show. She's pregnant, Dad. We're having a baby.'

Richard grinned. 'That's wonderful, John.'

'Yes, we're chuffed, but as I said, I'm not sure how Mel will take it.'

'She'll be pleased for you.'

'But, Dad, the baby will be born in January.'

Richard understood now. If their baby had been full term, it would have arrived in January, and though John's would be a year later, the reminder might still upset Mel. Still, there would be no hiding it from her, so trying to sound more assured than he felt, he said, 'It's been eight months now since we lost our baby, and I'm sure Mel will be able to cope.'

'I hope you're right, Dad. It would be awful if this set her back again.'

'Leave it with me. I'm off home now and I'll break it to her gently. I'm sure she'll be all right, and don't let it stop you coming round on Sunday as usual.'

'All right. We'll see you then.'

'Have you told Anne?'

'Not yet, but I'll ring her later.'

'Auntie Anne. I'm sure she'll be chuffed.'

'Yes, I think you're right. See you, Dad.'

'See you, son,' Richard said, and replaced the receiver. Bloody hell, he was going to be a grand-father: the thought made him feel both sad and old. He had hoped to be a father again, and though he'd hidden it well from John, this bit of news had come as a shock.

Would John tell Betty that she was going to be a grandmother? Richard doubted it, and though he'd managed to quash it until now, guilt rose. Yes, Betty had deserved to suffer, but it had gone on long enough. He'd have to talk to Mel, bring up the dreaded subject – try to persuade her that it was time to tell John and Anne the truth.

In the nursing home, Nora, the cook, flopped onto a chair by the long, wooden, well-scrubbed table.

She had time for a small break, but when all the crockery was returned there'd be a stack of washing up to do before she was finished for the day.

Nora liked this job, everyone was so friendly, but it really was hard work. She could do with a hand, if only someone to take on the never-ending piles of washing up. Everyone mucked in, she knew that, but it only extended to work upstairs. At least they had a daily cleaner but, with this house being the size it was, the kitchen only got a good going-over once a week, with everyday tasks left to her. With residents and staff, working here was like cooking three meals a day for a huge family, and the problem was she wasn't used to coping on her own. Her last job had been in a café, and though there had been a lot more meals to cook, she hadn't had to clear up afterwards, since that and the washing up had been left to other staff.

'Hello, Nora,' said Betty as she came in to place a small stack of trays, heaped with crockery, on the table. 'I'll be back with the rest in a minute.'

Nora heaved herself up. Her feet were playing up today, spilling over the side of her usually comfy slippers. 'I'll get the washing up done and then I'll be glad to get off home. At least it's Friday and I've got the weekend off.'

'What's wrong, Nora? You seem a bit out of sorts. Are your feet playing up again?'

Nora liked Betty, finding her a comfortable,

homely sort of woman who was easy to talk to. 'Yes, but keep it to yourself. I don't want Cheryl thinking I can't do the job.'

'You're doing fine, but maybe you could do with a bit of help down here. Why don't you have a word with Cheryl? I'm sure she'd be sympathetic.'

'No, no, if she thinks I can't manage, she might replace me.'

'Cheryl wouldn't do that.'

'At my age it isn't easy to find work and I can't afford to risk it. Don't worry, I'll manage.'

'I'm sorry I can't give you a hand, but until the residents are settled for the night, we can't leave them for long. I know Paula and I take it in turns to have breaks, but this is a busy time of the day.'

'I don't know how you do it. I might moan now and then about my workload, but I'd rather do this than look after that lot.'

'Oh, don't say that, Nora. They're lovely – well, most of the time – and you can't help growing fond of them.'

'Privileged, that's what they are. They live in this lovely house, are well cared for, which is more than you can say for most old folk.'

'They have to pay for their care, Nora.'

'They're still lucky. Take me for instance. I'm not rich, and when I can't take care of myself any more, I won't end my days in a place like this.'

'Haven't you any family?'

'No, since I lost my husband, there's just me.'

Val suddenly rushed into the room, her face as white as a sheet. 'Betty, come quickly, you're needed upstairs.'

'What's wrong?'

'It's Alicia. Cheryl has called the doctor, but . . . but I think it might be too late.'

'Oh no,' Betty cried, rushing from the kitchen.

Alone now, Nora shook her head. It was all right for Betty to say you grew fond of the residents, but it would be hard for them if this one died. Mind you, as they were all so old, it would be something they'd have to get used to.

At nine o'clock, still reeling with shock, Val walked through the basement kitchen to the small sitting room, Paula, Betty and Treacle following behind. She had managed, just to hold herself together until now, but at last allowed the tears to flow.

'Oh, love, don't,' Betty cried.

'I . . . I can't believe she's gone.'

Paula was crying too, her voice strained. 'When I walked in with Alicia's tray, I . . . I thought she was asleep.'

'She's been going downhill lately,' Betty consoled, 'and Doctor Harman has been called twice. There was a time when she would potter in the garden with Elizabeth, but she's hardly left her room for the past few weeks.'

'She . . . she seemed fine at lunch time,' Paula sobbed. 'She didn't eat much, but when I looked in later, she was having her usual afternoon nap. Oh no! You don't think she was . . . was already—?'

'Dead,' Betty finished for her. 'I don't know, but you heard what the doctor said. Alicia died quietly, and peacefully, in her sleep. She was eighty-two, a good age. Her heart just failed, and there was nothing he, or anyone else, could have done to save her.'

Val sniffed, managed to stop crying, then said, 'Come on, Treacle, I expect you're hungry and, come to that, none of us has had any dinner.'

'We didn't get the chance of a break, but I'm not hungry. What about you, Paula?'

'No, no, I don't want anything.'

As Val went into the kitchen, she was still fighting to control her feelings. Unlike Alicia, she wasn't old, but the thought of ending up dying alone horrified her. Would she always be living like this? A spinster – without a family around her? Stop it; stop thinking like that, she told herself. You've got Betty, Paula and Cheryl, who were as good as kin. Val gave Treacle a bowl of food then, going back into the sitting room, was unable to help voicing her thoughts. 'I know the residents are old, but when I took the job, I . . . I didn't think about this side of it.'

'It's hard, but I suppose losing them is inevitable.'

Paula sobbed, 'I can't do it, Betty. I can't face this again.'

'Paula, there's a call for you,' Cheryl said as she walked into the room. 'Someone called Lucy.'

Paula ran a hand across her face. 'I . . . I was supposed to have met her this evening, but . . . but with all that's happened the time flew and now it's too late.'

'Go and speak to her. I'm sure she'll understand.'

Val watched Paula leave the room, knowing the devastation on her face was a reflection of her own. Betty seemed to be fighting tears now, obviously holding them back to comfort both her and Paula.

'Paula was wonderful – you all were,' Cheryl said. 'I know it took longer than usual, but you managed to get everyone settled. I've left them in Jane's capable hands now.'

'Do you want anything to eat?' Val asked. 'I'm afraid the food that Nora left for us is ruined.'

'Oh dear, you didn't get your dinner breaks and must be starving.'

'No, we're not hungry, but what about you?'

'Sit down, Val. I'll make myself a sandwich in a minute,' said Cheryl.

'I don't know how you can eat,' Betty muttered.

'I'm upset about Alicia, but as a nurse I had to learn to cope with the loss of patients. If I hadn't, I couldn't have functioned and the other patients would have suffered.'

'But surely it's different now? Alicia had become like a part of the family, and . . . and,' there was a gasp, Betty finally breaking down, 'it reminds me of when I lost my mother.'

Val moved to her side, laying a hand on her shoulder. 'Don't, you'll start me off again.'

'Remember that Alicia was happy here,' Cheryl urged. 'She enjoyed pottering in the garden, until lately when she became very tired and spent more time in her room. After being such an active lady it must have been hard for her and, rather than lingering, she slipped peacefully away in her sleep.'

'Yes, yes, I suppose you're right,' Val murmured, 'but even Treacle seems to be feeling it. He's off his food too.'

'Let's take him for a walk,' Cheryl suggested. 'The fresh air will do us all good.'

Val nodded, scrubbing at her face, and Betty did the same. 'Paula might want to come too.'

'I'll grab a sandwich while we're waiting for her,' Cheryl said, going to the kitchen.

Cheryl forced down her feelings as she buttered two slices of bread. Alicia had been one of their first residents, and it had been awful to lose her, but as the only one who hadn't broken down, she had to hold herself and the others together. Mentally she calculated, sure that everything that could be done, had been done. Doctor Harman had been called and had been wonderful – though he too was upset that Alicia had passed away. Alicia's son had been

474

informed, the poor man dreadfully distraught when he arrived at the home. The death certificate had been signed and then given to the son to enable him to make arrangements for his mother's funeral.

What they needed now was closure. The other residents still needed care, and she hoped Betty and Paula would be up to it after their weekend off.

But when Paula came back downstairs, Cheryl couldn't help but worry. She was so young, with none of Cheryl's training, and though her eyes were now dry, she looked ready to break down again at any moment. 'I'm just going to eat this sandwich and then we're all going for a walk. Do come with us, Paula.'

'I can't. I know it's late, but my friend Lucy is on her way to see me. I tried to put her off, but she said it's urgent. You . . . you don't mind, do you?'

'Why should I mind? This is your home, Paula, and you're welcome to invite anyone to it.'

'I won't bring her in. We'll probably go for a walk too.'

Cheryl nodded and, as Paula went through to her bedroom, she sat down at the table, quickly eating her sandwich. What they needed was something else to think about, to focus on. She'd thought about a few things that could make the home run more smoothly: maybe they could sit down and thrash them all out. A lot would depend on the costs but, if put in place, there would be vast improvements.

* * *

Paula called goodbye as the others went out for a walk. She wasn't in the mood to see Lucy, but there'd been no putting her off. Lucy had been sympathetic about Alicia, but sounded agitated, insisting that she had to see her. Perhaps Myra had left her and she needed support. Mind you, in this state, Paula doubted she'd be much help, but at least they could cry on each other's shoulder.

A look in the mirror showed a wan face, devoid of make-up, but what did it matter? She felt that losing Alicia was her fault, tears now flooding her eyes again. Yes, she had looked in on Alicia that afternoon, but had only poked her head around the door. If Alicia had still been alive, and she'd looked properly – seen that she was ill, maybe, despite what Betty said – the doctor could have done something to save her. She'd wanted to be an auxiliary, had loved the job, but now felt hopeless, useless. Once Cheryl found out, she'd probably sack her, but at this moment, Paula knew she would welcome it.

Only fifteen minutes later there was a knock on the basement door and, surprised that Lucy had arrived so quickly, she went to answer it, saying as she pulled it open, 'That was fast. Did you get a taxi?' Her eyes rounded with shock. No – no, it couldn't be!

'I put my foot down 'cos Lucy said you might need a cuddle.'

'Keith!'

'I was waiting with Lucy in the café, but you didn't turn up.'

'With . . . with Lucy,' she stammered.

'She told me to come with her, said that if you saw me again, I might still have a chance. If I have, I'd love to give you that cuddle,' he said, opening his arms. 'You look like you need one.'

She stepped into them, sobbing, 'Oh, I do, I do.'

It was wonderful to be held, comforted, and for a long time they remained outside, arms locked around each other, until at last, Paula stopped crying. In his arms she felt no fear, just happiness, and didn't want to let him go. 'Do . . . do you want to come in?'

'Yeah, if you like.'

Paula knew how awful she must look and guessed that her eyes would be puffy from crying. She said hastily, 'Sit down, I won't be a tick.'

She dashed to the bathroom and quickly splashed cold water over her face, but saw little improvement. Keith was here. He was really here, wanting to know if he still had a chance. At last Paula smiled. Lucy had done this, brought them together – if she'd been there, Paula would have hugged her.

With little she could do to improve her appearance, she returned to the kitchen, finding herself shy as she walked in. 'Err . . . can I get you anything? Tea? Coffee?'

'Coffee would be great.'

Aware of Keith's eyes on her, Paula felt self-conscious as she made the drinks, her hands trembling as she placed them on the table. She avoided looking at him as she sat down, only saying, 'So . . . so you're not with Maureen now?'

'I wouldn't be here if I was.'

She at last looked up. Was Keith over Maureen? Or was he on the rebound? 'What happened?'

'She found someone else.'

'That must have been rotten for you.'

Keith was about to answer when the door opened, the others coming in, eyes widening when they saw Keith.

'Back already,' Paula said, jumping to her feet. 'Err, this . . . this is Keith. We used to work in the same factory.'

Val was the first to recover. 'We didn't feel like a long walk. Hello, Keith. I'm Val.'

'Nice to meet you,' he said.

Cheryl stepped forward, hand held out. 'I'm Cheryl and it's nice to meet you.'

Betty's eyes were narrowed with suspicion as she too introduced herself, then saying, 'So, Keith, why are you here?'

'I wanted to get back in touch with Paula.'

'What for?'

'Betty,' protested Paula, 'we're old friends.'

The atmosphere felt strained now, and as though sensing it too, Keith said, 'Well, I'd best be off.'

Both Val and Cheryl said goodbye, but Paula noted that Betty remained silent as she stepped outside with Keith, closing the door behind them.

His car wasn't far away, but as they walked towards it, Keith reached out to clutch her hand. 'Paula, I didn't get a chance to answer your question.'

'What question?'

'The one about Maureen and, just to set the record straight, no, it wasn't rotten for me when she chucked me in.'

'It . . . it wasn't?'

'Look, Maureen was all right, a bit of a laugh, but that was all.'

'When I worked at the factory, it looked like more than that to me.'

When they stopped by Keith's car, he turned to face her. 'I ain't proud of myself, but in truth, I only took Maureen out in the first place because I couldn't have you. Maybe I hoped it would make you jealous, but then you left, and it just became a sort of habit, that's all.'

'Oh Keith.'

'From the first day you started work in the factory, I knew there was only one girl for me. Please, munchkin, don't turn me down again.'

'I'm not going to,' she cried, throwing herself into his arms.

Chapter Forty-seven

What followed was a happier time for Paula, but it took Cheryl some time to convince her that she hadn't shown any negligence in her care of Alicia. Cheryl had worried that Paula would leave, but thankfully that hadn't happened.

When Paula started courting Keith, Betty had been difficult at first, but Cheryl understood why. Paula had become like a replacement daughter to Betty and she feared losing her. Keith was such a nice young man, bringing them flowers and helping out with odd repair jobs around the house. He was so obviously in love with Paula and trying so hard that Betty had finally thawed.

When Alicia died, it had been a hard time for all of them, but thankfully they had managed to move forward, all more aware that, with elderly residents, it was something that inevitably would happen again. Maybe they'd be more prepared next time, find it easier to cope – but she hoped it wouldn't be for some time yet.

With a wry smile, Cheryl kicked herself for not realising there was a dumbwaiter when she bought the house. It must have been boxed in years ago, but had now been uncovered, saving both Paula and Betty the job of running up and downstairs with trays. It made a huge difference, and with a dishwasher installed in the kitchen, both cooks were a lot happier. It had been short-sighted of her not to install one in the first place, but there had been no complaints from Betty when she'd been cook, or Nora, and it had taken Val to point out what a help one would be.

Alicia's room had been taken by their first male resident, William Penwith, a lovely elderly gentleman who was proving to be very popular with the women. It was November, and Cheryl's thoughts now turned towards Christmas. She wanted their first one in the nursing home to be special, with everyone – staff and residents alike – sharing a wonderful time.

'You're quiet, Cheryl,' said Val.

'I was just thinking.'

'Do you feel like sharing your thoughts?'

'I was thinking about this place, Christmas, and how we're going to celebrate.'

'Christmas yes, but when it comes to this place, don't you ever think about anything else?'

Cheryl had to laugh, then saying, 'Yes, I suppose I do come over as a bit obsessive.'

'Don't worry, I know how much it means to you, but don't you ever think about a boyfriend, marriage?'

'Not really. What's brought this on?'

Val shrugged. 'Perhaps seeing Paula with Keith, how happy she is.'

'I'm too busy to think about men, and anyway, they've never showed much interest in me.'

'I think they do, but for some reason you walk around with your eyes shut. Take now, for instance, you haven't even seen what's under your nose.'

Cheryl raised her eyebrows. 'Val, what *are* you talking about?'

'Doctor Harman.'

'What! But he's not interested in me.'

'Like I said, you walk around with your eyes shut.'

'But . . . but . . .'

'Yes, that's taken the wind out of your sails, hasn't it? Wake up, Cheryl. You're the only person who hasn't noticed how he looks at you.'

'Betty, did you hear that?' Cheryl squeaked as she came into the room.

'Hear what?'

'What Val just said about Doctor Harman.'

'That he likes you, yes, but I thought you knew.'

'I had no idea.'

'Well you know now.'

Cheryl felt her face flooding with colour. Oh, she'd

never be able to look the man in the eye again without blushing.

Val chuckled, 'That's brought some colour to your cheeks. Still, enough said. I think I'll take Treacle for a walk. Anyone want to join me?'

'Yes, I'll come,' Betty said, 'but we'd better wrap up warm. What about you, Cheryl?'

'Err . . . not this time. I think I'll have a bath.'

'Yes, and while you're soaking, think about your admirer,' Val teased.

'I'll do no such thing.'

'You're mad. He's lovely,' said Betty.

Cheryl huffed as she left the room, but after running a bath and sinking into it, she did indeed find herself thinking about Doctor Harman. He had lovely blue eyes and she loved the way they crinkled at the corners when he smiled. Stop it, don't be stupid, she chided herself. Val and Betty must be out of their minds. A man like Simon Harman would never be interested in her.

Richard felt sick to his stomach as he spoke to his wife. 'Mel, we've got to tell them.'

'Why? Loads of women have high blood pressure when they're pregnant and in most cases it's nothing to worry about.'

'That's not good enough, Mel. I've said it before: what if anencephaly is genetic?'

'And I've told you it isn't.'

Richard shook his head as he rose to his feet. 'I'm sorry, Mel, but this has gone on long enough. I'm going to see my son,' and, ignoring Mel's shout of outrage, he walked out of the house.

Since the day early in her pregnancy that Ulrika had said her blood pressure was high, he'd felt this dreadful horror of history repeating itself. Even when she'd been to the clinic and was thrilled to report that everything appeared fine, it hadn't eased his horror. They had a right to know – needed to know – the risk of anencephaly.

During the drive, Richard tried to rehearse his words, but in reality there would be no easy way to break this to them. He pulled up outside John and Ulrika's mews cottage, but remained in the car for a while, once again trying to gather his thoughts. Then slowly he got out, knocked on the door, his son opening it.

'Dad! What are you doing here?'

'I'm sorry, son, I should have thought to ring you first, but can we talk?'

John stood back to let him in and with a heavy heart, Richard stepped inside.

'Sit down, Dad.'

'Where's Ulrika?'

'She's tired and wanted an early night.'

'Is she all right?' Richard asked worriedly.

'Yes, she's fine, but what is it, Dad? I can see you're uptight about something.'

Richard took a deep breath, then began to talk, watching the range of expressions that ran across his son's face – until finally, he had said it all.

'But . . . but why didn't you tell us?'

'Mel didn't want you to know. She blamed herself – felt it was something she'd taken during the pregnancy.'

'And was it?'

'No, and the doctor convinced her of that,' Richard said, 'but it was eating her up. She refused to talk about it, and when you told me that Ulrika was pregnant, she still wouldn't let me tell you.'

John's head went down, and for a moment he said nothing. When he looked up, his eyes were hard, voice tightly controlled, 'So Mel wouldn't let you tell us – warn us that our baby might be at risk.'

'Yes, I'm afraid so.'

'And you went along with that?'

'I'm sorry, son, but since Mel lost our baby, things haven't been right between us. I've been trying, really trying, to make her see sense, but she gets so upset. I'm here now though. Telling you now.'

John leapt to his feet, his voice now high with anger. 'As Ulrika is nearly eight months pregnant, it's a bit bloody late.'

'What is wrong? John, why are you shouting?' Ulrika asked as she came into the room.

'It's all right, darling, go back to bed. My father is just leaving.'

Paula threw open the door, running into the basement flat, her eyes sparkling. 'Hello everyone.'

Val's smile was wry. 'I don't need to ask if you enjoyed your night off. Your face says it all.'

'We had a lovely time. Lucy invited us to her flat, and it was nice to meet Myra.'

Betty frowned. 'You've got a strange choice of friends.'

'Yes, but they include you,' Paula said, leaning forward from behind Betty to wrap arms around her neck. 'And you, Val, and you, Cheryl.'

'Get off you daft moo,' Betty said, 'and take that coat off. It feels damp.'

'It's raining,' Paula quipped, 'but yes, Mumsie, whatever you say, and I love you too.'

Betty felt her face flush with pleasure, but this was quickly followed by pain. Paula had called her Mumsie, said she loved her, and she loved her too, but if only it had been Anne saying those words. It was all right for Cheryl to talk about Christmas earlier, but Betty dreaded the memories that would be dredged up.

Somehow Betty knew she would have to get through it, paint a smile on her face for the residents, but she wished she had a magic wand that could wind time forward to a day long after Christmas. Or better still back: back to a time before she had caused those awful events – caused the death of a baby.

'Why the long face, Betty?' asked Cheryl.

'Oh, it's nothing,' she said dismissively. She didn't want to talk about it, her feelings, knowing that she would only get the usual platitudes. Time hadn't changed anything, and she knew now that it never would.

'Cocoa all round?' Paula asked.

'I'll do it,' Betty offered.

'No, you stay there,' she said, leaning forward again to kiss Betty on the cheek. 'At your age, we can't have you getting worn out.'

'My age!' Betty protested. 'I'm only a spring chicken.'

'Yeah, if you say so.'

In the face of Paula's happiness and affection, Betty's mood lifted. 'Enough of your lip. Just get the milk on.'

'Oh yeah, I forgot to tell you. I've found out why Mrs Wilson's daughter won't have anything to do with her.'

'She told me she'd disowned her grandchildren,' Betty remarked, 'but I didn't like to ask why.'

'It's because her daughter married a Jamaican.'

'And she told you that?'

'Yeah, she really opened up, said she wanted a young woman's perspective and asked me what I thought about mixed-race marriages.'

'What did you say?'

'I said that black men ain't my cup of tea, but if he was her daughter's choice, and the geezer made her happy, good luck to her.'

'How did she react to that?'

'She said she realises that now, but it's too late. Honestly, Betty, fancy disowning your grandchildren just because they're coffee-coloured.'

Betty found her mood lowering again. If only she had grandchildren, no matter what colour, she'd shower them with love. Yet if they ever had children, John and Anne would never let her near them. The thought was unbearable, and Betty's unhappiness rose to almost choke her.

'Paula, I've been thinking about Christmas,' Cheryl said. 'I want to make it special.'

Betty rose to her feet. 'I don't think I'll have any cocoa. I'm a bit tired so I'm off to bed.'

'Betty, are you all right?' Val asked.

'I'm fine,' she lied, and then calling goodnight was glad to get to her bedroom. With the pain of losing her children on her mind, she didn't want to talk about Christmas, didn't want to think about Christmas, but as she undressed and climbed into bed, she was haunted by the memories of last year.

Chapter Forty eight

Cheryl was delighted with how well things had gone. They had all shared Christmas dinner, staff and residents, but with Nora having two days off, Betty volunteered to cook the dinner, with the rest of them mucking in to give her a hand. It had been a job to drag her out of the kitchen, but when Cheryl had insisted, Betty joined them reluctantly.

The residents were now settled in their rooms, and in the basement sitting room, Cheryl looked at Betty, saw the sadness in her eyes, and understood why. In the days leading up to Christmas, Betty had looked anxiously at the post, but there hadn't been cards from either of her children. It obviously still weighed heavily in Betty's thoughts so, hoping to take her mind off it, Cheryl said, 'It's nice that Keith has taken Paula to meet his mother. I wonder how she's getting on.'

'Give them a chance. They've only just left,' Val said then, rubbing her tummy, added, 'I still feel like I'm bursting, but that was a wonderful dinner, Betty.'

'I couldn't agree more,' Cheryl agreed.

'How about a glass of sherry?'

'Yes, good idea.'

Val poured the drinks, and then passing out the glasses, she chinked hers with Cheryl's. 'To our first Christmas, and continuing success next year.'

'I'll drink to that.'

'It's a shame Doctor Harman couldn't join us.'

Cheryl went pink. 'I don't know how you had the nerve to ask him.'

'It only seemed polite, and he looked disappointed that he had to decline. Apparently he always spends Christmas with his sister and her family.'

'I think you were trying to matchmake again,' Betty said.

'Yes, well, if I leave it to those two they'll never get together.'

'Val, will you stop it?' Cheryl protested. 'I've told you, Simon isn't interested in me.'

'Oh, Simon now is it? Since when?'

'I don't know. We just sort of slipped into first-name terms.'

'Oh good, it'll be a date next.'

Cheryl tutted, refusing to be baited as she asked, 'Betty, is there enough meat left to serve it cold with mashed potatoes tomorrow?'

'For God's sake, surely we're not back to talking about this place again.'

'Leave her alone, Val, and yes, Cheryl, there's plenty of meat left.'

'Oh, I give up,' Val complained.

Cheryl smiled. Val didn't know it, but she had a feeling that Simon was indeed going to ask her out. She wanted to savour the thought, yet at the same time wondered if it was really what she wanted. The home had become everything to her – her life. She was happy, truly happy, and did she really need a man in her life – even one as nice as Simon Harman?

'All right?' Keith asked.

'Yes, but I'm nervous about meeting your mother.'

'It'll be fine, you'll see, and I don't suppose you've changed your mind about going round to Lucy's tomorrow night?'

'No, I haven't. It was nice of her to invite us.'

'I'm still not sure I want to spend Boxing Day with a couple of dikes.'

'Keith!' Paula protested.

'Yeah, yeah, I know, but if me mates saw me I'd never live it down.'

'So you've said before, but I'm just glad she sorted things out with Myra.'

'I still think she should find herself a bloke.'

'Keith, how many times have I got to tell you? Lucy doesn't fancy men.'

'It ain't natural.'

'Can't you just accept her the way she is? Here, why are you pulling over?'

Keith didn't answer until he had stopped the car. 'If Lucy is more like a bloke, I don't suppose anyone would want her as a bridesmaid.'

'I dunno, maybe. Why ask me?'

'Ain't it obvious?'

Her eyes rounded like saucers. 'You're . . . you're not asking me to . . . to . . . ?'

'Marry you,' Keith finished for her. 'Yes, I am, Paula.'

Still she stared at him, saying nothing, her face frozen in shock, until at last she stammered, 'I . . . I can't.'

'Don't say that. I know we ain't been courting for long but, as I told you, since the day you started work in the factory, I knew you were the one for me. I love you, and thought you loved me too.'

'I . . . I do.'

'Then marry me.'

'I . . . I can't. When you find out, you won't want me.'

'Find out what?'

She blurted it all out then, sobbing, but when she came to the end, Keith pulled her into his arms.

'I think I guessed, love, and it doesn't matter. Well, except to say that I'd like to get me hands on the bastard who did it to you.'

'You . . . you still want to marry me?'

'Of course I do. Now put me out of my misery and give me your answer? What's it to be? But if you don't want me old mum coming after you for breaking her only son's heart, it had better be yes.'

She took a juddering breath, smiled at last. 'Well, I don't fancy going up against your mum. Yes, I'd love to marry you.'

'Oh, Paula,' Keith said, dipping his head to give her a kiss.

It was after eleven when Paula came home, and Cheryl was the only one still up. 'There you are,' she said. 'I wanted to talk to you and was hoping you wouldn't be much longer. How did it go with Keith's mother?'

'Great, she's smashing, but where are Betty and Val?'

'They went to bed half an hour ago. Sit down, Paula. I know it's late, but this won't take long.'

'I was hoping they'd still be up,' she said, pulling out a seat.

'Paula, I've watched you work, seen how competent you are, and I've had an idea.'

'Oh yeah, what's that?'

'I think you should train to be a nurse.'

'Me, a nurse! Leave it out.'

'I think you'd be excellent.'

'Cheryl, thanks for saying that, but well, there ain't much point in talking about it.'

'Why not?'

Paula grinned, her eyes sparkling. ''Cos I'm getting married, and Keith wants to start a family straight away.'

Cheryl was so sad at the thought of losing Paula, and knew Betty and Val would be devastated too. Yet looking at the joy reflected in Paula's eyes, she couldn't help but be happy for her. 'That's wonderful. When is the happy day?'

'I know it might sound a bit quick, but Keith doesn't want to wait. We thought next spring.'

'It's going to be rather a short engagement, and not a lot of time to plan a wedding, but if that's what you both want, I'm happy for you.'

'We don't want a big affair, just family and maybe a few friends.'

Betty wandered into the room. 'Oh, I can't sleep. I think I'll make a cup of hot milk. Do you two want one?'

'Betty, you'd better sit down. Paula's got some news,' said Cheryl.

Paula didn't wait, grinning widely as she said, 'Guess what, Betty? I'm getting married.'

Betty's face drained of colour. 'Married! You're getting married! Oh, no, that means you'll be leaving me too! I can't bear it. I can't,' and, stricken, she fled back to her room.

'I didn't expect you to react like that,' Paula cried as she chased after Betty.

Cheryl ran a hand over her face. Slowly she rose to her feet, going into Betty's bedroom to see Paula sitting on the side of the bed and trying to comfort her.

'But you're not losing me,' Paula was saying. 'I'm getting married, not leaving the country. You'll still see lots of me, I promise.'

'Really?'

'Yes, really, now come on, buck up; after all, I'm gonna need help with planning this wedding. I couldn't do it without you.'

Betty sniffed, wiped her eyes and then said, 'I'm sorry, love. I don't know what came over me.'

Cheryl heaved a sigh of relief. It was going to be all right, and quietly she left the room. Val still had to be told, but her reaction was sure to be nothing like Betty's – at least she hoped not. Thoughts that she always struggled to keep at bay now rose in Cheryl's mind – what they had caused and why Betty's children wanted nothing to do with her.

But some good *had* come out of their plans. She had this house, had made it a home for all of them, and if Parker hadn't been put away, she doubted that Paula would be where she was now. It had given Paula the confidence to take up her life again, to start going out with Keith, and now she was getting married. Betty had taken the news badly, but it was wonderful really, and instead of feeling miserable, surely it was something to celebrate?

Chapter Forty-nine

It took Val some time, but by the end of January, she finally decided to speak her mind. When she had first been given the news that Paula was getting married, she'd been shocked, but happy for her at the same time. It was impossible not to share in Paula's joy, to join in with the wedding plans, but it was also awful to see how Betty was struggling to put on a brave face.

When Val saw the happy couple together, she was pleased to see how relaxed Paula appeared when Keith threw an arm around her, but they were the only displays of affection shown in front of them. There had been other times when Val had seen tension on Paula's face, and suspected she knew why.

One day, when she was alone with Paula in the sitting room, Val said, 'Paula, I hope you don't mind me asking, but have you told Keith?'

'Told him what?'

'About Ian Parker. What he did to you?'

'Yeah, he knows.'

'You may think it's none of my business, but I'm worried about you. Are you going to be all right? You know, on your wedding night.'

'Oh, Val, I'm glad you've brought it up. I admit it's been worrying me and in all honesty, I don't know. We . . . we haven't, well, done it yet. Keith's been wonderful, not pushing me or anything, but sometimes I wonder if I should let him go all the way. I mean, what if I can't?'

'Does he know how you feel?'

'I think so. We have lots of snogs, and I've got no problem with that. Keith's so gentle and I don't go all tense or anything, so . . . so do you think I'll be all right?'

'Darling, if it's worrying you that much, it'll spoil your wedding day. Maybe it's time, as you put it, to go all the way.'

'Blimey, I never expected you to suggest that. If Betty could hear you she'd have a fit.'

'Well she can't hear me.'

'Watcha, Betty,' said Paula, laughing when Val spun round to see no one behind her. 'Oh, you should see your face.'

'I'm glad you think it's funny. Seriously though, Paula, you should take my advice.'

'Maybe I will.'

'Yes, well, let me know how you get on.'

'What! You want all the details?'

'No, silly, just to know that it was . . . well . . . all right.'

'I knew what you meant,' Paula said as she rose to her feet, 'I was just having you on. Anyway, I'd best get ready. Keith will be here soon.'

Though relieved that the conversation had been easier than expected, Val was also a bit worried. If Paula took her advice, but found that she couldn't, that she froze, would Keith still want to marry her?

Paula was in Keith's arms, nervous but determined now. She whispered in his ear.

He reared back, astonished. 'What?'

'Keith, what if I can't? I . . . I need to find out, need to know before we get married. You want a proper wife, not someone who can't . . . well, do it.'

'So this is for my sake. No, Paula, I'd rather wait. Do it properly.'

'But, Keith.'

'Look, I know you're going to be nervous, but I don't want our first bit of slap and tickle to be in the back of a car.'

'I bet it hasn't stopped you before.'

'Maybe not, but you ain't some bird I've just taken out with nothing else in mind but getting into her knickers. I love you, Paula, you're going to be my wife, and, once we're married, if it doesn't work the first time, so what? We'll have all the time in the world.'

'I . . . I might never be able to do it.'

'What, with me so irresistible?'

Paula flung herself into his arms again. 'Oh Keith, I love you.'

'See, I told you, irresistible,' Keith chuckled.

And it turned out to be true, because, in the back of the car or not, Paula gave herself to Keith. He resisted at first, but when it finally came down to it, it was she who proved to be irresistible.

Chapter Fifty

Val was smiling as she sat in her office the next morning. When Paula came home last night she'd been so happy that one look at her face had been enough. Paula had thrown her a cheeky wink and Val had felt like applauding. She looked around her office now, brow creasing. Was it really less than a year since they'd all agreed to join Cheryl in this venture? It felt so much longer. First there'd been that dreadful Christmas, one they would never forget. They'd had a hard lesson, finding that, for Betty, revenge wasn't sweet and only brought heartache. It had been followed by Betty's breakdown, and then the months of hard work to get this place established. But they had done it, and now, hearing a ring on the doorbell, she went to answer it.

'Hello, Doctor. Cheryl's in with Mrs Wilson now. Go on up.'

'Thanks, Val, and please, like Cheryl, call me Simon.'

'All right, Simon it is.'

'Good,' he said, smiling at her before going upstairs.

Oh, he was a nice man, perfect for Cheryl, but so far nothing had come of what Val had hoped was a budding relationship. They were both shy, that was the problem, but with two of the residents coming down with colds, no doubt Cheryl would have to call him out more often this month.

Val returned to her office. With Paula getting married, and a chance of a relationship for Cheryl, she found herself thinking about her own future. Would she ever find love again? With her lack of a social life it seemed unlikely, but maybe it was time to make changes, to widen her circle. Perhaps she should try something new, take up a hobby, perhaps photography. She could join a night class, and there were sure to be men there with the same interest. Yes, she'd do that, and – who knows – maybe she'd find a chance of happiness too.

'Hello, Cheryl, can I come in?' Simon asked.

'Of course, and I'm sorry to call you out. I thought it was just a cold at first, but now I think it might be turning into bronchitis.'

'Hello, Mrs Wilson,' Simon said as he approached the bed. 'Do you mind if I listen to your chest?'

'I keep telling Cheryl that I'm fine, but she won't listen.'

'She's worried about you,' Simon said as he gently placed his stethoscope on the elderly woman's chest. He admired Cheryl – found her a good nurse, and her devotion to the residents was plain to see. In fact, she was so devoted he doubted she'd have any time for him, and the thought held him back from doing what he always wanted to do when he saw her, and that was to ask her out.

'Yes, Mrs Wilson, you have got a touch of bronchitis,' he said, 'but it's been caught early and a course of antibiotics will soon put you right.'

'Oh, good, I can get up then.'

'Not yet, Louise,' Cheryl said. 'You still need to rest.'

'But I promised William a game of chess.'

'I'm sure he'll understand,' Cheryl said as she firmly tucked the blankets around Louise. 'I'll be back to check on you soon.'

Louise looked petulant as they left the room, and out of earshot, Cheryl giggled. 'Honestly, since our only male resident was admitted, things haven't been the same. The women all vie for his attention and jealousy is rife.'

Simon laughed, 'At their age, too, but it's good to hear that it's never too late.'

'It's certainly perked them all up.'

Simon looked across at Cheryl, saw flushed cheeks, her cameo-like skin, and the sprinkle of freckles across her nose. If he didn't say something, this wonderful woman might be snapped up by someone else. Yet, as always, shyness held him back – until at last the question burst from his lips. 'Cheryl, I wonder if you'd consider having dinner with me?'

Her eyes widened, and then with a brilliant smile she said, 'Yes, I'd like that.'

'How about Saturday night? I could pick you up at eight.'

'That's fine,' but then hearing Louise's petulant call, she said, 'I must go.'

Simon was smiling as he walked downstairs. He'd done it and Saturday night couldn't come round fast enough.

Cheryl had been in to see Louise, completed the rest of her rounds, but after the initial excitement of being asked out had passed, she now wondered if she had made a mistake. She loved the residential home, what she'd achieved, and it meant so much to her. In the hall she paused for a moment, but then on impulse went to the office.

'Hello,' Val said as Cheryl walked in. 'What's up?'

Cheryl sat in front of the desk. 'Simon has asked me out to dinner.'

'Good. I was beginning to think he'd never get round to it.' Val's head tipped to one side. 'So why the long face?'

'I shouldn't have agreed.'

'Why not? I know you like him and I'm sure you'll have a wonderful time.'

'Val, I can't give up running the home. It means too much to me.'

'Cheryl, what on earth are you talking about? The man has asked you out to dinner, that's all.'

'Yes, I know, but what if . . . if we become serious? What if he eventually asks me to marry him?'

'Goodness, don't you think you're jumping the gun? You haven't been out to dinner yet, but you're already talking about marriage.'

'I know you think it's silly, but I don't want to lead him on.'

'Just take one step at a time. See what happens. It might not work out between you.'

'But what if it does?'

'All right, let's look ahead; imagine that one day Simon asks you to marry him. Now you know what sort of life he leads, how busy he is. He in turn knows you are equally busy, and, I'm sure, how much this place means to you.'

'He's still a man: he might expect me to give it up – to be a stay-at-home wife.'

'You don't know that, and to be honest I doubt it. There's no reason why you can't be a wife *and* run the home. You may want more time off, but can always take on extra staff.'

'You make it sound so easy.'

'And you're making it sound impossible.'

'What if he wants a family?'

Val sat back in her chair, shaking her head as she said, 'You haven't been out with him yet and I still can't believe we're having this conversation. All right, children, but you can always take on more staff, and don't forget you've got us.'

'Yes, I have, haven't I?' Cheryl said, her heart feeling lighter now. She smiled at Val, but then a thought crossed her mind. 'Do you ever regret not getting your own back on Mike Freeman?'

'I don't know why you're bringing this up again now, but no, I don't. What happened to Betty brought me to my senses and I realised that, in reality, I only had myself to blame.'

'Are you happy, Val? Do you like this job?'

'Yes, I'm happy, and yes, I love my work.'

'You don't regret leaving your flat?'

'Of course I don't. I might have been silly to seek revenge, but thankfully look what I've gained. I've three wonderful friends and who could ask for better ones. Now tell me, what's brought this on?'

'Oh, I don't know. The thought of change, I suppose.'

'Change is inevitable. For a start, Paula's getting married, but are we talking about Simon again?'

'Yes, I suppose we are, and he is rather cute isn't he?' Cheryl said as she rose to her feet.

'He's a dish and you'd be silly to let him go,' Val warned.

'Don't worry. I won't,' Cheryl replied. Val was right, she was being silly. She would take her advice, take one step at a time, and now found herself again looking forward to Saturday evening.

John looked at his baby daughter and felt a surge of love that almost took his breath away. He placed a finger on her palm, tiny fingers curling to hold on. God, she was beautiful, perfect, all his fears gone from the moment she'd been born. The doctors had told them there was nothing to worry about, that all tests had shown that the baby was fine, but still he worried, still unable to believe that his father had put Mel's lies before the welfare of their unborn baby.

Ulrika picked up a laden bag. 'I'm ready.'

'I'll take that,' John said. 'You carry the baby.'

He placed the bag in the boot and opened the passenger door for Ulrika, taking the baby while she climbed in. With infinite gentleness, John then placed their daughter in her arms again before going round to the driver's side. As he got behind the wheel, he turned to look at his wife and daughter. 'All set?'

'Yes, I am all set. We both are,' Ulrika said, smiling lovingly at the baby.

John gunned the engine to life, careful to look behind him before pulling away. He drove steadily, slowly, so aware of the precious cargo beside him. He thanked his lucky stars for the day he'd met

Ulrika, for her wisdom, her way of gently making him see another point of view. He'd been ready to cut his father from his life, just as he had his mother, but Ulrika had talked him round, as she always did. Her power to forgive never ceased to amaze him and showed the beauty of her soul. Ulrika had managed to talk Anne round too, and she'd be making this same journey tomorrow. He was glad, thankful that his wife had made them both see sense at last.

Val rose from her desk to answer the doorbell. She saw the young couple, but it took a moment before she recognised them. *Oh my God,* her mind screamed.

'Good afternoon. I understand my mother lives here, Elizabeth Grayson. Would it be possible to see her?'

Betty's son hadn't recognised her, yet Val remained frozen in shock, aware that he was holding a baby. *Don't just stand there! Say something.*

She then sensed someone behind her, Cheryl asking, 'Is there a problem, Val?'

'This . . . this is Betty's son and his wife. They . . . they want to see her.'

Cheryl too looked shocked, but maintained her equilibrium enough to say, 'In that case, don't leave them on the doorstep,' and, pushing Val to one side, she smiled at the young couple. 'Please, do come in.'

Still Val found herself unable to speak as she stood

back, unable to believe it, part wonder and part fear constricting her throat. Why had they come? Was it going to cause more pain for Betty? Oh, please, please, no.

As they stepped inside, Cheryl said, 'How lovely, you have a baby.'

'Yes, a girl.'

'Val, take them through to your office. I'll find Betty.'

With that Cheryl hurried away, whilst Val, still with a feeling of dread, led the couple to her office. The last time Betty had seen her son it had almost destroyed her, and at last the tightness in her throat eased. 'Why have you come?'

'I told you, to see my mother.'

'You . . . you're not going to—'

Val's words were cut off as the door opened and she spun round to see Betty walking into the room.

'John,' Betty gasped.

He moved towards her, a soft smile on his face. 'Hello, Mum. I thought you might like to meet your granddaughter. Her name is Elizabeth, Beth, and she's named after you,' he said, placing the baby in Betty's arms.

There was a sob, and then the tears fell, rolling down Betty's cheeks as she looked down at the baby. 'I . . . I don't deserve it.'

'Yes, you do. We all make mistakes, need forgiveness, and I realise that now. You were a wonderful mother, and I know you'll be the perfect grand-mother too.'

'Oh son,' Betty gasped, her eyes now swimming with happiness. 'Look, Val, look, Cheryl, isn't she lovely?'

Val realised that tears of emotion were streaming down her cheeks too. It had weighed so heavily on her that she had led Betty into gaining revenge, that it had driven her children away. She raised her eyes heavenward, thanking God that it could all be left behind them now, for this wonderful moment. 'She's gorgeous, Betty.'

With a soft smile, Betty kissed the baby's cheek. 'Hello, darling. Hello, Beth – my beautiful grand-daughter.'

Read on for an exclusive chapter of Kitty Neale's new novel, coming in summer 2009.

Chapter One

Battersea, South London, 1954

'Where do you think you're going?'

'School.'

'Not today you ain't,' Lily Jackson told her daughter. 'Take the pram out and go over to Chelsea again. I need some decent stuff for a change and the pickings are richer there.'

'But I had two days off last week, and Dad said . . .'

'Sod what your dad said! He hardly stumped up a penny on Friday. If we want to eat, finding me some decent stuff to flog is more important than flaming school. Anyway, you leave in a month so you might as well get used to doing a bit of graft for a change.'

Mavis felt the injustice of her mother's words. For as long as she could remember, after school, and every weekend, her task had been to take the pram out, begging for cast-offs. She hated it, along with her name. It had been her grandmother's, but even Mavis was better than her nickname. She knew her ears stuck out, that she wasn't clever, but every time they called her Dumbo, Mavis burned with shame. Oh, she'd be glad to leave school, dreamed of getting a job, of earning her own money. 'I . . . I won't mind going out to work.'

'Huh! Nobody in their right minds would employ a useless lump like you.'

'But . . . but . . .'

'But nothing. Now don't just stand there. Get a move on.'

'Can . . . can I take some grub with me?'

'Yeah, I suppose so, but there's only bread and dripping.'

Mavis hurried to cut two thick chunks of bread, spread them, and after filling a bottle of water from the tap, she opened the back door to put them into the large, deep, Silver Cross pram. It was a cold, damp February morning with a chill wind that penetrated her scant clothes. She hurried inside again to throw on her coat before wrapping a long, hand-knitted woollen scarf around her neck. 'I'm off, Mum.'

'About time too. Be careful with any glass or china, and don't show your face again until that pram's full.'

With a small nod, Mavis walked outside to the yard again and, gripping the pram handle she wheeled it out into the back alley. It was a long walk to Chelsea, but fearful of bumping into anyone she knew in the local streets, Mavis kept her head down as she hurried along to Lombard Road.

Tears stung her eyes. If her mother had suggested taking tomorrow off it wouldn't have been so bad, but now she'd miss the only lesson she looked forward to. Mavis had been clumsy at first, all fingers and thumbs, but Miss Harwood had been so patient with her. Now she loved sewing, could hold her own in class, and the dress she was making was almost finished.

Miss Harwood had praised her work, told her she could have a career in dressmaking, and for the first time in her life Mavis had felt special. There were only the finishing touches to complete before she could bring the dress home, but now it would be another week before she could show it to her mother. Mavis shivered with anticipation. The lovely dress would prove to her mum that she wasn't useless, and instead of shame, she would at last see pride on her face.

Lily was glad to see the back of her daughter. Mavis had been a lovely baby, a pretty toddler, with dark curly hair and big blue eyes like her father. She'd only had one flaw and that was large ears, but another one emerged soon after she started school. When other kids began to learn how to read and write, Mavis was left behind, and her clumsiness became more apparent. Simple things like catching a ball were beyond her, until one day Lily had to accept the truth. Her daughter might be pretty, but she was simple, daft, almost as bad as her father. But at least Ron could read. On that thought she scowled. Yes, Ron could read the racing form and write out a betting slip. Over the years they'd had row after row about his gambling, but nothing stopped him. In fact it just got worse, until almost every week his wage packet ended up down the greyhound track.

When Ron rolled home on Friday night, she had waited until he was asleep to search his pockets, hoping against hope that he hadn't blown the lot. All she'd found was a crumpled ten bob note along with a few coppers and, knowing her stock was low, she'd felt like braining him. She was sick of flogging other people's junk to make a few bob, with old clothes the worst. She had to wash and iron the stuff, tarting it up as best she could to sell down at the local market. Most weeks it made her enough to scrape by, but when she didn't, Lily thanked her lucky stars for her old mum. It wasn't right that she had to go to her for the occasional hand-out, but with Ron losing more than he ever won, sometimes she had no choice.

Lily took a last gulp of tea and then stoically rose to her feet. What was the matter with her? She didn't have time to sit here. She had work to do, the last pile of junk to sort out, but it wasn't up to much and hardly worth the bother. She just hoped that Mavis could cadge some decent stuff this time and that she didn't break it before fetching it home.

Ron stared at the foreman, his fists clenched in anger.

'Did you hear what I said, Jackson?'

'Yeah, I heard you.'

'Right then. Get a move on.'

'It ain't my job to dig out footings. I'm a hod carrier, not a labourer,' Ron snapped. He hated the foreman, the way he threw his weight around, and if he didn't bugger off, he'd flatten him.

'Your brickie hasn't turned up, and I'm not having you standing around doing nothing. Now do as I say and get to work.'

'Fuck off!'

'You're finished, Jackson. I want you off the site, and now!'

Ron raised his fist, ready to smash it into the foreman's face, but then felt a staying hand on his arm. Pete Culling had turned up, the bricklayer urging, 'Leave it, Ron. He ain't worth it. Come on, let's go.'

His head snapped round. 'Where the hell have you been?'

'I'll tell you later. Now are you coming?'

'Not until I've flattened this little weasel,' Ron spat,

but found as he turned his attention to the foreman that the man had already moved several feet away.

Pete laughed. 'Look at his face. He's shit scared and ready to do a runner. Don't waste your energy, mate, and anyway, sod this job. I've got something better lined up, a nice little earner.'

Ron felt his anger draining away but he scowled at the foreman, unwilling to leave without a parting shot. 'I ain't finished with you yet,' he shouted, 'so watch your back. As for this job, you can stick it where the sun don't shine.'

Laughing, the two men walked off the site, Ron asking, 'So, what's this nice little earner?'

'I heard about a bloke looking for teams and willing to pay top money. I went to meet up with him before I came on site this morning.'

'So that's why you were late.'

'Yeah, but when I showed up I didn't expect to hear you getting your marching orders.'

'You didn't have to leave. It was me who got the sack, not you,' Ron protested.

'Leave it out, mate. We're a team, and anyway, we *won't* be out of work. Let's go to the café and I'll fill you in. Not only that, I'm starving and could do with a decent breakfast.'

'All right, but no breakfast for me. Mind you, I won't say no to a cup of char.'

'Don't tell me you're skint again.'

'Of course I ain't,' Ron lied, 'it's just that Lily made

me a few sarnies for lunch and I ate them while waiting for you to turn up.'

'Don't give me that. I wasn't that late.'

Ron knew he hadn't fooled Pete. They knew each other too well and had worked together since getting demobbed. It hadn't been easy at first, coming back from the war to find half of London flattened and jobs scarce. Things had gradually improved and when at last rebuilding got underway, there was a demand for bricklaying teams. Nowadays they were never out of work and it looked like Pete had come up trumps again. He grinned ruefully. 'All right, I'm skint.'

'What was it? The dogs again?'

'Yeah, but I was doing all right. I picked a couple of winners, and then got the whisper of a surefire tip. I stuck the lot on Ascot Boy and he was doing all right, but then swung wide, fell and took another couple of dogs with him. Paul's Fun got through the gap to win by three-quarters of a length.'

'So you blew your wages again?'

'I had a few bob left, but after drowning me sorrows in the Queen's Head, I reckon Lily must have cleaned out me pockets when I rolled home.'

'Serves you right, Ron. I've said it before, gambling's a mug's game.'

'Look, I've had nothing but ear-bashings from Lily all weekend and don't need another one from you. I know I've got to knock the dogs on the head, and I will.'

'If you really mean it this time, I've got the answer,' Pete said as they walked into the café and up to the counter.

'What's that supposed to mean?'

'Watcha, Alfie. Tea and egg, bacon and beans with fried bread. Twice please,' Pete said, leaving Ron with his question unanswered.

'No, just a tea for me.'

'Ignore him, Alfie,' Pete said, and then taking the mugs of tea he walked over to a table.

'What did you do that for? I told you I didn't want anything to eat,' Ron said as he sat down opposite.

'It's my treat, and anyway, after hearing what I've got to say you'll need a full stomach when you tell Lily.'

'Tell her what?'

Pete took a gulp of tea, wiped the back of his hand across his mouth and then said, 'The new job's out of London.'

'Oh yeah. How far?'

'About thirty miles.'

'What! Leave it out, Pete. That's too far to travel.'

'Before you start doing your nut, hear me out. You've heard of these new town developments? Well, Bracknell in Berkshire is one of them. They're building houses for thousands of people, but with a shortage of tradesmen, it's behind schedule. That's where we come in. The bloke I met is looking for

crews, and the money is top whack. And if we put
the hours in, almost twice what we've been earning.'

Ron pursed his lips. 'It sounds good, but there's
still the problem of getting there. We'd have to be
up at the crack of dawn and Gawd knows what time
we'd get home.'

'There's accommodation on offer. It's only basic,
but to earn that sort of money, I'm willing to rough
it.'

'I dunno, mate,' Ron said doubtfully.

'It's the chance we've been waiting for. We've
always talked about starting up our own firm and
if you're willing to give up gambling, we could pool
our money; save enough to start up.'

'You'd take that risk on me?'

'We're mates, and after what you did for me, I'd
be willing to take the risk.'

Ron's head went down. During a beach landing
in France he'd seen Pete pinned down by gunfire
and unable to move. He ran back, grabbed Pete,
hauled him forward, but had taken a bullet in his
leg. It had only been a skimmer, a bit of a flesh wound,
and anyway, it was no more than Pete would have
done for him. Now his mate was willing to risk a
partnership, but could he do it? Ron agonised. Could
he give up gambling? 'I dunno, Pete. What if I let
you down?'

'You won't. There isn't a dog track in Bracknell,
and I reckon we'll be away long enough to get

gambling out of your system. It's time to take stock, Ron. If you don't pull your socks up you'll end up with nothing. Think about the future. We ain't getting any younger, and if we don't do this now, we never will.'

Two plates were put in front of them, and Ron's mouth salivated as the smell of fried bacon wafted up. Since rationing ended last year, there was more food about, and nothing could beat a good old fry-up, with a real egg instead of that powdered muck they'd been forced to eat. Mind you, with most of his money going down the dogs, there wasn't much on offer at home. Ron picked up his knife and fork, but as he cut into the bacon he felt a surge of shame. Lily would have loved a bit of bacon, but at best all she'd be eating was a bit of bread and dripping. He should be providing for his wife, and Mavis, but the pull of the race track always won; the thrill of watching the dogs, of picking a big winner. Some weeks he won a few bob, but then like an idiot he'd put it on another dog, only to lose it again. Pete was right. Lily was right. It was a mug's game, and he knew it.

Pete spoke and Ron was broken out of his reverie. 'Well, Ron, what do you think?'

'All right, let's give it a go, but Gawd knows what Lily's going to say.'

Chapter Two

When Mavis passed her gran's house in Lombard Road, she hadn't been able to resist popping in. Her reward was an egg sandwich which she munched as she sat by the fire.

'So, you're out with the pram again?'

'Yes. Mum needs more stock and wants me to try Chelsea.'

'And judging by the look on your face, you ain't happy about it.'

'I'd rather go to school.'

'Blame your dad. If he didn't blow all his money on gambling, she wouldn't have to flog her guts out. The least you can do is give her a hand.'

'I know,' Mavis placated and, though reluctant to leave the warmth of the fire, she finished her sandwich then rose to her feet. 'That was lovely, Gran, but I'd better go.'

Her gran stood up too, swaying a little, prompting Mavis to ask, 'Are you all right?'

'Yes, I'm fine. You're getting as bad as your mother, fussing over me all the time, but as I told her yesterday, I'm as fit as a flea.'

Mavis doubted this was true. Her gran had once been chubby and red-cheeked, but for the past six months the weight had been dropping off her. 'Gran, you're looking really thin. Have you been to the doctor's yet?'

'No, and I don't intend to either. As I told your mother, there's nothing wrong with losing a bit of weight. Now go on, bugger off and leave me in peace.'

The sting was taken out of this comment by a swift hug and a kiss on the cheek, which Mavis returned before asking, 'Do you need anything from the shops?'

'If you pass the pie and mash shop on your way home, I wouldn't say no to a portion of jellied eels. Hang on, I'll just get me purse.'

With the money in her pocket, Mavis waved goodbye, still worried about her gran as she pushed the pram along. Unlike her mother, Granny Mavis wasn't slow in showing affection. Mavis knew she was stupid, useless, fit for nothing as her mother always said, but her gran made her feel loved and wanted. Mavis knew she'd be lost without her, and was frightened that she really was ill; tears flooded her eyes as she turned the corner.

'Be careful, girl.'

'I . . . I'm sorry, Mrs Fine,' Mavis stammered as she hastily veered to one side.

'Where are you off to? It's Monday morning. Surely you should be on your way to school?'

'My . . . my mum needs more stock.'

Edith Fine's neck stretched with indignation. 'Don't your parents realise how important your education is? I made sure my son never missed a day at school and now look at him. He's a Civil Servant and doing really well. You'll learn nothing trawling the streets. As I'm going past your house, I think I'll have a word with your mother.'

'Oh no, please, don't do that! I leave school in a month and . . . and it's not as if a day off will make much difference.'

The woman's face softened imperceptibly, her tone a little kinder. 'No, I suppose not, but despite your difficulties I'm sure you're bright. I think you just need a bit of extra help and it's a shame you aren't getting it.'

Once again Mavis felt her cheeks burning. She hated it that Mrs Fine knew about her failings; until last year the woman had been the school secretary. Anxious to get away, she stuttered, 'I think my English teacher has given up on me.'

'What about your parents? Have they tried?'

'Err . . . yes,' Mavis lied, and to avoid any more questions, she added, 'I . . . I really must go now.'

525

'Very well, but watch where you're going with that pram. You nearly had me off my feet.'

With this curt comment Mrs Fine walked away, her back bent and walking stick tapping the pavement. Mavis, too, resumed her journey. She had always been in awe of Edith Fine, and on their encounters found her changing personality bewildering. She could be very strict, blunt, and opinionated, yet underlying this there was sometimes kindness. She and her son lived in Ellington Avenue, only a ten-minute walk from her own home in Bullen Street, but the difference between the two was stark. Ellington Avenue was tree-lined, with bay-fronted houses that had gardens back and front. In complete contrast the houses in Bullen Street were flat-fronted, two-up two-down terraces, with just small, concrete back yards. There were no trees, and the only view was of the dismal houses opposite.

Mavis had been out so many times with the pram that she knew every road, lane, street and avenue in the whole area, but Ellington Avenue was one of her favourites, especially in May when the trees blossomed into froths of pink and white.

At last Mavis reached Battersea Bridge, the river grey, sluggish, and the wind stinging her cheeks as she walked to the other side. On Cheyne Walk now, she hesitated while deciding which direction to take. She could cross to Beaufort Street; go along to Brompton Road and try some of the houses around there. Or she could walk along Chelsea Embankment to Grosvenor Road, and maybe into Pimlico. These were both routes she had chosen before, but as her last forage had been around the Brompton Road area, she decided to try the latter.

Mavis set off, immune now to the looks of pity or disdain from people she passed, her one hope that it wouldn't take all day to fill the pram.

Edith Fine was deep in thought. Despite Mavis Jackson's inability to read and write she was sure that she was bright, and not only that, the girl was pretty. Yes, but was Mavis malleable? There was only one way she could think of to find out, and now raising the handle of her cane, Edith rapped loudly on the door. Despite the pain, she managed to keep her back straight and her head high when it was opened.

'Blimey, Edith Fine, and to what do I owe this honour?'

Edith hid her feelings of disdain as she looked at Mavis's mother. The woman was a mess, her peroxide blonde hair resembling straw and her clothes totally unsuitable for a woman in her mid-thirties. 'I'd like a word with you about your daughter.'

'Why? What's she been up to?'

'Other than the fact that Mavis isn't in school, nothing, but as she's leaving soon I think it's time you thought about her future.'

Lily's neck stretched with indignation. 'Now listen, lady, you may have been the school secretary but that doesn't give you the right to tell me what to do about my daughter.'

'No, I'm not trying to do that,' Edith said hastily, and hating that she had to affect an air of humility, she nevertheless forced her tone to sound contrite. 'Oh dear, I'm so sorry, but we seem to have got off on the wrong foot. You see, I came to see you about offering Mavis a job.'

'A job? What sort of job?'

'I'd rather not discuss it on the doorstep. May I come in?'

'Yeah, I suppose so,' Lily said, 'but you'll have to excuse the mess.'

Edith was unable to help her eyebrows rising as she went inside. The room was a mess, with piles of junk spread over the linoleum. She could see old, rusted saucepans in one heap, a frying pan black with grease, and amongst the jumble, a few odd pieces of cutlery. In another pile she saw china, mostly chipped, and in her opinion, only fit for the dustbin.

'You'd best sit down,' Lily said.

There was a sheet of newspaper on the table on top of which Edith saw an old, dented kettle which Lily had obviously been trying to polish up, one side now marginally better than the other. Edith pulled out a chair and looked at it fastidiously before sitting down.

'Right, what's this about a job?' Lily asked as she too sat down.

'I'm afraid it's only part time, but I'd like Mavis to work for me. You see, in my early thirties I was diagnosed with Multiple Sclerosis, and due to relapses, I had to give up work last year.'

'Yeah, I'd heard, but didn't know why.'

Edith ignored the interruption. She wanted to get this over with, to leave this dirty house and who knew how many germs behind. 'I'm only forty now, but the disease is progressing, so much so that I need help around the house and with cooking. With your agreement, I'd like Mavis for two hours a day, and an hour at weekends.'

'Two hours a day ain't much of a job, and anyway, Mavis is a clumsy cow. I don't think you could trust her not to break anything.'

'I'm sure she'd be fine with simple tasks *and* I can teach her to be less clumsy. It's just a matter of training.'

'Leave it out. I know my daughter and gave up on her years ago.'

'I'm willing to take the risk. I'll also pay her one shilling and sixpence an hour, which is a good rate for a young, unskilled domestic worker.'

'It ain't bad, but I want her to work for me when she leaves school.'

'Surely you could spare her for a couple of hours?'

Lily's eyes narrowed in thought, and then she

began to count on her fingers. 'I make it twelve hours in total, and she'd earn eighteen bob. Yeah, all right, for that money I can spare her, but I warned you, so don't come complaining to me if she breaks anything.'

'I won't. I'd like to show Mavis her duties before she starts. Would you send her round to see me?'

'Yeah, but there's no hurry. She doesn't leave school until the end of term.'

'I really could do with her before then. Could she perhaps do an hour after school, and two on Saturdays and Sundays?'

'Yeah, but she can't start today. It'll have to be tomorrow.'

'That's fine.'

'I'll send her round to see you later. After she's had her dinner.'

'Thank you,' Edith said, but as she stood up a muscle spasm caused her to gasp in pain. For a moment her vision blurred and she felt off balance, but then she reached out to grasp her cane, the moment thankfully passing. She walked slowly to the door, saying as she was shown out, 'Goodbye, Mrs Jackson.'

'Bye,' she chirped back.

When the door closed behind her, Edith heaved in a breath of fresh air. She'd done it. The first stage of her plan was in place. She just hoped Mavis was the perfect choice.

* * *

Lily picked up the half-polished kettle, her mind twisting and turning as she started on the other side. Edith Fine's visit had given her food for thought, and if the woman really could teach Mavis to be less clumsy, it would make all the difference. Could she? Could she really do it? Edith Fine had sounded so sure of herself and maybe she was right. Maybe it *was* down to training.

Lily knew she should have tried harder with Mavis, but busy trying to make ends meet, she just hadn't had the time or patience. When Mavis left school, she'd planned to put her to work, sending her out most days with the pram, and using her on other days to tart up any metal stuff. With more stock it would increase profits, but now there might be an alternative. Lily didn't want to count her chickens before they were hatched, but with a possible light at the end of the tunnel, she attacked the kettle with renewed vigour. Of course if Ron would stop gambling they'd be in clover, but that was a pipe dream. However, this new turn of events could well be real, and soon she might be able to take it easy – have a bit of time to put her feet up for a change.

By the end of another hour, Lily's arms were aching, but at last she had a pile of now shiny saucepans to flog, not that she'd get much for them. Her sigh was heavy as she washed the muck off her hands. The door swung open and Lily spun around, her eyes widening. 'Bloody hell, Ron! What are you doing home?'

'We got laid off.'

'Why? What did you do this time?' Lily asked in exasperation as she hastily dried her hands.

'I fell out with the foreman, but before you do your nut, don't worry. Pete has already found us another job and the pay's a lot better.'

'Is it now? Knowing you, I doubt I'll see any of it.'

Ron moved closer, pulling her into his arms. 'Yes you will, love. Things are going to change, you'll see.'

Lily at first stiffened as Ron's lips caressed her neck, but sixteen years of marriage hadn't dimmed her passion for this man. He might be a gambler, his wages gone most weeks before she saw a penny, but his body never failed to thrill her. She moved her hands upwards, felt his muscles ripple, and melted. It was always the same. She would threaten to leave him, but then be left helpless with desire at his touch. Well, not this time she thought, fighting her emotions and pulling away. 'No, Ron.'

'Come on, Lily, you know you don't mean it,' he urged, pulling her close again, the hardness of his desire obvious as he pressed against her.

It was almost her undoing, but once again she fought her feelings. 'I said no!'

'Lily . . . Lily, we should make the most of this. When I'm working away we won't see each other for months.'

Ron's words were like a dash of cold water. 'Working away! What do you mean?'

'Oh shit, I didn't mean to blurt it out like that. I'd planned to tell you when you were feeling all warm and cosy after a bit of slap and tickle.'

'Oh, I see, soften me up first and then break the news. Well, forget it. You can tell me now.'

With a sigh, Ron released her. 'All right, but you ain't gonna like it,' he said, taking a seat before going on to tell her about the job in Bracknell.

Lily sat down too, heard him out, only speaking when he came to an end. 'So let me get this straight. You're saying that if you take this job you'll be able to give up gambling, and not only that, you and Pete are going to pool your money, saving up enough to go into partnership?'

'You've got it in one. I know being apart is gonna be rotten, but I'll send you money every week.'

'That'll be a change. I get sod all off you now.'

'I know, love, I know, but I really am going to give up gambling this time. And don't forget, without me to keep, you'll be quids in.'

'Why can't you come home at weekends?'

''Cos we're going to put in as much overtime as we can. The more hours we work, the more we'll earn, and by the end of the contract, Pete thinks we'll have enough to buy a van and all the stuff we'll need, mixers and such, to start up our own firm.'

Lily's mind was racing. If Ron really did mean it this time, their lives would be transformed. He'd be able to go into partnership with Pete, and the money would come rolling in. Oh, what was the matter with her? It was a silly dream. Ron would never give up gambling – years of broken promises were enough to prove that. 'It's all pie in the sky,' she snapped. 'As soon as you get your first pay packet you'll be down the dog track.'

'Ah, that's just it. I won't be able to. There's no greyhound racing in Bracknell.'

For a moment Lily dared to believe, but then common sense prevailed. 'You'd find a track somewhere, or something else to gamble on. It's a sickness with you, Ron, and you know it.'

'Yes, but this time I really do want the cure. Pete and me will be in the same accommodation, and if I'm tempted he'll keep me on the straight and narrow, you'll see.'

'I won't be there to see it though. You could be up to anything and I wouldn't know.'

'All right, you don't trust me and I can understand that, but surely you trust Pete?'

'Yes, he's a good bloke, but he ain't your keeper. If you really want to give up gambling, it's down to you.'

'Lily, I promise you, cross my heart and hope to die, I really am going to make it this time,' Ron said as he stood up to pull her into his arms again. 'I don't deserve you, I know that, but I'll make you proud this time.'

Once again his lips caressed her neck, and this time Lily didn't pull away. Ron lifted her up with ease, cupping her legs in his arms as he carried her upstairs.

Chapter Three

Mavis was so tired, her feet throbbing and the pram three-quarters full as she knocked on the last door in the street. The houses were large, several steps leading up to the front doors, but she'd had many shut in her face. She'd also narrowly avoided a copper on his beat by diving out of sight. But if she got a few things from this last house, with any luck she could make her way home. Fingers crossed she waited, and when the door opened, Mavis found herself confronted by a wizened old woman who was bundled up in what looked like several jumpers and a cardigan.

Blimey, Mavis thought, she looks scruffier than me, but taking a deep breath she said politely, 'I'm sorry to bother you, but have you got any household items or clothes that you want to get rid of?'

'Get rid of! Do you mean sell them to you?'

Mavis told the usual lie, one her mother had

advised. 'Oh no, I don't want to buy anything. I'm collecting for charity, stuff to pass on to the Salvation Army.'

'I see,' the tiny woman said. 'In that case, you'd better come in and I'll see what I can find.'

It was unusual to be invited in, but Mavis followed her inside, along a hall and into a living room. There was no fire lit in the huge grate; the room was freezing and she could see an old quilt draped over a chair that had been pushed to one side. Was that where the old lady had been sitting? Was it all she had for warmth? Mavis's eyes flicked around the rest of the huge room, seeing peeling wallpaper and an absence of any pictures or ornaments.

'I haven't got much, my dear, but perhaps these candlesticks,' the woman said as she reached up to remove them from the mantelshelf, handing them to Mavis.

Mavis hadn't noticed them, but though old and dirty, she was sure they were silver. Shame flooded through her. This might be a huge house, the outside appearance one of wealth, but even her small home in Bullen Street had a little more comfort. 'No, no, I can't take these. I'm sure they're valuable.'

'Really? Are you sure?'

'Yes, look, now I've rubbed here you can see the silver hallmark.'

'In that case they have some value and I'm afraid I'll have to keep them, but surely I can find something for the Salvation Army. Let's have a look in the kitchen.'

Once again Mavis followed the old woman, but found the kitchen as austere as the living room. Oh, this was dreadful, she thought, the poor woman must be penniless to live like this. Cupboards were opened, most empty, including the pantry. Once again Mavis was swamped with guilt. She had lied to the woman, and now all she wanted was to get away. 'It's all right. It doesn't matter. I've collected loads of stuff already and I really must go now.'

'But it's such a worthy cause and I'd like to help,' she insisted, pulling something from a bottom cupboard. 'What about this?'

Mavis carefully took the biscuit barrel, its metal lid black with dirt. 'Thank you. This is fine and more than enough,' she said, and before the old lady could protest she fled the kitchen, ran down the hall, pulling the door closed behind her, before almost skidding down the few stairs and onto the pavement.

Pram full or not, Mavis just wanted to go home. She had looked with envy at the large houses, imagined the luxurious interiors, but seeing inside one was a revelation. That poor old woman had nothing, yet was still prepared to donate something to charity.

Mavis put the biscuit barrel in the pram and then, deciding to risk her mother's wrath, she started the long walk home. Oh, if only she didn't have to do this. If only she could leave school and find a job, but as her mother always pointed out, nobody in their right mind would employ her. Downcast, she trudged along, worn out and hungry by the time she reached Bullen Street.

Lily was feeling warm and mellow. Ron was sitting by the fire, his feet on the surround, and so full of his plans that she was beginning to feel that he really could make it this time.

When the back door opened and Mavis walked in she said, 'So, you're back. Let's see how you got on.'

'The pram isn't full.'

'I told you not to come back until it was.'

'Have a heart, love,' Ron protested. 'Look at her. She looks frozen.'

Lily ignored Ron as she marched out to the yard. She rummaged through the pram, relieved to see that Mavis hadn't broken anything, and saw a few things that would show a bit of profit. She could have done with more. It was just as well she had other plans now, but seeing what looked like a half-decent biscuit barrel, Lily felt a surge of pleasure as she gave it a closer inspection. The rest of the stuff could wait until tomorrow, but in case of rain, Lily threw a cover over the pram.

Mavis was hunched over the fire when she went

back inside, her eyes nervous, and for once Lily was kind. 'You did all right, and this is a really good find,' she said, holding up the biscuit barrel. 'If I'm not mistaken, it's really old and the lid's made of silver.'

'Oh no! I'll have to take it back.'

'Take it back! Are you mad?'

'But, Mum, the old lady who gave it to me is really poor. I only took it because I didn't think it was worth anything.'

'I can't believe I'm hearing this. If it hasn't escaped your notice, you daft cow, we're poor too.'

'But she didn't even have a fire going, and there was hardly any food in her pantry.'

'Oh, and I've got a lot in mine, have I?' Lily said sarcastically. 'We're so well off that all we've got for dinner is an egg, with a bit of bubble and squeak.'

'Things are gonna get better, love, you know that,' Ron cajoled.

'Yeah, so you say.'

'Lily, I promise, I'll send you five pounds a week, without fail.'

'Five quid! From what you said, you'll be earning nearly three times that.'

'I'll have to pay a bit for lodgings, and I told you, the more money Pete and me can pool, the sooner we can set up on our own. Blimey, love, once we do that, the money will come rolling in.'

'Does that mean I can return the biscuit barrel?' Mavis asked eagerly.

'No, you bloody well can't! What your dad's talking about is just pie in the sky and may never happen. In the meantime, if we want to eat tomorrow, I'll need to sell this, and fast. In fact, while I'm cooking dinner, you can have a go at cleaning it up.' Lily kept her expression stern and thankfully there were no further protests from Mavis. 'You know what a clumsy cow you are, so just polish the lid. I don't want any scratches, so make sure you use a soft cloth.'

While Mavis did her bidding, Lily started on their dinner, unable to help doing a mental calculation as she worked. If she really did get five quid a week from Ron, along with the money that Mavis could potentially bring in, for the first time in years she'd be in clover. She flicked a glance at her husband, saw that he had dozed off, and her expression hardened. What was the matter with her? She couldn't rely on Ron. As always, he'd let her down again.

Mavis couldn't stop her mouth from salivating. She'd eaten her bread and dripping at midday and now the smell of her mother's cooking made her stomach growl with hunger. She saw that under the grime the ceramic pattern on the outside of the barrel was a circle of black ponies with a blue border on the top and bottom. She took off the lid, polishing it carefully, the handle too, pleased to see how it began to gleam. When Mavis thought it shiny enough to please her mother, she said, 'Look, Mum, what do you think?'

'Yeah, very nice,' Lily said, her eyes squinting to see the hallmark. 'I don't know much about the date letters, but I think it's early.' She then put the lid down to pick up the barrel, and upending it, she pointed out the maker's mark on the bottom. 'Look at that, it's Royal Doulton. Well done, girl, it's as I thought and this is worth a good few bob.'

It was rare that Mavis received praise from her mother, and though unable to return the barrel, she couldn't help feeling a glow of pleasure. At least she hadn't accepted the silver candlesticks, Mavis thought, assuaging her guilt. 'Right, dinner's ready so lay the table,' her mum then ordered as she placed the barrel carefully on the dresser. 'Ron! Ron, come on, wake up.'

Mavis quickly placed cutlery on the table, smiling when her mother spoke kindly again. 'Look at him, out for the count. I've a good mind to leave him like that and it'll be all the more bubble and squeak for us.'

'I heard that,' he said, stretching his arms before standing up. He then kissed Lily on the cheek and smiled cheekily. 'Come on, woman. Feed me.'

'I'll do more than feed you if you ain't careful.'

'Is that a threat or a promise?' he asked, winking at Mavis as he took a seat at the table.

Oh, this was so nice, Mavis thought. Her mother

was in a good mood, her father joking. She wished it could always be like this. Mavis then saw her mother holding out two plates.

'Be careful giving this to hungryguts,' she said, 'and that one's yours.'

Mavis laid her father's dinner in front of him, and then quickly sat down to eat, the food rapidly disappearing off her plate. They were all quiet as they ate, but as Mavis finished her last mouthful, her mother spoke once again.

'Right, Mavis. You've finished your dinner so get yourself round to Edith Fine's house. You'll be working for her after school tomorrow and she wants to show you your so-called duties.'

'Mrs Fine? I . . . I'll be working for her?' Mavis stammered. 'But . . . but what does she want me to do?'

'From what she said, a bit of cleaning, and you can get that look off your face. You ain't fit for much, even domestic work, but the woman thinks she can train you.'

'Lily, there's no need to talk to her like that . . .'

'Go on, jump to her defence as usual.'

Mavis hung her head. Things were back to normal, her parents rowing, but nevertheless her thoughts raced. She wasn't sure that she wanted to work for Mrs Fine, yet surely it was better than taking the pram out? Oh, but would her mother expect her to do that too? 'What about stock – the pram?'

'That depends on your father. If he's true to his word and sends me five quid a week, we can knock it on the head. If he doesn't, well, you'll have to keep finding me stock.'

Mavis suddenly latched on to her mother's words. '*Send* it. What does that mean? Won't you be here, Dad?'

'No, from tomorrow I'll be working away, but your mother needn't worry. I said she'd get her money and I meant it.'

'Yeah, and pigs might fly.'

'I'll make you eat your words, Lily. You'll see.'

Before her mother could respond again, Mavis hastily broke in, 'Will you be away for a long time, Dad?'

'I'm afraid so, love, at least six months, maybe more, but it's all for a good cause.'

'But . . .'

'Mavis, that's enough. I said get yourself round to Edith Fine's. Now!'

Desolately, Mavis pushed her chair back. She knew better than to argue with her mother, and now the only person who ever came to her defence was leaving and, from what he said, for a long time. Mavis took her coat from the hook, unable to help blurting out as she shrugged it on, 'Oh, Dad, please don't go.'

'I've got to, love. It'll be the making of us, you'll see, and when I come back things are going to be different. I'll have me own business, making a packet, and your mother will never have to work again.'

Mavis saw the look of derision on her mother's face, and like her, doubted it was true. She knew her father was a gambler, had heard so many rows, followed by his promises – ones that he never kept. Yet she loved her dad, dreaded him leaving, and tears stung her eyes as she stepped outside. What would happen to her now?

2 FOR 1 DAYS OUT FOR ALL AVON READERS!

AVON are offering all readers of 'Desperate Measures' 2 for 1 days out on a number of fantastic attractions across the UK and Ireland. 2 for 1 day out attractions range from castles to caves, railways to roller coasters, wildlife parks to nature reserves and science centres to stately homes.

HOW TO USE 2 FOR 1 DAY OUT

1. Choose your destination from the list of venues provided on www.avon-books.co.uk
2. Call the venue beforehand to check availability and any restrictions. Inform the venue that you will be taking advantage of a TLC 2 for 1 Day Out voucher. The voucher entitles you, a friend or a family member to free admission for one person when accompanied by an adult paying full price.
3. Download a voucher from the website.
4. Take your voucher and a copy of the book 'Desperate Measures' and its original till receipt to your chosen attraction and present it at the time of entry. Valid for one person only.

SOME ADVICE BEFORE YOU SET OFF

1. Some attraction facilities or special events may be limited by weather conditions.
2. Many attractions do not allow pets.
3. Not all child ticket prices have the same age limit – each attraction sets its own.
4. Most attractions close on Christmas Day and New Year's Day.
5. Attractions will not accept TLC 2 for 1 Days Out vouchers on Bank Holiday weekends.
6. Vouchers may only be applicable to children; this is dependent on the venue. Please clarify this with the venue beforehand.
7. Please read the Terms & Conditions carefully.

TERMS & CONDITIONS

1. This offer is open to all UK residents aged 18 years or over. This offer is not available to employees of HarperCollins or its subsidiaries, TLC Marketing plc or agencies appointed by TLC and their immediate families.
2. The voucher entitles the bearer to one free day out entry, when accompanied by another adult paying the full price.
3. Proof of purchase is required, therefore a copy of the book 'Desperate Measures' and the book's original till receipt must be presented along with the voucher. If this is not produced, you must pay the full price for the day out entry session.

4. Only one voucher may be used per person. The voucher claimant may not claim another voucher at a participating venue.
5. All additional customers will pay the full price and all future bookings will be charged at the full price.
6. Voucher valid until April 30th 2009.
7. Offer excludes Public Holidays and Bank Holidays.
8. The offer is based on advance bookings only and is subject to promotional availability at participating venues.
9. Customers must call the venue in advance of their visit, stating that they are in possession of a 'TLC 2 for 1 day out voucher' to check availability, discuss the usage of the offer (restrictions may apply) and book their day out.
10. The instructions listed at the back of the book, on the website and on the voucher form part of these terms and conditions.
11. If you fail to cancel your booking within 48 hours of the appointment, or do not show at the venue, a cancellation charge may be incurred.
12. The list of participating venues remains subject to change. Please contact your chosen venue to confirm continual availability of the offer.
13. Participating venues are all contracted to participate in the 2 for 1 day out offer.
14. Participating venues reserve the right to vary prices, times and offer availability (e.g. public holidays).
15. Prices (if any) and information presented are valid at the time of going to press and could be subject to change.
16. Neither the Promoter, nor its agents or distributors can accept liability for lost, stolen or damaged vouchers and reserves the right to withdraw or amend any details and/or offers.
17. The voucher may only be used once. Photocopied, scanned, damaged or illegible vouchers will not be accepted.
18. The 2 for 1 day out voucher has no monetary value, is non-transferable, cannot be resold and cannot be used in conjunction with any other promotional offer or redeemed in whole or part for cash.
19. In the event of large promotional uplift, venues reserve the right to book voucher holders up to 4 months from date of calling to make a promotional booking.
20. Neither TLC, its agents or distributors and the Promoter will in any circumstances be responsible or liable to compensate the purchaser or other bearer, or accept any liability for (a) any non-acceptance by a venue of this voucher or (b) any inability by the bearer to use this voucher properly or at all or (c) the contents, accuracy or use of either this voucher or the venue listing, nor will any of them be liable for any personal loss or injury occurring at the venue, and (d) TLC, its agents and distributors and the Promoter do not guarantee the quality and/or availability of the

FAMILY BETRAYAL

Kitty Neale

Every family has its dark secrets . . .

MENACING . . .

The Drapers rule the streets of South London. Everyone's afraid of them – and that's just how they like it.

But when tempers flare and a family feud spirals out of control, tragedy strikes, leaving eldest son Danny in charge.

MANIPULATED . . .

But he has shocking plans for the family business and Petula, the baby of the family, becomes the scapegoat for the Drapers' dirty dealings.

MISSING . . .

Years later, and the once united family has now split up. Petula returns to the place she once called home to face her family as well as her demons, unleashing a terrible secret that could destroy them once and for all . . .

Praise for Kitty Neale:

'Full of drama and heartache.' *Closer*

'A gritty tale.' *Bella*

ISBN: 978-1-84756-022-3

NOBODY'S GIRL

Kitty Neale

Abandoned and alone, you'll do *anything* to survive . . .

ABANDONED . . .

On the cold stone steps of an orphanage, just hours old and clutching the object which was to give her her name, Pearl Button had a hard start to life.

ALONE . . .

Now 16, she's finally managed to escape. Finding work at a nearby café, Pearl is thrilled to start earning her own money, even if she must contend with sharp-tongued owner Dolly Dolby and her menacing son Kevin.

AT RISK . . .

Soon though, Pearl's life is thrown into jeopardy when she becomes tangled up in the murky South London underworld, while at the orphanage where Pearl spent her wretched childhood, a terrible secret is about to be unleashed . . .

'Heartbreakingly poignant and joltingly realistic. A book that fans of misery lit won't want to miss.' Annie Groves, author of *Some Sunny Day*.

ISBN: 978-1-84756-005-6

SINS OF THE FATHER

Kitty Neale

Emma Chambers has a way out of the poverty-stricken life she lives – but it might just destroy her to take it . . .

When 17-year-old Emma Chambers is left to look after her siblings after her mother dies in childbirth, life is tough. With not enough food – not to mention money – to go around, plus the vile temper of her drunken father to contend with, the future looks bleak.

Until Emma is offered a way out and a chance to save her family. She can swap a life of abject poverty and drudgery for one of comfort and even luxury – so long as she marries her landlord Horace Bell. Over 20 years her senior, it's not a match she relishes but she has no choice.

All too soon she becomes wise to Horace's sadistic demands. Night after night, Emma wonders how she can escape his advances. Then, on hearing the news that she is pregnant, he leaves her – threatening to sell the house beneath her.

Beside herself with worry, Emma practically stumbles across a woman lying in the gutter one day. She has been badly attacked. Emma takes in Doris and discovers she is a prostitute – and an idea begins to form in her mind. For years, men have taken advantage of her. Now it's time to turn the tables.

Emma becomes a successful and steely businesswoman. But then tragedy strikes when her young daughter Tinker is kidnapped – and it's discovered that someone has been keeping tabs on Emma all these years . . .

ISBN: 978-1-84756-021-6

ORPHANS OF WAR

Leah Fleming

The ones you leave behind are the ones that stay with you forever . . .

When Madeleine Belfield loses her family and her home in the Blitz, she is sent to live with relatives in the Yorkshire Dales.

En route, Maddy befriends Gloria Conley and her brother Sid, abandoned by their desperate mother. Although Maddy and Gloria are chalk and cheese, they soon vow to be 'forever friends'.

Maddy slowly adjusts to her new life. Eager to help with the war effort, her Aunt Plum has opened up a home for 'difficult' evacuees and Maddy and Gloria quickly become part of a motley crew, including headstrong Greg and flighty Enid.

The friendship endures into adulthood, until a tragic experience tears them apart. Desperate to escape her memories, Maddy flees to London.

Years later, Fate reunites them all. But a visit back to Yorkshire reveals the truth about the past - a revelation with unimaginable consequences.

ISBN: 978-1-84756-023-0